— LOST LEGACY BOOK ONE —

THE LAST WISH

ALANA KAY

ISBN: 979-8-9912918-0-4 (Ebook edition)
ISBN: 979-8-9912918-1-1 (Paperback edition)

Library of Congress Control Number: 2024916697

First edition 2024

The story, all names, characters, and incidents portrayed in this production are fictitious. No identification with actual persons (living or deceased), places, buildings, and products is intended or should be inferred.

Cover by: Miblart

Published by Fate Unbound Publishing LLC
Los Angeles, CA

Visit the author's website at www.alanakayauthor.com

A gentleman holds my hand. A man pulls my hair. A soulmate will do both.

ALESSANDRA TORRE

THE LAST WISH

CHAPTER
ONE

SHEENA

A muscle in my back spasms. I shrug it off, just like I ignore each new float that pops up in the parade of injustices in my life. I rake ketchup and stray fries off the plate in my hand and toss it into the industrial sink in front of me. It lands with a dull clang, and I stifle a groan.

Back hurts, Sheena? Tough shit. At least you're still alive.

The rules I've lived by for the last eight years are simple: no pity, trust no one, keep it moving. With those guidelines in place, I've found myself the temporary resident of twenty-one—make that twenty-two—states since this nightmare began. Unfortunately, the places I've hunkered down aren't on anyone's list of top tourist destinations.

I target locations where no one dreams, and boy, did I hit the jackpot here. The people in this town don't dare to wish for anything better, and if they do, they keep those thoughts carefully protected inside their own heads, surrounded by metaphorical barbed wire and literal 'fuck off' energy.

Another chipped plate follows the same path as the first.

I work at Styx, a grimy bar in Backwoods, Wyoming. That's not a joke. It's the actual name of the town, or settlement, or whatever you want to label a hellhole so small and unremarkable it doesn't even get a dot on the damn map. Serving more grit and grease than anything else, I would wonder how it stays in business if I didn't know for a fact it's the only place to get a drink for miles around.

Styx is a dump for sure, but it's paradise to me for three reasons. One, it pays cash; two, people rarely make eye contact; and three, no one ever asks questions. I've been working here for four months, which is practically tenure compared to my normal gigs. So far, there's been an almost suspicious lack of red flags. If I believed in luck, or justice, or any other fairytale concepts, I might be feeling optimistic for once.

Too bad I don't believe in anything anymore—except for my rules.

A quick glance at the plastic clock on the wall tells me there's less than an hour left in my shift. Just fifty minutes until I can crawl back to the ratty mattress in my rented RV and pretend my life is different.

A shuffling sound from the front room catches my attention.

The line cook, who doubles as the creator of most of the grit and grease, grunts and dips his chin toward the bar. I grunt back, happy enough with our prehistoric method of communication. He may be a walking health hazard, but he's never tried to be my friend or get in my pants. Those are two green flags in his favor.

Abandoning the dirty dishes, I shove through the swinging saloon doors that separate the back of house from the front. Dim lighting, chipped tables, and watered down liquor decorate the space. I guess you could call it a dining room, but I'd like to see anyone manage that with a straight face.

I take a few steps forward and icy dread trickles down my spine. Something isn't right. I freeze and take stock of my surroundings.

Two strangers are standing by the bar. Even from fifteen feet back, I can tell they don't belong. One is probably the biggest man I've ever seen in real life. While his size isn't all that out of the ordinary—they grow big in the West, after all—he doesn't blend in. For starters, he's not filthy. Clean curls, clean clothes . . . I can tell that even with his back to me. Unlike the rest of the clientele who stumble into Styx, there are no obvious holes or stains on his shirt. To top it off, his posture screams confidence. With his shoulders back, chest up, and head held high, he looks like he's never had life chew him up and spit him out just because it could.

Maybe I'm overreacting, but his sudden appearance puts me on guard, activating the instincts that have kept me alive for the better part of a decade. With every hair on the back of my neck tingling and standing on end, I shift my focus to the second stranger.

This one is facing me, and on paper, he doesn't seem that scary. Actually, he looks like he wandered away from his fraternity and stumbled into this bar by mistake. He's got on a backwards cap and designer sunglasses, and he's baring his shiny white teeth at me in what I can only assume is supposed to be a disarming smile.

Red flag for sure.

Some useless, primitive part of my brain left over from a bygone era notices that he's also really hot. Since I don't have a death wish, I discard that like the useless trash it is. The frat boy is watching me expectantly, but I avoid eye contact and pull out my notepad.

"What can I get for you?" I ask. I'm pleased with how bored I sound, but the big guy whips around like I slapped him. His eyes drill into me like he can read all my secrets with a look.

Shit. Maybe he can.

When he growls at me, adrenaline floods my body. Through my rising panic, a low electrical current hums to life between us like one of my arteries has been replaced with a live wire. I've never experienced anything like it. It tugs at me, urging me to move closer to him, until self-preservation overrides the impulse, screaming at me to run instead. The notepad buckles in my grip.

"We'll just have two of whatever you have on tap," the frat guy says.

His voice should be illegal. Deep, smoky, and inviting, the sound washes over me like a caress. Against my better judgment, my head snaps up to get another look at the source. Big mistake. He's even more gorgeous up close, flashing that megawatt smile at me. His black eyes are a bottomless pool of heated promises. As for the giant, he's as golden as the frat boy is dark. Together, they are devastatingly beautiful.

I nod to acknowledge I heard their order. Inside, I feel dazed. Heat spreads across my skin, but my heart turns to ice.

Things are starting to add up, and I don't like the results. Black eyes, growling, an electric buzz in my chest . . . Not only do these guys not fit in at this bar, I have a sneaking suspicion they also don't fit into the standard genetic code. *Not human. Get out.*

My body goes on autopilot as I walk through my next steps, never taking my eyes off the two strangers. When they face away from me and start up a hushed argument, I seize the opening. Maybe this head start will be enough.

I slap my cheek harshly as I dart out of the employee exit; I can't panic right now. The terror is overwhelming, but I've got to get past it or I'm fucked. I'm not sixteen anymore. I won't be taken by surprise again.

The alien tugging sensation in my chest mixes with the adrenaline coursing through my veins and makes me feel sick. I choke back bile as I jog across the parking lot to my car, checking over my shoulder as I run. This could be it for me.

It meaning the day I've dreaded—when the self-preservation instincts that have kept me just one step ahead finally run out. My exhausting life on the run will be over if I'm caught. For a second, the idea fills me with relief. Running to live and living to run takes a toll. At twenty-four years old, I already feel tired down to my bones.

I slap myself again. Fuck that defeatist attitude.

I'm Sheena May. I don't dwell, and I certainly don't give up. There just isn't time, plus it violates my rules.

No pity. Trust no one. Keep it moving.

With one last glance behind me, I hop into my battered Toyota Corolla and tear out of the bar parking lot. Two miles down the road, I pull up alongside the ragged RV I've called home for the last few months. I throw the car in park, leave it running, and sprint inside. I drop to my knees next to the bed to retrieve the faded go-bag from underneath. It's already packed with a few hundred bucks in cash, a first aid kit yellowed with age, some nondescript cheap clothes, and a box of name-brand tampons.

The essentials I need to start over . . . again.

I've run this drill many times. I should be out of here in less than ninety seconds if everything goes according to plan.

Turning to the small cabinet on my left, I toss cans of soup, protein bars, and unopened packs of beef jerky into the duffle. It's not much, but I've certainly had less.

Time to go.

I study the interior of the rusty RV one last time, feeling a brief pang at having to leave it behind. Satisfied there's nothing lying around that might trace back to me, I hoist the bag over my shoulder and hightail it out of there. I don't bother locking the door. Every second matters, and I won't be back.

Securing my seatbelt, I stomp on the gas. I'm five miles down the highway before I allow myself to draw a deep breath and think about what just happened.

Those men. Something about them was both familiar and off. I'm positive I've never seen them before, but the way the big guy looked at me, that instant connection—well, something about it wasn't normal.

Maybe someone with less baggage would find it exhilarating, but I've had more than enough excitement to last me a lifetime.

After my introduction to the supernatural as a kid, I learned to never slow down or ask questions. Nothing—and I mean absolutely nothing—is worth putting my freedom in jeopardy.

No, my rules are in place for a reason, and I won't be breaking them today. Rubbing my chest, I ignore the aching pull and glance down at the weathered old atlas I keep stuffed in the glove box.

Colorado might be nice this time of year.

CHAPTER
TWO

SHEENA

Steam curls up from the engine in wispy spirals, an ominous sign I'm going nowhere fast.

This car has made it 200,643 miles, but it's choosing now as the perfect time to give up?

Just my luck.

I squint at the setting sun as a chill settles low in my gut. Though I crossed into Colorado a while ago, I'm still a few miles outside of the town I'm heading for according to the map. I won't make it there before dark with this complication. That means I've got to roll the dice on two shitty options and cross my fingers that nothing goes wrong.

Who am I kidding? Something always goes wrong.

Now I've got to decide which choice is least likely to get me killed: sleeping out here in the open or walking into a strange place after dark with no set destination.

Looking again at the horizon, I'm a little disappointed when the town doesn't magically materialize. A twist of my neck shows there are no promising options in the direction I came from either —only a whole lot of nothing. No cars have passed by since I've been stuck on the side of the road. Not that I would flag someone down for help anyway, but the lack of traffic is a good indicator that this place is incredibly remote.

The electric current snaps in my chest, refusing to be ignored.

It's not painful, but it is distracting. At first, I thought it was the product of my fear and adrenaline, but it hasn't stopped sizzling beneath the surface of my skin since I encountered those guys.

Did they do something to me?

Suspicion flares up, joining the frothy cocktail of feelings bubbling inside me. The combination turns my stomach. It reminds me of the one time I tried jungle juice at a house party in high school.

Shelving that useless memory, I eye the sun as it sinks lower in the sky, and then close my eyes to think. When I imagine hunkering down in the exposed car overnight, the wave of fear threatens to level me. That settles it, so I open my eyes and fall back on rule number three.

Keep it moving.

Shouldering my duffle, I pocket the keys to the car. She may have let me down today, but I can't afford to hold that against her. Maybe I'll come back and sell the old rust bucket for parts once I get settled. With that happy thought, my optimism tank is now running on fumes, so I head toward the town, ignoring the way cold tension spreads throughout me with each step I take away from the car.

After a mile or so, the rhythmic repetition of my walking lulls me into a sense of comfort. Since I left Wyoming, I've only managed a few quick naps to keep me going behind the wheel, and the exhaustion is catching up with me. I stifle a yawn and shift the bag to my opposite shoulder, kicking myself for packing so many cans.

As I watch the last few rays of the sun disappear one by one, I feel a prickle of awareness on the back of my neck. Alone, stranded on the side of the road, I'm now bathed in shadow and second-guessing my decision to hoof it in the dark.

Please let me actually be alone.

Peering at my surroundings, I notice nothing out of the ordinary. My other senses don't seem to believe my eyes. They're screaming at me to hide, but it's not like I have a lot of options. There are no big rocks or trees near me, and my visibility is close to nonexistent now.

"Well, what do we have here?" A raspy voice breaks the silence, and my heart jumps into my mouth. Spinning, I'm stunned to find a grimy man just a few feet behind me.

Where the fuck did he come from?

"Pretty little thing like you shouldn't be on her own in the dark like this." He spits on the ground. "I reckon that was your car broken down a few miles back." He points back in the direction I came from, his hungry grin revealing one fake gold tooth and a host of real, stained ones.

The man takes a step toward me. I take a step back.

When his grin gets even wider, I brace for a fight. He may think stumbling across a stranded woman in the dark is his lucky day, but I'm determined to make him regret it.

I finger the knife I have tucked inside the waistband of my jeans and paste a brittle smile on my face. Maybe I can talk my way out of this.

"Car trouble," I explain, doing my best to sell my lie by starting with the truth. "My cousin is on his way to pick me up, but I wanted to watch the sunset and stretch my legs instead of waiting in the car." I giggle and shrug like I'm only just realizing this was a silly idea. "Thanks for checking on me, mister, but he'll be here any minute."

The creep considers my bluff, his sharp eyes taking in my worn, faded outfit. As he looks me over, his smile fades. I grit my teeth; the message is coming through loud and clear. He's done pretending, which means I am too. When he takes a deep sniff of the air, I could swear his eyes glow yellow in the gloom.

"Yeah, I think you're a liar. But even if you're not, I'll be done long before your cousin gets here." He licks his lips, and I let some of the disgust I'm feeling show on my face. "Fuck, you smell like dinner. Surely I won't get in trouble for just a little taste." He crouches as he speaks, and I whip my knife out, dropping my duffle along with all pretense of politeness. I've never actually stabbed someone before, but I'm fully prepared to gut him if he comes closer.

At the sight of my knife, he hesitates, and then winks at me.

"I like it when they fight back." The chilling words have barely left his mouth when he lunges, erasing the space between us faster than I would have thought humanly possible. Even though I'm prepared, he moves so quickly it throws off my aim. Instead of burying the knife in his chest, I slice him in the cheek instead.

The cut gushes blood, but it doesn't stop him. He growls, enraged, and backhands me as I stumble to put more distance between us. I feel the blow down to my toes. Through sheer desperation, I manage to keep myself upright. It's over for me if he gets me on the ground.

The disgusting son of a bitch circles me, wiping the blood from his face as he sends me another twisted smile. I'm horrified to realize I wasn't imagining it earlier; his eyes are definitely glowing now. They're the eerie yellow of things that go bump in the night. A few years ago, I might have panicked at the sight, but I'm a different person now. He's not the first monster I've faced.

Stand your ground, Sheena.

When he charges again, I'm ready for it. Instead of guarding myself, I put all my focus into plunging the knife into his heart. I commit to the strike, putting all of my power behind it. As the blade nears his chest, he jerks to the side and throws my aim off again. The knife sinks into his shoulder with a sickening squish. Before I'm able to pull it out, he lurches away.

He stares down at the wound, and I see my chance to run. I only make it a few steps before I'm wrenched backwards by my hair. My scalp explodes with pain. He yanks my head up, a feral look blazing in his yellow eyes. Something sharp rips into the skin of my ribs, but I can't look down to see what cut me while he's holding my ponytail like a leash. With his face now just inches from mine, I watch in horror as his teeth warp and morph into jagged points.

He's going to tear out my throat. I'm going to die here on the side of the road.

The realization enrages me. I haven't spent this long on the run only to die at the hands of this piece of shit. With a final desperate surge of energy, I slam my head face first into his nose.

The move stuns me, my vision fading in and out like a strobe effect. That must be why I think there are headlights joining the black dots in my field of vision. Or maybe I'm just hallucinating because the last thing I see before I pass out is a lion charging toward me. My vision tunnels, and my legs collapse.

I'm out before I hit the ground.

GIDEON

We were almost too late.

Callum catches the waitress, and I turn my rage onto the partially shifted stranger. He's a dead man walking. I shred through the vagrant coyote like wet tissue paper. He tries to fully shift, but his heartbeat is too slow, his body done for. When I sink my teeth into his throat and tear it out, I watch the life fade from his eyes with monstrous satisfaction.

It scares me a little.

Then I remember the fear I felt when we drove up and saw the tiny woman fighting for her life. The bastard was trying to get her on the ground. Her desperation to get away from this sicko may be the only reason she survived as long as she did.

No, I'm fresh out of regret for my actions.

Relaxing my jaw, I let the vermin's body drop from my mouth

into the dirt. The ground is muddy now from blood that doesn't all belong to him. That makes me want to kill him again.

I have to force myself to turn my back on the mangled corpse and pad back toward Callum. He's holding the woman, cradling her gently to his chest like she might shatter.

Blood seeps through her t-shirt, and in my animal form, I can already spot bruises forming on her face. A whine escapes my mouth, primal rage threatening to take over. I wrench back control with pure force of will and shift back to my human form.

The change takes longer than it has in years. By the time I'm standing on two feet again, I'm trembling from the effort. Fuck. *Fuck.* I'm losing it. Ever since I saw her in that disgusting bar, I've been spiraling out of control. I pull the knife out of the asshole's body, toss it in the SUV, and suck in a deep breath.

All I smell is blood . . . and her.

Callum transfers the woman to my arms without a word. Feeling her alive against me quiets some of my panic, which makes no logical sense. I don't know her. I don't even know what she is. She's obviously not a human like she was pretending to be or a shifter like me. The only thing I know for sure is that she's my fated mate. It's ridiculous.

I've never said a damn word to her, but I know she's my destiny.

When Callum and I walked into that bar, our intention was to ask if there had been any disappearances recently. It was the eighth town we'd stopped in, and we both felt like we were close to a solid lead. Neither of us expected her.

Man, I've fucked this entire investigation up.

Cal is too nice to call me on it, but I'm not supposed to scare off potential informants by growling at them or starting supernatural rumors. Too bad the mate bond didn't seem too fussed about flying under the radar.

Callum is quiet now, but I know he's thinking through what has to be done. Now that his arms are free, he drags the body away from the road and further into the dark. With no other option, I carry the woman to the SUV, noticing how small she is when I lay her gently across the back seat. Even covered in bruises and blood, she's beautiful. She has pale skin and a dusting of freckles on her nose. Some of her dark brown hair is loose from the struggle. I brush one tangled strand back towards her ponytail, feeling a massive knot forming on her forehead.

What if the hair tie is pulling on her scalp?

That's only going to make her head hurt worse. Gently, I work the band out of her hair and use it to pull my own messy curls back into a loose bun. Now I feel silly. Why the hell did I do that, and what the fuck am I going to say if she wakes up and sees it? 'Yeah, sorry ma'am, I killed that guy, put you in my car, and then stole your rubber band.' That's going to go over great. Shit, I'm completely out of my depth here.

Where is Callum?

As if I summoned him with my thoughts, he appears, tossing the woman's duffle bag into the back of the SUV and handing me a pack of wipes and a towel. I nod in thanks, glad to be given something to do besides spiral. Once I've mopped away the worst of the blood, I slip on the hoodie and sweatpants he has ready for me.

"You got rid of the coyote shifter?" I grunt. He nods.

"I left the body for the other animals to take care of. It will be gone before the sun's up." Callum glances at my hair, then the back seat. He hesitates, meeting my eyes in the glow of the overhead light.

"You got to her in time, Gideon. She's going to be okay now." He lays his hand on my back, and I accept the simple comfort gladly, pulling him into a hug. It's not something I do often, but I need my best friend right now.

Sucking in a breath, Callum's familiar spicy scent mixes with the woman's floral smell. Combined, they feel like home. I breathe in deeper. The air fills my lungs, and I gag. Another smell is ruining their scent. It's gamey and sharp, mixed with the acrid stench of cigarettes.

The coyote wasn't alone.

"He's got backup," I snarl, pulling back from the hug. Callum stiffens, and we both look out into the dark. Even with my eyesight, there's nothing to see. This new enemy is smart enough to stay hidden.

Still, Callum doesn't question my instinct. "Random or traffickers?" He whispers.

I shake my head. I can't tell unless I shift back again. I'm reaching for my shirt to do just that when Callum grabs my arm.

"We don't know what we're up against." He looks again at the back seat. "We need to get her out of here."

I want to argue with him. My rage is back, along with the burning desire to finish this. Never in my life have I felt the urge to spill blood this intensely. I look at the back seat and all that fury fades. One mistake and she could be taken or killed.

I can't risk that.

There's no getting around this awkward situation. Since the woman hasn't woken up in the last thirty seconds, we're going to have to drive off without talking to her first.

"It feels weird to just take her, Callum," I admit out loud. He runs his fingers through his hair, and I see a flash of the panic I'm feeling reflected in his eyes.

"She's out cold. We can't exactly ask her permission."

He's right, but I have a bad feeling about it. I may not be sold on having a mate bond with a complete stranger, but abducting her while she's passed out . . . Even I know that's a bad beginning.

"Shit." That one word sums up the entire situation.

"Yeah, well, let's just hope she prefers a temporary kidnapping to certain death." Callum sounds as frustrated as I feel, but when he looks down at her, his tone softens. "We'll explain. She'll be fine, man. Hell, maybe she's the lead we need to track those assholes down. From the looks of that busted RV, she's used to running."

When we tracked her to the vehicle using the directional pull in my freaking chest, we found the hunk of metal drenched in her scent. A glass jar full of wildflowers was the only sign anyone lived there at all. I don't like thinking of her as a lead *or* my mate, but Callum is right . . . We're out of options.

I sigh, sniffing the air again and hoping for better luck. I don't get it. The stench is still there, stronger now. It's definitely a predator.

Out of time.

"Okay, let's go," I say. We climb into the car without another word and peel out.

Even though we're leaving one mess behind, I can't help feeling like we're driving straight towards another.

LYSANDER

I LICK MY LIPS, tasting salt from my sweat and a hint of nicotine. She's so close. I can still feel the power of her blood from my hiding place. My hands twitch, and I pinch at the denim of my worn jeans to keep my bones from shifting. The bitch got lucky, escaping me again.

I grind my teeth and pull out another cigarette.

There's no doubt I've enjoyed the hunt so far. Watching her taste a freedom she can't enjoy gives me a rush like nothing else. She's so weak, so scared. Yeah, watching her run is the only drug I need. Besides my smokes.

We're waiting on the same thing, she and I—a fate she can't outrun. She may dread the day I close in and toss her back in a cage where she belongs, but that won't stop it from happening.

Her fear, my anticipation . . . That just makes it sweeter.

Still, even though the game's been fun, it's time to wrap it up. This latest fuck up complicates things, and I don't have time for it. I need the money and the power now. Having my weapon fall into someone else's hands isn't part of my plan.

I almost ruined it all when those two assholes loaded her up. I recognized the enclave heirs. Shit, anyone would. Spoiled, pampered, and privileged. It's about time they learned a lesson about taking what doesn't belong to them and leaving nothing for the rest of us.

They've never felt the throbbing twist of hunger in their bellies, never had to fight for the scraps left behind. They deserve what's coming to them, but the timing isn't right.

As the taillights of the fancy SUV disappear into the dark, I follow the smell of blood away from the road. As I suspected, I find my scout torn to shreds. I'm not mad he's dead. Those pricks just saved me time by killing that pathetic coyote for me. None of this would have happened if the fool had just followed my orders. Serves me right for trusting a dog to do a wolf's job.

Standing over the corpse, I take another drag of my cigarette to clear my head.

I've been locked in on her scent for eight years. There's nowhere on this planet she could go that I wouldn't find her. The enclave sniffing around my business makes things complicated, but I like a challenge. I drop the glowing cherry on the scout's shredded torso. It flickers a few times before the congealed blood snuffs the tiny flame out.

She can enjoy her freedom for now. It won't be lasting much longer than that spark.

CHAPTER
THREE

GIDEON

It's late when we pull up to our cabin. I crack my neck, but it doesn't do a thing to clear my thoughts. My head was on a hinge during the drive, constantly watching the back seat for movement. Besides the times when we hit a few bumps or potholes, her body didn't move once. I feel a little dumb, because I couldn't stop myself from checking. I had to be sure she was okay.

I keep telling myself it's good she hasn't woken up yet. Explaining why we followed her and brought her home without asking isn't going to be easy, but the waiting is eating me alive.

Callum turns the car off, and the overhead light flickers to life automatically. He checks the back seat and sighs.

"Do you think anyone followed us?" I ask, giving into the urge and looking back again.

"We were careful, so I doubt it." Cal's voice is sluggish. He scrubs his hand across his face, but there's no way it helps with the exhaustion or the anxiety. As the garage door closes behind us, I unclip my seatbelt and slide out. We unload the car in silence, starting with the stranger. I lay her gently on the leather sectional, while Callum grabs the bags. It's dark in the living room, but I can still see the bruise on her face swelling and starting to turn purple. Rage bubbles up, burning away how tired I am.

Callum flips on the light, and soft, recessed lighting highlights the worst of the damage. It doesn't look that serious, but no matter how many times I tell myself that, I can't control my reaction.

"You should feed her some of your blood, so she won't wake up in pain," I demand. Callum shakes his head like I'm losing it.

"Dude, she might not wake up in pain, but I don't think any of us are ready for her to *drink my blood*." He's not wrong, but she's *hurt*. Doesn't he understand? Can't he see? My nails dig into the back of the couch, and Callum must see I'm about to argue because he cuts me off before I can start.

"I mean, seriously," he snorts. "You want this girl to wake up in a strange house with two guys she doesn't know *and* the inexplicable urge to hump the sofa?"

I grumble, knowing he's right. Callum just smiles, lifting her shirt a couple of inches to take in the scratches on her side. His smile drops when he sees the drying blood. The cuts aren't deep, but she's going to feel them for a while. I stare at her, lost in thought.

Callum shuffles back into the room with a first aid kit, and I realize with shock that I didn't even notice him leave. Shit. I should have been taking care of her, but I'm just staring like an idiot.

He gently cleans her side with antiseptic, laying a soft, breathable bandage over the worst spots. Callum touches her like she's made of glass, and I can't look away. I'm watching him so closely that I don't see her wake up. Nope, the only clue I get is her gasp, loud in the quiet of our living room. Her eyes flash with panic. I whine, and Callum freezes.

Oh fuck.

SHEENA

My HEAD IS POUNDING. It's the only thing I notice at first, my mind fuzzy and disoriented as I come to a little more with each throb. It takes real effort to force my eyelids into the upright position. Jesus, I'm not sure they've ever been heavier. Adding insult to injury, my only reward for prying them open is a glimpse of some dated wood paneling.

Before I can focus on that for too long, a sting in my side makes me gasp. The sharp inhale floods my nose with the subtle smell of leather. Two things become clear at once: I'm not in my RV, and I'm not alone.

Goddammit. The guys from the bar. They've taken me.

They're standing over me and staring like . . . I'm the threat? Who the hell kidnaps someone and then has the audacity to feel awkward about it? That makes almost as little sense as my mental state. Maybe I have a concussion because an odd wave of calm settles over me as soon as I recognize them. If these guys went to the trouble to track me down and bring me to some unknown location, the only thing I should feel is panic.

I feel like I've been body snatched by an idiot.

Did they drug me? The possibility brings back some of the fear I've been missing. It's a relief to feel my heart race again as I take stock of my body. The strange buzzing that's been driving me crazy since I left the bar is mostly gone, but my side hurts. I lift my shirt with trembling hands to find there are several carefully secured pieces of gauze staring back at me.

The fight flies back into my head in frightening detail. His glowing yellow eyes devouring me, sharp nails scoring my side, and the taste of blood in my mouth after he backhanded me. I suck in a sharp breath, and my ribs ache from the sudden movement.

My fear roars back in at full power, lending me the strength to stand on wobbly legs. I back away from them both, scanning the room for a way to escape. Maybe they'll let me.

"It's okay. You're safe," the one with black eyes whispers. *Liar.* "I promise no one will hurt you." *More bullshit.* I learned a long time ago words are only worth the breath it takes to say them.

He holds his hands out in front of himself. If it's supposed to make me feel calm, it's not working. I watch him closely, waiting for the attack. He's standing so still, it's like he's avoiding spooking a skittish, wild animal. Maybe that's what I am to him—just prey, bruised, hyperventilating, and helpless in his house. He can think what he wants, but I won't make it easy on him. Still, if he thinks his lies are working, maybe he'll drop his guard.

I just need to give myself space to run.

When I try to speak, my voice comes out in a low, garbled rasp. It hurts. The giant one darts in front of me with a glass of water, holding it out without a word. If they were going to kill me, surely they would have done it earlier and not wasted time with poison. I take the water, gulping it down all at once as he stares in silence.

In my hurry, some of the water drips from the corner of my mouth. I wipe it away with the back of my left hand and tighten my grip on the glass. It's the only weapon I have. Maybe I can throw it or break it and use the sharp pieces to fight back.

I'll need to play this carefully. Testing my voice again, I keep the volume low and my tone calm.

"Why am I here?" I ask.

They exchange an uncomfortable glance. I retreat a step, trying to figure out the best path to the door without being obvious.

"We saw that guy attacking you. We were worried he might have a pack nearby, and since you were unconscious, we couldn't really ask permission." The frat bro shrugs his shoulders like he's embarrassed. I'm not buying it. No one with that many visible tattoos has any business pretending to be a boy next door.

He ramps up the excuses like he's sensing my skepticism.

"We loaded you up and brought you here so that you'd be safe." He smiles. "I'm Callum, by the way—Callum Casanell. That's Gideon Therion." There's no way he just gave me their real names . . . Unless he plans to kill me before it even matters. Silently, I think of them as the mouth and the muscle. The big guy has yet to say a word in front of me. The other guy talks a good game; I'll give him that. Plus, his smile is dazzling, but it's not so blinding that I don't notice what he's deliberately leaving out.

"Okay, sure." I narrow my eyes. "But why were you even there? I ran into you in a bar in the middle of nowhere, only for you to ride in and save the day hundreds of miles away." I pause for dramatic effect, letting a quiver slip into my voice as if the thought is only just now occurring to me. "Were you following me?"

I need to tread carefully. I want answers, but I also can't risk antagonizing these guys. There's bravery, which isn't really part of my repertoire anyway, and then there's doing what you have to do to survive. In my experience, the two rarely go hand in hand.

The mouthy one who claims his name is Callum grimaces, and the mountain of a man—Gideon—steps closer to me. Internally, I tense to run, letting my real fear show on my face. Maybe they aren't the kind of men who hurt women. I haven't met many of those, but surely they exist. Either way, it doesn't change my plans. I won't be taking the time to find out what kind of men they are, so it's best if they underestimate me.

"It's complicated . . ." Callum trails off, hesitantly continuing when I glare. "We were following you. That's true, but it's not what you think."

He has no idea what I think, but his excuses aren't cutting it. Like he can sense that I'm not buying it, he rushes on. "You seemed freaked out at the bar. We wanted to make sure you were alright."

Is he serious, right now?

It's true that I was freaked out, but if he thinks that tiny detail is enough to explain two strangers following me hundreds of miles, he's got another thing coming. This story has more holes than a goddamn colander.

Still, why deny kidnapping me after the fact? I'm here—wherever that is—armed only with a kitchen glass. Even at full strength, I'm no match for either of them in a fight, much less both. Maybe they don't know what they're doing, but it's been my experience that kidnappers don't go to the trouble of hiding their intentions at this stage.

I don't have a rule that applies here. That makes my skin crawl.

Fuck it. I'm just going to go for it and test them.

I clear my throat.

"Look, I can't just stay quiet when my safety is on the line." I sidestep cautiously towards what I hope is the front door. "Thanks for stepping in to help me." I smile, feeling both of them tracking my every move. "I'll be forever grateful that you stopped that . . . man." I stumble over the word, but push past it, because this is the moment of truth. "Now, if you can point me toward the nearest town, I'll get out of your hair."

I hold my breath, but I don't have to wait long for a genuine reaction.

A growl erupts from the giant's throat, draining whatever blood was left in my face. Something about the rush of fear combined with that noise sends my mind hurtling back to the moment on the side of the road. Similar animalistic sounds came from both my attacker and the *lion* that rescued me.

Shaking my head, I replay the memory once, twice, four times, reaching the same impossible conclusion each time. *How can that be real?* I must have a serious head injury because there's no way this man could be a lion. I know there are a lot of things that are difficult to explain in this world, but a fucking lion?

My back bumps against the wall, and I shudder. I didn't even realize I was retreating. Now, I'm cornered by two dangerous— men? That term might not even apply to this situation.

Suddenly, I feel like part of the bad end of the food chain.

This is terrible.

But if they want to kill me, I'm going to kick, scream, and bite the entire time, no matter how much bigger their teeth happen to be.

The talkative one steps forward. He seems on edge, which is frankly ridiculous and a little offensive. It's not like two strangers just followed *him* into the boonies and tossed *him* in the back of their car.

"Okay, everyone, just take a breath and stay calm." He glances nervously at the big guy before focusing back on me. "Ma'am—sorry, we don't even know your name, but Gideon feels he has a . . . connection with you."

I tense against the wall. Did I imagine him hesitating before saying the word connection? It doesn't matter. They're clearly delusional.

Ignoring the mouthpiece, I turn my focus to the bigger threat, the muscle. The giant looks like he's about to have a meltdown. He keeps tugging on his curls, while his irises are flashing from brown to an unnatural golden color. He's clearly malfunctioning. Something tells me I don't want to be anywhere near him if he fully loses it.

Sucking in a breath, I try to think. I need to be careful with this, but I'm tired of the lies. With my back literally against the wall, I have no choice but to push back.

"Stay away from me," I warn, hating the slight panic in my voice. To my shock, both men listen, freezing where they are.

"We won't hurt you."

"You say that, but you . . . kidnapped me," I hiss, clenching my hands to stop them from shaking. "You followed me hundreds of miles because he feels like we have a connection?" I point at the big guy, and then yank my hand back to my side when the other one grimaces. He opens his mouth, but it's too late to stop now. I need answers.

"I need to know why I saw glowing yellow eyes in a man's face and a lion running loose in Colorado." Neither of them reacts to that insane sentence, and I feel a rush of relief that I'm not actually going crazy.

"Explain. Please." I let the demand hang there as the tense silence builds. It drags on. One second. Two. Ten.

"You know about supernaturals." The big guy speaks for the first time, and my whole body jolts. Is that a statement or a question? I can't tell, but his voice is low and grumbly. It sends another shiver down my spine. My body buzzes to life. I've got to be in shock or suffering a mental break because I'm almost turned on right now.

Callum throws himself down into an armchair with a groan, covering his face with one hand. I lean against the wall, letting it support my weight while I grapple with how to respond.

"Are you saying you're not human?" I ask. I mean to come across as skeptically sane, but I really just sound like a mouse caught in a trap. The *lion*—Gideon—flops down on the couch with a huff.

"Right. Neither is Cal." He raises one eyebrow and stares me down. "And neither are you."

I manage not to flinch from pure force of habit. He can't know. No one knows. I've been so careful.

I force a brittle laugh.

"Okay, I don't know what fantasy novel you're living in, but I'm just a normal, *human* woman with bad taste in men." I shrug. "There's absolutely nothing special about me."

Even as the lies roll off my tongue, it's clear they don't believe me. Gideon actually looks at me like my response disappoints him, but the next words out of Callum's mouth destroy my hope of keeping them completely in the dark.

"I don't know what you are and you don't have to tell me. But you don't have to pretend. We could sense it from ten feet away."

I prepare to hold my ground, then reconsider. He said I didn't have to tell them anything. I can't risk accidentally revealing something to these strangers by continuing to lie. The partial truth is my best bet.

"As you guessed, Gideon is a shifter," Callum says. He looks at his friend and shakes his head slightly before focusing back on me. "He can pick his form, but he prefers the lion you saw before. I'm a little different." He scratches the back of his neck, his eyes boring a hole into the glass in my hand as he continues. "I'm . . . a demon. I'm not evil or anything. It's just how my kind are categorized."

He finishes the explanation in a rush, and I blink in shock. I can't believe he's telling me this. They don't even know me. It's the stupid kind of risk only a person completely confident in their ability to protect themselves would take. I've never had that luxury. In fact—wait, why is this man blushing? *Is he embarrassed?*

It's so ridiculous that I blame my shock for what happens next.

"Do you turn red and sprout a tail?" I tease, eying him up and down deliberately. I'm not sure which of us is more stunned by my joke. The demon's mouth drops open, then his entire expression turns predatory. Within seconds, I find myself the full target of the most intense smolder I've ever seen.

The wall is holding me up for a different reason now.

Gideon groans loudly, breaking our tense, embarrassing stare-off and dragging a pillow over his lap.

"Knock it off, you slut. This conversation is hard enough without a fucking hard on." His complaint registers in my short-circuiting brain. *Did he really just call me a slut?*

Before I can express my outrage, Callum turns the hypnotic expression toward his friend. Gideon freezes, but recovers quickly, lobbing the pillow at the demon's face to break the connection. They both laugh, and even though I'm confused, scared, and oddly overheated, I'm tempted to join in.

It's official. I've actually lost my mind.

The events of the last twenty-four hours are catching up to me as my exhaustion overpowers my survival instincts. Like they can sense the change, they both face me again. The full focus of their combined attention is intense.

"Look, I'm sure you're about to pass out," Callum says. "If you want to crash here, I swear nothing and no one will touch you as long as you want to stay. I give you my word." All the laughter is gone from his voice. I feel his black eyes searching my face.

I let my eyelids slip shut. I can't think straight while he's staring at me like that. To my shock, I think I might believe him. I do my standard safety assessment. My stomach churns. It's horribly risky, but these guys might actually be my best option for now.

Admittedly, my odds aren't great either way. It's dark. I don't know where I am. My adrenaline is wearing off, and I've barely slept at all since leaving the bar.

This decision could be the last one I ever make, but what choice do I have? Gritting my teeth, I give them both a hesitant nod. The look they exchange is so relieved I almost tell them I've changed my mind.

My eyelids droop. I'll reassess after a few hours of sleep.

When Callum leads me up the stairs and down the hall, I follow on autopilot, noting the exits. He leaves awkwardly after showing me to a cozy guest bedroom with an attached bathroom.

I find it stocked with towels and products. Even though I can barely keep my eyes open, I lock the door and take a quick shower. It's been so long since I've had access to hot water, I'm not about to waste the luxury. Gently, I wash the grime off of my body and take stock of the clusters of bruises, being extra careful to keep the bandages dry around my scrapes.

I've had worse, but I can tell I'll be feeling this fight for a while. I wash out my hair, letting the conditioner sit on the long, dark strands for a few minutes before rinsing it out.

Five minutes later, I'm running a comb through the tangles in my hair and grimacing as I slide back into my filthy clothes. When I return to the bedroom, I could cry with relief. My duffle is sitting neatly by the bed. It looks shabby compared to the rest of the room, but that bag holds everything I own.

Still, I don't like that one of them came in here to drop it off while I was vulnerable in the shower. I reach for the bag, then freeze. The pocketknife I stabbed the drifter with is propped on top. I grab it with shaky fingers. Memories of blood trickling down the hilt onto my hand flood my brain.

It's going to be gross . . . except it isn't.

Someone cleaned the blood from the blade and made sure I would find it first thing. It's a small gesture. The knife wouldn't do a damn thing against an actual lion, but somehow I feel better. Not enough to get lulled into a false sense of complacency, though.

No, I'm completely aware of how outgunned I am. That's why I lock the bedroom door and slide a nearby chair under the knob. It probably won't hold them for long, but I can't get the heavy armoire to budge. At the least, I hope my preparations will buy me enough time to defend myself.

Rifling through my ratty assortment of things, I find what I'm looking for and slide into a worn, oversized t-shirt and shorts. Whether I need to fight or flee, I'd rather not do either in tattered, blood-soaked clothes.

Maybe I won't have to.

It's nothing but wishful thinking. I'd be better off banning thoughts like that.

Sinking into the soft down of the pillow top mattress, I breathe deeply for the first time in more than a day. It's like resting on a cloud. The duvet cover is even giving me a false sense of security with how it wraps around me, cocooning me away from the rest of the world. This bed is literally to die for. I can only hope fate doesn't actually expect me to pay up.

I fall into a sleep that's free of nightmares but filled with sexy men staring at me.

It's disturbing, even in my dreams.

CHAPTER
FOUR

GIDEON

The birds are chirping, the sun is shining, and I couldn't ask for a better day to run. Too bad my mind is a million miles away. I finish stretching and take off anyway.

Each morning, I wind my way up and down the mountain trail, sometimes fast, sometimes slow. The altitude was a bitch at first, but I'm used to it now. The exercise is great for burning off my energy and keeping my animal in check.

Cal and I picked this spot for our cabin because it feels wild. We're in Colorado; it doesn't take long to get to the mountains no matter where you live here, but this section of the Rockies is literally our backyard.

My arms pump as I dig deeper. Faster. Harder. If I push hard enough maybe I'll be able to outrun all the shit in my head.

Despite the breeze, I'm working up a sweat today. I should be enjoying myself, but instead I feel like I'm about to miss a step and swan dive off the side off the cliff. Seriously, my brain is more twisted than a corn maze right now, and I've never been great with puzzles.

I up my pace, feeling the burn from my calves to my quads. I trip over a loose rock. It's easy to regain my balance, but the rock isn't so lucky. It disappears over the edge, swallowed up by the morning mist.

If I'd ever stopped to consider what I wanted from the gods before maybe it would be her. But it's literally never crossed my mind. I picture the waitress, my mate, in my head. Dark hair, dark circles under her eyes, and a level of exhaustion that goes a hell of a lot deeper than a few sleepless nights. She's beautiful and tough, but something about her seems fragile, like I could break her with one wrong move.

I don't do well around fragile things. My mom has always joked about needing to tie things down to keep me from knocking them over. While I've grown into my size now, it's not like I've had much practice with breakable people.

She's not what I need, not even a little bit. My brain knows this, but my body and soul don't care. Even now, there's a tug in my chest, pushing me to turn around and go back to her. The longer I spend scrambling up this trail, the more frustrated it gets.

How can my body know we're made for each other when I have absolutely no idea what she is?

She doesn't smell like a shifter, but she doesn't feel like a demon or fae. I guess she could be a witch, but magic leaves a residue behind that's almost impossible to mask—even for the most powerful magic users.

Part of me wants to just throw all my cards on the table. If I tell her what she is to me, we could decide what to do together. Except that would send her running. I know that in my gut.

She might actually be the least trusting person I've ever met. That's saying something, considering the dodgy nature of most supernaturals. If I come right out and tell her everything, I'll never see her again.

I'm not ready to face that, so I can't risk complete honesty yet. But I also don't want to lie to her. Everything in me rebels against the idea of keeping secrets from my mate. That's why I've let Callum do the talking. He's better with words anyway, and I'm likely to give something away or scare her into running again if I take over.

After she went to bed, Callum and I hammered out a game plan with three simple objectives. Number one: don't scare her off. Number two: figure out what she is. Number three: find out who is hunting her and rip them into tiny pieces.

This approach requires patience. Based on how well I slept last night knowing she was safe under my roof, it will be worth it in the long run. A sharp pinch hits my chest, so I give in and turn around.

Making my way down the mountain, I feel a little more confident. We may not even know her name, but I trust Callum with my life. If he thinks baby steps are the key to earning her trust, I'll tiptoe around for as long as it takes. Fated mates are practically a myth. I'm not about to be the first one in history to spit on a gift from the gods.

The house comes into view, and I slow down to let my body cool off.

I toe my trail shoes off and kick them out of the porch walkway, pulling my shirt off and using it to wipe away my sweat. Walking into the kitchen, I see her standing at the coffee pot.

Despite the cooldown, my heart damn near beats itself out of my chest when she looks me over from head to toe. The feeling of her eyes running over my skin makes me want to do something incredibly stupid like snatch her up and nibble on her neck.

I do neither, thank the gods. But I can't resist testing her reaction to me by reaching over her head to grab a coffee mug. As I expect, she freezes when I flex my bare abs and arms.

"Good morning," I mutter.

I don't think she even hears me. She's watching a bead of sweat trickle down my chest like it's the most interesting thing she's ever seen. Her green eyes track the progress of the drop until it disappears into the waistband of my sweatpants.

She wants me.

The thought makes me want to roar in triumph and sweep her

off her feet. I hold myself back again, willing myself not to get a boner and ruin the moment.

I guess unflappable self-control is my new fucking superpower.

Take that, mom.

SHEENA

BLOOD RUSHES to my cheeks, and my heart hums shamelessly in my chest.

This man is dangerous, and I've just made a fool of myself. I'm not sure which is worse. He must have some kind of mind-control power because there's no reason I should be objectifying a complete stranger.

Christ, I stared at that man like he was a piece of meat. All he was trying to do was get some coffee. Part of me is embarrassed, but the other part is still obsessing over his sweaty muscles and how tiny he makes me feel. Seriously, is it even natural to be that tall?

I should be scared, so why do I want to get closer? I blame my deranged behavior on the stress of the last twenty-four hours.

Gideon watches me silently from a safe distance away, sipping his coffee from a swiveling chrome barstool. Since he's studying me, I return the favor. Dark blonde hair falls in messy curls around his ears, and there's some stubble built up on his jaw. I can't tell what he's thinking, but if I had to guess, he's probably worried his houseguest is about to jump him.

For a second, I imagine what it would feel like to cross the room and press my lips to his. Would they be soft or is a man of his size incapable of being gentle? A shiver runs down my spine.

Oh my god, I did it again.

When I see him smirking behind his coffee cup, I mentally slap myself. I've got to snap out of it.

After the best night of sleep I've had in years, I decided this was a good chance to find out more about the supernatural world. Ever since I was violently tossed into the middle of it, I've been wildly unprepared. Maybe if I understood more about what was going on, I'd have an easier time staying out of it. Either way, as long as I feel safe here, this is a rare opportunity for me.

I clear my throat.

"So, you're a shapeshifter, Gideon?" When he smiles at me, it encourages me to keep going. "How long have you known about that?"

His smile doesn't fade, but he looks confused now.

I'm just relieved he's not mad.

"I've always known," he explains. "Both my parents are omnis. My dad prefers birds of prey, but my mom likes cats."

His deep voice rolls over me and his eyes twinkle. More bare skin appears in the corner of my vision. I blink a few times. *What did he say?*

"You always were a momma's boy." Callum dodges Gideon's playful punch as he joins us in the kitchen, his husky chuckle echoing around the room.

My mouth goes dry. He's shirtless too.

Jesus, does no one in this house fully dress themselves?

I'm just trying to drink my coffee and mind my own business, and this guy is strutting around in nothing but athletic shorts and a backwards cap, his tattooed chest and arms on display, just asking me to . . .

Goddammit.

Heat rushes to my cheeks. I've now lived long enough to see myself become a walking, talking, waving in the wind, red flag. I add shame to the growing list of unpleasant emotions churning in my gut.

It's not fair.

"Good morning . . .?" The demon—his word, not mine—looks at me with a friendly smile. There's an obvious question lingering at the end of his greeting. He's asking for my name. Do I dare give it to him?

I'm surprised when I realize I want to share this small piece of me.

"I'm Sheena."

When I give them my name, part of me expects something terrible to happen. When it doesn't, my exhale comes out ragged. It's noticeable, and I'm a little embarrassed. It's just a name. Everyone has one, but it's one of the few things I own. After guarding every piece of myself for years, I desperately want to hear someone say it with a fraction of warmth.

If my breathing is over the top, his smile makes my reaction look tame. Callum knocks me off kilter yet again with his white, gleaming teeth and genuine joy.

A wave of fear sinks into my heart. I can't let them become important. My rules are clear.

Gideon slips off the stool. He's surprisingly graceful for a man his size, but it's impossible not to notice when he moves. He walks over to me, transferring his coffee mug to his left hand and reaching out with his right.

It hangs in the air between us waiting for me to decide.

He could snap my arm like a twig. Something tells me he won't.

I slide my hand into Gideon's outstretched one. His fingers and palm are rough with calluses, and my hand disappears, completely swallowed by his size. He shakes our clasped hands up and down gently.

"It's a pleasure to meet you, Sheena," he rumbles. My eyes drift shut, overwhelmed by the sound. My name has never sounded so perfect.

The buzzing in my chest goes silent.

I suck in a breath.

Romantic fantasies are a thing of my past—the hopes of a lonely child that pain forced me to outgrow. Given my experiences, I learned long ago that happily ever after only belongs in storybooks. But there's something about the way I feel right now . . .

I guess I get why some people risk everything for a chance to feel.

Like they know how difficult it was for me to give them my name, neither man asks any follow-up questions. Instead, Callum digs through the cabinets, pulling out a pan and asking me what my favorite omelet ingredients are. Though I don't register words leaving my mouth, I must say something, because before I know it, I'm sitting at the kitchen table with a steaming breakfast in front of me. It's the best thing I've eaten in years.

I feel like the foundation I've built my life on is crumbling beneath me, but the banter between Gideon and Callum is easy and light.

"You've known each other for a long time then?" I ask, clinging to their normalcy and hoping it rubs off on me.

Gideon smiles as he chews an enormous bite, and Callum takes over seamlessly. He's clearly used to speaking up when his friend can't.

"Since we were born, actually." Callum smiles at Gideon, a genuine expression that shows off his perfect teeth. "Our parents went to school together and now lead the same enclave. Lots of kids didn't trust me because of my . . . heritage, but Gideon always shut them up. Before I knew it, I was stuck with him."

The giant blonde man looks almost embarrassed, a rosy blush spreading up his neck and across his cheeks.

"Yeah, well, kids are dumb." Gideon clears his throat. "I knew you were pack from the start."

Watching Callum from the corner of my eye, I can see the words sink in. There's a moment of silence as he stares across the table at his friend.

"Anyway, we went to the academy together . . ." Callum trails off when he notices my confused look. "Starfall Academy. It sounds pretentious as fuck, but supernaturals are pretty big on traditions. Students learn how to handle their powers and choose vocational skills that will benefit their enclave. Pretty much everyone goes there."

Except me, apparently.

Gideon nods and picks up where Callum left off.

"Yeah, think of it as an undergrad program for everyone who isn't quite human." He smiles at me warmly, dimples popping up again on his cheeks. "I bet you would have been there at the same time as us. We graduated four years ago."

There it is. Another optional opportunity to share more about myself. It's a kind gesture, and I'm honestly tempted, but I don't take him up on it.

"It sounds like a magical place. Do you like the work you do now?" I'm obviously fishing for info, but neither of them calls me out on it. Gideon shrugs.

"It's interesting, I guess. Especially when we get to investigate stuff. We don't patrol or arrest people for public nudity after they shift or anything dumb like that, but there is crime." Gideon scratches the back of his neck. "Recently, we're looking into a possible case of trafficking."

He's watching me carefully now, and I realize I might not be the only one fishing.

"We're trying to figure out if it's a group of human zealots or some supernatural gang snatching up women with no protection."

I gulp and feel my skin pebble.

What he's describing sounds so familiar that I feel like someone dropped a cube of ice down the back of my shirt. It also wasn't subtle at all. I expect to feel panic, and maybe I would if it wasn't for the obvious worry radiating off of him.

Is he worried about me?

No one has looked at me like that since I was a teenager, not since—I stop that train of thought in its tracks. I need to act normal. Absolutely no good can come of me taking a trip down memory lane right now.

A sharp, unexpected zap in my chest cavity makes me jump. I

rub the heel of my hand over my heart to ease the pressure, and Gideon tracks the movement with burning golden eyes. His stare, the buzzing in my chest . . . It's all too intense. I can't do this. Staying here was a mistake.

I look to the door and brace to run, but I never get the chance. Gideon stands, yanking me into his hard body roughly for—a hug. He folds me into his chest and wraps himself around me like a blanket. As if we're not strangers who just met. Like he knew I was on the verge of a nervous breakdown and about to sprint from the room screaming.

He can't just put his hands on me like this.

I'm bracing to push back and make a run for it when I notice the maddening live wire in my chest has finally gone quiet. The peace is so unexpected and wonderful that instead of shoving him away, I breathe a sigh of relief and relax into his chest.

"Sorry, Sheena. Just trying to give the connection what it needs," he rumbles near my ear. I feel the words against my cheek. One big hand cradles the back of my head gently, and I can hear his heart thumping beneath his skin. It's a reassuring sound, and despite everything, I try to turn my brain off and accept the comfort of it.

I can always run later. Once I figure out what he's hiding.

A clatter at the sink makes me jump and I lift my head to see Callum washing dishes. He's got his back to us, a flimsy attempt to give us some privacy, but blood rushes to my face, anyway. He must think I'm some sort of weak woman with the common sense of a fruit fly.

Hell, I practically just climbed his best friend in the kitchen minutes after revealing my name. I stiffen and try to pull away. I don't get far.

"Cal, leave the dishes for a second. It's group hug time," Gideon insists, pulling my head back into his chest. I hear a soft chuckle a second before more warm skin molds to my back. Tattooed arms stretch past me to wrap around Gideon as well.

I'm surrounded.

A shiver runs down my spine, but for once I'm not scared. While Callum is a lot taller than me, he's significantly shorter than the blonde giant that is Gideon. Callum tucks his chin on top of my head like he's done it a million times.

"You are such a cuddler, dude," he mutters. "Sheena, keep an eye on him. He'll find any excuse to snuggle and try to make it mandatory." Callum's words are playful but filled with affection. It's obvious he doesn't mind.

"It's nice," I murmur, surprised to find I mostly mean it. "No one's ever . . ." I trail off, embarrassed to admit it's been a long time since I mattered enough to anyone to be held. The sudden tension in both of their bodies tells me they got the message loud and clear.

"Get used to it," Gideon says as he pulls back gently. "I've got a hug with your name on it ready whenever you want."

It's a little awkward, but neither of them makes a big deal about it. They both simply unravel their limbs and move over to the sink like nothing happened. I stare for a few minutes, trying to process.

The door is right there. They have their backs turned, but something tells me I'm not done here. Trusting my gut, I grab the drying towel hanging from the oven door and step up to the sink.

Gideon hands me the first dish with a smile, and we finish them all in companionable silence. Once the skillet is stowed under the stove, Callum turns to look at me.

"Do you want to rest today or explore?" He glances at my waist. "I know you're pretty bruised up, but I figured you might want to take a look around."

Is he this trusting? Maybe it's a trap, but I can hardly pass up a chance to get my bearings in the daylight in case I need to run.

Twisting my torso, I feel the tug of my torn skin. While I'm still a little achy, the worst of the pain is gone. "I think I can handle a little exploring." I smile at him, and for a split second, I swear I see something moving in his eyes. By the time I blink to get a better look, all I see is the unusual black color I noticed last night.

"That's great, Sheena." He says my name again. The sound both unnerves me and feels nice. "We can start with the house, see how you feel, and then check out some of the best trails." Callum glances at Gideon.

"You coming, or do you have other urgent plans?" There's something about his smirk that makes me feel like I'm missing the punch line of a joke.

"I'm just going to take a shower really quick, but I'll meet you guys outside," Gideon says. In a flash, he disappears around the corner, then I hear him galloping up the stairs.

With laughter in his eyes, Callum shows me around the main level.

We return to the cozy living room. I see the couch I regained consciousness on—before I was given a guest bedroom to sleep in —and a stone fireplace next to it that I failed to notice yesterday.

There's also a wraparound porch with various entry points around the floor. Callum shows me each of them, including one that jams easily. He shows me how to lift the door slightly to get it to open, then he points out a hidden key under a pot in case I get locked out.

He's definitely too trusting.

I trail after him, taking in the home gym off the side of the garage. There are weights, a rower, an elliptical machine, and a couple of treadmills. Though I pick up a faint smell of sweat and disinfectant, it's not gross. Black mats cover the floor, and one side is sectioned off for what I can only assume is a sparring zone. I see some boxing gloves dangling from a hook next to some wraps and a haphazard stack of towels.

"We spend a lot of time in here." He picks up a stray towel and tosses it into a hamper in the corner. "You're welcome to use anything you want. If there's anything you want to change or add, just let us know."

I nod, like it's not crazy as hell that this complete stranger just offered to let me take over his home gym.

He shows me the rest of the house, including what I now

know are five bedrooms upstairs, before leaving me to get ready for the outdoors tour.

I slip into a pair of worn jeans, forcing myself not to overthink things. The rips in the knees come more from rough use than fashion, but they fit perfectly. Tying a flannel around my waist in case I get cold, I shove my feet into the sturdy hiking books I wear on the run. A look at the clock shows it's been almost half an hour since we finished the dishes. I make my way downstairs and out to the porch.

The view takes my breath away.

Since I've been forced to travel so much in my life, you'd think I'd be numb to the beauty of just being outside. Despite it all, I still go misty eyed when I look at the mountains. They are so strong, so old, so dependable. The longer I stare up at them, the more they lend me their strength. Maybe that's stupid, but I can't help feeling a little more capable.

The screen door opens with a subtle whine and both men join me. Gideon's cheeks are a little red, and there's something about Callum's smirk that makes me even surer that I'm missing a joke. I search for something—anything—to say, but come up blank. Thankfully, I'm saved when Gideon grins down at me and throws his arm over my shoulder.

"Let's take the ATVs." Gideon's deep voice booms with enthusiasm.

I can barely keep up with his long strides. When I try, the raw scrapes on my ribs pull painfully.

"Slow down, you Neanderthal. She's like three feet tall," Callum shouts from behind us. While I'm grateful he said something about the pace, I narrow my eyes at his wording.

"I'm five foot two, actually," I sputter. "Probably an inch taller in these shoes." I stomp the dusty ground to illustrate my point. There's a tiny pause, then they both burst out laughing. I grind to a halt and their laughter dies down as they exchange glances.

"It's a very respectable height," Callum backtracks. "Practically average for a woman, I think . . ." He says the words with a straight face, but my eyes narrow when Gideon can't quite hide how his lips are twitching.

"Yes, yes, Sheena is so tall." He rolls his eyes as I glare at him. "The only reason I'm doing *this* is because I want to . . ." Gideon hoists me onto his back so quickly my head spins, wrapping his giant hands under my thighs. Suddenly, I'm seven feet tall and riding on the back of a giant with no impulse control. "Not because I'm worried we won't make it back by dark at this pace."

I gasp and demand he put me down, but he just pretends he can't hear me. Instead, he takes off at a bouncy trot, forcing me to grip his shoulders or risk backflipping to my death in the dirt. When I glance over my shoulder for backup, Callum just smirks and matches his jog to ours.

Maybe a quarter of a mile later, we reach a clearing with a small, well-kept barn. Callum places a steadying hand on my back as I slide down to the ground. When I take a step away and turn to face him, he laughs at my wide-eyed, exasperated look.

"I told you, he's a cuddler," Callum explains, grinning like that even begins to describe the wild, unsanctioned piggyback ride through the woods.

I shake my head. This day is getting weirder by the hour.

CALLUM

I SHOULDN'T HAVE TOUCHED HER.

Sheena's cheeks are rosy. Her dark hair is a little tangled after the jog through the woods. She looks torn between annoyance and embarrassment, and I want to kiss the look right off her face.

I'm a fool.

This is Gideon's *mate*. Literally some fated, magical, 'their souls are designed for each other' type of shit. Sure, they might not be together yet, but I know what she is to him—what they will be to each other. It's practically destiny.

There's just one problem: I still want to kiss her.

I hate myself for it, but my incubus doesn't care. It's his fucking fault that I want to push Sheena up against a tree and make her moan and scream until her voice goes hoarse. It's definitely his fault that I want to lay her down on top of the ATV and lick her until she's a dripping, whimpering mess, begging for permission to come on my face.

Honestly, that's all pretty standard issue incubus stuff. But kissing away the embarrassment on her face? I'm not sure I can blame that on demonic nature.

My chest feels tight, the ever-present seed of anxiety in my gut growing exponentially as it feeds on what ifs until I can feel it twisting around my organs like a parasitic vine. What if I ruin everything? What if I lose my best friend? What if I prove everyone right about me?

Lingering lust burns inside me and my power hums beneath my skin, poking, prodding, singeing me from the inside out as it looks for an outlet. I want to gag.

I can't fuck her, can't kiss her, can't ruin this for Gideon. She's off limits. Full stop. Past, present, or future—no matter how much we would both like it.

I close my eyes and picture all that long, dark hair wrapped around my fist as I pump into—no.

Stop it, Callum. We can't have her.

I repeat it like a mantra. Shit, I'll keep reminding myself and my demon as long as it takes to banish the dirty thoughts in my head.

I'm in control. *I'm in control, dammit.*

My body doesn't get the message. Gods. It's been years since a daydream made me hard, but here I am about to hop on an ATV with a stiffy. I'm disgusted with myself.

Unable to meet Gideon's eyes, I shuffle into the barn, giving both of them my back and urging my body to cool off. Grabbing the keys from the lockbox, I toss one set in Gideon's direction and settle on top of my four-wheeler.

I can feel them both watching me. The vine of anxiety inside me sprouts thorns.

I've got to have space. Now.

Without a word, I crank up the ATV and back it out of the barn. I'm acting like an asshole, but I need a minute. It's not like I can even explain what's going on. That would be even worse.

Sheena's suspicious expression brands the side of my face as I take off. She's just waiting for us to give her a reason to leave. Now I've given her one. Gideon is going to kick my ass, and I deserve it.

The cool wind beats against my face, and the vine loosens its hold enough for me to suck in a thread of crisp, wispy oxygen. The air may be thinner up here, but the view is worth the extra effort from my lungs.

Maybe I can salvage this.

When the hum of their engine joins mine, I try to just enjoy the ride. Unable to resist, I glance over my shoulder. Sheena is riding in front, short enough that Gideon can see over the top of her head with no problem. But with the way her body is pressed against him, I can sense the effect it's having on my friend.

A shiny blue helmet protects Sheena's head, while Gideon's massive arms rest securely on either side of her body—a barrier against the occasional overgrown branches crowding the trail. We've had that helmet forever but never touched it. I'm not surprised Gideon made her put it on, but I wish he hadn't—I can't make out her expression behind the tinted visor.

They look so good together.

Seeing Gideon folded around her like that is enough to make me hot all over again. I've obviously gone too long without feeding. My demon sees the makings of a delicious meal. I see the beginning of my end.

WE RIDE FOR ABOUT AN HOUR, exploring the trails around our home. It's relaxing, and some of my unhinged urges fade to the background by the time we reach our favorite spot in front of a small pond. Nestled along the side of the mountain, the water is cold enough to take your breath away year round. It's mostly made up of the runoff of melting snow from the mountain peaks. Despite the temperature, it's both gorgeous and peaceful.

After the way I saw Sheena staring at the mountains this morning, I hope she likes it.

Climbing off my ride, I give my hungry incubus one last lecture. I'll be damned if I screw a friend over because of a lack of self-control. Plus, this woman seems like she's been through enough already.

I pop open the storage compartment, pulling out the quilt we brought along and laying it on the ground. By focusing completely on the task, I avoid looking at either of them for a full minute. Too bad I can still feel the way she watches me.

She knows something is up.

While a heavy silence lingers between Sheena and I, Gideon makes up for it by talking a mile a minute. He points out the mountain range, the pond, the melting snow, and some random shit about the fuel efficiency of the ATV that I didn't even know. I've never seen him so nervous, chattering like a fourteen-year-old on his first date. Sheena takes pity on him and asks how we found this spot, a soft smile tugging at the corners of her lips.

Meanwhile, I plop down on the blanket and stare at the horizon like it's the only thing I've ever cared about in my life. I dread finding out what this woman thinks of me now.

When they come over and join me on the quilt, Sheena settles on the very edge. Gideon takes one look at her hovering by the damp ground and drags her into the center of the blanket, right between his legs. *Oh, for fuck's sake.*

Since that was a weird ass thing to do, Sheena noticeably stiffens.

"I'm sorry. That was . . ." Gideon stammers, keeping his hands at his sides awkwardly. "I was just . . . there's dirt on the ground."

I burst out laughing, unable to hold it in.

Sheena jumps at the loud sound, then relaxes against him, smirking.

"Makes sense, since we are outside."

Gideon's tan gives way to a mottled, red blush, and he narrows his eyes at me as I continue to laugh. But for once, I've done something right because I can literally see the tension leaving Sheena's body.

It's clear she's unused to physical affection. Gideon, on the other hand, is tactile in the extreme. He pretty much groups everyone he meets into two categories: people he wants to hug or people he wants to kill. He's got to tread lightly, or she's going to bolt.

"Do you want to see me shift?" His question catches us both off guard. That's the opposite of treading lightly. Sheena's jaw drops, and I laugh again.

"Damn, you just dropped that on her," I say when he glares at me. He shrugs and hops to his feet.

"I just thought she might want to see, since last time . . ." He stops abruptly, realizing he's just shoved his giant foot in his mouth again.

I'm about to attempt damage control when Sheena giggles.

"It's okay. I *am* curious," she admits. "Can you really turn into anything?" Her big green eyes look up at him, and he gulps. I resist rolling my eyes. He's such a goner.

"Any animal, as long as I've seen it." He puffs out his chest, and I hide my smile. It's adorable watching him try to impress her.

"What about like unicorns or dragons?" She teases, but neither of us corrects her. When Gideon steps back and pulls off his shirt with one hand, Sheena is gaping at him in wide-eyed disbelief.

"Wait, they're real? Are you serious?" By the time she gets the second question out, her voice is barely more than a squeak.

When his pants hit the ground, so does her jaw. I choke on another laugh and ignore the zip of heat that shoots through me as she tries to look anywhere but his crotch and fails miserably. Gideon notices, slipping his thumb into the waistband of his boxer briefs with a grin so big I can see both his dimples.

Sheena sputters, and I take pity on her.

"He's kidding," I say, tossing a pinecone at his junk. Gideon catches the projectile easily with his shifter reflexes and hurls it back at me. I bat it away and grin.

"Dragons are real, though. I just haven't seen one," Gideon insists. "I'm not sure about unicorns." He's bouncing up and down now with excitement as Sheena blinks up at him with her mouth hanging open.

"What would you like him to shift into?" I ask, keeping my voice low.

"Well, if I can't see a unicorn, I don't know." Her eyes lick up his bare skin, like she can't help checking him out. "Why don't you show me your favorite?"

Oh gods.

I don't even have time to suggest that maybe this isn't such a good idea before Gideon vanishes. He squats down as a man, then his body contorts and twists, and a lion stands in front of us. The entire process takes less than a second, but it wasn't always that way. I wince as I remember dozens of painful, lengthy attempts to shift when he first started.

Sheena stares at the lion, amazement and fear warring for dominance on her face. The cat is huge. He's almost as tall as me —at least eleven feet long, and a total fucking showboat. There's prancing, tail swishing, and a roar that makes goose bumps spread along the delicate curve of Sheena's neck.

When Gideon crouches down and prepares to pounce, my heart jumps to my throat. He launches straight towards her face and I panic. Why didn't we even consider weird animal reactions to the mate bond?

Before I can throw myself between the two of them, Gideon's

lion changes to a fluffy bunny in mid-air. Landing at the edge of the quilt, he hops the rest of the distance to Sheena, nose and tail wiggling. I can hear her heart pounding from several feet away. She stares down at the tiny, brown rabbit and its violently twitching nose as it feels the anxiety in the air.

This was . . . a joke?

I'm going to kill him.

"He . . . What?" Sheena stutters, looking to me for answers.

"He's an idiot," I sigh, feeling my pulse return to normal as I relax back on my propped arms. The bunny shifts to a puppy then, complete with tiny ears, tiny feet, and a tiny, pitiful whine. The dog, much like the man, is so full of shit. There's no way Sheena will fall for—nope, I was wrong. She's eating his act up like a hot fudge sundae.

She scoops the puppy up, cradling him to her chest and pressing kisses to his fuzzy head. He licks her cheek and she giggles. I narrow my eyes at Gideon, watching the goofy grin spread across his canine mouth as she lavishes him with attention. He's playing her like a fiddle, but it's nice to see her relax.

I close my eyes, enjoying the peaceful quiet. I might have drifted off to sleep if Sheena's soft voice didn't bring me back.

"It's beautiful out here," she whispers. "I don't want to wear out my welcome, Callum."

There's tension in her voice that wasn't there a moment ago. I open my eyes to see her staring out at the water, a faint furrow in her forehead.

She takes my breath away.

"Let us worry about that," I tell her, watching Gideon's puppy squirm in her lap. He doesn't like the direction this conversation is taking, and I can't say I blame him. Even if I never completely understand the mate bond, I can see he's already getting attached. *Shit.* He deserves a chance.

I've got to convince her to stay.

"Sheena, the house, this land." I point at the view all around us. "In a lot of ways, it's our sanctuary. It could be the same for you." She looks at me then, her big green eyes studying my face. I will her to feel my sincerity. Part of me wants to keep talking. I can spit lists of logical arguments all day, but instinct tells me to shut up and let her think.

The silence stretches between us, but it's comfortable. My offer is out there; the choice is hers now. When it's time to pack up and head back, I stand, offering her my hand. She slips her fingers along my palm with no hesitation. Need rips through me like a tidal wave, but I'm firmly in control now.

I'm more than an incubus. More than a monster. I'm a man, a loyal friend with responsibilities, and godsdammit, I'd rather die than put that look of fear back on her face.

To pacify my hungry demon, I tug her to her feet and press a kiss to her knuckles. I soak up her peachy blush. Her reaction quiets the raging urge I have to lay her back down on the picnic quilt.

For a blink, it feels like we're the only people on this planet.

Only when dog-Gideon tilts his head to the side and yips do I remember we're not alone. He shifts back into a naked man, and Sheena's blush spreads like a wildfire. Yanking her hand from mine, she turns her back politely until he's dressed, completely missing the silent conversation between Gideon and I. It involves a lot of raised eyebrows and shrugging, but I know I'm fucked. He's definitely going to bring this up later.

During the ride home, I try to think of a way to explain, but I get nowhere. My mind is too busy replaying the stupid hand kiss to figure out how I'm going to tell my best friend I want the girl who's meant to be his.

CHAPTER
FIVE

SHENA

Some sweet sixteen.

I shove at the wall of bitterness inside me, but it doesn't budge. Will I always be alone? It's not like I want much. I know I can't have a house on the hill complete with two happy parents, a pair of siblings, and a spotted dog, but it would be nice to experience something like the other kids at school. A party, a present—shit, even a hug would be cool. A tear trickles out of the corner of my eye. It slides down my cheek, then falls, sinking into the scratchy polyester sheets. I roll over, burying my face in the lumpy twin mattress and slamming my fist into the bed. It was dumb to think things would change.

Another year gone. Another foster family making my life hell.

This was supposed to be my best year yet. School was going okay, and I had Quaid. He showed up in middle school—a stranger that somehow became my lifeline. We were going to become more this year because I was finally going to tell him how I felt. I never got the chance. Something changed for him. Now the walls are closing in, and I don't even have my friend anymore.

Quaid has been giving me the cold shoulder for a few weeks. He's always been moody, though, so I gave him space. I expected him to pull *his head out of his ass today to wish me a happy birthday. No such luck. When I waved in the hallway, he turned his back on me like I was a contagious disease. It was so obvious a few girls nearby even giggled, and a tiny piece of my heart shattered on the chipped linoleum floor. Even now, the humiliation rushes back in, burning my cheeks. I lift my head from the mattress, sucking in some air.*

"I wish things were different," I whisper into the dark, hoping that fairy godmothers are real and something, or someone, will step in to rescue me. For a solid minute, I hold my breath and put all my hope in the fantasy.

As usual, I'm disappointed. Nothing changes. Except . . . wait . . . something seems different. I feel a breeze and hear a faint thud. My heart races. The heat was stifling earlier, so maybe I left the window open. Fighting the urge to close my eyes again and hide under the covers, I reach a shaky hand out towards the lamp on my bedside table.

My fingers never reach the switch. A bony hand clamps down on my wrist. Another one covers my mouth.

The instincts I've honed while living in a roster of shitty foster homes tells me I've only got one chance. I fight like hell. This life is crap, but it's all I've got. If they get me out of this house, I'll just become another statistic, a rumored runaway no one bothers to look for.

The hand over my mouth is too tight for me to scream, but that's not the only way to make noise. So I thrash, kicking out with my legs and ramming the rickety headboard against the wall. The lamp smashes on the floor.

"Gods, get a hold of her." The man's raspy voice makes me fight even harder against the disembodied hands pressing against me. His voice is somehow both oily and rough. I shudder at the sound. Faint light from the streetlight outside my window gives me a glimpse of a skull mask. I try to scream again, but only a small, muffled squeak escapes. Maybe I've done enough because someone's stomping down the narrow hallway to my room. My foster mother's shrill voice is music to my ears as she throws the door open without knocking, light flooding the room.

"Sheena, you slut, do you have some boy in here? Keep quiet, or you'll be sleeping in the—" Rebecca's tirade cuts off abruptly when she

sees two masked men dressed in all black holding me pinned to the bed. Her eyes go wide as she takes in the skull masks.

The man with his hand over my mouth glances at his partner and shrugs. "Might as well test her out now." The other man grunts, lifts his head and locks his cold, yellow eyes with mine.

"I wish that woman would leave this room, erase your existence, and forget she ever had a foster child." What the hell is he talking about? Rebecca is a piece of shit, but she'll call the cops and—my body erupts with burning pain. Through the agony, I watch as she leaves the room without a word, her eyes vacant. Please, don't go. I want to beg her for help, but I can't.

The door closes with a final, familiar thud. I'm confused, terrified, and the burning won't stop. I will my body to keep fighting, but it doesn't listen. Lying limp on the mattress, my attackers high five over my body as I struggle to see through the spots dotting my vision.

"Ten years of hunting, and we've finally hit the jackpot." Yellow eyes' voice is the last thing I hear before another wave of pain drags me under.

I GASP, sitting up with a start on an unfamiliar bed. Even all these years later, dreaming of the night they took me still leaves me terrified. I shake my head, but I know from experience I won't be able to dislodge the memories that easily. Sweaty strands of hair cling to the side of my neck. My breath escapes in frantic, irregular puffs as my hands tremble.

I can't have a panic attack here. I go through my grounding checklist; a combination of trial and error and PTSD tips I found online at a public library a few years back. Assuring myself I'm not back in that room, I reach out for the duvet, feeling its softness under my fingertips. This material is cool and light, nothing like the cheap bedding I grew up with. I grip it tightly.

Inhaling deeply, I smell the coconut shampoo I used before bed. It mixes with the salty tang of my sweat, but it's different enough from the past that my breathing slows. Then I wiggle my toes one by one and list as many animated movies as I can think of. The longer I list them, the more I'm able to claw myself back to a place of calm.

Once I've pushed the panic attack back, I time my breaths—inhaling for five seconds, holding for five more, then blowing out the air for a final five. By the time I'm done, I'm exhausted. I sink back into the pillows, trembling both from the nightmare and the decisions I need to make.

My rules tell me I should cut my losses and run.

There's just one problem: I don't want to.

Today was nice. Fun, even. Riding ATVs through the mountains with Gideon and Callum made me feel fifteen again. Back then, I was the kind of girl who dared to dream of a better life and a love that could conquer anything. That girl was naive. She died the night she turned sixteen. I'd be better off if I left her and her hopeful fantasies buried in the past.

As always, the nightmare was horrible. But it was also an important reminder. I'm being hunted. I can't forget that, no matter how drawn I am to these guys.

That's another problem . . . I see how they look at me. If I'm not careful, I could come between them. A shiver runs through my body. From Gideon's messy, blonde curls and constant touches to Callum's dark gaze and brooding intensity, I'm completely sucked in. I want them in a way that's both unfamiliar to me and threatening as hell to my survival.

I've literally never had a positive sexual experience, so I'm not sure why my dormant libido is kicking into gear now. Seriously, a few of the fantasies I had today would make the erotica section of a used bookstore blush. I'd do well to remember that their loyalty is to each other. Any tug of war would end with me as the ultimate loser.

Even if I'm the only person I can count on, being lonely is better than being dead. Tears burn behind my eyes, but I don't let them fall. I stopped crying over boys the day I turned sixteen, right around the time I learned that if I want to be safe, I have to save myself.

GIDEON

I LAY ON MY BACK, listening to her toss and turn through the wall. Racing breaths, gasps, and the occasional whimper. Sheena has nightmares. Fucked up ones from the sound of it. Each sound makes it harder for me not to kick off my covers and kick down her door.

But how the hell can I help without scaring her more? I have no business kicking down any doors, much less hers. That room needs to be her safe space. I won't take that away. I can't—even if every tooth in my mouth grinds to dust from the effort it takes me to stay in my own bed.

She cries out again. The bond rips and tears at my heart until I feel like it might actually yank the organ out of my chest. Claws replace my fingernails and leave little punctures in the bedding as I fight with everything I've got to resist the pull to go to her. I'm holding on for now, but there's nothing left over to control my animal side. I can replace the damn covers, but if my mate leaves, something tells me I'll have lost a piece of myself I'll never be able to get back.

I can't fucking fight her dreams for her, but the people who hurt her . . . They're going to pay.

I'll gut them like that coyote, toss their bodies in shallow graves, and lay their hearts at her feet so she can stomp on them.

That crazed thought breaks through my bloodlust, and I shake my head to clear it. Why the hell would she want a bloody, disgusting heart? I'm really losing it.

My senses are all over the place, and I'm wondering if I can even trust them at this point. I didn't want to tell Callum in front of Sheena, but while I was shifted as a puppy earlier, I thought I smelled wolf. My nose wasn't at its best in that form, but I could have sworn—no, it's impossible, especially in my territory. It's got to be my nervous system going haywire over the mate bond.

Stick to the plan, Gideon.

No scaring her, no pushing for details, no growling, and absolutely no literal bloody gifts. I'm starting to like her, and I don't think it's just the magical pull or my instincts to protect. No, under all the fear, there's someone sweet and maybe just a little wild. We got glimpses of that Sheena today, but if I ever want to earn her trust, I need to be someone new, someone better.

My claws retract, and my mind drifts to my second problem: Callum.

He wants her too. It's obvious, even if he's trying to hide it from me. Sure, maybe it will wear off for him, but can I deal if it doesn't? I picture Sheena in my mind, wavy brown hair hanging down her back, a dusting of freckles across her nose, and gentle curves I'm fucking desperate to map with my hands.

Then, I imagine Callum. Dark, dangerous, and dragging the weight of the world's judgment behind him everywhere he goes. I see his arms—lean muscles covered in the tattoos he got to piss off his dad—reaching out to wrap around her, his fingers rubbing all the places I just know will make her moan his name.

My eyes snap open.

I'm not jealous; I'm hard as a fucking rock. It's just a dirty daydream, but could I *share* her with him in real life? The woman the gods created just for me. If the legends are true, Sheena is the person who literally completes my very soul. Sharing her shouldn't work, so why can't I stop imagining it? Sheena trapped between us, writhing in pleasure and screaming our names. Sheena begging us both for more, her green eyes blown wide with lust as we fuck her in tandem.

Gods fucking dammit.

The urge to slip my hand down into my boxers is nearly impossible to resist. I'm about to give into it—even though I know it's a total creep move and Callum will know what's happening—

when a sob comes through the wall. My erection fades away to nothing.

She's afraid. Sheena, the woman I'm getting to know and obsessing over, is scared. What's left of my lust disappears so fast I can barely believe it was there to begin with. New plan. I'll keep working on my weaknesses, but I also need to play to my strengths, which don't include dwelling, brooding, or over-thinking shit.

First, I'll find the source of her fear and kill it. Second, I'll convince her I'm part of her future. If Callum is also part of it, we'll figure that out when we get there. Hell, if it means someone I trust helps me protect her and rails her into happily ever after by my side, that's a win-win, right?

We can do this.

I stay awake until her breathing levels off and the tossing and turning stops. Once I'm sure she's left the nightmares behind, I'm finally able to drop my guard enough to sleep.

LIKE WE'RE STUCK in a time loop, I find Sheena fiddling with the coffee maker again when I come in from my morning run. I look her over, but I try not to be obvious about it. One look shows me the nightmare carved deep, purple half moons beneath her eyes. The emerald green color of her eyes is duller somehow; the sparkle I noticed in the mountains long gone.

I want to put it back.

"How did you sleep?" I ask. The answer is obvious, but just because I've decided to be patient doesn't mean I can't push a little.

"The bed is very comfortable," she says, neatly dodging the question and tossing a fake smile in my direction. "Would you like some coffee?"

I grunt, ignoring the need to call her on her bullshit.

Sheena passes me a mug, and I take a sip, surprised to find it's exactly how I like it—sugar and creamer with some coffee on the side. I raise an eyebrow at her, and a blush floods her cheeks.

"I've worked at a lot of hole-in-the-wall diners. Remembering a coffee order is basically my top skill." She taps her temple and avoids direct eye contact while wiping down the counter. I'm not even sure where she got that dishrag. I've never seen it before in my life.

"You don't have to do chores, Sheena." I fight to keep the frown off my face. "You're our guest here, but this is your home for as long as you want."

Green flames spark to life in her eyes, and she's clearly opening her mouth to argue when Callum appears out of the shadows. She jumps, and I glare at him for startling her. He just rolls his eyes at me and makes his way to her side.

"Time to check those scrapes," Callum says.

She squints at the first aid kit in his hand and looks like she's winding up to argue again. I go with my gut. Before she can say whatever she's thinking, I lift her up on the counter and smack a kiss to her cheek.

"Let him check you over, Sheena. You won't win an argument with a demon." I kiss her other cheek and wink at her as she sputters. "Plus, coyotes are gross. You don't want an infection, do you?"

Blood rushes to her face, and I want to cheer as she grumbles something under her breath about how we're working her up on purpose. I duck my head into the fridge so she won't notice my smile, then I pretend to rummage around for food while watching her through the crack in the door.

Callum ignores Sheena's outrage completely, calmly wedging himself into the space between her legs and reaching for her shirt with a raised eyebrow. She huffs, lifting the fabric herself so he can get a look at her side. The bruises have changed to a sickly yellow already, confirming that she's definitely healing faster than a human would, but not as fast as a shifter or demon. Nothing new there. We already knew she wasn't human or like us.

Callum removes the gauze next, revealing the raw, angry scratches. I frown. Based on the bruises, I expected the healing to be further along. I look to Callum, but he doesn't comment or acknowledge my concern. Fucker.

Nope, he just sprays antiseptic on the scrapes and blows soothingly on the area. Goose bumps spread across Sheena's skin, and her breathing speeds up.

That's when I realize I'm still staring through the crack in the refrigerator door. They can't see me, but—*oh shit*—by the time I realize my mistake, it's already too late. The damn thing beeps at top volume, complaining loudly about how long I've been holding it open. I slam the door with way more force than necessary, bottles rattling as the beeping mercifully stops.

Now I'm standing here empty-handed and red in the face as they both stare.

"Can't find what you're looking for?" Sheena asks, laughter coating her voice. My embarrassment melts. I don't even care that she's laughing at me; I want to hear more of the sound. Wrenching the refrigerator door back open, I pull a carton of eggs out of the bottom shelf.

"Couldn't decide if I wanted an omelet or just toast this morning," I lie, plotting my revenge against the snitch-ass appliance. They both accept my explanation without comment, but I know Cal is going to give me shit for it later.

He tells Sheena she doesn't need a bandage anymore as long as she avoids reopening the scrapes. She thanks him, then hops down from the counter and walks over to me. We stand in comfortable silence, chopping veggies side by side. It's peaceful, domestic, and so chill that I barely notice the pull in my chest demanding I rush in and claim her.

Cal's phone goes off while we're eating. Sheena jumps, but we all pretend not to notice. Callum looks at the screen and sighs. He answers the call without getting up. The fingers of his free hand start to drum anxiously against the table as I shovel a bit of omelet into my mouth. Seeing his tell almost makes me groan. There's no way I can make it through even a secondhand Dimitri lecture without getting indigestion.

I'm about to glare at Callum for choosing to do this here until I realize he's making a deliberate point by not leaving to hide the call. He's proving to Sheena that she can trust us by showing her he trusts her. It's smart.

Knowing it's the right move doesn't help my frustration, though. This whole interrogation is bullshit, and Cal is a saint for even answering the phone.

We've already followed protocol and submitted a written report on the Wyoming lead. Obviously, we left Sheena out of it, but it's not like our fathers have any way of knowing that. No, this is standard Dimitri bullying. Callum's father never misses a chance to browbeat his oldest son. With no arrests and no immediate leads on the traffickers, he's determined to blame him. This call is just his way of getting a few hits in disguised as 'hands-on leadership.'

Sheena holds herself completely still as she listens, only relaxing slightly once Callum explains how the bar was a dead end without mentioning her. When he's finished, Dimitri kicks off the lecture. I can't make out what he's saying, but the tone comes through loud and clear. Fucking prick. By the time he's satisfied, Callum's jaw is clenched so tightly I worry he's going to chip a tooth.

"Understood. We'll check it out." Callum ends the call.

Heartburn grips my chest. "What the fuck does he want now?"

"There's another lead." Callum stares at his plate without blinking. "Near Boulder this time."

Callum may sound calm, but I know better. He's spiraling, and not just from talking to his dad. We can't take Sheena on a mission to some shady supernatural corner of our territory. We're going to have to leave her here, alone in the house with no protection but plenty of time to convince herself to take off again.

I risk a glance her way, but her poker face is damn good.

"Okay, what's our move?" I focus back on Callum, pretending like there's nothing off. He sighs, fiddling with the phone.

"Some low-level shifters are missing." He darts a look at Sheena, worry digging harsh lines in his face. "At first, it was women on their own, but then the pattern changed." He hesitates, then focuses back on me as he continues.

"They took a wolf from the local pack. It's hard to say whether they got sloppy or overconfident, but they made a mistake. She's well connected. The only reason we know about the other disappearances at all is because the alpha heard about them while tearing the town apart looking for his niece."

I let out a low whistle. You don't snatch an alpha's niece unless you have a death wish, especially if you're trying to fly under the radar. While every species is a little different, women are almost universally protected within shifter hierarchies.

This is a mess. I don't bother hiding my concern when I turn my focus back to Sheena. Her face is still slack, but I'm not fooled, not when I can hear her heart beating out of her chest. I don't think she even realizes she's shredding her napkin into tiny pieces. My heartburn flares back to life. I desperately need to burp, but now doesn't feel like the time.

Callum drops his phone on the table with a clatter and takes Sheena's hands in his, stopping the napkin massacre.

"We won't be gone long," Callum whispers. "We'll show you how to work the security system and leave you with a gun." There's no sign she's even hearing him, but he doesn't stop. "This place is off the grid. No one has any reason to believe you're here."

That does it.

Her head snaps up, pupils blown wide as the black consumes the vivid green. I can practically taste her fear. I get why she may be uncomfortable, but this degree of terror seems a little extreme. Still, I'm opening my mouth to tell her we won't go—that we won't leave her alone for even a second—when Callum takes hold of her chair. He yanks it towards him. The wooden legs screech against the tile in a horrible way before the sound cuts off abruptly.

"You're tough and smart. You don't need help from me or Gideon, but it's yours if you want it." Callum cradles Sheena's face in his hands. His thumb grazes her bottom lip, and only then do I notice how they're both trembling.

"Sheena," he whispers. "It's your choice." His conviction makes each word sound like a promise.

Fuck, this is make or break.

I sit helplessly, taking the tension in my body out on the fork in my hand. It bends in half while we both wait for her answer.

Sheena stares into Callum's dark eyes, clearly searching for something. He holds the eye contact. Neither of them so much as blink as she reads him. When she finally finds whatever she's looking for and clears her throat, I hide the mangled fork under the table.

"I was taken," she whispers, her voice haunted. "I still don't know who they were or how they found me. One night, I was in my twin bed crying over a boy. The next, I was in a cage." She trails off, sucking in an uneven breath.

I wait for rage to overpower me, but it doesn't. The anger is still there simmering deep in my gut, but my overwhelming instinct right now is to comfort the woman in front of me. I'm clearly not the only one feeling that way because Callum pulls her carefully onto his lap.

I take her now vacant seat and lay a tentative hand on her back. She doesn't seem to notice, too lost in her past to focus on either of us.

"These people you're looking for—they sound a lot like the group that hunts me," Sheena says. I stiffen at that; the need to hunt them down and rip out their spines builds inside of me.

"No matter where I hide, they always catch up." Her breath hitches. "I don't want to bring any trouble down on you, so I'll head out today. It may take time, but they will find me. They always do."

Her focus returns to us. She tries to climb out of Callum's lap, but he's not having it and neither am I. He shoots me a warning look over her shoulder, but it's too late.

"You're not leaving," I snarl at her. "We'll track them down and gut them like the cowardly monsters they are." I'm roaring now, too consumed with rage over what happened to her to control myself. "You don't need to go anywhere."

Callum clears his throat.

"What Gideon means to say is, our job is to protect supernaturals in this territory, Sheena. We would never toss you out to avoid trouble."

She must hear him, but she doesn't react to his declaration. Instead, she turns in his lap to study me. Sheena's face is blank and impossible for me to read. Panic stings my skin. Any second now, she will run screaming from this kitchen, and it will be all my fault. Even knowing this, I can't stop the feral rumblings escaping my mouth. Maybe I can beg forgiveness. Maybe I can—

"Okay. I'll stay," Sheena says.

Wait. She can't possibly mean that. Right?

Sheena erases the distance between us, gently cupping my jaw in her hand. It's the first time she's touched me deliberately in my human form. I'll remember it until the day I die.

"As long as you're both fine with it, I'll stay," she repeats, glancing over her shoulder at Callum.

He's watching me closely, like he's preparing to snatch her out of my reach if I lose control again. Callum is familiar with my temper, but I could never hurt Sheena. I felt the truth of that deep in my bones the second she touched my face. Still, I give him a nod, and some of the tightness in his expression disappears.

"Of course. I meant what I said earlier—you can belong here if you want to," he tells her. "But, given what you've just shared, I think we should talk more if you're up for it."

Godsdammit, Callum.

The tension comes back, ratcheted up to about a million now, and I can't stand it any longer. Scooping her out of his lap, I ignore her surprised squeak, and carry her towards the living room.

"Gideon!" Callum's voice is exasperated, but I don't stop.

"If we're going to have super intense story time, followed by super boring strategy time, then we're at least going to be comfortable," I yell back at him, sinking down into the deep leather couch cushions and dropping Sheena beside me.

I'd rather have her in my lap, but I can tell she needs to feel some kind of control over her space right now. So I drag a warm, fuzzy blanket off the arm of the couch, cover us both, and hold the edge up, gesturing impatiently to Callum as he trails after us. He purses his lips, but sits down beside Sheena like I knew he would, sliding under the blanket without complaint. Once she's nestled safely between us, I finally feel like I can breathe again.

Thank the gods she's too distracted to notice me fussing.

"What do you want to know?"

Sheena gets right to the point, but her voice sounds tired, like the thought of digging all this back up is exhausting. I hate that she has to relive it, but Callum is right to push. If this group is the same one that took her, it's even more important that we track them down fast.

"Whatever you're comfortable sharing," Callum says. "Focus on anything that could help us figure out if it's the same group." Sheena nods once, staring at her hands while she plays with a tassel on the end of the blanket.

"They always wore masks. Halloween, skulls, and monster stuff." She frowns slightly. "They abducted me and held me hostage in Virginia. That's where I escaped from, at least, so I guess it's far-fetched to think it could be the same group. But in the years since my escape, I've felt them coming for me."

She's defensive. Almost like she expects us to call her paranoid, but I nod instead.

"I saw one of them back in Texas a few years back," she admits. "I ignored the warning feeling. It was stupid, but I had a pretty decent setup going. He got so close . . . When I noticed, he was watching me like it was a game." She shudders and wraps her arms around herself. "I use that memory to remind myself about what can happen when I ignore my gut."

When she reaches for the blanket's tassel again, I grab her hand in mine.

"You were right to listen to that feeling," I say, leaning into the need to reassure her. "In this world, your instincts and intuitions are just as important as sight or smell. They will keep you alive when nothing else will."

Her fingers tighten around mine, a silent thank you.

"Before I got away, they kept me carefully guarded but mostly unhurt. Because of . . . why they wanted me . . . I was really weak." She hurries on, but I don't miss her pause. "I only got away because they were planning something big and wanted me strong."

She takes a deep, shaky breath, but neither of us pushes her to elaborate. I draw shapes on the back of her hand with my thumb instead, trying to help her relax.

"I stopped fighting back after a while, so they only had one guard watching me. The night I escaped, I pretended to be asleep." Her bottom lip trembles, but her green eyes are blazing. I can't look away from her. "I waited until he turned around, and then I jumped on his back and wrapped the chain around his throat. It took so long," she whispers. "Longer than I expected. I thought I might pass out before he did. When he finally fell, I ran, and I haven't looked back."

When she stops talking this time, the bones in my hand are fucking throbbing. When I realize the pressure is coming from her and not me, I squeeze back gently. She can break every bone in my hand if it helps her forget.

"I don't know what I am," her voice has a brittle edge now. "But I promised myself that night I would tell no one what I can do. I understand if that's a deal breaker. I'm sorry to keep it from you two, but I just can't put myself at risk again."

Her last words are defiant, and it's sexy as hell. Instead of telling her I think her stubborn streak is hot, I stay quiet and listen as Callum takes over. He tells her she doesn't have to share any more details about herself, that she was brave and smart.

Callum has a way with words, and I feel the tension draining from Sheena's body as he reassures her. Once she's boneless on the couch, he asks her some simple follow-up questions. She's able to add some vague details about height, weight, accents, and tattoos, but when he asks about abilities, she hesitates.

"I never saw anyone . . . change or anything, but they didn't feel human," she says. Callum accepts that with a nod.

Not hunters then. Part of me is relieved to hear that psycho cult isn't involved. Instead, it sounds exactly like the trafficking group we're chasing now—a supernatural gang betraying their own community for profit. It's fucked.

When Callum asks if anyone else was held hostage with her, Sheena's tension returns tenfold along with a healthy serving of the earlier defiance. She says she didn't see anyone else. Although, she believes there may have been others based on sounds she overheard. Callum doesn't press on the obvious sore spot, but the conversation is still grueling.

Eventually, he stops asking questions and flips the TV to some mindless comedy. We pretend to watch it, but no one is invested. Within minutes, Sheena drifts off to sleep cuddled into my side, the laugh track playing in the background.

CHAPTER
SIX

SHEENA

I wake up slowly to the rumble of two deep voices. Lying on my side, my head is pillowed in one lap while my legs are stretched carefully across another. Memories of the last few hours trickle in, but the familiar panic doesn't come.

I told them about my captivity. I gave up a piece of my past to two men I barely know.

The last part of that thought doesn't feel true anymore. I feel like I know these guys. Maybe not their favorite foods or pet peeves, but their morals—those I feel like I've got a decent grasp of already. Why else would I feel so light after sharing a secret that's haunted my every breath for the better part of a decade?

Maybe they won't betray me. Maybe I don't have to carry this burden alone. After bearing the weight for so long, laying it down is intoxicating. Do I dare trust them with the truth about my abilities? The tiny hairs on the back of my neck stand up as fear rolls in, overwhelming me with its familiar intensity.

Bitterness follows in its wake. *Nice try, Sheena.* Maybe I can adapt some of my rules to fit this new reality, but my promises to myself . . . No, those I have to keep. I should have known better.

"Callum, I swear to the gods, I'll kill them. One by one, crushing their hope for survival. Once I've butchered the last one, I'll scatter the pieces along the mountainside for the vultures to fight over. No one will find them. No one will remember their names."

Good LORD.

I open my eyes just enough to see Gideon deliver the tail end of what's got to be the longest, most deranged collection of words I've ever heard him string together. Gone are the dimples and teasing smiles. Logic tells me I should be terrified, but his brutal talk of revenge on my behalf makes my blood pump instead. Shit, I'm probably deranged too.

Callum groans, and the sound makes my skin pebble.

"Yes, they will all die. Lots of regret, pain, agony, blah blah blah." Callum raises his voice to talk over Gideon's growl. "They'll get what's coming to them. I swear it, Gideon, but not before we get answers and make sure this can't happen to anyone else. Promise me you won't be so blinded by this psycho revenge boner you're rocking right now that you lose sight of the goal."

Gideon huffs, his massive arms crossed over his chest as he glares at his best friend. Callum seems both amused and irritated, and I get the feeling I've missed the first few rounds of this argument while I napped.

"I fucking heard you the first three times, dude."

"Okay, wonderful. What did I say then?"

"Godsdammit," Gideon hisses. "No murder until we follow all the leads. I got it. Now, let me fantasize about revenge."

I snort, then freeze. Gideon's impatience and Callum's exasperation made me forget I was pretending to still be asleep.

"We've got a little spy on our hands, Gideon," Callum says. I clench my eyes shut tightly, making it even more obvious I'm awake and listening in.

"Hmm, her eyes are closed, though. How can we know she's really awake?" Gideon asks. Fingers clamp down on my ankle, and then someone tickles the arch of my foot. I lose it. My eyes fly open, and I kick my other leg up, desperate to escape. My shin narrowly misses Callum's stupidly perfect nose. He dodges back with a wide grin of triumph.

"Our little spy is ticklish. We'll keep that in mind for the next time we need answers." Callum stops tormenting my foot, but his dark eyes are still sparkling with laughter.

Gideon's pained groan makes us both turn to look at him.

"Dude, the next time you decide to tickle her, can you at least warn me so I can prepare to have her bouncing around in my lap?"

I blink a few times as I process what he just said. With dawning horror, I figure out his meaning when I notice something hard poking the back of my head. I sit up so fast my muscles aren't ready to keep me upright, and I fall back down like one of those weird inflatable tube things you see waving in the wind outside used car dealerships.

Callum pulls me back up, but something intense is dueling with the amusement in his eyes now. I don't dare try to identify it.

Gideon places a throw pillow on his lap, hiding the evidence with a dimpled grin. I'm mortified. I'm blushing so hard I can feel my heartbeat pulsing in my face. Meanwhile, Gideon looks like he doesn't mind at all.

Where should I even look?

I settle on the TV, which is still playing some mindless comedy. I try to focus, but the laugh track seems forced; and I can't stop thinking about the fact that Gideon is sitting right next to me—huge, handsome, and horny.

Just minutes ago, I woke to him describing how he wanted to dismember my captors and spread their body parts across a mountain range. It shouldn't be hot. So why does my skin feel so tight?

I lean forward to give myself a little space, but I can't stop thinking about how good it would feel to erase it instead. I'm sure neither of the men on this couch would have any problem making me feel wanted.

Clenching my thighs together, I suck in a deep breath as someone curses. I'm too focused on getting my body and brain under control to figure out who. When a big hand trails up my back, rubbing softly, I shudder. It's probably supposed to be soothing, but I'm too worked up.

"Sheena, if you want something—anything at all—it's yours." Callum purrs directly into my ear. Another shiver rocks me. "Gideon would be happy to take care of any needs you may have."

The hand on my back slides slowly up each bump of my spine, ending its journey with a slow, sensual caress along the back of my neck.

"It would stop whenever you want it to. No strings, no expectations, just a chance for you to feel good and get rid of some of that stress." Callum's words sink into my body like a drug, so soft and seductive. I arch into the phantom touch.

It isn't enough.

If he stops, maybe I could think.

If he stops, I might die.

I'm not sure how long I teeter on the knife's edge before something in me snaps. Whipping my head around, I find Gideon bathed in the fading light of the late afternoon sun. If I feel out of control—he looks it. Eyes wild, fists clenched at his side, he's staring at me like it's taking everything he has not to reach out and grab me. His bottom lip is slightly puffy, and I imagine him nibbling on it.

Jealously churns in my gut. I want to replace his teeth with my tongue.

Like he can sense my thoughts, I watch as molten gold burns away the deep brown of his eyes. He looks half starved and three-fourths feral, and some buried instinct inside of me yearns to satiate his hunger.

Before I even make a conscious decision, I've dislodged Gideon's throw pillow and straddled his lap. The last thing I hear before I crush my lips to his is another one of those low, possessive rumbles.

Okay . . . I've heard people describing first kisses before, saying it felt like Earth moved beneath them. I've always rolled my eyes because it sounds ridiculous to think two tiny beings could affect the gravitational pull of an entire planet.

Now I get it.

When my lips touch his, everything changes. Granted, I can't tell if any tectonic plates shift, but what's actually happening is just as scary. Instead of relief from the tension that's been building between us, I swear I'm catching fire.

Gideon's lips are soft and utterly destructive. He kisses me with a single-minded focus, like there's nothing else he'd rather be doing. His fingers weave among the strands of my hair, tugging gently to put my head where he wants it. It's so intense I feel my whole body shaking.

"Can I stay?" Callum's pained voice barely registers in my mind until Gideon separates our lips to answer.

"Yeah, man—take whatever you need."

I don't have time to make sense of the exchange as Gideon's lips immediately latch on to the sensitive skin of my neck. I moan and grind down on his lap, shamelessly looking for friction. He answers my unspoken demand, moving his hands from my hair to my waist, helping me rub against him in a rhythm that makes my body sing.

We're still fully clothed, but this is by far the sexiest thing I've ever done in my life. None of the drunken make outs from my high school years or the unsatisfying one-night stands on the run ever came close to this heat.

Maybe I'll feel differently later, but it doesn't scare me.

Callum said I was in control and could stop at any point, and despite myself, I believe him. Despite all my fears and best intentions, I'm starting to trust them both.

"Does he feel good?" Callum's whisper in my ear surprises me, but I can't stop the groan that escapes in response.

"Why don't you take his shirt off?" It's a brilliant suggestion. I yank Gideon's shirt over his head, tossing it out of the way. Now there's nothing stopping me from sinking my fingers into the coiled muscles he's been tormenting me with every morning after his runs.

He twitches a little beneath my touch, and I smile against his mouth. Maybe I'm not the only one here who's a little ticklish. Still, I want him closer to me, not squirming away. I latch one hand onto his shoulder and bury the other in his wild curls. They are as soft as they look. I lose myself in his kiss and the rough grind of my jeans against his running shorts. It feels good, but I need more. Desperate, I turn my head back to Callum, hoping for another suggestion.

He doesn't make me wait.

"I bet it would feel good if you took your shirt off, too," he says.

I pause. I'm not wearing a bra. Nerves skitter along my skin at the thought of being so vulnerable. A glance at the reassuring heat in Gideon's eyes gives me a surge of bravery. Before I can second guess myself, I peel my shirt off. Callum assists me when it gets caught in my hair on the way over my head.

I don't have time to feel embarrassed because Gideon is looking at me like I'm Christmas morning. He reaches for me like he can't help himself, but pauses to make eye contact. I nod, and then the space between us is gone.

His enormous hands cup my bare skin like I'm precious, like I could vanish at any second. His fingertips are callous and rough. My nipples pebble under his gentle exploration. When he rolls the tips carefully between his fingers, my pleasure spikes, passion pulling me under as I arch into his hands and gasp for breath.

I slump slightly, overwhelmed with sensation, until Callum's hands find my waist. Somehow, he helps me find the perfect rhythm, the perfect friction, as I ride his friend on the couch. His hands never wander, but the filthy secrets he whispers in my ear stoke the bonfire burning inside me. Each word and every stroke drag me closer to the edge.

The demon explains in explicit detail all the things he wants to do to me, punctuated with detailed compliments about how perfect I am. I soak up the praise, hoping one day I'll be brave enough to ask him to follow through on some of these promises.

When he tells me to let go, my orgasm crests, and I writhe between them, chest heaving, a wild cry escaping my mouth. Gideon swallows the sound with a hungry, open-mouthed kiss, stiffening beneath me.

He presses a kiss to my sweaty brow.

"Okay, don't judge me for that." He groans. "You're just so sexy." Gideon crushes my naked chest to his, letting out a tremendous sigh. "I swear I'll last longer next time." I chuckle then, realizing why he's embarrassed.

"I can't make the same promise," I tease, relaxing into the cuddle.

The air conditioning kicks on with a distant hum. Cool air blows across my back and a shiver rattles down my spine. I feel a little self-conscious about my topless state, but before I can get too embarrassed, Callum drops Gideon's massive shirt over my head. When I swivel my head to thank him, my mouth drops open instead.

He's so hopelessly beautiful I can't even understand what I'm seeing.

The dark circles under his eyes are gone, and his skin is . . . glowing? Some of his sharper edges seem smoother somehow. Callum looks like the glossy cover of an airbrushed magazine come to life.

"It's not fair, is it? Fucking incubus demon," Gideon mutters good-naturedly, like he's used to staring at perfection. "I was going to ask if you got what you needed, Cal, but it's obvious you're all charged up."

Callum smiles at Gideon's statement, a light blush staining his olive skin. He doesn't look away from me, though. A tiny furrow pops up between his eyebrows as I catalogue all the subtle changes to his appearance.

After a moment, he clears his throat and breaks our eye contact.

"I didn't mention it earlier because there's a lot of suspicion about my kind," he admits. "Like Gideon said, I'm an incubus demon. I consume lust and sexual energy to survive, and you both just fed me a three-course meal."

He delivers that explanation like he's gearing up for a confrontation. His gaze locks on me again, except now it's devoid of the earlier softness. Callum is clearly waiting for me to freak out or something, but—besides surprise over his appearance—I'm not overly concerned.

I am, however, curious about what he can do and why he expects a fight. "Your abilities," I begin. "I assume they can be more predatory, too?"

Gideon tenses against me, but Callum seems both relieved and angered by my question.

"I can burn someone alive with desire. I can make them so desperate to please me they'd walk off a cliff without question," Callum scoffs. The sound is as bitter as it is beautiful. It shows me more clearly than any words could how much he hates this part of himself. He can't hide his self-loathing from me, not when its echo has haunted me for years. When I simply nod in response, he blinks slowly and tilts his head.

"Aren't you going to ask me if I did that to you?" He points at me. "Accuse me of making you so horny you humped my friend's cock until you creamed your jeans?"

I flush at his crude characterization and cut him off with my hand.

"I'm going to stop you there. If I thought you would try something like that, Callum, I would be out the door already."

He narrows his eyes at me. I roll my own. His attitude is ruining my post orgasm buzz, so I give him what he obviously wants.

"Fine. Since you're obviously desperate for me to question your character, I will. Callum, would you ever use your power to influence or control my body?"

"I would never do that to either of you without your consent," Callum insists, his voice earnest, all the anger gone and replaced with a kind of sad resignation. He doesn't think I'll believe him.

I gently climb out of Gideon's lap, compassion for the incubus demon welling up in my chest. He may look like a stereotypical sexy villain, but it's becoming clear that I'm not the only person in this house with baggage. Standing up on my tiptoes, I press a soft kiss to the corner of his perfect lips.

"Then there's no problem," I assure him. He says nothing, his face frozen in a blank mask of confusion.

He's not the only one.

CALLUM

HOLY FUCK. Holy *fuck*. I slam my bedroom door, tripping over my own feet as I stumble to the mirror.

I look like a god and feel like a monster.

Power buzzes beneath my skin. I think I could legitimately move a mountain or compel an auditorium full of people to get themselves off in public if I tried. Still, even if I did that, I can't imagine the lust rush could top what I just experienced. I barely touched Sheena, and I feel stronger than I have in years.

Fuck, this is bad. If I can't resist her, can't stop myself from going back for more . . . I clench my trembling hands, hating how the tremors damn me as nothing more than an addict, desperate for his next fix.

I don't like feeding my demon, can't even remember the last time I bothered, but this reaction seems extreme. *Other.*

Like ice melting on my skin or nails raking down my back, it's a godsdamn fucking rush. My cock goes rock hard as I think about what could have happened if we'd taken it further. For a stupid, indulgent moment, I let myself marinate in an alternate ending.

My hands around her waist. Driving her down until I bottom out inside of her again and again. Pushing her to the edge of madness until she's so mindless with pleasure that she doesn't know if she wants to beg me for more or beg me to stop.

Shaking my head, I try to clear the filthy thoughts. They aren't doing a godsdamn thing to discourage my erection or my guilt.

I promised Sheena I would never use my abilities on her without her consent, but if she were to give me that kind of trust, the possibilities would be endless.

She won't. You can't. Gideon . . .

I shake my head, stepping closer to the mirror to distract myself with how creepy my face looks. There isn't a single blemish. Not a damn thing. I look like some wannabe influencer who's been through ten rounds of fillers and filters. The dark circles, the slight bags I woke up with this morning, and the faint laugh lines I've had for several years are all gone.

I'm parasitic perfection, unnatural, dangerous, and primed to hunt.

Incubus demons are notorious for their beauty. For me, my appearance has always been the one thing I couldn't ignore, marking me as a predator against my will and serving as a barrier to true connection.

My trembling fist itches to shatter the glass and destroy my reflection, but the door clicks open before I can strike. Gideon steps inside without knocking, shutting the door behind him, then scanning my face thoroughly.

If I look unhinged, he looks shell-shocked.

My shoulders slump. He's here to kick my ass, and I won't try to stop him. After all, I put my hands on his mate. We study each other in the tense silence, his unruly curls sticking out in every direction from where Sheena pulled on them as she chased her pleasure on his lap.

Fuck. I've got to stop thinking about that or I'm going to pop another hard on just in time to get the shit beat out of me.

"Dude. Your face . . ." Gideon shakes his head, his long strides erasing the distance between us.

"Yeah, it's weird," I mutter, hating how awkward this feels. We both sound like we've never strung together a complete thought in our lives. But how can I tell Gideon—the one person who's never left my side—that I want the woman who's meant to be his?

I could lose him over this.

"I'm so sorry," I tell him, the words spilling out of me in my desperation. It's true. I am sorry, but it's a hell of a lot more complicated than that. Maybe, if I find the right words, I can make him understand that—

"Sorry for what?" He groans. "That was so hot. I came in my pants like a teenager." His eyes flash golden, then he studies me like I'm a math problem that won't add up. I open my mouth to says gods know what, but I don't get the chance.

"Anyway, I'm here to hammer out a game plan for tomorrow. I don't think Sheena is up for talking more about the traffickers tonight."

I hold up my hand to shut him up.

"Wait. Wait. Gideon, I *touched* your mate. Saw her come . . ." I cringe, bracing for the punch.

He nods slowly, concern for me on his face. Shit, he must not have noticed how bad it was in the moment. I rake my hands through my hair. I have to tell him, have to let him know how far out of line I was earlier.

"Dude, I whispered all kinds of dirty shit in her ear," I admit. "I told her I wanted her to ride my face until her legs collapsed and I drowned."

He growls at that, reaching down to adjust himself.

"Stop making me picture that. I just put on clean shorts." Gideon chuckles.

The sound abruptly cuts off when he notices whatever look is on my face.

"Gods, you're fully freaking out right now, Cal."

When I nod, he rolls his eyes. It reminds me of Sheena's reaction to my explanation of the dangers of incubus powers.

"I need you to help me hold it together," Gideon says. "Maybe that's not fair, but I can't figure this out without you. You expect me to lose my shit, mark my territory, tell you to fuck off. Well, I won't."

I don't know how to respond. I'm too hung up on him admitting he needs me.

"Yes, she's my mate, but I don't own her." He grabs my shoulders with both hands. "We're getting to know each other."

Gideon's forehead furrows. I know this look. He wants me to understand—to help him articulate his thoughts, and normally, I would, but I've never been more confused. When I gesture for him to go on, he throws his hands up.

"Shit, I'm so bad at explaining. I liked seeing your hands on her. I loved hearing you whispering all that sexy stuff in her ear." Gideon grins. "But maybe cut it out sooner next time, so I don't blow in my pants again and give her the impression I can't last."

I gape at him like a startled goldfish. "I don't understand," I say. *Can he really mean . . .? He can't be suggesting what I think he is.*

"Callum, I want her to be mine, but that doesn't mean she can't be yours too." He points at my ridiculous expression; his own is uncharacteristically serious. "You want her. And it's obvious your demon is a big fan. But if it's just sex, you need to figure that out now because I won't have her hurt again."

Could I really have her too? Share her with my best friend? His words play on repeat in my head, each one piercing a new hole in my defenses. I can't pretend the thought of Sheena's curvy body pressed between us, gasping, and completely at our mercy isn't fucking with my intentions.

I study Gideon, unsure how to respond to the bombshell he just dropped on me. The future he's describing sounds perfect, too good to be true even, but if it means I get more time . . .

The trembling in my hands gets worse as I hold my secret in.

My incubus has long felt possessive of Gideon, but I've never admitted that out loud. A part of me has always lived in fear of the day when our paths would split. If there's even a chance to prevent that, I have to take it.

"If she's interested, we can try," I say, clapping him on the back. I'll stick around for as long as they both want me. I just can't get attached or forget the truth.

They're meant for each other, but an incubus always ends up alone.

———

As soon as the sun peaks through my window, I give up trying to sleep, toss some things in a bag, and brace myself to head downstairs. A quick glance at the mirror shows that my sleepless night went a long way toward making my face look more normal.

I'll take it.

Gideon and I head out to investigate the new lead today. My eyes may feel gritty and tired, but my anxiety is well rested and ready to put in some work this morning. It's so bad I have to order myself to stop doom listing worst-case scenarios. Every time I think about leaving Sheena alone, my chest gets tight. *Something could happen to her, or she could decide to leave.*

On top of that, I'm worried about what we'll find in Boulder. This lead could easily fall flat or expand into a complete shit storm. If it's not the same group that took Sheena when she was a kid, then we've got two dangerous—potentially rival—criminal organizations to deal with. If it is those masked assholes, then we've got some serious justice to hand out.

Shuffling into the kitchen, I drop my duffle bag by the door next to Gideon's and follow the sound of voices out onto the porch. Sheena is standing in the yard bathed in sunshine, wearing the devil's own sick idea of shorts. The sight of her holding a 9mm pistol and listening earnestly to Gideon's instructions on how to grip it replace all my anxious thoughts with horny nonsense.

I may have to kick my own ass.

Instead of saying any of my thoughts out loud, I walk across the yard and offer a suggestion about her stance. She blushes but makes the change with no comment, her nose wrinkling in concentration. After a tiny hesitation, she pulls the trigger. Once I'm able to peel my eyes away from her to look at the target, I'm surprised to see she hit the edge on her first try.

Good eyesight and a steady hand are a given for most supernatural species, so this doesn't give us any new clues about her heritage. I tell myself it doesn't matter. She'll trust us enough to share more about herself one day.

Sheena fires off a few more shots before Gideon is satisfied with her accuracy and confidence. After taking the gun back, he walks her back to the house. He shows her how to work the security system, where the keys to the spare car are, and the safe room we installed in case of emergencies a few years back.

He keeps all the explanations short and serious, the smiling man from last night nowhere to be found. I know he's worried too, but I hope Sheena doesn't feel like he's acting cold towards her after what I'm referring to as 'the couch incident' in my head.

Gideon puts the pistol in a case and hands it to her, along with three preloaded clips. There's a little pink in Sheena's cheeks, but I can't see any other signs of embarrassment. She seems to be taking all of this in stride.

He watches her for a long, tense moment, then snaps, grabbing her up in a bear hug that lifts her feet completely off the ground. To her credit, she rolls with it, wrapping her legs around Gideon's waist like she's done it a thousand times before.

"I know it's moving fast," he groans. "I'm freaked out too, but please, don't leave. We can figure it out together."

When Sheena runs one hand through his curls, he grips her even tighter.

"I'm not going anywhere, Gideon," she says, her tone soft but adamant.

It's not a promise exactly, but I believe her. It seems he does too because some of the tension leaves his body.

"Be careful—both of you." Her voice trembles, and she turns her head to include me in the warning. "If these are the same guys . . . They're dangerous and not exactly worried about collateral damage."

I hear the hitch in her breathing, hating that her fear is back, but I'm touched that she's worrying about me at all. When I catch Gideon's eye, his normally brown irises are glowing a faint golden in the morning light. I dip my chin, knowing instinctively that we're back in sync. We'll take care of this threat no matter how bloody it gets, then come back to her.

Gideon sets Sheena down, then gives her a kiss that starts friendly enough but borders on obscene by the time he's done. My heart pounds as two trickles of lust seep into me from their goodbye kiss alone. I want to kiss her too, but I settle for a hug and a peck on the cheek. Now isn't the time to make a mess in her head or mine.

We'll have plenty of time for that later.

CHAPTER
SEVEN

GIDEON

Whoever picked this song should die.

The only thing getting me through this bullshit waste of time is a fantasy of me planting my foot in the dusty ass speaker and punting it across the room. Anything to end the tinny twang of the classic country deep cuts. Each one is worse than the last.

I just want to go home.

Instead, I'm stuffed into an old, grimy booth with scarred wood and frayed vinyl seats. My legs don't fucking fit, and I'm worried if I stretch too much, I'm going to crack the rickety thing in half. To make matters worse, the floor is wet, the beer is sour, and every time I turn my head to the right, there's a smell that makes my eyes water.

My mood is so bad I've been sidelined.

Cal ordered me to stay in this booth and stop making eye contact. I bitched about it but agreed, mainly because I know he's right. Just last week, I would have been all over this investigation, but now all I want to do is get back to Sheena . . . or break something. Knowing she deserves answers is the only thing keeping me in this booth.

So I sip my piss poor beer in silence like a good soldier and watch Callum work the room. He's using his influence to make the workers and regulars more likely to answer his questions. Part of me wants to pull my phone out and record him because this shit is actually hilarious. Callum is stronger than normal thanks to the energy boost he got from Sheena. While that sounds great on paper, he's not used to the extra juice, so he's going too hard.

People keep touching him. I've seen half a dozen men and women grope his ass, squeeze his arms, or rub his back. One of the half naked waitresses even slipped him her panties. As soon as her back was turned, he tossed them in a trashcan, his jaw so tense he could crack a tooth. I laughed so hard I snorted beer up my nose.

He fucking hates it.

Even though I'm distracted, I know the moment he learns something worth knowing. Callum straightens up and sends a powerful wave of influence towards the already glassy-eyed bartender. Their conversation lasts another five minutes, then he peels her off of his arm and pays the tab. She blinks with confusion as he walks away but doesn't stop him.

It's the sign I've been waiting for, so I untuck myself from the booth and trail after him, leaving my unfinished pint behind. I only hope the information leads us to someone I can shred. Then we can go home.

Callum is already in the driver's seat when I get to the SUV, so I hop in and buckle up, checking the glove compartment for my gun. I prefer to go in shifted, but it never hurts to be prepared. I'm expecting him to start talking and driving immediately, but the only sound in the cab is the slide of my magazine as I check my weapon over.

"Well? What did she say?" I finally ask, jamming the full clip back into place.

"Two of their staff members are missing." Callum's voice

shakes with anger. "Bartender was going to leave it at that, but I could tell she knew more. The owner sold those girls out for cash."

He slams his palm into the steering wheel three times before he's calm enough to say more. "The bartender—the blonde one—overheard where they took them and wanted to come clean, but she was too scared she'd find herself in a cage too if she said anything. She only talked because she heard about the alpha's niece and didn't want to catch a stray bullet for hiding what she knew."

I've heard more than enough.

"Let's torch the place." I reach for the door handle, already imagining all the ways we can make the owner of this shit hole pay.

"You know we can't do that." Callum whips his head around to face me in the dark. He grabs my arm, and I barely hold in my growl. "Gideon, the bartender saw *masks*."

One word. That's all it takes to throw my bones and tendons into chaos. Each one spasms. My entire body rocks with the urge to shift.

I tell myself anyone could wear masks, that it makes sense to hide your identity if you're involved in trafficking innocent people. Too bad logic doesn't do a damn thing to help me chill.

I'll tear them to pieces and piss on the remains. I'll—

A rough punch to my shoulder rips me away from my thoughts of murder and revenge. I snarl, glaring at my friend in the dim light of the nearby bar. I try to convince myself it would be a bad idea to return the favor.

"Focus, man," Callum snaps. "We don't know what we're walking into here, and our priority has to be saving those women. *After* we make that happen, we can hunt these fuckers down and get revenge for Sheena."

We'll burn them alive; make them beg for her forgiveness . . .

Absently, I hear grinding metal.

"Calm down or you're useless to her." Callum's harsh words

penetrate the red fog choking my brain, giving me time to suck in a deep breath. I hold it until my lungs are empty and my mind clears of everything but my need for fresh oxygen.

My eyes catch the ruined door handle. The metal is covered in claw marks.

Sheena deserves a better mate. Cal deserves a better partner.

I breathe in just enough to keep from blacking out and look down at the floor.

"Cut that shit out, too." Callum threads his fingers roughly into my hair, yanking my head upright. "You don't get to feel like shit over how hard you fight to protect."

His black eyes sear mine. Combined with the tension on my scalp—I can't fucking take the intensity anymore. It feels too much like my earlier rage.

"You telling me how to feel now, too? Bossy." I joke to lighten the mood.

He immediately rolls his eyes, releasing my hair and cranking the engine. With one last look at the bar, he throws the SUV into gear and backs out.

"Put your fucking seatbelt on."

I grin at his tone, clipping the buckle and looking up just in time to see a muscle tick in his jaw. The tiny movement reminds me just how angry he is about this too. My emotions may burn hotter than his, but I know better than to think he doesn't have them.

As far as demons go, Cal is pretty laid back, but shit like this . . . It gets to him.

We live in a brutal world of power, greed, and blood. If you don't have a supernatural leg up, you better be close to someone who does. It's why I can't truly blame the bartender for her cowardice. She's just trying to survive.

Our enclave's territory stretches from Colorado to Idaho, each foot carved out over decades of fighting. If we don't defend these communities, we lose them. It's that simple. These fuckers need to know they can't take our people and get away with it.

We stop about a mile from the coordinates the bartender overheard, grab our weapons, and share our location with the enclave just in case. We decide to go the rest of the way on foot and rely on our senses to warn us if anyone is nearby.

The field is covered with the type of grass that rustles noisily in the wind and hides a fuck ton of holes in the ground. We have to focus on our feet to avoid twisting an ankle. Still, we're pretty quiet. The only sounds that break the silence are swishing grass and the occasional hoot of an owl.

After what feels like a lifetime of walking, a big barn appears in the darkness. There's a soft glow emanating from the rough cracks in the walls, and the thing looks like it's one strong kick away from returning to a pile of wood on the ground.

Callum's night vision isn't quite as good as mine. When he sends a questioning look at me, I shake my head. Even with my supernatural eyesight, I can't make out much more from here. I focus instead on what I can hear and smell, closing my eyes to remove distractions. With one sense removed, the others heighten.

A gust of wind blows our way, bringing with it the unmistakable stench of piss, shit, and unwashed bodies. I wrinkle my nose, separating the scents and trying not to gag. There are several types of shifter—all lower tiers. Now that I've isolated my targets, I can make out the rumble of multiple male voices. Two . . . no, three men, unless I missed someone, and the faint sound of a woman crying. My nostrils flair as a tremor rocks my body. This is definitely the place.

Time to crack some heads.

Opening my eyes, I hand Callum my pistol and strip off my sweats and t-shirt, stuffing them inside his backpack. When he claps his hand on my arm, my vision tunnels. By the time I get my rage under control, he's leveling me with a concerned look.

He wants reassurance that I'm not going to do anything reckless.

I nod shortly, not sure I actually mean it, then funnel all my angry energy into shifting into a rat. While I'm not usually a fan of transforming into prey animals, my omni nature really comes in handy sometimes, especially in moments where I need to be stealthy.

Everyone would notice a lion. But a sniveling rodent? No one blinks twice. The only thing I have to worry about now is getting spotted by one of those owls we heard on the way in.

Wasting no time, I scurry towards the barn, feeling dirt beneath my paws and blades of grass brushing against my flanks. It takes all of thirty seconds to cross the field and find a crack in the wall to peek through.

Three men sit huddled around a bottle of whiskey and a dog-eared set of playing cards. There are several cheap skull masks lying on the ground near their feet. Bingo. My nose twitches. In this form, the stench is impossible to miss, but two of them smell like wolves to me. The third may be some kind of bird shifter, but the B.O. makes it hard to know for sure.

Their backs are turned to three captive women stuffed naked in a single dog kennel. Thankfully, they all appear to be alive.

Two seem like prey shifters, maybe rabbits or squirrels. Both are common enough in this area but often lack protection. They must be the missing bar employees. The third woman is slightly bigger than the other two, and she's not acting scared. She's angry.

The alpha wolf's niece.

I'm about to go report my findings to Callum when one of the smaller shifters slumps against the side of the cage. Her scream rips through the night, loud, agonized, and raspy. With the way the others don't even flinch, this isn't the first time.

These assholes have electrified the cage.

The captives can't even rest without fear of immediate—totally fucking unnecessary—pain. The smallest woman curls herself in a tight ball, her muscles trembling as tears roll down her face.

Laughter from the three shits playing cards drowns out her whimpers. I grind my teeth. They've sealed their fate.

Without another thought, I rush around the corner at a dead sprint, transforming from rat to lion mid-stride. My organs grow, my bones elongate, and the sharp pain that rips into me as I'm remade only fuels my rage.

As I crash through the barn door, I rip the heads from the shoulders of the first two vermin in my path with no resistance. My teeth and claws tear through their skin like butter.

Most colors are absent from my vision in this form, but every line is crisp as I sentence them to death for their crimes. I watch the life fade from their eyes with satisfaction, tasting iron from their blood on my tongue. When I turn to the sole survivor, urine runs down his leg.

Pathetic. He's right to fear me. I am retribution.

I step toward the remaining trafficker. He's looking around wildly, desperate for an escape route, but there's nowhere to run. Instead of removing his guts and spreading them across the floor like I want to, I plant one massive paw against his throat and pin him to the ground. The color of his face changes depending on how hard I push. Pink, red, purple. When a blood vessel shatters in his left eye, I'm disappointed. He's no match for me.

Callum curses behind me.

"Chill out. You're going to do brain damage." He smacks me in the flank. My lion considers taking a bite out of him to teach him respect, but ultimately, we decide against it and flick him with our tail instead.

I reluctantly let up on the remaining shifter's throat. He's out cold now, fresh blood and bruises mottling skin coated with old layers of dirt and grime. The women in the corner are weeping hysterically, terrified by the violence I just brought down on their behalf.

They'll get over it . . . Probably.

"We need to get out of here." Callum studies the inside of the barn with narrowed eyes. "This is just a drop point. Let's help these women, then we'll take this guy back to the compound for questioning."

He's in boring problem-solving mode now, so I just chuff in agreement, giving the shifter one last shove. I accidentally draw blood. *Oops.* I lift my paw gingerly, lick it clean, and then transform back into my human form.

Cal tosses me my clothes, and we make quick work of checking the barn for anything we may have missed. There's nothing much here, just a few guns, some small wads of cash, and a handful of loose pills. I'm most interested in the abandoned masks, which we bag up.

"We're here to help you, give you some safe options . . ." I hear Callum say as he gently leads the women out of the cage. I leave him to it. Of the two of us, he's not quite as frightening, plus he's got influence at his disposal if they start freaking out.

While he's reassuring them they're safe now, I stuff the prisoner into his new home, the electric dog kennel, and load it into the SUV. He's still out cold, but he's in for a rude dose of karma in a few hours.

Payback's a bitch.

Two of the women ask to be returned to the same town they were taken from. We offer to relocate them somewhere safer, but they both say they'd be more comfortable where they came from. I don't get it, but I'm not here to argue. The third, the alpha's niece, asks to use my phone. Her pack promises to pick her up from the bar.

Cal helps them to the car, handing them blankets to wrap around themselves. I try to be patient with their slow progress, but shit, I'm ready to go.

Once they're settled, I torch the barn and we head out. Hopefully, this will send a message to the traffickers they won't be able to ignore.

Now that my adrenaline is wearing off, I can't ignore the throbbing in my chest any longer. The unsealed bond isn't happy with how far I am from Sheena.

It also isn't thrilled with how the female wolf shifter in the back seat keeps touching me. If she weren't traumatized, I'd shut that shit down real quick. I don't want to make her night any worse by biting her head off. But when she runs her hand over my shoulder for the tenth time, I've had enough.

"I'm taken," I bark.

She recoils like I slapped her, a slight pout curling her lips. Her disappointment doesn't last long, though. Within five minutes, she's staring at Callum like water in the desert. He narrows his eyes at me in annoyance, but I just shrug, returning to my thoughts about Sheena and our bond.

It's way too soon to even think about making it permanent, especially since I haven't figured out how to explain the whole mate thing to her yet. I'm worried the 'until death do us part' bit will freak her out. If I just come right out and ask her to seal a bond more permanent than marriage, she's going to run for it. I wouldn't blame her if she did.

I've only heard of one or two mated pairs in the world, and they're ancient even in supernatural terms. That's another thing we haven't talked to Sheena about. Most of us live a few hundred years with aging slowing dramatically somewhere in the mid to late twenties. How do you even bring that up to someone who fears their future more than anything else?

I rub my chest with the heel of my hand, trying to ease the ache. It doesn't help. The throb has been getting worse since we left, and I can only hope it's not this uncomfortable for Sheena. Callum glances at me a few times with concern, but I know he won't say anything in front of strangers.

When we finally pull back into the bar parking lot, the two smaller women vanish into the night within seconds. Not a word of thanks, but I can't blame them for being jumpy. Prey shifters have to be careful at the best of times, and these two have more reasons than most to avoid more powerful creatures.

On the opposite side of the spectrum, the wolf pack's representative won't shut up about how thankful he is, clapping Callum on the back half a dozen times as he bundles the alpha's niece up into their tricked out Jeep. I choose to stay in our SUV. I'm hurting too much to care if it makes me look like an arrogant dick.

Once Cal slides back into the driver's seat, I sigh with relief, ready to go. He puts his hand on the gearshift, then lets it fall back to his lap, turning to face me.

"We'll need to hunt the bar owner down eventually," I say before he can speak. "There have to be consequences for selling out."

He nods, but I can tell by the stubborn glint in his eyes he won't be sidetracked.

"You're hurting."

I grunt an affirmative, and he puffs out a loud breath.

"They'll be able to tell, Gideon. It will bring up questions we aren't ready to answer."

I grunt again. He's right of course, but I don't know what the fuck I'm supposed to do about it. Nothing gets past our dads, and since we haven't been home in months, I'm sure they'll make it a point to be all over our business when we stop by to drop off the trafficker.

"I'll just stay in the car," I mutter.

"Yeah, like they wouldn't just immediately send someone to drag you out." Callum snorts, then hesitates. " . . . I could take the edge off."

My jaw literally drops. I can't help it. It's not often he truly shocks me, but this makes the list.

"How would you getting me off solve our problems, Cal?" I ask, too curious to feel any type of way about the suggestion.

"Gods. I'm not offering to suck you off or something." He runs his fingers through his hair, clearly flustered. "I'm just saying I can give you something else to focus on, so you aren't fixating on the bond."

He's embarrassed now, and I feel bad. Callum rarely uses or even mentions his abilities. He's ashamed of his nature and the way people view it.

"Okay." I agree with a shrug. There's no point in overthinking things. He's my best friend. That's not about to change, and him feeling comfortable with himself is way overdue.

"Okay? Just like that?" Callum asks.

He's staring at me now with an intensity I'm not used to. I fight the urge to squirm in my seat. "Well, yeah. I trust you, and they are nosy." I bat my eyelashes and fan myself dramatically with my hand. "I don't want to answer anyone's fucking questions. Give me another feeling to focus on, Callum."

I'm rewarded with another eye roll as he reaches for me with his right hand. When I see his fingers shaking in the dim light of the cab, I erase the last bit of distance between us myself. His fingers spread wide across my chest, evenly spaced, with his palm directly over my heart.

He so rarely uses his magic around anyone, but now I've got a front row seat. I can see every dark shadow dancing in his eyes. His cheekbones sharpen, drawing attention to the deepening hollows of his face. It's savage, terrifying, and hypnotic. I can't look away.

Before I think better of it, I'm reaching for him and exploring the shifting planes of his face. He closes his eyes, then leans into my hand. I feel the exact moment he pushes his power into me.

The throbbing sting of the bond fades, but only because I'm now hyper aware of every other nerve in my body. I'm not exactly horny, but every sensation is intense. The way my shirt shifts over my nipples, the air conditioning blowing against my lips, Cal's skin under my fingertips.

The sensitivity is overwhelming, but he was right. It's easier to ignore than the painful throbbing in my chest. It'll take effort, but I'll be able to act normal when we get to the compound.

Black eyes flicker open and lock with mine. When Callum pulls his hand gently away from my chest, I nearly gasp at the feeling.

"Don't worry," he says. "She's still in there. I just numbed the sensations around your heart for a little while and gave you something else to feel." His voice is deeper than usual, and I watch with fascination as the shadows and sharp edges fade from his face. Some of the laugh lines I'm used to seeing are back now, too.

"Yeah, I can tell," I chuckle, flicking the air vent closed. "I can make this work."

Callum makes no comment, but I see him smirking as we back out. He's still grinning when we merge onto the interstate a few minutes later.

"Kinky fucker," I mutter, needing to break the silence.

He laughs then, long and loud. Despite our destination, I can't help joining in.

By the time we pull up to the enclave, our laughter is long gone. The gate opens without protest, and we pass under the carved awning into the stone courtyard.

Cal sighs.

This is harder on him than it is on me. My parents were tough, and they taught me to be the same. I spent my childhood preparing for a life of leadership, but I know they love me and want me to be happy more than anything else.

Callum doesn't have the same luxury.

I glance up at the enormous compound we grew up in. Seeing it again for the first time in months is always a strange feeling. Massive and utilitarian on the outside, it sprawls further than the eye can see, both above and below ground.

The building itself is a hollow square frame with three wings divided among the leadership factions, plus another wing for storing weapons and, at times like these, hostages. The sides surround a massive outdoor space, which is used for training and fun. It has a hedge maze, a fountain, and a sparring ring.

It's weird as hell to be back, but it's home.

There are signs of construction, which I can only assume is the fae faction making itself comfortable. That alliance is new and fragile. If my father is to be believed, it will add to the strength of the enclave and the entire region. While I'm not a big fan of the fae I've met, any additional stability can only be a good thing, especially when you're dealing with supes who can level entire blocks when they have a bad day.

Callum backs the SUV into a garage near the holding facilities. We don't make it a habit of detaining anyone, but the rooms are there for a reason.

I get out of the passenger side, kicking the door closed and nodding to one of my dad's guards. When I saunter to the back of the vehicle and pop the back hatch, I'm disappointed to find our prisoner is still out cold. I had hoped he would wake up so we could shock him a few times before handing him over. No such luck.

I turn the electricity off on the cage and hoist it out of the back with Cal's help. Together, we carry it through the narrow hallway to the nearest holding room and toss it none too gently inside.

"Son, where the hell have you been?" My father's booming voice puts a smile on my face. He pulls me into a crushing hug.

Hiding the mate bond from him is going to make this a long night.

CALLUM

Gideon's dad blows into the room with the force of a hurricane, grabbing his son up in a hug so tight it makes my bones ache just watching. Then it's my turn. Joshua releases Gideon and crushes me in a similar hug. I cling for a second and hope he doesn't notice.

By the time he pulls back, my eyes are gritty, and my emotions are raw. Joshua was there for me in ways my father refused to be. I would endure hours of uncomfortable affection in his home before I would offend him.

As if he can read my mind, the older shifter ruffles my hair like I'm still a little boy, then claps me on the back so hard I worry he's knocked one of my teeth loose. I'm twenty-six years old, but I guess some things never change.

"Welcome home, boys. What did you bring us?" He turns his brown eyes—so similar to Gideon's—toward the holding room and peers at the prisoner through the two-way mirror. "Gods, did you slam his neck in a door or something?"

I laugh and point at his son.

"The kitty cat was a little heavy-handed with the capture."

Joshua turns back to his son, raising his eyebrows in a silent demand. It's a look I've seen on his face a thousand times. Predictably, Gideon gives no shits. In fact, he looks less sorry than I've ever seen anyone look, crossing his arms over his chest and glaring at me.

"He had it coming, dad," he growls. "They were keeping those shifters naked in an electric dog kennel." Joshua's amusement flips to outrage in a flash. I've never seen them look so alike.

"It's a wonder you didn't rip his head off, then. We'll have a long conversation with this one when he wakes up," Joshua says. "For now, let's leave him in there to think about what he's done. Your mothers are very excited to have you both home." His smile returns as quickly as it disappeared, and he throws an arm around each of our shoulders.

It doesn't escape my notice that he omits my father. There's no love lost between us, and Joshua knows better than to push us together these days. No, that ship sailed a long time ago—the second I didn't manifest as a nightmare demon like the rest of the family.

Joshua and Gideon keep up a steady conversation as we walk back to the residential part of the complex. Their chatter is punctuated by loud laughter and probing questions, which Gideon narrowly dodges.

When we enter the shifter wing of the compound, some of my anxiety fades. As a teen, I spent more time in this home than the demon quarters. We gravitate towards the kitchen the same way we always used to, where Gideon's mom, Sarah, immediately fusses over her son. She stands on her tiptoes to examine how long Gideon's hair is, exclaiming her surprise, before pressing excited kisses to both his cheeks.

Too late, I notice Sarah isn't the only mother in the room.

My mom rises from her spot at the table, looking uncomfortable with Sarah's exuberant display of affection for her son. Not a strand of her blonde hair is out of place. As usual, her greeting for me is about as warm as falling sleet.

"Hello, mother." Despite the familiar stab of sadness that comes whenever I see her, I bend down to kiss one of her pale cheeks. I couldn't be what she wanted in a son, and she couldn't be what I needed in a mother. It is what it is, but the pain doesn't seem to be something I've grown out of yet.

"It's good to see you, son." Her voice is crisp, the words unflinchingly polite. She might as well be speaking to a casual acquaintance, but I won't wilt. She nods firmly, and I reflexively mirror her actions, keeping my cool until the woman I actually want to see swoops in to save me.

"Mallory, look how handsome our boys are," Sarah exclaims, jostling Gideon out of the way to reach me. She presses a warm kiss to my cheek, and I fold her gently in my arms. As always, her hug makes everything a little better.

Unlike my mother, Sarah is a tall woman, which is common among omni-shifters. At five foot ten, she's just a couple of inches shorter than me. That makes her easy to hug and hard to avoid.

Sarah clasps my face in her hands and looks me over thoroughly; there's no escaping her perceptive gaze. I try to look normal, but just like when we were boys, nothing gets past her. Whatever she sees in my expression makes her eyes sharpen. *Fuck me.* Now, it's just a toss-up over whether she keeps her observations to herself or makes them a family discussion.

Sarah tilts her head to give her son a narrow-eyed look, then swivels back to me. The gods only know what conclusion she comes to, but when her mouth splits into a wide, terrifying smile, I'm scared shitless.

Sliding out of her clutches, I drop into a chair and reach for one of her famous chocolate chip cookies. It melts in my mouth. Maybe if I never stop chewing, she won't be able to question me.

We make small talk for the next few minutes, while Gideon tries to distract his mom with questions about her and Mallory's gardens. My mother offers a handful of tepid remarks, but she seems uncomfortable and out of place sitting around a simple wooden table in the cozy kitchen.

It's just not her aesthetic. No, Mallory is more evening gowns and formal sitting rooms. I doubt she's ever baked a batch of cookies in her life.

"Where is everyone?" I stiffen as I hear my brother's voice coming from the living room. The cookie sours in my gut when Ciprian walks into the kitchen followed closely by our father.

"Why are you all grubbing around in the kitchen like the help?" Ciprian asks, glancing at me as he snatches a cookie for himself. "Now that you've finally crawled out of your cabin in the woods to give us a report, let's hear it, brother."

The golden child earns a reproachful look from our mother for speaking with his mouth full, but her eyes hold a fondness she hasn't directed at me in a decade.

"Ciprian," my father drawls. "Perhaps a formal setting would be more appropriate for this conversation."

Ignoring my little brother's look of annoyance, he offers Gideon his hand without even looking at me. It's a deliberate slight. I'm his fucking son.

Gideon shoots me a worried look as he returns the handshake, but it's not his fault. Even if affection holds no sway with my father, etiquette dictates he should greet me first. But Dimitri Casanell's priorities have always been crystal clear. I'm way too used to coming in last place to anyone and everything to be hurt by his calculated micro aggressions. It's not worth getting worked up over.

When father finally turns to greet me, I deny him the courtesy of standing. Instead, I give his hand a brief shake, and then slap my brother's greedy fingers away from the platter of cookies.

Ciprian looks more like our parents every time I see him. He's pale and blonde, with neatly waving hair and sparkling white teeth. If I look like a dark, evil demon cliché, then all three of them look like some sort of pop culture caricature of angels.

They would hate that comparison, but it fits. Except in the eyes. There, unfortunately, lies a genetic marker that was impossible to dodge, even for me. While my mother has soft, gray eyes, my father's are as black as obsidian. Both Ciprian and I share that feature. Our soulless void eyes are anything but angelic.

Clearing my throat, I pull my gaze away from my family and address Joshua directly because one, I'd rather talk to him, and two, I know it will piss my father off.

"We were right to worry. There is a supernatural gang trafficking in weaker species. Besides the alpha wolf's niece, the women we rescued outside of Boulder were prey shifters living with no protection to speak of. They were easy pickings."

Sarah makes a distressed sound, but I already know what she's winding up to ask.

"We offered them the protection of the enclave, but they didn't want to leave." I run a hand through my hair. "Neither of them have ever been more than fifty miles away from where they were born."

Sarah pinches her eyebrows together. "I believe you, sweetheart . . . but were you scary?"

I picture Gideon's massive lion teeth dripping with blood and the heads literally rolling around on the floor of the barn.

"Of course not. We rescued them and were nice as hell," I assure her, but she's not convinced. From the look on her face, I can tell she doesn't want to drop it.

"The captives aren't important," Gideon jumps in. "The guys I . . . err . . . neutralized were vermin, low-level puppets. There's no way they were pulling the strings."

"You think someone with power is organizing these traffickers from the shadows? Snatching people up in our territory?" Joshua's voice rumbles like a landslide, and I'm reminded why he's a scary fucker to most people.

When we both nod, Joshua turns to my father. "We'll have a talk with the puppet, Dimitri. If this goes as deep as the boys suspect, they'll need help."

Oh, fuck no.

Both Gideon and I protest, but Joshua silences us with a look.

"If you think I will put either of your lives at risk to protect your foolish pride, you've got another thing coming." He pins us both under the weight of his stare. "If the enclave determines backup is called for, you will both accept the help and say 'thank you' with smiles on your faces." By the end of his rant, he's red in the face.

Sarah places a soothing hand on his arm.

"Of course, the boys will take reinforcements if it's too dangerous. Don't get yourself worked up, darling." Her words are calm, but her narrowed eyes are back on us in obvious warning.

I feel like a moth pinned to some scientist's board.

Now I'm even more certain she knows something is going on. She's sparing us right now, but it won't be long until we face her questions head on. That's a lot more intimidating than her husband's bluster.

As we talk well into the night, I dodge barb after barb from my brother, enduring his constant attempts to put me in my place.

As if I could ever forget.

I'm Callum—black sheep, disappointment extraordinaire, and displaced heir to the Hall of Nightmares.

When we finally retire for the night, Gideon and I leave the cozy kitchen to return to our childhood bedrooms. Gideon's room is just down the hall, but mine is in the marble tomb that masquerades as the demon wing. A chill settles over my skin.

After exchanging perfunctory goodnights with my parents, I close my bedroom door in my brother's face. With any luck, the insufferable shit won't be part of the backup team Joshua threatened us with.

When I slide under the covers, I think about Sheena's pretty blushing cheeks and Sarah's curious looks. It's clear now, we haven't buried our secrets well enough, and eventually, some of them will come to light.

My phone dings, and I grapple with it, seeing an incoming message from Gideon.

My mom thinks we are ducking

fucking*

Come again?

Lol that's EXACTLY what she thinks is going on

Be serious. Why would she think that?

I am. She's always thought we had a thing.

That look she gave us after your face was all sexed up healthy… she thinks she knows what's going on. That's why she didn't ask.

Every time we come home, some crazy shit happens

It's OK. Mom doesn't care

Don't you?

Care? Not as much as you do apparently.

Dude

You're such a prude

We can talk more tomorrow. I want to go home to our girl. Leave by 7a?

Sure thing

That's just wonderful.

My mind races, anxiety pressing against my lungs.

Now the woman who is the closest thing I have to a real mom thinks I'm in a sexual relationship with her only child. I can only imagine what my father would say if Sarah shared her theory.

Things are already tangled enough, but I can't help feeling like this mess is just getting started. After thrashing around in the sheets for what feels like hours, I fall into an uneasy sleep. Even as I drift off, I'm mindful of the nightmares all around me.

Thank the gods none of them know Sheena exists.

CHAPTER
EIGHT

QUAID

I stare at the ashes of what used to be a barn and consider stomping through the mess. After weeks of hunting, we finally closed in on a truly vile group of shifters, only to find someone else got to them first. Now we're at a literal dead end. The few bones that survived the fire are too badly damaged to be of any use to my trackers.

An ugly suspicion swirls low in my stomach.

This was no accident.

While some of the dry grass around the perimeter is scorched, someone obviously went to a lot of trouble to make sure the flames didn't spread. My boss won't be happy to hear there's another party involved, especially one that appears to be even more powerful than these dead shifters.

A member of my team curses from somewhere behind me, but I don't bother looking to see who it is. I understand their frustration. We failed to put the traffickers down. It doesn't matter that they ended up dead, anyway. Hunter hands didn't end their lives; a failure is a failure.

That's our singular purpose, but I lost sight of it once during my first assignment. A dumb kid, I got sucked in too deep, forgetting the rules I was raised by. I botched the entire mission. She's the sole blemish on my spotless record, a bruise that never quite heals. Most of the time, I can forget my failure, but then something like this happens, and the pain of remembering takes my breath away.

"There's nothing here for us. Move out," I shout. The team follows my lead without question, and we load into our nondescript all-terrain vehicles, leaving the ashes of the barn behind. I'll find out who did this and take them down.

I won't hesitate this time.

The only good supernatural is a dead one.

SHEENA

AFTER YEARS SPENT almost exclusively in my own company, you would think I could handle two days by myself. Apparently not. Things are so chaotic in my head I actually regret not accepting Callum's offer to get me a cell phone to keep in touch.

Ugh. Who am I?

Tossing the remote down on the coffee table, I throw myself back against the couch . . . aka the scene of the crime.

Time to examine the new Sheena.

She's incapable of being alone for forty-eight hours, panting over not one but two men she barely knows, and prone to dramatic third person internal monologues. I bet this Sheena gives up all of her darkest secrets by the third date, too. Jesus, she sounds like the type of person who takes drinks from strangers and screams 'yolo' while straddling a mechanical bull. *Oh, no . . . a* chilling thought occurs to me. *Is the new Sheena a good time?*

I pull the cozy blanket over my face and groan.

Surely a few nights in a comfortable bed and an orgasm didn't give me a complete personality transplant. I just need to dig a little deeper for the familiar.

I recognize myself in the gnawing fear that things are just way too good to be true. It's been working overtime since I came here. Also, the prickly sensation skittering up and down my arms since I covered my eyes . . . That's all the old me. I yank the blanket down, grimly satisfied, and check all the visible exits. All clear. For now.

With a sigh, I sit up, enjoying how the buttery leather of the couch feels against my bare skin. Physically, I'm okay. My bruises are almost gone, and the scratches from the attack have faded to dim pink lines along my ribs.

I'm restless; what am I supposed to do with all this free time? I consider going down to the gym and getting a workout in, but that doesn't sound very fun to any version of Sheena. I'm used to working hard to keep enough cash to stay on the run, but I've never been a huge fan of structured exercise.

Lying around in this nice ass house is feeding my paranoia.

A car door slams, interrupting my internal ramblings—they're home. I jump to my feet, but stop when I don't hear the thud of a second door closing. I'm probably being paranoid, but I'd rather look like a skittish fool than a dead dumbass.

My fingers feel frozen, but I reach for the small pistol anyway, gripping it lightly like Gideon showed me. With my left hand, I fumble with the remote until it clicks over to the security feed. A blonde man is standing next to an unfamiliar pickup truck.

Who the fuck is this?

He's surveying the house with an arrogant sneer. Even from the grainy security footage, I can tell he's eerily perfect. Inhuman. I watch, scarcely daring to breathe as he heaves a sigh so deep it registers on the camera. When he pulls something out of his pocket and marches towards the front door, the icy feeling spreads from my fingers to encase my entire body.

My skin is numb, but my mind is racing. *Did Callum and*

Gideon sell me out? I don't want to believe that, but denial is for the stupid, and I have bigger things to worry about right now.

Fight or flight? Over the years, I've learned to run when I'm in danger. No questions asked. The only difference this time . . . I don't want to leave. *Fight it is.* Without giving my brain a chance to second-guess the decision, I hurry into the hall, pointing the gun at the front door just as it swings open. Fear and adrenaline threaten to drag me under, but I'm proud to say my hands only tremble a little.

As soon as the blonde guy spots me, he freezes with the key in his hand and stares. His jaw drops. His cold black eyes survey me from head to toe, only pausing briefly in their examination when they get to the gun in my hands. Shaking his head, he kicks the door closed, and his shocked look morphs into a grin I can only describe as triumphant.

"Oh my *GODS!* I knew they were full of shit. Oh, just wait until I tell the parents that Cal shacked up with some nobody." He points at me gleefully. "I mean, don't take offense. You're hot as fuck, but I can only assume you're some kind of bunny rabbit shifter with a sob story and shallow pockets."

Why do people always say 'no offense' before spewing the most offensive things they can come up with?

Blood rushes to my face, and I wait patiently for him to shut up. When he finally gets tired of hearing himself talk, I flick the safety off on the gun. In the silence, the click is deafening. Some of the delight fades from his eyes, replaced with a calculating gleam.

"Did you just now turn the safety off? I'm fully in the fucking house, babe. You should have shot me on the porch."

He has a point there, but it just makes me mad. When he takes a step toward me, I hold my ground and narrow my eyes. He stops and sighs.

"Look, I don't know who you are, but you're pointing a gun at me in my big brother's house. That's a mistake."

Wait, what? There's no way.

"You're Callum's brother?" I look him over, searching for similarities as he nods.

I'm prepared to call bullshit until I notice the pitch black eyes narrowed on me. I've only ever seen eyes like that on one other person.

Oh fuck, is he here because something happened to them?

"Is Callum okay? Is Gideon? I haven't heard from them since they left. Have you talked to them?" I don't trust this guy, but I need to know what he knows more than I need him dead.

"Yes, yes, and yes." He ticks each one off with his fingers. "I think that covers all your questions." I scowl as he dips into a bow that's as mocking as it is arrogant. "I'm Ciprian Casanell. Now, who the fuck are you?"

I'm saved from answering by the sound of gravel churning in the driveway. Gideon and Callum must recognize the truck because they are out of the SUV in a heartbeat, storming up the porch steps, flinging open the door, and jumping in Ciprian's face.

"You snuck out at the crack of dawn to case my fucking house?" Callum screams in his brother's face. "You're such a piece of shit."

Seeing Callum and Ciprian side by side, I notice more similarities. The cut of their jaws, the curve of their lower lips, and the way they flail their arms when they yell. Because I'm watching so closely, I catch Ciprian subtly flinching away from his brother's anger before he joins him in hurling accusations.

"Hey, baby," Gideon says, pulling my attention to him. "It's good to see you. How about you hand me that gun?"

I blink a few times and realize I still have a death grip on the pistol. So much for holding it lightly. My arms are shaking from the weight, so I flip the safety on and hand the weapon butt first to Gideon. He sets it down on the entry table, then scoops me up, both of us completely ignoring the screaming siblings.

Once I'm wrapped up in his hug, the constant pressure on my chest vanishes with one final throb. I cling to him like a little kid. It would embarrass me if he weren't holding me just as tightly.

"I'm glad you're back," I admit, blood rushing to my face a second before he presses his lips to mine.

Now that it's happened a few times, I'm sensing a theme to Gideon's kisses. He puts everything he feels into them. Each one is so different; it's like we're having a wordless conversation. This particular kiss starts off soft. It tells me he was afraid when he saw me holding the gun, and even now, he's trying not to scare me. Once I'm kissing him back, he really dives in, one big hand sliding under my ass to support my weight.

It's a possessive touch. He's telling me he missed me.

The pressure increases, and my feet leave the ground as he shuffles us both backwards. Now my literal back is against the literal wall, and Gideon uses that leverage to grind against me. It reminds me of the couch, but I'm not brave enough to admit to myself what he's trying to say with that move.

I also don't want him to stop.

"Don't fucking look at her."

Callum's hissed demand breaks me from my lust bubble, and I pull back from Gideon to look at the two warring brothers.

"Boiling hot." Ciprian fans himself dramatically. "I give you a seven out of ten for that display, Gideon. Don't stop on my account," he croons, holding lecherous eye contact with me the entire time.

I can't help rolling my eyes.

Ciprian is objectively good looking. I can see that, but his appearance does absolutely nothing for me, especially when his goal is clearly to wind his brother up. Gideon just laughs, letting my body slide to the ground much more slowly than necessary. He makes sure I feel every inch of him during the descent.

"Runt, I would say I'm surprised to see you here, but I'm not. What's it going to take for you to leave with your mouth closed?" Gideon asks.

Again, I watch another weird look flicker across Ciprian's face. *Did the question hurt his feelings?* This is some complex sibling drama. As an orphan dropped outside a fire station, I'm not exactly qualified to decipher these dynamics.

Ciprian ignores the question, turning to face his brother and prodding obnoxiously at his face. "I see now why the broody, under-eye bags are gone. Her lust must be a top of the line moisturizer, big brother, if just watching her climb him juiced you up this much."

Callum slaps his brother's hand away and steps around him to give me a deliberate hug. I wouldn't have minded a kiss, but I don't want the first time that happens to be in front of some scheming relative with a chip on his shoulder. After holding my own during the confrontation and the electric kiss with Gideon, I'm feeling pretty confident. Maybe that's why I raise my voice and stir the pot.

"Callum, your brother is kind of a prick."

"Yeah, believe me, I know." He shakes his head. "Why are you here, Ciprian?"

A tense silence follows the question, broken finally by a loud sigh.

"You were obviously hiding something at the compound. You marched in after six months of ghosting us all, looking better than I've seen you look in years but acting twice as worried. I knew something was up, so I beat you back here to find out what."

He turns to me then, the black of his eyes unnerving in their intensity. "Thank you for feeding my brother." There's a gravity to his tone that makes my eyebrows furrow. At first, I don't understand what he means. When it clicks, my face floods with heat.

"Stop embarrassing her," Callum snaps. "It's not like that."

My face flushes. He's right, but does he have to deny it so aggressively? I can't help feeling disappointed. From the look on Ciprian's face, I'm not the only one, although it's impossible to tell why he gives a shit.

"Well, why isn't it like that?" He demands. "And while we're on the subject, you've been starving yourself for years. You're wasting away. Every time I see you, you look more like a corn-husk than a demon of fucking."

Callum opens his mouth, but his brother isn't finished.

"What's up with that, anyway? Can't stand to get your dick wet because you're in love with your best friend?" Ciprian crosses his arms. While he's obviously still trying to rile Callum up, the concern in his eyes is now unmistakable.

"Dude." Gideon laughs. "I fucking told you the family thinks we're fucking."

Callum's face turns red, and he opens his mouth. I just know there's about to be more yelling, and I've reached my limit with that. Making a decision, I step between them, clearing my throat and putting one hand over the other in the universal time-out gesture. It actually works. I suspect the silence won't last long, so I jump into the arena while I have their attention.

"Hi, my name is Sheena." I shake Ciprian's hand emphatically. "You must be Callum's brother—who I've only just learned exists."

He returns my handshake, staring down at me with a twinkle in his eyes.

"Your brother and Gideon saved my life, and they are letting me stay here while I figure things out. I'm not really sorry that I pointed a gun at you, but I would appreciate it if you wouldn't mention meeting me. A lot of people want me dead." I suck in a deep breath and eye Callum with concern. "I'm also interested in hearing more about why you think your brother is starving himself."

By the time I finish my speech, I'm a little out of breath and a lot nervous. While I kept the details vague, I'm still taking a risk by trusting this man at all. My gut tells me it's okay, though, and I'm a big believer in listening to what's being said without words.

I just watched an intense argument, cluttered with insults and male posturing, but it was all bullshit. The brothers' relationship may smell like a bucket of hot garbage, but it's still a bucket they both care enough about to fight over.

Ciprian rocks back on his heels and cocks his head to the side as we assess each other. I refuse to flinch under his stare. Ten long seconds pass, then he gives me a nod so small I wonder if I've imagined it. A heartbeat later, he presses an extravagant kiss to my knuckles and dances out of Gideon's reach. Blinking slowly, I pull back my hand. I'm pretty sure I just reached a silent understanding with a demon I held at gunpoint.

"It's a pleasure to meet you, Sheena," he says. "I have a feeling we're going to be the best of friends, and I would never rat out a friend. Come sit with me. I'll give you all the dirt on this dynamic duo."

Since this doesn't seem to be negotiable, I accept the cease-fire offer and follow him to the living room. At first, Callum hovers near us. Once it becomes clear his brother isn't going to murder me or call their mom, he leaves the room. Ciprian is obviously a troublemaker, but I can't deny his energy is infectious.

He explains that Callum often resists using his powers, which makes him physically weaker than he should be. That's concerning, but I don't comment. When Ciprian asks about me, I give him the heavily redacted version of my story. He doesn't protest the obvious plot holes, which surprises me, but he does make me laugh almost constantly.

By the time he stands to leave, I'm actually sad to see him go.

He scribbles his number on a pad of paper and gives it to me. "Call me if things get out of hand," Ciprian says. I fold the paper carefully, slipping it into my pocket, but commit to nothing.

He leaves without saying goodbye to the guys.

I head back into the kitchen to find Callum and Gideon making sandwiches. From the innocent looks on both their faces, it's obvious they've been eavesdropping. I lift myself onto a barstool and wait until they both look over at me.

"Callum, your brother loves you very much," I declare with a grin. Gideon laughs, Callum groans, and before I know it, I'm squealing and dodging thrown chips.

I'm so glad they are home.

As we eat lunch together, I refuse to let the thought rattle me and enjoy a few moments of normalcy. I know it won't last. It can't. As soon as we finish here, we'll have to have a serious talk.

After I've cleaned and dried the last plate and handed it to Callum to put away, I look up at them expectantly. My foot taps, and Gideon looks at his watch.

"Almost thirty-six minutes. You held back longer than I expected."

I swat at him with the dishtowel, but he's too fast for me and dodges easily. "You two are the worst." I groan. "What happened? Did you find the traffickers?"

My bare foot stomps the kitchen tile, which does nothing but make me feel like a complete jackass. Callum grins down at me and calmly slides the plate in the cabinet, but it's Gideon who finally starts talking and puts me out of my misery.

"Hmm, let's see, we drank some really gross beer. Cal convinced a bartender to give up the gang . . . Then things finally got interesting. I did surveillance as a rat, before decapitating as a lion." His dimples disappear, and his face turns serious. "The enclave is interrogating the one we left alive now to see if he gives up his bosses."

I blink a few times.

There's a lot to unpack in that, but unfortunately, my brain is stuck on one part.

"How did you convince the bartender?" I ask, trying to look nonchalant.

I think I'm nailing it until I notice Gideon trying to hide his smile. Great. Now I sound jealous. I expect Callum to get mad about the question. After all, it's none of my business. Instead, he just stares at me like a shark observes a seal.

He advances. I retreat until I feel the edge of the counter pressing against my back. Callum has me caged in. His tattooed arms block my escape on both sides. I'm trapped, and there's blood in the water. Absently, I notice Gideon leave the room, an enormous grin on his face. I'm alone with a demon.

"What do you want to know, Sheena?" Callum whispers. "Are you asking if I convinced her like this?" His lips brush the shell of my ear ever so slightly.

I suck in a breath, but keep my mouth shut. His hands slide from the counter to my waist. He lifts me up to perch on the edge, putting us at eye level. I have nowhere to hide.

"Maybe you're asking if it happened like this?" His lips move to my neck, where he drops open-mouthed kisses along the sensitive skin of my throat. My eyes fall closed, a full body shiver rakes down my spine.

I might be embarrassed if this wasn't so obviously getting to him too. I hear the fast, deep thumping of his heart as his hands explore my body. His little phantom touches are systematically setting me on fire. My every nerve ending perks up to demand his attention.

Callum's thumbs explore the sensitive skin of my inner thighs where my shorts cut off. I have to force myself not to squirm at the touch. He dips his calloused fingertips just beneath the frayed denim, teasing us both.

I inch my thighs further apart in an obvious invitation. But instead of taking me up on it, Callum stops touching me.

My eyes snap open to find his face is just inches away from mine.

"What do you want to know, Sheena?"

It's a command disguised as a question, but for a moment, I can't remember what started this whole thing. By the time my brain catches up, my own questions are bubbling up to demand answers.

"Did you touch her? Did she feed you?" I lock eyes with him. "Callum, did you kiss her?"

Everything that was better left unsaid pours out of me. I fear his answers; I don't have any right to make demands of him, but the demon doesn't call me on it.

He actually seems pleased by my obvious jealousy.

"No . . . I didn't." His voice is husky. "I'd rather kiss you."

Callum never breaks eye contact, and I swear I'm melting into a puddle on the counter.

My mind and body are buzzing so much I can't think of a single word to say. So I do what I've been thinking about since I first saw him standing in front of the bar top at Styx.

I touch him.

With trembling fingers, I explore his perfect face. I bury one hand in his dark, messy hair, and run my nails along his scalp. Power consumes me when he shudders at my touch. With the thumb of my other hand, I gently graze his full bottom lip. His Adam's apple bobs, and my mouth goes dry, but I don't stop. Not this time. When I finally press my lips to his, the pressure is so faint it's almost a whisper.

I feel the moment his control breaks.

With a groan, Callum takes over the kiss. I'm a passenger now, and all I can do is hold on for the ride. He kisses me so thoroughly I don't even think my lips belong to me anymore. They're just an extension of him. He nibbles, sucks, and licks at the seam of my mouth, and I answer every unspoken demand.

If Gideon's kisses tell me what he's feeling, Callum's make me feel brave and strong—like I can have anything and everything I want. All I have to do is reach out and take it. When he finally pulls back, we're both gasping for breath.

I could get used to this.

CHAPTER
NINE

This is getting too complicated.

It's been several days since Callum broke my brain on the kitchen counter. Now that my body has cooled, my thoughts are burning out of control. Not only do I like two guys, but I'm also keeping dangerous secrets from them.

Now that I'm emotionally involved, my rules are making me feel guilty.

As a kid, loyalty wasn't some moral dilemma for me. I gave it to anyone who treated me with kindness, but after Quaid, after the abduction, I changed. My only loyalty is to myself now. I haven't felt bad about that in years, but with my head full of secrets, my stomach is tied in knots.

Can I trust them? It's tempting, but I can't betray the promise I made to myself as a terrified teen.

With a sigh, I roll over until I'm face down on the mattress. It fits around me like a cloud, stealing some of my tension. This house is starting to feel like home.

Keep it moving.

My inner voice blares the warning, but all I want to do is hit mute. If I had died in that coyote shifter attack last week, no one on this planet would have known or cared. Isolation once meant peace and safety to me. I'm not so sure now.

Flopping onto my back, I touch my lips. Callum kissed me like he would care if something bad happened to me. Sprawled on that counter, I felt like a queen on a throne, experiencing the rush of chasing after something I want.

Then, there's Gideon. The way I gravitate toward him . . . It's like my body needs his to function. I thought he felt the same way. Though he kissed the breath out of me when they got home, he also left me alone in the kitchen with an incubus demon. *Shouldn't he be jealous?*

My body doesn't care either way. It wants them both.

I yank the covers over my face, sinking into the homemade cocoon and letting it quiet some of the extraneous noise. It's a childish habit, but burrowing under covers is something I've always done when I need to think. Why am I so rattled, anyway? I've had a few one-night stands over the years, but none of them did much for me. In fact, my mostly dressed moments with Callum and Gideon were steamier than anything I've experienced naked.

Ugh. This isn't working.

When the heat under the covers becomes unbearable, I throw them back with a huff. Maybe I'm not a virgin, but my body is pulling me toward something I'm not sure I'm ready for. Now would be a great time to have a friend to talk things through with, but I'm an island—forever destined to have my own back—and also melodramatic as hell apparently.

Glancing over at my nightstand, the shiny new phone pulls me in. I caved and let the guys buy it for me. Being stuck here with no idea what was going on sent me into a doom spiral I don't want to repeat.

It's a concession I made only after they agreed to let me pay them back. Callum sourly accepted one hundred dollars from my dwindling supply of cash as a down payment. He didn't argue, but he did glare at the money like it offended him. Gideon just stormed out of the room without a word. I plan to keep a close eye on my bag to make sure the money doesn't mysteriously reappear.

Looking at the new phone gives me an insane idea. I jump up, digging through the pockets of my discarded shorts for the scrap of paper Ciprian gave me. Before I can question my sanity any further, I enter the numbers and press the green button. A suspicious voice answers after two rings.

"Who is this?"

"You said to call if I needed help." *This was a terrible idea.*

"Sheena?" Ciprian seems surprised to hear from me. I don't blame him. This is definitely not what he meant when he made that offer.

"Yeah . . ." *Why did I do this? I should hang up.*

"What's wrong? Is someone hurt?" He's completely focused now, and I feel like an idiot. *If I hang up now, he'll call Callum or Gideon.*

"No, everyone's okay," I sputter. "There's nothing really wrong . . . I just need a sounding board and you're the only person I could think of."

I'm mortified, but he just chuckles drily.

"My condolences on that, babe. I'll do my best. What's going on?"

Fuck it.

"Have you ever liked two people?" The question tumbles out of my mouth and I cringe, relieved that at least he can't see me. If I'm lucky, maybe he didn't even hear—

His scoff erases that hope.

"You sound like a kid with a crush. Do you mean, 'have I ever wanted to fuck two people?'"

Jesus Christ. The question is crass and blunt. I cover my face with my hand, and the silence stretches out uncomfortably until Ciprian groans.

"Look, if you can't even say the word 'fuck'—you're not ready to fuck Gideon, much less my brother. You're also going to get a bill for any therapy I need if this friendship involves disturbing conversations about my only sibling."

I roll my eyes, forgetting he can't see me.

"Quit being so dramatic. You're not helping at all. Just tell me —am I a slut for wanting them both?" I ask. A snort follows my question.

"First, no woman is a slut for going after what she wants while communicating honestly. Second, have they asked you to choose?"

What's he getting at?

"Well, no. We haven't really talked about it." I pause, trying to figure out how to word things without traumatizing him. "I've had . . . moments with them. Separately and together," I explain.

"Please, no details. My brother is going to owe me so much for this," he grumbles, clearing his throat. "Sheena, I expect they prefer you want them both. Monogamy isn't really mandatory in our community, and it's unheard of for an incubus. But Callum— he's not really built to sleep around."

"What should I do?" I say, my voice small. *I was so brave on that counter, but do I dare reach out and take what I want?*

"Umm, have a damn conversation and maybe some fun. You don't have to buy the car just because you take it for a test ride. Just please, and I can't emphasize this enough, don't tell me about it afterwards."

"Thanks, Ciprian," I murmur.

Can it really be that simple? I still have some thinking to do, but the conversation did actually help. He's right. It's not like I'm agreeing to some kind of lifelong commitment.

"Any time, bestie."

His tone is sarcastic, but the nickname makes me smile. *I'm going soft.*

After he hangs up, I crawl into bed. Though it's not late, I can barely keep my eyes open. It's weird, but fatigue doesn't always make sense, I guess, and there have been a lot of changes in my life. Sinking into the bed, I enjoy the cool feeling as I drift off.

My skin tingles, but it's not the sheets. Something else is . . . here. My sleepy brain struggles to make sense of the feeling.

It's not something at all. It's . . .

Danger.

Someone is watching me.

My brain demands I wake up, but my body is too far gone. I sink deeper into sleep, my heart racing helplessly.

GIDEON

I LISTEN TO SHEENA thrash around in her sleep through the wall. Another nightmare. Proof that a past like hers doesn't always go away quietly. I've been giving her space during these episodes, but tonight, the bond is screaming at me to comfort her.

She whimpers, and I'm on my feet.

I tiptoe down the hall, opening her door gently. The last thing I want to do is scare her more, but I can't just leave her to fight her fears alone. She's curled up in a tight ball in the middle of the big bed, flipping back and forth, a light sheen of sweat glistening on her forehead.

A breeze moves the hair on her cheek.

Wait, what? Why is the window open? The curtains are blowing in the breeze, bathing the room in the humid summer air. *No wonder she's sweating.* I slide the panel shut and flick the lock. It's not safe for her to sleep with the window open, even if we are on the second floor.

When she whimpers again, I forget all about the window and move to the side of the bed. Looking down at her, I hesitate. I'm scared to make it worse, but seeing her like this is terrible.

She flinches. Then her whole body stiffens in terror.

"Baby, wake up. It's a dream," I whisper.

That's it. I can't leave her like this. I crawl in beside her, wrapping her up in my arms. She doesn't wake, but her body relaxes. I'm clueless about what I should do, so I go with my gut and start talking. I tell her she's safe and that I won't let anything happen to her.

When her breathing finally levels out, I slip quietly from the bed, checking the window on my way out. It's just as I left it.

The oppressive humidity from earlier has escalated to a pop-up storm. Lightning crackles in the distance. Sheena doesn't stir. For a while, I stand there watching raindrops slide down the glass in patterns, each one slightly different than the one that came before it.

I hope it dies down soon.

I check the latch one more time. Satisfied it's secure, I make my way back to my room, hoping Sheena will sleep until morning without having to face any more nightmares from her past.

CHAPTER
TEN

LYSANDER

One more minute and I would have had her.

I stand at the edge of the woods and look up at her window as rain soaks me to the bone. It's time for that overgrown boy and the sex demon to die, so I can recoup my losses and take back what's mine. First, they attacked my shipment. Now, they're keeping her, my *property,* away from me like they have some right to her.

If I had known those two enclave fools were going after my men earlier, I would have taken her while they were gone. Instead, I wasted the best chance I've had in years. Rage boils inside me at the missed opportunity.

I'm growing tired of this hunt. The storm does nothing to cool my fury.

I want to charge into that house and grab her, but I didn't get to where I am today by making hasty decisions. No, my victory will have to wait until another day.

Backing slowly into the woods, I shift into my wolf form and return to my hideout. I shake the rain from my fur and curl up under the overhanging rock as I consider my options. I'll get another chance, and when it comes, I'll be ready.

She'll be mine again soon.

CHAPTER
ELEVEN

GIDEON

Fuck rain.

It's still gross outside, so instead of climbing a mountain, I'm stuck inside running on the treadmill like a hamster on a wheel. The spinning belt is a cheap substitute for what I really need, but I'm hoping a good workout will make me feel more settled. I have the machine set to simulate running in the mountains.

The difficulty changes every few minutes, but it's not really working for me. Sheena's nightmares, the mate secret, the traffickers, the cell phone—it's all starting to get to me.

Sheena walks into the gym wearing sweatpants and a black sports bra. The pace and incline on my treadmill kicks up a notch at the same time she bends down to stretch, and I literally miss a step. She looks so good I stumble, almost falling off the back of the belt.

Sheena pretends not to notice. With a small wave and a poorly disguised smirk, she climbs on the elliptical . . . Something I'm pretty sure she hasn't done since she's been here.

What's she playing at?

Determined not to drool, I push harder, trying and failing not to watch her workout. There's just one problem. Her new phone is resting in the little cubby on the machine, taunting me, reminding me of her refusal to accept it as a gift.

Why won't she let me make her life easier?

Seeing her hand over a huge chunk of the money she scraped together to survive makes me mad as hell. I know Cal didn't like it either, but he didn't fight her on it. Still, something about it makes me feel unsettled.

If she doesn't need me, how can I convince her to stick around?

I want to slap myself for thinking like a caveman. Now that I'm getting to know her, I can't imagine rejecting the mate bond. She's important to me, but she could leave. I could lose her, and the very idea makes me sick.

My strength as an omni-shifter has always been a selling point for me in the dating pool, but Sheena doesn't care about that. If anything, my position in the enclave and the supernatural world is a red flag after her experiences on the run.

I'm starting from behind, and I don't like it. Somehow, I've got to get her to fall for me without all the bullshit . . . The problem is I don't have the first idea how.

After about ten minutes, Sheena steps off the elliptical, sweat glistening on her face and lower back. I watch as she clumsily rolls a clean set of boxing wraps around her hands. She stops and starts over a few times, glancing down at her phone repeatedly. *What is she doing?* Then it hits me. She's watching a video tutorial on how to wrap her knuckles.

Fuck. Why didn't she ask me?

I want to help, but this is the perfect opportunity for me to show her I'm not a lunatic. I can resist breathing down her neck. I can. I keep my running pace steady as she slides her hands into the gloves. When she struggles to fasten the left one with the right one already on, I swear I don't even think about jumping off the treadmill to help. Sheena approaches the heavy bag and throws a punch. Her stance is all wrong.

I can't take it any longer. She could hurt herself with form like that. Before I even decide to move, I'm launching myself across the room.

"Let me help. Please." I cringe at my strangled demand.

When she turns around, the triumphant grin on her face stuns me.

"I'm amazed that you held out so long," Sheena says. "I would love to have your help, Gideon." She glances back at the treadmill belt, which is still spinning like a top. "If you're finished with your run, of course."

A suspicion creeps into my mind.

"You did it on purpose." I narrow my eyes at her as I walk over to switch the treadmill off. "All that fumbling with the wraps. The shitty ass punch. You were baiting me all along."

Her devious grin flips to a frown.

"My punch wasn't shitty. I don't need your help," she huffs, fire blazing in her eyes. Her temper is so damn hot that I don't really care anymore if she came down here to goad me. Nope, I just want to see more of it.

So I throw down a challenge.

"If you don't need my help, you're going to have to prove it, baby." I crowd her space, my chest just inches from hers. "Make me back up."

She stiffens at first, then gives me a tense nod, her nose in the air. Still, when I step closer and bump our chests together, she takes half a step back. Her first instinct is to run. While that really pisses her off, it isn't actually a bad move.

"That's okay, retreat can be strategic," I tell her, letting her keep the space she took back. "If your opponent is bigger than you, you'll need to be that much smarter and faster."

I correct her stance, and she listens carefully, making adjustments and moving to stay out of my reach. I circle her for a while, letting her get used to moving her feet and maintaining the distance.

"That's good. I'm going to come at you a little harder now. Watch for an opening, and when you see it, don't hold back."

I show her the motions a few times, shadowboxing in the space between us. She copies the movements, concentrating intensely the entire time. When I leave an obvious hole in my guard, she throws a quick jab, but she doesn't put much force behind it. The hit glances weakly off my upper arm and leaves her exposed.

"What was that? If I was napping, that hit wouldn't even wake me up."

"I don't want to hurt you," she hisses, eyes flashing when I chuckle in response. She thinks I'm mocking her. Before I can explain, an idea pops into my head. It's fucking brilliant.

"If you think you're so tough, let's make a deal," I say. Her foot taps, but I can see she's interested now. "I'll let you pay us back for the phone . . . if you can actually hurt me."

Sheena brings her fists back up, determination lining every inch of her body.

"I'll take your deal, but you need to remember I'm a grown woman. You don't *let* me do a damn thing, and I don't want a sugar daddy. You can't just get mad and storm off every time you don't get your way."

There it is.

She's mad at me for leaving during the tussle over the phone last night. I knew things were off between us, but I thought she was pissed that I wanted to pay, not because I stormed out. I'm just relieved that the gloves are coming off now. Metaphorically speaking, at least. It also gives me a chance to get what I want.

I thump my gloves together and bounce on the balls of my feet.

"You're right, I wanted to buy you that phone. I stormed off because you wouldn't let me. Now, make me pay, baby." I growl the words. She shivers at the sound. Yeah, she likes that, even if she doesn't want to admit it.

"The only thing you're going to pay for is your macho bullshit."

She circles me then, determination fueling her as she searches for an opening. When she lashes out, she's fast, but she telegraphs her intentions. I easily dodge.

"Okay, that was good, but you showed me where you were going to attack with your eyes."

She nods, doubling down with an intensity that makes me burn for her. I want her to look at me with that single-minded focus.

She's clearly been paying attention. It doesn't take long before I actually have to concentrate to defend against her hits. Unfortunately for her, she's running out of steam, unused to the energy needed for extended sparring.

"Pretend this is an actual fight," I suggest. "The longer it goes on, the worse your odds get. Remember, being able to defend yourself could save your life."

She takes my advice to heart, charging at me with a flurry of flying fists. I'm not expecting it, and a couple of the blows get past my guard.

When her body collides with mine at full force, I'm so much bigger that she bounces right off. I experience the whole thing in slow motion, reaching for her as she falls and twisting to let my body take the brunt of the impact. We hit the mat hard, and I grunt when she lands on top of me.

"Did it hurt?" Sheena asks.

I open my eyes to see her earnest, hopeful expression staring down at me from where she's perched on my chest. Just like that, I'm a goner. No power on Earth or in any of the realms could convince me to disappoint her right now.

Godsdammit, I never stood a chance.

"It hurt so fucking bad." I groan and clutch my ribs. Sheena seems both suspicious and pleased, but she doesn't call me out for my bad acting. "That was a hell of a hit, but if you're fighting someone who really wants to hurt you, try not to end up on the ground where they can get their hands on you."

I illustrate my point by dragging my hands up the back of her thighs and cupping her ass. She blushes bright red, but makes no move to get up.

"But I won," she whispers.

"Yeah, baby, you did." I watch a drop of sweat slowly trickle down her neck. It slides over the curve of one breast and vanishes into her sports bra. I want to chase it with my tongue.

She's so perfect.

Suddenly, I'm desperate to make her believe that. Tugging off her boxing gloves, I kiss her wrapped knuckles. Her cheeks turn pink, and she squirms against my obvious erection. It's digging into her stomach now. There's no way she can't feel it.

"You won't say anything else about the phone?"

"What phone?" I twist my face in confusion, and I'm rewarded with her giggle. Lifting my head, I rest my face against her chest. She sucks in a breath.

"What are you doing?"

"I lost and I'm hurt. I need comfort," I murmur the words into her cleavage, shifting my face until I feel one of her nipples pebble against my nose.

"I'm all sweaty," she protests, but doesn't push me away.

"I know." I lick the swell of one breast and hum at the taste. "You're delicious."

Sheena lets out a small gasp. When she pushes her chest more firmly into my face, I don't feel like I lost anymore. Slipping my thumbs under the edges of her sports bra, I lift my head to look into her eyes.

"Please?"

The animal inside me doesn't want to beg, but I'm in charge right now, dammit, and nothing is more important than Sheena's comfort.

After a brief pause, she nods. As I peel her bra off, I never once look away from her green eyes. Only once I've tossed the damp fabric to the side do I look my fill. I can't stop the rumble in my chest. Her breasts are full and still heaving slightly from exertion, tipped with perfect, rosy pink nipples. I'll never get tired of looking at her.

"You're everything," I manage, nearly choking on the gravel in my throat.

Rolling her on the mat, I brace my weight on one hand, lifting the other to tease her right breast. I run my blunt nails all around her sensitive skin, careful to touch everywhere but her nipple. Sweat long forgotten, I watch as she slowly goes wild beneath me, skin pebbling, chest heaving, back arching as she tries to get my fingers where she wants them.

Emotion hits me like a truck.

Seeing her trust me with her body like this . . . Gods, I've never been given anything I wanted more. In this moment, I don't think there's anything I wouldn't do to make her feel good.

I roll her tight nipple between my fingers. After minutes of my gentle touches, the rough movement makes her whine. The sound feeds my fucking soul, but I want more, so I play with her until she's thrashing around on the floor. When I replace my hand with my mouth, she gives me more delicious noises.

It's not enough.

Sliding my newly freed hand down her body, I pause at the waistband of her sweatpants, wondering if I'm pushing her too far, too fast.

"Gideon, touch me, please," she begs.

Thank fuck.

Determined to never make her wait for anything, I slide my hand into her pants. The only thing underneath the worn fabric is a soaking wet woman. I thank every god I can remember for this moment. The pleasure I feel just touching her is so intense, I'm actually terrified I'll come in my pants with absolutely no stimulation at all.

I rein myself in and explore her gently, letting her get used to my touch. Stroke by stroke, I add to her tension, building it layer by layer until finally, I slide my index finger inside her at the same I rub a firm circle over her clit.

That's all it takes.

She wails, back arching as her inner muscles spasm around my finger. So gorgeous, so sexy. An army of men couldn't stop me from kissing her right now. Our mouths move together perfectly as she rides out the aftershocks. When I'm finally able to drag my lips away from hers, she's staring at me in wonder.

"Your eyes, they're golden." She cradles my face in one small hand.

"I'm sorry if it scared you." I blink a few times, leaning into her touch. "My shifter really liked that sound you made," I explain, feeling sheepish about my lack of control.

"Don't be sorry. You don't have to hide from me."

My heart swells in my chest, and I kiss her again desperately. If I don't, I know I'm going to crack and beg her to tell me everything.

When she reaches shyly inside my athletic shorts and wraps her tiny fingers around me, I know I can't possibly last long.

After barely a minute of her careful strokes, I shoot off like a rocket in my pants, groaning and collapsing on top of her. When I try to lift my weight, she holds me in place with a strength that surprises me.

"I don't want to crush you, baby."

"Just a little longer." She sounds hesitant but happy, so I collapse into the cuddle, burying my face in her neck. My entire body feels relaxed like the tension I've been carrying for months is gone. There's no point denying it anymore. I'm in this now, and I don't care how long it takes her to catch up.

She's mine.

SHEENA

THE HOT SPRAY of the shower pounds down on me. I stand as still as a statue, but my mind makes up for my lack of physical movement by replaying what happened in the gym on repeat. A helpful exercise for absolutely no one.

Okay, this is fine, Sheena. Everything is fine.

So what if Gideon taught me some self-defense moves, then put on some sort of clinic in nipple play? He's a talented guy, and I'm glad I got to experience his skills firsthand. Right? I can have an orgasm and also play it cool. Casual even. We're just two buddies who clung to each other like the planets aligned when we touched.

It didn't feel casual.

I run the soapy loofah over my body, feeling a latent tingle as I wash my breasts. My brain might be working overtime, but my body feels languid and content. The throb in my chest is gone. Instead, my heart is humming like the connection is pleased that we helped each other come. I scoff and turn the water off.

Of course, the mystical voodoo thread in my chest is a shameless hussy.

I'm not sure why I'm making such a big deal out of this. It was hot, and I wouldn't mind a repeat performance. I'm a modern woman, goddammit. *Why can't I get off without freaking out?*

Towel drying my hair, I slip into a comfy matching set of sweats, which mysteriously appeared in my closet the other day along with several other outfits. *Something else to add to my tab.* Or it would be if Gideon would stop pretending to have no idea where the clothes came from.

A grin spreads across my face. I sprawl in the chair by my window and grab my phone. Maybe a second opinion will help.

> Ciprian... oh my god... something just happened

> Wait. Stop. Which one?

Gideon

K. Plz continue

He was teaching me to box. Then we weren't boxing anymore.

Nice. How big was it?

...I didn't see. Just felt... but it seems to be in proportion to the rest of him

Of course it is

We didn't even take our pants off and it's the hottest thing that's ever happened to me

Good for Gideon. Didn't know he had it in him.

I can't believe I'm telling you all this

That's what besties do. You just don't know because of you know... being fucking kidnapped.

Title of your sex tape: when the caged girl cums

A startled laugh bubbles out of my mouth, and the sound momentarily stuns me. It's the only time I've ever felt an ounce of humor in connection to my abduction. But I still ignore Ciprian's next two texts and let him sweat for the audacity of that comment.

I'm about to type a response and put him out of his misery when an incoming call pops up. I swipe to answer, letting out a plaintive sniffle instead of saying hello.

"Okay, I took it too far," he says. "I won't joke about it anymore."

He sounds remorseful, and even though we barely know each other, I can actually picture his face scrunching up. I let the silence stretch on.

"Shit, Sheena, I'm really sorry. I won't make any more comments about your abduction or your sexcapades."

"It's fine," I say. "Just letting you sweat." He lets out an outraged squawk. I laugh out loud.

"Just for that, I hope they are both absolute duds in bed."

"Well, from what I've experienced so far, I think you're out of luck there." I can't help the smug tone of my voice.

"Don't be crass," he scolds.

"Me, crass? Have you talked to yourself?" I laugh again, enjoying the banter.

"I'm just trying to desensitize you, babe. It's a rough world out there." Ciprian is teasing, but there's an element of truth to it. Maybe having a friend like him will be good for me.

"So, did he finger you or eat you out?"

Never mind, this friendship is an actual nightmare.

"I thought you didn't want details," I sputter.

"You're right. Gideon isn't my brother, but it's still too close for comfort. How do you feel now . . . like emotionally?" He asks this question like it's somehow dirtier than the first.

I roll my eyes even though he can't see me.

"I don't know. It's weird. My head is spinning, but my body is completely relaxed. Even the throbbing in my chest has stopped. Now it's just like this gentle hum—"

"What the fuck? Stop." Ciprian interrupts me mid-thought, his voice so loud in my ear that I flinch. "Are you fated mates? Did Gideon bite you?"

I stare at the phone, confused both by his questions and his frantic tone.

"Why would he bite me?" I stand up, feeling nervous all of a sudden. "Ciprian, what do you mean? Mates?"

The pause on the other end of the line makes my skin crawl. My heart is pounding. I have no idea what he's talking about, but my gut says it's important.

"Has Gideon mentioned the throbbing or humming?" Ciprian

ignores my questions and asks another of his own. His voice is cautious, but it has an undercurrent of excitement now. It's obvious that he's holding himself back, and I don't fucking like it.

We may be getting along great, but we only just met. Even though I need answers, I can't forget where his loyalty ultimately lies. I look at my closed door, wondering if Callum and Gideon can hear me talking.

I think back on our earlier conversations and lower my voice just in case. "Gideon didn't say anything about how it feels, just that he felt a connection with me when we met. Do you know what that means?" I ask, trying to dial back the frenetic energy buzzing inside my chest. I get no response.

"Ciprian," I shout. Then I check the connection. The call is still going. I'm about to yell at him again when he sighs down the line.

"I'm a dead man. Those shady bastards are going to skin me alive."

"Wait. Why would they be mad? What's the big deal?"

I start to pace, keeping to the far side of the room, away from the door. My cool is long gone now, adrenaline surging through my veins as my fight or flight instincts kick into overdrive.

"I can only speculate," Ciprian says. "And before you ask, no, I'm not going to do that with this. I will tell you that some bonds in our world are incredibly rare." He pauses, then I hear him sigh again. "Sheena. You need to talk to Gideon about this. He's the only one who can answer your questions. Call me if you need me."

I barely absorb the last bit over the roaring in my head. Absently, I hear myself say something noncommittal before disconnecting the call.

My content feeling from earlier is gone. Both my body and mind are on high alert now. I missed something monumental because I didn't know the right questions to ask. That ends now.

I walk down the stairs, forcing myself not to run. They lied to me, and I'm scared, but I don't know why I feel so betrayed. I only met them a week ago. So why does my heart feel like it's cracking into pieces? I rub my chest to ease the sudden return of the ache.

When I step into the kitchen, I find them both prepping dinner. Gideon looks up and gives me such a sweet smile I have to remind myself he's been keeping something from me. Something so huge it even shocked Ciprian. Gideon's smile fades as he processes whatever look is on my face.

"Sheena, is everything—"

"What's a fated mate?" I cut him off, my voice sharp.

Both of them look shocked by the question, so I know I'm on the right track. My heart sinks, beating violently in my chest.

"Where did you hear that?" Callum asks, looking suspicious.

"I'm asking the questions this time," I snap. "Gideon, why has my chest been throbbing since we met?"

He steps toward me then, arms outstretched. I retreat, and his eyes fill with hurt and something that looks a lot like panic.

"It's complicated." Callum tries again. "Remember how I told you Gideon thought you two had a special connection?"

I hold my hand up to stop him.

"I need Gideon to answer my questions." I pin Callum with my stare. "I want Gideon to give me honesty. Can Gideon not speak for himself?"

Callum takes a step back and Gideon looks lost, his arms still partially reaching out to me. I lock eyes with him, waiting out the tense silence with my arms crossed over my chest. When he stays silent, I double down.

"I will walk out that door and never look back if you don't explain this to me right now. No one gets to control me again." My voice breaks, but I can't stop. "Half-truths aren't good enough. Not when this bullshit world of yours has the power to destroy me."

Tears are rolling down my face now, but I ignore them. What he says next will determine if I ever cry over him again. Gideon takes another step toward me.

"Sheena, I swear I never lied." Gideon's voice is husky and

raw. I can hear the fear in his words. "I was scared. Didn't want to scare you off." He runs his fingers through his curls, the strands still messy and tangled from my fingers earlier.

"Fuck." His shout startles me, and I take an involuntary step back. Gideon tracks my movement, his face crumpling. "Baby, I'm not good at explaining. I wish I could tell you how I really feel."

The words are my worst nightmare come to life.

No. God, no. Please. But it's too late. I feel the moment my powers activate. It's like I'm both in my body and outside of it. Energy shoots out of every pore in an explosion that I have no control over. One second, Gideon and Callum are staring at me with shock and horror. The next, my hair floats, my eyes burn, and words pour out of Gideon like he's possessed.

"Sheena, you are my fated mate. It's an old, traditional term for a rare magical bond. It can never encompass how I feel about you, but in simple words, it means you are the being who completes my soul. The perfect complement to everything I am. In this vast universe with creatures of all kinds, we were designed to be each other's shelter and peace. You're my perfect partner."

I'm frozen in mid-air, terror consuming my thoughts while magic pours out of my body. Gideon's eyes well up with tears, but his voice is robotic. Though I'm compelling him to say these things, I'm as powerless as him. Against my will, against his . . . A careless wish has stripped us both of consent and damned us at the same time.

"You're upset, and I understand that, but I couldn't risk telling you the truth and driving you away." Gideon steps up to me then, his brow furrowed like he's fighting the control of my magic. "When we first met, you ran from me, didn't give me a chance. You didn't know what was going on then. You were understandably afraid, but I've lived in terror ever since . . . Knowing that I could be forced to watch you leave me again."

I can barely make sense of his words. All I know is he hid this from me, omitting information in order to keep me here. He may not have locked the doors, but he chose not to be completely honest. A fated mate bond, a magical tether controlling me . . .

Oh god, did he touch me earlier as another way to tie me to him?

Gideon brushes the tears from my cheeks. My body wants to flinch away from his touch, but I can't move. He's still under the compulsion of his own wish, but he's also clearly reading something in my expression because he drops his hand and steps back. His gold, glowing eyes beg me to understand even as he gives me space.

"You're not a hostage, Sheena. You could leave me behind at any time. The bond still hurts because it isn't sealed yet. You can believe what you want about me, but I would never do that without your consent. Yes, you're my fated mate—a rare gift from the gods—but you don't have to accept the bond. You have the power to reject me."

My tears are dripping down my face now, each one falling faster than the last. Gideon stares at them as they collect in a puddle on the kitchen tile.

"I've never been good with words, baby. I act first, think later, and you were looking for a reason to leave. If I had told you at the start, you wouldn't have given us a chance. Is it so wrong that I wanted to buy some time to give you a reason to stay?"

Gideon sags slightly, like he's finally exhausted all the words in his arsenal. His wish has come true, I certainly understand now.

His secret is out . . . and so is mine.

As the compulsion ends, Gideon blinks a few times and then looks in stunned silence from me to Callum.

My feet slam back to the floor. I stumble as the power rushing from my body cuts off abruptly. Without it, I'm weak and vulnerable. I know what happens next. Violent trembling starts in my hands and slowly spreads up my arms until my entire body shakes like a leaf. I'll lose consciousness soon. Already my thoughts are blurry. This time I won't get away.

No pity. Trust no one. Keep it moving. In my stupidity, I thought I'd outgrown my rules. I'm paying for it now. I beg my feet to move, but it's as though I'm stuck in quicksand, sinking deeper by the second.

Then the room tilts and everything goes dark.

CHAPTER
TWELVE

CALLUM

What the hell just happened? How did we go from fated mate damage control to floating hair and trancelike magic?

"Sheena, wake up, baby. Sheena!"

Gideon's earlier robotic speech, which will haunt my nightmares for years to come, is long gone. With the way he's yelling now, it's clear he has moved fully into the freaking the fuck out stage. I'm not far behind him if I'm being honest.

"Callum, help me!" His frantic roar finally pushes me to move.

I kneel down beside them. "Calm down, man. She's breathing —see, her chest is moving. Feel her pulse." Gideon does as I ask, gently pressing two fingers to her throat.

"She's going to be fine," I assure him, slumping to the floor and leaning my head against the cabinet. Physically, I believe that, but mentally and emotionally? I'm not so sure. This is a mess.

"Let's take her up to her room," I suggest. Gideon grunts, scooping Sheena up in his arms and taking off up the stairs. I trail after him, trying to organize my thoughts.

Sheena is incredibly powerful. The way her face morphed was

distinctly demonic, but I didn't recognize any of the major power types. It couldn't be witch magic. The aura isn't the same. And both Gideon and Sheena looked like puppets . . .

What the fuck is she?

From the look of dread on her face just before her magic activated, she knew what was about to happen. I want to yell at her and call her a hypocrite for hiding this from us. She fucking tore into us for not telling her about the mate bond, but this is just as big if not bigger. But the terror on her face . . . She wasn't faking that. Internally, I groan at how quickly this spiraled out of control.

As Gideon slides Sheena under the covers, I notice her phone light up on the bedside table with an incoming call. My brother's name flashes across the screen. *Why is he calling?* I gesture for Gideon to follow me out of the room as I swipe to answer the call.

Immediately, Ciprian starts talking a mile a minute. "Well, what happened? Are you really his mate? You've left me on read here, Sheena. I'm freaking out."

I should have known. Why is he always at the root of my problems?

"What did you do?" I demand, having already heard more than enough to confirm his involvement. My question is met with dead silence on the other end of the line, and I snap. "Ciprian, I'm not fucking around here. What did you do? Are you trying to fuck her or fuck me over? She doesn't need your shit."

I'm getting madder by the second, and my brother just gave me a target for it all.

It doesn't take long for him to clap back.

"Get off your fucking high horse. You and Gideon always decide you know best. Sheena is my friend, and you've been lying to her." Ciprian sounds cold and furious, but I'm used to his brand of bitter bullshit.

"Of course, you would try to make trouble for me." I scoff. "You just can't resist sticking your nose in my business. I'm not a nightmare, so of course I have no right to privacy and deserve to be forever alone."

He hisses. I can practically see him rolling his eyes through the phone.

"Don't be dramatic, brother. You don't really believe that."

How dare he? My hand clenches around the phone, and Gideon watches me with wide eyes. I'm too far gone to hold back now. I start to pace, cutting a path along the hallway. I'm too tense to stand still.

"Why wouldn't I believe the truth?" I snap. "You've hated me ever since my powers manifested."

"Oh, so we're actually going to talk about this?" Ciprian has the nerve to laugh. "Alright. Let's fucking go. Are you talking about how you conveniently forgot you had a little brother? When you packed up and took off with Gideon without a word, and left me alone to deal with mom and dad? That time, Callum?" Ciprian's voice trembles with anger and a whole bunch of other shit I can't identify.

I pause. He's never once talked about how things were for him.

"It wasn't like that. You know it wasn't," I say. I didn't think about how me leaving would impact him, but he had manifested as a nightmare by that time. Our parents' pride and joy. I knew he would be fine. "I had to get out. And ever since I left, you've been on their side—out to get me at every opportunity," I grind the words out, breathing heavier with each one.

"You know what? Not everything revolves around you, Callum. If you don't want a brother, you don't have to have one." Ciprian's emotionless voice makes my stomach feel hollow and unsettled. I don't know what to say.

"Please." Ciprian sighs. "Put Sheena on the phone. I'm worried about my friend." He sounds sincere, but now I'm reminded of how he went behind my back and told her things she should have heard from us.

"I can't," I admit. "She's asleep right now. But I'll tell her you called."

"Bullshit. I talked to her less than an hour ago, and she was upset. Now you're telling me she just fucking fell asleep? What did you do to her?"

Is he accusing me of hurting her now? Does he think so little of me?

Before I can shout at him some more, Gideon snatches the phone from my hand and turns his back on me. With my sensitive hearing, I can still make out both sides of the conversation.

"Ciprian, it's Gideon. Sheena confronted me about the mate bond. We argued, I tried to explain, then . . . shit got really fucking weird."

"What do you mean shit got weird?"

Gideon runs his free hand through his hair roughly and groans. "I don't know how to explain it. She was glowing, then she passed out, and I'm freaking out now, man. Has she told you anything about her powers? I'm not asking you to betray her trust, but I have no idea if she's going to be okay."

Ciprian lets out a string of curses. "No, she hasn't said anything about that. Just that those masked assholes abducted her. I didn't want to ask. I think talking about it still fucks her up."

"Yeah, we haven't pushed either, but now I wonder if we should have. I don't know how to help her."

"Sheena doesn't seem that fragile, Gideon. Listening to you try to communicate—no matter how bad it was—isn't going to take her out."

Gideon huffs out a laugh. Fuck my brother for being the one to reassure him.

"I wasn't trying to start trouble. I swear," Ciprian says. "She was just telling me about how her chest felt different after you got her off. It sounded like the mate stories your mom used to read to us, and I got excited for you both. I started running my mouth before I realized you hadn't told her." My brother's tone is sheepish, but he sounds genuine. My stomach churns. Maybe I jumped to conclusions.

"No hard feelings. It was messy, but I came clean," Gideon says. "I'm sure we'll work things out once she wakes up."

Gideon agrees to keep Ciprian updated on Sheena's condition, then hangs up. When he turns to look at me, his eyes are brimming with worry, regret, and just a splash of judgment.

"Now isn't the time, but shit, Callum, I don't think he's always out to get you."

I groan and massage my temples. "Don't start, please."

"He's family. That's all I'm saying."

"Yeah, and when has that fact ever mattered to any of them?" My voice sounds bleak even to me. "Anyway, can we unpack my childhood trauma later? We've kind of got a lot going on right now." He nods, but I can tell from the stubborn set of his jaw that we will be discussing this later.

We both look at the door to Sheena's room, and Gideon hangs his head. "What if we blew it, Cal? The way she looked at us." He shudders, tugging again on his hair. "She was scared to death."

I close the distance between us, pulling him into a hug.

"We'll fix it," I reassure him.

"I need her, you know?" His grip on me is crushing, but I don't pull away. "I know it seems crazy fast, but she fits."

My heart twists for him. Gideon isn't used to feeling vulnerable, even emotionally. Sheena isn't the only one who's scared here.

"I get it," I mutter, thumping him on the back a few times. "Let's go wait for her to wake up. We can apologize, and then we'll go from there."

I pull back from the hug, pleased to see Gideon standing a little straighter.

Together, we tiptoe down the hallway, gently opening her door. It turns out there was no reason to be quiet.

Sheena is long gone.

SHEENA

I SLIDE DOWN THE GUTTER, limbs shaking violently as the wind gusts around me. My head is still throbbing from using my powers. Every few seconds, I have to wipe away the blood dripping from my nose. It's a miracle I don't fall and break every bone in my body, but somehow I make it to the bottom with just a few bumps and scrapes.

I have to get away. This is my only chance.

I woke up in the bed to the sound of Callum interrogating Ciprian. Eavesdropping on that angry exchange finally forced me to listen to my instincts and not my irrational feelings. I didn't catch the entire conversation, but I heard enough to make the decision to run.

Staying here was a mistake. It's clear Callum doesn't trust me, and Gideon didn't bother to tell me we're magical soul mates. Neither of those things matters now that they know what I can do. I won't be caged again.

Another drop of blood trickles down my chin. It hits the ground like a grisly exclamation point, emphasizing just how serious my situation is.

I don't have a name for whatever my power is, but it's unnatural, and it drains me. Even though it's been years since anyone forced me to grant a wish, I can tell I'm weaker this time around. I won't make it much farther on foot.

Where is that barn?

It's hard to navigate in the dark. Nothing looks familiar. But I need to find those ATVs and use one to get away. My conscience burns. I don't want to steal from them, but I'm desperate. I don't have a car, and I abandoned my worn hiking boots in my hurry to put distance between the house and me.

Once again, I'm starting over with almost nothing, just my duffle and the will to survive. My head throbs in time with my footsteps. But the hardest pain to ignore is the throbbing in my heart. The more ground I cover, the more it aches. With only a few minutes' head start, I can't afford to stop or rest yet. I tune out the pain.

No pity.

I think of the words that poured out of Gideon in the kitchen and my guilt flairs stronger. He wished to explain in a way that made me understand. I feel bad for turning his fear into reality, but I know it won't stop there.

This ability, this curse I'm afflicted with—it makes people insane. No one should be able to access their wildest dreams by saying a handful of words. That kind of power, hovering on the tip of your tongue—it creates a hunger that's impossible to satiate. Nobody can resist that.

Maybe Gideon wouldn't use me to give himself riches or dominate someone else, but what about couching his weaknesses? Sure, it was an accident this time, but that eloquent explanation wasn't real. It wasn't his choice.

Trust no one.

Part of me knows leaving and denying him a chance to prove himself isn't fair, but neither is life. If it was, I wouldn't have been dropped at a fire station as a newborn, my best friend wouldn't have abandoned me in high school, and no one would have kidnapped me in the first place. If life was fair, this cursed power wouldn't exist at all and I wouldn't need to run.

Keep it moving.

GIDEON

HER DUFFLE IS GONE, but her boots remain on the porch. Sheena's tattered shoes are the only sign in the entire house that she was ever here.

She left me.

The realization nearly brings me to my knees, but I'm not actually surprised. Sheena is a runner. I was right not to trust her to stay. While this rejection hurts, I can survive it. Better it happened now, before the bond sealed. If she'd decided things were too hard down the road, the agony could have actually killed me.

I wanted to be the reason she took a risk.

Callum is obsessing over what happened in the kitchen, but I don't give a flying fuck about that. At the end of the day, floating hair and glowing eyes don't matter. If she doesn't think what we have is worth fighting for, then our future will never outweigh her past.

"We have to go get her," Callum says, checking his phone and heading towards the door. "She has no transportation, and there's another storm coming."

He keeps shooting glances at me like I'm the one acting weird, but he's not seeing the full picture. We never stood a chance. Our biggest mistake was ever thinking we did.

"If she wants to leave, that's on her." I shrug, trying to look unaffected. "I told her she had a choice. She's made it." I crack open a beer, sitting at the counter and ignoring the gut wrenching fear I feel at the thought of her being alone outside and exposed to the elements.

"Look, it's shitty that she took off," Callum says, frowning at me. "But I think we can assume panic is driving her right now. She freaked the fuck out. We need to make sure she's okay, then, once it's less raw, we can put everything out on the table and sort through it together."

"Were you not in that room with me?" I gesture towards the kitchen with the beer bottle. "I put it all on the table already, and she fucking left. I'm not going to chase her around in the dark like a jackass."

"I was there," he snaps. "In fact, I was the only one not possessed at the time, and I still don't know what the fuck happened in there. Think about this, man. I know you're upset, but I don't want you to wake up tomorrow with regrets."

I take a big swig of the beer as if my heart isn't shredded.

"I have thought about it. She's thought about it. Maybe *you* need to think about it. She climbed down a fucking gutter in her pajamas, Cal. I think she was pretty clear about where she stands."

"But, Gideon—"

I snarl at him then. I can't help it. Why can't he understand that there's nothing left to talk about? I poured my heart out to her in the kitchen. She knew how worried I was about her leaving and still chose to walk away. I can do the same with this conversation.

Callum sighs as I look away. When he speaks again, his voice is gentle like he's talking to an injured animal. "You're both making a mistake. Don't let pride get in your way."

After that parting shot, I hear the door slam shut behind him. I listen to his footsteps disappear into the night while I drain what's left of my drink.

He doesn't get it.

It's not pride that's holding me back, but self-preservation. She's already broken my heart once. I can't give her the chance to do it again.

SHEENA

I FEEL THE EXACT MOMENT Gideon realizes I'm gone. The pain literally brings me to my knees. Damp leaves cushion my fall. It takes a full, precious minute for me to struggle back to my feet. I was a fool not to question this connection sooner. Now that I know what it is, it's painfully obvious it isn't normal.

Despite the added agony in my chest, I force myself to keep going. *They will come for me now that they know about my abilities.* Tears and blood drip to the forest floor as I descend the mountain.

After about fifteen minutes, my bravado crumbles.

I'm seeing spots now, and it's beyond difficult to navigate. I can't seem to focus. I should have reached the little barn already, which tells me I must have missed it somewhere in the dark. As both warmth and hope leech out of me, I wander aimlessly ahead on autopilot.

I'm getting rained on now, and I'm not dressed for it. Each

gust of wind slices through my clothes, lashing my skin like a whip. My body is so numb I can't even feel the fear that consumed me just half an hour ago. When a wolf howl cuts through the wind, my whole body shivers.

That sounded close.

I scan the trees. Instead of a four-legged predator, I see Callum stomping towards me on two. Even in the dark, I can tell he's dripping wet and pissed all the way off.

"I didn't want to scare you." His voice is cold and angry, and even though I'm determined to be brave, I jerk back from the sound. The involuntary movement knocks me off balance and I stumble.

"Shit, Sheena," the demon curses, grabbing my arms and steadying me. "I know you're freaked out, but this is the stupidest stunt I've seen in my fucking life. It's not safe out here."

"Let me go, Callum," I demand, trying and failing to sound tough. I can barely hear my own voice over the wind and rain. He ignores my protests, draping a huge jacket over my shoulders. I shrug my arms in and push off of him.

"Quit fighting me," he snaps, zipping the front of the jacket and yanking the hood over my soaked hair. "If you still want to go tomorrow, you can take my fucking car." Through the spots in my vision, I see him wave what looks like keys in front of my face. "But you're not about to walk down this mountain in the dark, leaving a blood trail behind you and attracting every predator within a ten-mile radius."

He thinks I'm crazy. Maybe he's right, but if I could just make him understand.

"Keys are just keys," I slur my way through the words. "Now that you know what I can do, I'll never be free."

"I don't know shit." His brow furrows as he looks down at me. "Gods, did you hit your head or something climbing down the gutter? You're not a hostage." He glances over his shoulder. "We are, however, both at risk of falling off a cliff or getting eaten by a mountain lion." He kicks at a branch, then runs his fingers through his wet hair.

"Look, full disclosure, I'm really fucking mad at you right now, but I don't want you dead. Can we at least go back to the house to argue? You're as pale as a ghost, and I'm freezing my ass off."

Staring up at Callum in the dark, I want to believe him so badly. A demon I barely know who has the power to make me want him. I trusted him when he promised he would never use his magic to control me, but that was before he knew what I could do. Surely, with the ability to make his every wish come true standing right in front of him, he'll consider that promise null and void. If he used his incubus powers right now, I would fall in line immediately. So what is he waiting for?

He's not the kind of person to break a promise . . .

It's a dangerous thought, but I can't get rid of it. Seconds tick by, then minutes. Callum doesn't say another word, just waits in silence for me to make my decision. My resolve melts in the face of the rain and his patience.

"Okay. Let's go back to the house," I stutter. He's right. My body is shutting down, and I couldn't even make it to the barn.

After waiting for god knows how long for me to make a decision, Callum wastes no time now. He sweeps me up in his arms, tucking me tightly into his chest. I cling instinctively to his body heat.

"Shit, Sheena, you're freezing," he grumbles, sounding a little scared. "I could warm you up, but I don't understand what's happening to your body. It might make things worse." He takes off at a slow jog, his long strides making quick work of the rough terrain. "Hold on, okay? I left the ATV on the trail nearby."

I nod and another howl cuts through the night. The sound is frenzied and so close it's practically on top of us. I shiver again, but it has nothing to do with the cold this time.

"You're okay, sweetheart," Callum whispers, sitting me down

carefully on the four-wheeler and climbing on behind me. "I'm going to get you out of here."

"Gideon?" I'm barely coherent, but he knows what I'm asking.

"Back at the house." He doesn't elaborate. He doesn't need to. Those four words say more than enough. The pain in my heart sizzles and pops, and I tuck my face into Callum's neck.

Neither of us tries to speak again. Callum starts the engine. Its loud rumble drowns out some of the raging storm.

I should be relieved. Instead, my skin is crawling. I have the sickening feeling that we're being watched. Lifting my head weakly, I look back into the dark woods.

Yellow eyes stare back at me, cruel and unblinking.

They're impossible to forget. The same stare has haunted my nightmares for eight years. I try to warn Callum, to tell him there's a monster behind us, but my body fails me.

He found me. Now we're all going to die.

CHAPTER
THIRTEEN

CALLUM

Sheena stiffens in my arms, then goes limp. Finding her in situations that leave her bloody and unconscious is getting really old.

I flex my foot, shifting gears and upping our pace. With the weather and terrain, I'm stretching both my senses and the engine to the limit. Obviously, I don't want to wrap us around a tree, but she's so cold. I can't shake the feeling that I need to get us back to the house as quickly as possible.

We're back in half the time it took me to find her. I whip the ATV to a stop by the porch and climb off with Sheena cradled in my arms. We're both soaking wet, and the position is awkward, but she doesn't stir at all, even as I juggle her in my arms to open the door.

I'm scared of the physical toll her magic took on her body. It doesn't make sense. If I spend too much energy without consuming lust to replace it, I feel fatigued, maybe even a little nauseous. But I don't think Sheena has used her power in years. The nosebleed, the fact that she collapsed like a rag doll—that's not normal for any supernatural species I've ever heard of.

Maybe she's sick.

That thought sends a chill down my spine, and I tuck Sheena a little tighter into my chest. If she stays, she's going to have to tell us something tomorrow. I'm fucking over this secret drama.

Gideon is lying on the couch doing his best to appear uninterested. As I stomp past him, his nostrils flair. "Blood," he shouts, lurching to his feet. I roll my eyes as he vaults over the couch with a growl.

"Yeah, she's got a nosebleed," I say, raising my eyebrows. "Her power output really drained her. Maybe that's normal for her, maybe it's not. I don't know why you care, though. I thought you were done."

Another angry sound escapes his throat. Gideon is as stubborn as they come, but he won't like the thought that something might be wrong with her. Too bad I've known all his buttons since third grade.

"I'm taking her to my room." I step around him. "I want to be close in case she wakes up and needs something."

His eyes flare golden, but he says nothing.

"If you don't want to deal with it," I say, applying some strategic pressure with a blank look. "I can tell her you're not interested and help her pack up in the morning."

An enraged roar explodes behind me as I hide my grin and climb the stairs. Gideon doesn't follow me up, but that's fine. I gave him plenty to think about.

I lay Sheena down on my bed. She looks good there, like she belongs, but I can't focus on that. My incubus may burn for her, but someone has to remain logical if we're going to untangle this mess tomorrow.

I slip her shoes off, clean the blood from her face, and swap her wet clothes out for some of my coziest sweats. If she still wants to leave tomorrow, I'll keep my promise and help her. Even if it hurts.

After a quick shower to shake off the cold, I throw on a pair of flannel pants and climb into bed beside her. Sheena's hair lays in chaotic tangles across the pillow; it's so wet it looks black in the darkness of the room. She looks innocent and peaceful in her sleep. The small smiles, the teasing smirks, and the frozen, fear-filled expressions all fade away, leaving behind a beautiful but exhausted woman.

She's my filthiest fantasy and Gideon's fated destiny. I have no right to want her, but I'm starting to fear that I no longer have a choice.

I WAKE UP with Sheena wrapped in my arms, her back to my chest. From her shallow breathing and the rigid way she holds herself, she's already awake and no doubt feeling prickly about our bodies' decision to cuddle up in our sleep.

"Good morning," I manage to say. I'm determined not to let her overthinking screw us over right away. She turns her emerald eyes to me, and I'm relieved to see that they're cautious but clear.

"You came to get me," she whispers. It's a prompt, not a question. I think I'm starting to be able to read her tells. She still sounds wary, but some of the fear is gone from her voice.

"I did." I tuck a strand of her hair behind her ear. "Things got out of control yesterday. We all need to talk. Figure this shit out."

Sheena huffs at that, but I don't acknowledge her skepticism. I'm on a mission now, and nothing is going to get in my way.

"Why am I in here?" She looks around my room, unable to hide her curiosity as she checks out my space. I sit up, pushing back the covers. I'm only slightly irritated when she doesn't seem to notice my naked chest at all.

"I didn't want you waking up in the middle of the night and bailing out the window again. I think you can agree we all deserve some answers."

Sheena looks at me then, searching my face for a long moment. Her silence unnerves me, so I do my best to return the favor, hopping out of bed and stretching.

"No time like the present, I guess," I say, faking a yawn. "Let's go find Gideon and hash this shit out. If you want to take off after, I'll give you the keys to our spare car. You can walk right out of the front door, no acrobatics required. I know you didn't want to leave your boots behind."

"You don't have to give me a car, Callum." Sheena sits up. "Neither of you owe me anything. If you just drop me off near a main road, I'll be fine." She trails off at whatever look must be on my face.

Is she fucking for real with this shit?

"I told you last night I'd give you a car. I know life has taught you differently, but you can trust me." She doesn't argue, which is a small win. But I can't tell if she actually believes me or not.

I get dressed in silence, making no effort to hide my body from her. I would never use my powers to control her, but there's nothing wrong with giving her a little taste of what she'll be leaving behind.

A tingle runs down my spine.

Lust. Sheena's lust. I drink it in. Even this small taste of her desire is delicious. Our eyes lock. Her pride won't let her back down from me, so I put on a show, knowing she's glued to my every move. I slowly pull up the zipper of my jeans. Her eyes stay frozen on my crotch.

"I can take them back off if you want," I tease her, loving the blush that floods her pale cheeks.

She jumps out of bed, swaying slightly on her feet and grabbing the nearest bedpost. I'm prepared to help her, but her vertigo passes quickly. Irritation and embarrassment war for control on her face, but standing there in my room, wearing my baggy sweats, she's what my dreams are made of.

I can't believe how badly I want to beg her to stay.

I chuckle to cover my desperation. She storms from the room then, tossing her long, tangled hair over one shoulder. Good. I prefer her sassiness to her fear and apathy.

I trail behind her as she rounds the corner and barrels right into Gideon. He's shirtless, as usual. Instead of wrapping her up in a hug, he sets her back from him in a way he's never done before. Sheena's face wilts, and she shifts her weight uncomfortably.

I'm clearly fighting an uphill battle here. The path forward is littered with obstacles for all three of us, but I don't know how to fix things if neither of them is willing to get out of their own way.

"Living room?" Gideon asks, ignoring Sheena completely by looking over the top of her head at me.

"Sounds good to me." The chipper note I force into my voice is obviously fake, but no one calls me on it. Walking around them, I hand Sheena her phone as I pass her and lead our procession down the stairs. "Ciprian has been trying to get in touch with you. He's threatening to come up here if he doesn't hear back by lunch."

"Okay. Thanks . . ." Sheena murmurs.

I sigh, tired of the eggshells we're all stomping around on.

It might take a miracle to fix this.

SHEENA

MY FACE IS STILL BURNING from Callum's teasing. Why is he acting like we aren't teetering on the edge of disaster?

I scrape my hair into a rough bun on the top of my head as I walk down the stairs. The strands are coarse and twisted from the storm last night. It probably looks like a family of birds are nesting in it, but that doesn't matter right now.

I don't think I can fix this, and I'm not sure I should. Hell, the brief look I had of Gideon's face outside of Callum's room made that clear. I've been around ice cubes that were warmer.

In the living room, I perch on the edge of the couch while Gideon folds his massive body into a lounge chair. Callum the Oblivious slaps his thighs as takes a seat on the other end of the couch. He's put several feet of space between us, so we're all positioned in a rough triangle.

"I guess I'll kick things off," Callum says, cutting into the tense silence. "Sheena, to start, can you tell us what we should do to avoid accidentally triggering your powers again? I don't want you to get hurt, or Gideon to end up floating off to space or something." He's making light of it, which is kind, I guess, but I can't find any humor in the situation.

"It's pretty simple," I begin, staring at my hands. "No saying 'I wish.' That's the only catalyst I know of." I look up, bracing myself. It's the first time I've uttered that phrase out loud since I turned sixteen. I wait, terrified . . .

Callum just nods, meeting my eyes with a gentle look in his own. "From what I could tell, it hurt you when it activated. Was what happened yesterday a normal reaction?"

I blink in surprise.

He noticed that? My magic is excruciatingly painful, as if whatever compels me to grant wishes is peeled directly from my essence.

"Yes, it always hurts. Some times are worse than others, but it always leaves me weak," I say, wringing my hands. I never thought I'd talk about this. I don't even like thinking about it.

"Are you some kind of mind-controlling demon?" Gideon demands, speaking for the first time. I cringe at the bite in his tone.

"I didn't control your mind," I snap, allowing my anger to surface and protect me. "You're the one who made the wish. It's not like I had a choice." I sit up straighter on the couch, daring him with a look to keep blaming this whole mess on me.

"So you're just going to act like you didn't run for the hills the second I told you how I felt?" He scoffs. It's an ugly sound coming from his normally laughing mouth.

Unexpectedly, tears burn behind my eyes. I stand to leave.

"Of course. Things get hard and you run. Totally on brand,"

Gideon says. He points behind him. "You might as well use the door this time. I'd hate to have to replace the gutter."

Asshole.

Even if there's an element of truth to his accusations, it's not like I didn't have reasons to leave. Before I can decide whether to fight back or run from the room, Callum steps in again.

"Cut the reactionary shit out—both of you. If you keep this up, we're not going to get anywhere." Callum turns to me. "Sheena, why did you leave?"

I'm so on edge that I actually decide to answer. "I heard you yelling at Ciprian," I say, meeting his stare. "I knew you were mad that I didn't tell you everything. Once you saw what I could do . . . It wasn't safe here anymore." I look back and forth between the two of them. "Eventually, you'll both get tired of me, and then you'll either sell me out or use my powers for your gain—"

Before I can finish, Gideon explodes, knocking the heavy chair over as he jumps to his feet.

"That's bullshit," he roars. "You're my mate. I'd rather sell my fucking soul than betray you. I told you exactly how I felt in that kitchen, poured my damn heart out at your feet, and you *left me.*"

I flinch back from the force of his accusations, stunned speechless.

He stomps out of the room, angling his face away from me, but it isn't fast enough to hide all the hurt I see hiding beneath his anger.

The silence that follows drags on until I'm desperate and can't take it anymore. "Am I wrong?" I ask Callum, afraid I already know the answer.

"Honestly, we all messed up." He rakes a hand over his face, some of his forced, positive mask falling away. "I understand why you don't trust this world; it's only ever hurt you. I also get why you didn't tell us you have some super rare wishing power."

He slides across the couch cushions, erasing the space between us and reaching out to take one of my hands in both of his. "I was mad at first, that's true," Callum says. "I felt like you didn't tell us because you were plotting something. Then, after I realized Ciprian was involved, I freaked out. He and I . . . We have some issues to work through, but that isn't your fault."

I nod, relieved he's explaining the anger I overheard in their conversation.

"I know Gideon is upset right now, but we still want you to stay. I promise you—we will figure this out together, but there has to be trust." He pauses, looking deep into my eyes. "If you get scared again, that's okay. Talk to us. Gideon won't be able to handle it if you leave again, and neither will I."

Callum's words are his own—no magic, no coercion. Just sincerity. Unable to hold back, I launch myself into his lap, pressing my lips to his. It's practically an attack, but if he's surprised, he doesn't show it. His soft lips immediately respond, dancing gracefully against mine. I sink my hands into his hair, and we leisurely make out on the couch like teenagers. When I finally pull away for breath a few minutes later, I know exactly what to say.

"I'm sorry, Callum," I whisper.

"Me too."

He presses one last kiss to my lips, then helps me stand. We both know I have another apology to make.

CHAPTER
FOURTEEN

SHEENA

After a much needed shower, I find Gideon in the gym, running on the treadmill like the devil is at his heels. He sees me walk in, but he makes no move to slow down or acknowledge I'm there. I clear my throat. Nothing. Gathering my courage, I decide to dive in even though he's ignoring me.

"I know you're upset with me, but I have some things I'd like to say if that's okay with you."

A grunt is all I get in response, but at least he's not yelling at me to get out.

"First of all, I'm sorry I ran. I've kept my abilities hidden since I escaped. Having them spill out when I was already freaking out—well, it was too much for me. It was easier to run than stay and put myself at risk." He's listening, but he doesn't break stride, his powerful legs pumping at a pace that would be an all-out sprint if I attempted it.

"When Ciprian mentioned that we might be mates, I panicked. I was mad you kept it from me, then I was terrified that a connection to me would corrupt you or get us killed. Being here with you felt like the universe was finally cutting me some slack. I was afraid the mate bond would change that."

He slams his hand down on the treadmill's emergency stop button with a violent smack. The belt comes to a whirring halt. He's still dead silent, so I press on.

"I'm also sorry that my powers stole your free will. It might have been your wish, but you didn't know that would happen; and I'm sure those aren't the words you'd have chosen to say to me without magic interfering. I would do it differently if I could."

Gideon steps off the machine. I can feel him towering over me, his eyes burning holes in my skin. I don't look up for fear of what I'll see. I can't stop until I'm done.

"When you made the wish, I hated your words because they weren't you. They were some mystical bullshit—the easy way out. I wanted to hear from *you*," I say, finally daring to look up at him.

His handsome face is still serious, no dimples in sight, but the anger is finally gone. He cups my chin with one gigantic hand, and I hold my breath.

"You're going to stay?" Gideon asks.

I think about it, then I nod.

"If you want me to, I will."

He steps closer, crowding me in a way that makes me feel safe.

"You want to hear my real words, baby?" As soon as I nod, he continues on in a low rumble. "You're mine. I'm yours. No more secrets. We'll figure everything else out later."

His speech is simple but perfect, and he leaves absolutely no room for misunderstanding. When I agree with him, he lifts me until we're at eye level, pressing his forehead to mine. Our hearts are as close together as they can possibly get, and within seconds, they beat in sync.

I don't feel even a hint of fear as Gideon carries me up the stairs.

GIDEON

HOW FAST can I climb these stairs and get this woman into bed?

We pass Callum as I carry Sheena up to my room. He's smirking at us like he just won the lottery. The smug fucker is about to get a delicious, secondhand power rush, and he knows it.

Once I get her to my room, I kick the door closed. With the way it rattles the entire wall, I might have used a little too much force, but I give absolutely zero fucks.

"Are you in some kind of hurry?" Sheena teases, her green eyes sparkling. I can smell how excited she is, and I'm desperate to show her just how compatible we really are.

"Damn right I'm in a hurry. We just had our first fight, baby. I've got to show you how sorry I am by making you come all over my face." I nip at her neck, reveling in her little gasp of shock.

"Gideon, you don't have to . . . do that."

She sounds nervous, and I can't help teasing her. I lift my mouth away from the soft skin of her throat and pretend to be confused. "Do what? You'll have to be more specific."

"Gideon, please."

"Yes, now we're on the right track." I grin. "Gideon, please . . . what? Drown in your pussy? Gladly. Spend the rest of the day finding all the spots that make you scream? Sign me up." I nuzzle the tip of my nose against hers. "Is that what you meant, Sheena?"

Her face is so red now. I can see her blush disappearing under the collar of the sweatshirt she's wearing. It's fucking adorable.

"Yes, I mean, sure. I mean, ugh, I don't want you to feel obligated—"

"Baby, there are plenty of things I feel obligated to do. Taking out the trash, doing my taxes, talking to my dad about classic cars . . . Finding the best ways to make you squirt is something I'm dying to do." I nibble on her lips, living for the little moan she tries to hide. "Think of it as a higher calling."

She laughs at that, shaking her head.

"You know, you act like you don't have a way with words, but that's some serious dirty talk," Sheena says as she leans back on the bed, resting her elbows on the mattress, a challenge burning in her eyes.

"You like that, baby? Did it make you wet?" I stare down at her sweatpants as I run my index finger along the waistband, noting how her breathing picks up.

"Why don't you find out?" Her words are barely a whisper, but they're all I need.

I slide my finger into her panties, pleased to find she's as soaked as I imagined. She arches into my touch, but I tease her, running the tip of my finger everywhere except where she wants it. Soon, she's thrusting her hips up, demanding more. I keep up the light touches until she's grumbling with frustration.

"Gideon, please."

I stare up at her as she says it again. *Gods, I love hearing those words.*

"Do you need something, baby?" I attempt an innocent face, but she's not having it.

"Yes, obviously, I need to come." She sits up fully then, gripping my hair roughly with her fingers. A single bead of sweat drips down her temple. I can't resist licking it away.

"Put your hands behind your head, grip the sheets, and don't let go," I demand. "If you hold on tight, I'll give you what you want."

Her pupils dilate. She takes a second to consider my order, before she rips off her sweatshirt and flops back so fast I don't know if I want to laugh or cheer. Sheena fists the sheets, her eyes drifting closed, chest heaving. It's so sexy.

I get rid of her pants in record time.

She's gorgeous. Perfection. She looks like a full meal, and I don't give her time to feel self-conscious, diving right in to enjoy my feast. I start gently, letting her get used to the pressure of my tongue and savoring her taste. She squirms beneath me, but she doesn't let go of the sheets.

"Good girl," I growl the words against her clit, then slip two fingers inside her, curling them until I find the spot I'm looking for. I tap against it firmly, sucking her clit into my mouth at the same time. She digs both of her heels into the bed and arches her back to get as close to my mouth as possible, whining and bucking against my tongue.

Her orgasm hits us both like a tidal wave.

Sheena's entire body bows, except for her inner muscles, which clench and flutter around my fingers. Her eyes shoot open, glowing purple and locking onto me as she screams. I stroke her gently as she comes down, then lick my lips and fingers thoroughly.

"That's one," I tell her. "For not telling you about the mate bond." I kiss her soft, silky thigh, enjoying the moment her eyes widen when she makes sense of my words.

Before she can speak, I dive in again, enjoying the way her legs squeeze my head like she can't help herself. She can crush my head like a fucking grape for all I care; I'll die happily with my tongue buried inside her.

When she comes again, I give her a second to breathe and another apology.

"That one is for not going after you, for not fighting for us." Her fingers let go of the sheets and burrow down into my curly hair. She runs her nails along my scalp. Everything feels so right.

I bring her over the edge two more times before I'm satisfied—once for yelling at her in the living room and again for giving her the silent treatment in the gym. By the time I'm done, her damp hair is falling out of its messy bun and sticking to her temple. Her arms tremble violently. I kiss my way up her body, pressing soft kisses to her cheek, her forehead, and finally, her lips.

"Your eyes are purple, baby." They flash brighter, turning a vibrant color that reminds me of royalty. It's beautiful.

When her eyes widen and her hands come up to feel her face, I can tell she's about to panic. "That's nothing to worry about," I assure her. "What color are my eyes?"

"Golden," she rasps the word. "Like treasure." Her voice is hoarse from screaming, and she seems embarrassed.

"Speaking of treasure," I hum. "I've had my appetizer. Now it's time for the main course."

Sheena wastes no time reaching for my gym shorts. I watch as she peels them down my thighs. When she moves to take me into her mouth, I gently pull her away.

"Not this time," I say, stopping her before she can return the favor.

Her face falls, and I feel a sting through the bond. She thinks I'm rejecting her, but that's not it at all. "I'll finish in your mouth some other time," I assure her.

I need to watch her face. I need to know she's as desperate for me as I am for her.

"I need you to ride me first."

The bond hums with excitement. Sheena scrambles on top of me eagerly as I lay back on the bed.

When she lines herself up and sinks down on my dick, I feel like I'm coming home from three lifetimes of war. It's an ice pack for my bruised heart. We both groan at the sensation.

It's so perfect that I'm suddenly terrified I'll come before I'm even fully inside her. I think of cold nights, gross rain, fighting stances, and Cal being mad at me. *Fuck. Why did that make my dick twitch?* Suddenly, I can't think of anything at all because the woman who's my perfect match in every way is bouncing up and down on my cock.

I look down at where we're joined, just as she takes my entire length inside her. She's so fucking beautiful. It's a mesmerizing view. I save it to my personal highlight reel.

Gasping her name; I ignore the urge to make the bond permanent as my orgasm builds. If I bite her, it won't be during our first time, right after our first fight.

When she throws her head back, sobbing around another powerful climax, I can't hold back any longer and come harder than I have in my entire life. It takes everything out of me, and I melt into the mattress. Sheena falls on top of my chest, breathing heavily into my neck, her arms curled around me.

If I could bottle this feeling, I would. But not to sell. I'd keep it all to myself because this woman is perfect, and she's mine.

SHEENA

Twelve hours ago, I was careening down a slippery mountain, dripping blood, and having a complete mental breakdown. Fast forward five orgasms later, and I'm collapsed in a boneless heap on top of Gideon. If the traffickers kicked down the door right now, I don't even know if I could sit up, much less run away.

For some reason, I'm not too worried about it.

"Why don't you have any blankets on your bed?" I ask. I noticed it when he first tossed me on the mattress, but it didn't seem like the time to bring it up.

"I get hot when I sleep." He presses a kiss to my temple. "Seems like too much trouble to kick them off, so I don't bother."

His skin is warm where it's pressed against mine, and I can feel his chest moving while he talks. The rumble is comforting and sends a tingle down my exhausted body. *The way he talked to me earlier*. He may not think he has a way with words, but my body disagrees.

"Should I worry about the purple eyes?" I ask.

"Nah." Gideon yawns. "It's sexy. Just a horny supernatural thing." He sounds like he's about to fall asleep, but I need to know more.

"Okay, but it didn't feel like I was being drained." I prop myself up on my elbow to look into his eyes. Gideon sighs.

"You weren't using your powers—you were just raw, baby," he says. "You know how we all look human, most of the time . . . but we're not?"

I nod, following his train of thought.

"Sometimes, when we experience something intense—whether it's emotional or physical—our true self gets closer to the surface. Since we were both feeling a lot, our eyes reflected that. Literally." He scratches his head, looking to see if I understand.

"That actually makes sense," I tell him. Immediately, his smile perks up, both dimples making an appearance. I smile back.

"Can you tell me anything else about the mate bond?" I trace a few patterns around his heart, realizing mine hasn't hurt since we reconciled in the gym.

"It's really rare. Like, one in million rare," he begins, and I snort.

"I mean—purple and golden eyes—it all seems like a fairy tale to me," I joke.

"I guess so." He chuckles. "I never really put much thought into finding a mate before, you know? When we walked into that pub looking for leads, I was in a mood. The floor was sticky, I had a headache . . . Then, wham." He claps his hands together. "It was like lightning struck. I took one look at you and I just knew."

Gideon's hold around me tightens, and I feel safe in his arms.

"I thought of a million things to say to you," he says. "But none of them were good enough. Then you were just gone."

I grimace at that even though there's no judgment in his voice.

"I don't ever want you to be so scared that you have to run," Gideon says, his voice dropping an octave. "I won't let anyone else touch you unless you want them to."

I shiver.

He smirks, cupping my bare ass in one of his big hands. Immediately, my body gets ideas.

"Good god. How can I be ready to go again?" I ask.

He grins, shifting his hand until he's cupping me exactly where I need him.

"You're not human. This is pretty standard, baby."

Gideon kisses my lips with a gentleness that takes my breath away. Then he slips two fingers back inside me. He gradually works me back to the edge with his hand as we make out.

When I finally explode, it's slow and intense, and I'm shocked to see that I've soaked the bed. We both stare down at the mess, me with mortification and Gideon with heat burning in his golden eyes.

"That was—"

"Fucking incredible," he interrupts me.

Gideon scoops me up and hauls me to the bathroom. Like his bedroom, it's clearly designed for a bachelor. There's no hand towel or conditioner in sight, but thankfully, it appears to be clean. My survey of the room is interrupted by Gideon dropping me on the counter. I hiss when my bare ass hits the cold marble of the sink, but then I'm hissing for another reason when he kneels down and starts eating me out again.

The moment I notice what he's doing, my entire body turns red. He's not just trying to get me off . . . No, he's cleaning me up. This gorgeous, cuddle-obsessed man is licking all the juices from my thighs and pussy like he can't stand to waste even a drop. The realization sends me hurtling straight into another orgasm.

I'm so sensitive now, I don't think I can stand more. When I grab onto his curls and yank his head back forcefully, Gideon grins up at me. He's crouched between my legs, while I sprawl naked on his counter. He looks enraptured, and I feel more powerful than I've ever felt before. It's the most hedonistic thing I've ever seen. I don't even need to look in the mirror to know my eyes are purple yet again.

I slide off the counter, suddenly desperate to make him feel just as good. I turn the spray of the shower on, wait for it to heat, and then push him under the water. He's double my weight and more than a foot taller, but he follows my lead without complaint. It makes me melt. As warm water rains down on us, I lose another piece of my heart to him.

I kiss him eagerly, while my fingers map the hard ridges of his back and the chiseled grooves of his abs. He's strong, but with each touch of my hands, I take him apart. Now he's the one trembling.

Falling to my knees, I wrap my lips around his cock. I have very little experience with this and he's massive, so I can't fit him all in my mouth. But his groans still make me feel like I'm doing an amazing job. I wrap my hand around the base and swirl my tongue around the tip, reveling in the sounds he makes.

A grunt here, a gasp there, the tightening of his fingers in my wet hair.

Looking up into his eyes, he takes my breath away. Gideon's eyes are glowing, his jaw is clenched, and his head is thrown back with pleasure—he's stunning. I feel like I'm making love to a living, breathing work of art.

Gideon taps my head in warning, but I'm not going anywhere. I hollow my cheeks, sucking him to the back of my throat with one final push. He comes with a shout, tugging sharply on my hair as he finds his release. I rock back on my heels and catch my breath. But it's not long before he yanks me to my feet and presses a deep kiss to my mouth.

When we both pull back for air, he slumps against the wall.

Laughing, we wash each other's hair and bodies as fast as possible in water that's gone tepid, then frigid by the end. When we finally step out of the shower, Gideon wraps me in the only towel he can find, choosing to stand naked as the day he was born, dripping and shivering from the cold.

Who says chivalry is dead?

I catch sight of my violet eyes in the mirror and think back to his earlier explanation. I do feel like my true self is closer to the surface. After spending so many years hating all the things that made me different, it's a happy realization.

My heart thumps joyfully in my chest as I follow him out of the bathroom.

Maybe everything is going to be fine.

CALLUM

SHEENA AND GIDEON come downstairs around lunchtime holding hands and smiling at each other. I expect to feel jealous, but seeing them both happy after last night's explosive mess unravels the knot in my chest.

"I put a lasagna in the oven about an hour ago," I tell them. "It should be ready in a few minutes."

As if on cue, Sheena's stomach growls loudly. She chuckles, putting her hand over it. "Thank you." She pauses before meeting my eyes. "I'm going to let Ciprian know I'm okay, then I'll come eat."

I fight to keep any reaction off my face at the mention of my brother. *Troublesome little shit.* My poker face must be pretty good because Sheena just smiles softly at me before going out to the porch and curling up in a chair out there.

Once I hear the door slide shut with a soft snick, I turn my grin on Gideon, raising my eyebrows.

"Don't fucking start," he grumbles, but his smile is so big I can see half of his teeth. He sinks into the couch cushions next to me like an oversized starfish, tossing his head back and grunting as his joints crack.

I glance pointedly at the clock.

"You've been gone for hours, that's all. I guess you had a lot to talk about," I tease him. "Maybe you had to go over the *sensitive* bits a few times and *hammer* out the details before you both were *satisfied.*"

I block the throw pillow Gideon swings at my head, snatching it from him and tucking it under my arm.

"We cleared up our shit," he says.

I hide a smile at that incredibly on-brand statement. Simple, to the point, and completely without details. Typical Gideon.

"That's good, man. I'm glad you worked it out. You both deserve to be happy."

He lifts his head at that, a shadow crossing his face. "I'm

worried about why her powers made her sick," he says. "She doesn't actually know what she is, so we're flying blind here. I don't like that."

Uncertainty gnaws at my gut.

"We need information, but we have to be careful about how we get it or we'll put her at risk."

"I know," he huffs, watching me closely. "I don't want to say it, but . . ."

"Just don't," I groan, tugging on a loose string dangling from the pillow.

"Callum, come on." Gideon whips out the tone he only uses when he thinks I'm being unreasonable.

I hold up a hand. I already know what he's suggesting.

"No, please. Don't say it." I cover my head with the pillow. It's childish, but I don't want to hear—

"We may need to go to the enclave. Bring our parents in."

That. I didn't want to hear that.

"Gideon, we just saw my parents. Twice in one month is asking way too much," I whine.

"What other options do we have? We can't just post about it online and hope we get some helpful replies."

I remove the pillow, so Gideon can see me rolling my eyes at that ridiculous suggestion.

"They will be insufferable if we ask for their help. You know that, right?"

"It might not be that bad," he says. "Maybe they'll surprise you."

He's being ever so cheerful about this—probably because he just got laid and can't even imagine anything unpleasant.

"Oh," I seethe. "That's not the problem. They surprise me all the fucking time. Just never in a good way." He doesn't look convinced, so I bring out the big guns. "Seriously, do you think Sheena is ready to be tossed in the middle of that madhouse?"

"What madhouse?" Sheena asks, walking into the room with a smile.

It's nice to see her relaxed. How can we explain this without—

"We need to know what you are, so we can figure out why your powers made you so sick." Gideon barrels in with all the finesse of a stampeding buffalo. My fingers twitch around the pillow. "Our parents might know something that can help."

Sheena frowns, dropping down on the couch between us. As soon as she's within reach, Gideon tugs her insistently to his side.

"But I don't plan to ever use my powers again," she says, her forehead creasing as she mulls things over. "Why would I need to worry about the side effects?"

"Because it was fucking scary, baby," he admits. "You just dropped like a rock. Then you felt like shit for hours. What if you're sick, and your magic made it worse?"

Shit. I'm being selfish. He's right; we need answers even if it means going back to the compound.

"We don't want to leave your safety up to chance," I toss in before she can argue.

Sheena glances up at Gideon, her cheeks bright red. "What would you tell your parents about . . . us?"

It's a smart but loaded question, hurdling this conversation straight into define-the-relationship territory with no warning. Sheena seems like she wants to disappear into the couch, while Gideon . . . Gods, Gideon looks like he just attended his coronation as king of the fucking world.

"I would tell my parents that you're ours," he blurts. "Mine and Cal's."

His declaration is met with complete silence. In fact, the only thing I can hear is the roaring in my own head. I'm not sure who is more surprised—Sheena or me. We both stare at him like a zoo animal that's escaped its enclosure, then look everywhere except at each other.

"I want to tell them about the mate stuff too, but I get it if you're not ready for all that," Gideon says.

I can't believe he's still including me. He and I have talked about sharing her, but not on this level. And telling our parents would be a huge step. After being with Gideon, I have no idea if Sheena is even still interested in me. The knot is back in my gut, but this time it's twice as large. *Damn his big mouth.*

"What's wrong?" Gideon demands, looking back and forth between the two of us. When we don't respond quickly enough for him, he fills the silence himself. "You're both horny for each other."

Sheena shoots him a scandalized look, but his stubborn streak has been activated. There's no stopping him now. "Why are you both acting shy and shit? Callum charged down the mountain after you in the middle of a rainstorm. He wants you, Sheena."

"Gods, I can speak for myself—"

"It was a light rain—"

Sheena and I talk over the top of each other, then cut off abruptly. Tension ripples between us in waves. Gideon drums his fingers on his knee, looking unnecessarily pleased with himself.

"You know, everyone says I'm bad with words, but you two are the ones that can't even admit you want each other."

He stares me down. Sheena is clearly at a loss, her mouth opening and closing like a malfunctioning garage door. Meeting Gideon's eyes, I widen my own and look pointedly between the two of them. He has the audacity to laugh.

"You think because Sheena and I took things to the next level and talked about being mates that you're out now? It wasn't a race, dude." He looks at me like I'm some kind of idiot. It's infuriating enough to get me past the awkwardness.

"Obviously," I snap. "But I don't want to insert myself into your mystical universe bond and get in the way." I toss my hands up, annoyed that he's pushing this, and also feeling incredibly vulnerable that Sheena still hasn't said anything.

Gideon levels me with a flat-eyed stare.

"First, you couldn't get in the way. Second, I don't think Sheena would mind you *inserting* yourself." He bumps her with his shoulder to punctuate the innuendo, but she just squirms further into the couch.

"You're making her uncomfortable," I scold him, but Gideon just waves me off.

"Callum, do you want to be with Sheena?"

I have no way to dodge, not with her staring straight at me now. The vivid green of her eyes pins me in place.

"Fuck, of course I do," I shout, glaring at my former best friend.

Now that he's gotten the reaction he was looking for, Gideon ignores me, turning his focus on Sheena.

"Baby, do you want to be with Callum?"

The silence stretches so far I can feel the air thin around us. I die a million painful deaths waiting for Sheena to speak. Abruptly, she throws Gideon's arm off her shoulder and stands to face us.

"Yes, dammit, I want you both," Sheena admits, blushing bright red. "Now that we've settled that in the most awkward way possible, can we eat the lasagna? I'm starving."

She shuffles into the kitchen without waiting for a response, grumbling under her breath about Gideon's lack of tact.

I heave in some much needed oxygen, throwing my head back in relief while Gideon chuckles. Sheena may be embarrassed, but now I'm incredibly grateful my friend kept pushing. When we stand to follow her, I grab his arm to stop him and clear my throat. "Thanks . . . for saving room for me," I sputter and look at my feet. "You've never had to, but you always have."

I think of all the times Gideon has had my back, and a lump forms in my throat. I swallow around it and meet his eyes. They flash golden as he looks at me.

"I never saved room, Cal. The space was always yours."

Gideon speaks like it's chiseled in stone or a basic fact of life. Like the sky is blue and I belong with him. Without making a big deal about it, he tosses his arm over my shoulder and steers me toward the kitchen.

"Now, come on. We need to eat and figure out what to do about the parents."

CHAPTER
FIFTEEN

SHEENA

I can't believe I agreed to this. It's been almost a week since Gideon and I made things official, and ever since, I've been letting my rules slide to give this relationship a real shot at success. Now I'm buckled into the back seat of their SUV on the way to meet their parents, which even after half a dozen conversations, feels like an insane thing to do.

Maybe I've lost my mind.

The back tire hits a bump, jostling me.

Maybe it was just all the good sex.

Blood rushes to my face. I wonder if I'll ever stop blushing when I think about the intimate details of my sex life. It would be easier if I could be more brazen about the entire thing, especially since I want to take that step with Callum too.

I squirm against the leather seats as I picture it. I mean—he's an actual sex demon, so I'm sure it will be phenomenal. Part of me worries I won't be able to keep up, or that he'll be disappointed. Another part of me can't wait to roll up my sleeves, drop my panties, and give it my best shot.

A month ago, I was in the middle of a yearlong dry spell with no interest in changing that. Now, I'm counting the minutes until I end up on my back again.

"What are you thinking about?" Callum asks, looking at me in the rearview mirror with a knowing grin.

"You know exactly what she's thinking about." Gideon jumps in before I can answer. "And if she keeps it up, I'm going to wreck this car or pull over to join her in the back seat."

He growls at me, and the sound immediately makes me wet. I cross my legs.

"How can you possibly know what I'm thinking?" I go on the defensive. "You can't read my mind . . . Can you?"

"No, Sheena." Callum snorts. "But I can sense lust, and Gideon is basically an animal. My nose is nowhere near as sensitive as his, and even I can smell you."

Oh. That's mortifying.

"Let's change the subject," I demand, trying unsuccessfully to get my arousal under control. "Actually, let's just go back home. I don't feel sick at all. This is completely unnecessary."

"I promise they will love you."

Gideon sounds sincere, but I don't share his optimism.

"You can't know that. I'm broke and broken—not exactly the kind of girl you take home to meet your parents." Both of them start to argue, but I hold up my hand and cut them off. "Then, if they decide to be cool with the fact that I have nothing to offer . . . We're just going to tell them their precious sons have to share me? I wouldn't be surprised if they throw me out."

"You're not broken," Callum whispers gently. "You're one of the strongest people I know."

"And they won't give a shit about the sharing," Gideon says, thrumming his fingers on the steering wheel. "My mom already thinks I'm bending Cal over every night."

"Wait. Why would she assume you're always on top?" Callum turns to him, laughing. "I'm an incubus demon for fuck's sake."

"Right. If you wanted it, all you'd have to do is ask," Gideon teases, glancing at Callum in the passenger seat, then looking back at the road.

I'm not sure if he caught it or not, but I could swear Callum's black eyes turned a shade darker at the suggestion. I don't blame him. The thought of the two of them together makes my desire come roaring back to life. I curse both of them as I shift in my seat.

"Someone likes that idea."

Gideon's voice is pure sex. I close my eyes to pull myself together, but it doesn't help. Instead, my brain supplies me with a lot of graphic sexual images of the two of them wrapped around each other.

"If you both don't stop, I'm going to have to introduce Sheena to my parents with a hard on," Callum warns. "And if that happens, I'm going to make damn sure you both are every bit as uncomfortable as I am."

"It's his fault, not mine." I hurl the words at Gideon, pointing my finger at him in accusation.

My shifter seems like he's having a blast, dimples flashing as he grins and starts whistling tunelessly. He's the picture of innocence, but I'm not buying it.

We stop talking then, and I focus on the best way to make a good impression, realizing I don't have the first idea how to dazzle anyone's parents.

Before I can get too worked up, we're passing through a gate and veering left down an enormous cobblestone driveway. I catch glimpses of buildings, a fountain, and tall hedges as we go. We finally stop at another massive building. Gideon parks the SUV, then Callum opens my door. I slide out and do my best not to fidget or stare. This place is stunning. They definitely undersold it.

"You said this was a home," I hiss, frantically scraping a spot of mud off of my boot onto the stone. "I'm not sure what this is exactly, but it's not like any home I've ever seen."

Gideon looks at the sprawling structure as if he's trying to see it through my eyes. "Yeah, it's big. Our families have their own living spaces, but a lot of other people live here too."

"And many of them have nowhere else to go," Callum explains. "There are a bunch of other areas used for operations and training, too."

"Boring stuff like that," Gideon says.

I think I hear Callum murmur something about dungeons under his breath. Before I can ask, I hear a set of footsteps coming up behind me.

"Just think of it as an ostentatious, mixed-use development." At the sound of the familiar voice, I spin around so fast I almost trip.

"Careful, bestie," Ciprian teases, smiling as I rush forward to give him a hug.

"The house isn't the only thing that's ostentatious. Are you wearing slacks?" Callum asks, pointing at his brother.

Ciprian tilts his head cheekily. "I had these custom made to cup my ass just right. What do you think, babe?" He twists to show me the back of his tight, black pants.

"No one will be able to look away," I assure him, choking on a laugh and giving him a thumbs-up.

He ignores his brother's scowl and throws his arm around my shoulder, grinning. "Come inside now, Little Red Riding Hood. It's time to meet the big bad wolves."

I stop in my tracks, ice trickling down my spine.

"Wait, no one mentioned wolves." I turn to question Gideon about what I'm walking into. "I thought your parents had an affinity for birds and cats?"

He smiles down at me, shaking his head. "There aren't any wolves staying here that I know of."

"He's right." Ciprian laughs. "Just some nightmare demons living next to an over-capacity, cage-free animal shelter." He leans in closer. "And we've got fairies now."

Callum twists his head toward his brother with a scowl. "How's that going?"

"So far, it's been a heaping pile of painfully polite small talk." Ciprian rubs his chin. His tone is light, but the tension I'm feeling from all three of them makes me certain I'm missing some kind of context here.

"I'd prefer we save those introductions for another visit," Callum says, looking around the courtyard with narrowed eyes.

For once, Ciprian seems to agree with him because he nods his head and ushers me forward. He keeps up a steady stream of chatter about people I've never heard of while he leads me towards the nearest entrance.

"My family lives in this wing," Gideon says, slipping his hand in mine as we climb the stairs.

At the top, Callum reaches for the heavy, ornate door, but it opens on its own.

A man steps out. He's tall, elegant, and full of stunning, sharp edges as though his entire body was carved from marble. I assume he has Asian heritage until I notice the gracefully pointed ears on display beneath his black, neatly coiffed hair. After spending time with Callum and Gideon, I thought I would never be stunned by another good-looking man again, but this guy . . . He's so otherworldly flawless, it scares me.

Gideon's hand tightens around mine. Ciprian's arm, which was draped lazily over my shoulders, twitches twice as the man stares me down. He studies me like a specimen under a microscope. I shudder.

"Idris, it's good to see you again." Callum breaks the silence. His words are perfectly polite, but his tone is cold.

This must be one of the fae I wasn't supposed to meet.

Idris gives Callum a curt nod, but his icy blue eyes never leave mine. I take an involuntary step back, but I don't dare look away from him. I know danger when I see it, and life taught me early on never to take your eyes off an enemy.

Our silent standoff shatters when Gideon lets loose a vicious, warning snarl and a tall woman bursts through the door. The fae just looks at Gideon and smiles, his lips slowly peeling back to reveal flawless white teeth. It's not a friendly expression.

"Gideon, watch your mouth." The woman steps gracefully

around Idris with a boisterous, dimpled smile and plants an enthusiastic kiss on my mate's cheek.

This is clearly Gideon's mom, and god only knows what she thinks of this weird display. Her son is still squeezing my hand in a death grip, and Ciprian is glued to my other side, so I have nowhere to go when she turns her excitement on me.

"Darling, Gideon has told me almost nothing about you, so I know you're important. Please, come in. I'm not sure why you're all hovering in the doorway." Somehow, she extracts me from both Ciprian and Gideon with no effort. I follow her into the house, blinking like a little lost duckling.

"Idris, are you heading out, or would you like to stay for tea?" She tosses him a smile over her shoulder and some of the malice melts from his expression.

"Sarah, your offer is more than kind, but this is a family affair. I wouldn't dream of intruding."

When he speaks for the first time, it's all old-world charm, tinted with a slight accent I don't recognize. His voice is smooth and thick. It reminds me of melted chocolate and rolling around on silk sheets. I blink that comparison away, wondering where it came from.

I've never even slept on silk sheets for god's sake.

Idris bows low in my direction before gliding down the stairs.

Ciprian whistles and shudders dramatically. "That was weird as fuck."

"Shut up, he can still hear you." Callum smacks him in the arm.

Sarah smiles indulgently at both of them, interlocking her arm with mine and grinning down conspiratorially at me. "Sweetheart, it's obvious you're with two of my sweet boys, but what about my darling Ciprian?"

I replay her words three times before they truly compute, then my jaw drops, both from the insinuation and her casual acceptance.

"Shit, Sarah. Absolutely not." Ciprian grimaces at her, taking a step out of Callum's reach to avoid another swat. "Sheena is my friend. Everyone knows if you bang your bestie, things get messy." He swings his head around, wiggling his eyebrows at his brother and Gideon. They ignore his antics. Sarah looks amused.

"Mom, this is Sheena." Gideon finally introduces us, sounding both exasperated and amused.

"It's wonderful to meet you, ma'am," I sputter. "You have a lovely home." I gesture to the empty corner by the door and immediately feel like a total idiot. Her lip twitches, but she doesn't laugh at me.

"Oh, sweetie, there's no 'ma'am' in this wing. Call me Sarah. I'm sure we're going to be the best of friends."

She leads me out of the foyer then, and again I find myself moving without realizing it. It's quickly becoming clear that Sarah is a force of nature all on her own. All three men leave me to my fate, trailing behind like dutiful puppies.

We walk through a series of lavish hallways and hop on a golden, ornate elevator. As I look left and right in astonishment, I worry my eyes are bugging out of my head more with each incredible thing I see. Sarah keeps up a steady yet calming stream of chatter, bringing each of us into the conversation seamlessly. Seriously, it's like she has a doctorate in diffusing tension.

By the time we step into a set of rooms that look more lived in, I'm almost comfortable around her. This part of the compound has cheerful earth tones punctuated here and there by bright pops of color. It's tasteful, eclectic, and warm—perfectly matching the woman next to me.

"Boys, will you be staying in your rooms here or in the other wing?" She includes both brothers in her question, and I see them eye each other warily.

"I'll be staying here with Sheena if that's alright with you, Sarah," Callum says.

She nods, a pleased smile on her face.

"Unfortunately, I'll be heading back to the House of Horrors later," Ciprian quips, earning a sharp look from his brother.

"The Hall of Nightmares," Sarah explains for my benefit. "That's the official name of the demon wing, dear."

Ciprian wanders away, clearly comfortable in the Therion home, while the rest of us settle around the cozy living room.

"No cookies this close to dinner," Sarah calls out, ignoring the groan that comes from around the corner in response.

"What if I share with Sheena?" Ciprian asks as he stomps back into view. "Seriously, if she goes another minute without trying your chocolate chip cookies, it might kill her."

Sarah shakes her head at his attempt to negotiate, then agrees with a smile. Ciprian's smirk is triumphant, and he offers me what's clearly the smaller half of a cookie. I reach for it, only to change direction at the last second, swiping the bigger half from his other hand. He sputters, outraged, but I stuff the gooey treat into my mouth before he can retaliate.

"That's the last time I'll be sharing with you," he whines, throwing himself down on the couch next to Sarah and looking to her for sympathy.

"You'll have to excuse him, Sheena. He's the youngest, so I'm afraid we spoiled him a little." She smiles fondly at the blonde demon. "He was just such a darling little baby."

Ciprian preens under her attention, throwing smug looks at Callum and Gideon. "Yes, Sheena, my birth was a blessing for the entire region."

I groan at his antics, finishing the cookie and ignoring his giant ego.

"Sarah, I hesitate to agree with Ciprian—for obvious reasons— but that's the best cookie I've ever had," I tell her. "I would love the recipe if you're willing to share it." Both Callum and Gideon perk up at that.

"Of course, dear. Do you bake?" There's genuine interest in her question, and my guard drops another notch.

"Not as much as I'd like," I admit. "But one of my diner jobs required baking pies every day. I got pretty good at that."

We make small talk for the next few minutes until Callum clears his throat. We all look his way.

"Sarah, what's the deal with Idris?" His voice is wary, but Gideon's mom seems unsurprised by the question.

"It's going amazingly well, dear. He and his companions finished moving in just a few days ago. So far, the alliance is holding strong." She looks at me then, including me in the conversation. "I'll admit I questioned the move at first, myself, but we're hopeful having the fae as part of the enclave will bring more stability."

"I don't trust him," Gideon grumbles. "And I don't like the way he stared at Sheena."

I'm glad I wasn't the only one who thought that interaction was strange.

"Oh, sweetie, I'm sure it was nothing." Sarah pats her son's arm. "He's just intense. After all that he's been through, it's not surprising."

Gideon still doesn't look convinced, but his mom seems confident everything is fine.

When we head over to the Hall of Nightmares for dinner, I'm still thinking about Idris' cold, blue stare. Even now, as we navigate the dim labyrinth of corridors, I can still feel his eyes on me.

———

IDRIS

THERE IS A DJINN at the enclave.

Walking across the courtyard, the click of the stones under my shoes grates on my nerves. The expensive leather pinches my feet. I feel a pang of longing for the lush grass of my homeland and the way my bare toes would sink into the earth there. Suffocating that insipid sentiment, I remind myself forcefully that those days are behind me now.

As for the djinn . . . It's been decades since I've seen one. I thought they had all been hunted to extinction. *Why would she reveal herself to a compound teeming with supernaturals?*

I could feel the creature's power radiating across the threshold. It was on the tip of my tongue to test her and make a wish, but if she were bound, those words would have been the last ones I ever uttered.

With the way those boys clung to her like vines to a trellis, it's clear she's under their protection. It will not be enough. She's not safe, nor is anyone in her immediate orbit. An unbound djinn— gods, if she were to fall into the wrong hands, her magic could destroy realms.

Which begs the question: how can I use this to my advantage?

After I ensure I'm seen entering the fae section of the compound, I wait for a few hours to pass, then cloak myself in a heavy glamour. I'm nearly invisible. If anyone looks directly at me, they won't see anything, except perhaps a slight rippling of the air when I move.

Satisfied with the disguise, I sidle soundlessly back to the shifter domain. The gods are on my side for once, and I encounter the group just as they're walking toward the Hall of Nightmares. A pretentious name for what's essentially a gauche, gothic shrine to a bygone era.

They keep up a steady stream of chatter as they walk, so I trail after them, hoping to learn something interesting. The young demon is trying desperately to get attention from the older one. It could be interesting to find the source of that familial tension and exploit it, but I don't have the time for side projects right now.

"Ciprian, keep your grubby hands off my girl," the incubus demon snaps. *What was his name again? Calvin or Cornelius or something?*

"Dude. Why so greedy? It's not like you aren't already sharing her."

Both the incubus and the enormous shifter swing for the blonde, but he dodges.

"Stop trying to rile them up," the djinn demands, groaning.

Her voice is low and melodic in the dim corridor. Hearing it for the first time sends shivers down my spine, but that's nothing compared to how the calculating gleam in her eyes affects me.

"If you keep antagonizing them, I might let something slip about your winged problem." That veiled threat obviously hits its mark because the nightmare swings his head around, glaring down at her.

"I told you that under the best friend confidentiality clause. It's a binding contract, in case you were unaware," he insists, making a laugh bubble out of her. It's rich, throaty, and entirely too sensual for a woman wearing dirty hiking boots.

"I don't remember signing anything." She taps her chin with her pointer finger. "You also never said it was a secret."

"Oh my shit, Sheena. It was implied. Like the time you told me about what Gideon can do with his tongue."

The djinn cringes, but the shifter seems amused. "My mom is right there, man," he says.

Sarah laughs at that. She's been a quiet but shrewd observer up until this point, much like myself.

"It's okay, dear. It's comforting for me to know my son isn't a selfish lover." She pats him on the back and beams down at the djinn.

"Umm. Nothing to worry about there, Sarah," the djinn says. Her face is so red now her blush is visible even in the dimly lit corridor. She looks like she'd rather be anywhere else.

As soon as Sarah turns back to lead the group on, the three of them converge on the blonde troublemaker, hissing and swatting at him. He has the nerve to look aggrieved, and I'm surprised to find myself genuinely amused by their scuffle.

Unfortunately, I've learned almost nothing helpful, except that two of the males are sharing her physically. That is not uncommon in the supernatural world, hardly worth even noting, but the variable does interest me. Perhaps she will have a better chance of survival if she collects a powerful group of lovers.

"Sheena, my son tells me you've had some trouble recently.

Are you feeling better?" At the question, I immediately perk up, eager to hear her answer.

"Yes, it's been a hard few years," she says. A shiver rolls down her spine. "I do feel better, though. Thank you for asking." The big shifter steps closer to her, rubbing his chest and looking pained by her reaction.

I smell fear in the air.

"We're hoping you might have information that could help us keep Sheena safe, mom." The shifter wraps a protective arm around her. Sarah promises to do whatever she can, her curiosity bleeding through her polite tone.

I watch them disappear into the Casanell's private residence and consider my next move. If they have questions for the leaders of the enclave, that includes me now.

It seems tonight is the perfect time to take the demons up on their standing dinner invitation.

CHAPTER
SIXTEEN

GIDEON

I feel like we're at the highest point of a roller coaster, dangling over the edge, waiting to drop into complete chaos. Sheena's nerves are obvious, and Callum's tension gets worse with each step we take toward his childhood home.

My parents expect a lot from me, but they also make it clear their priority is my happiness. Instead of support, Cal learned at the most difficult time of his life that his parents' favor was conditional and out of his control.

We warned Sheena that his parents are assholes, so she's prepared, but if they make her or Callum uncomfortable, I'm going to lose my shit. Dimitri may be one of the leaders of this enclave, but I'm next in line, and I won't put up with any disrespect.

Glancing around at the dark living space, I repress a shiver. I hate spending time here. It's just so godsdamn Halloween. Dark fabrics, dark wallpaper, dark art. Seriously, turn a light on or something. I'm no interior designer, but what does it say about you when your coziest room screams 'the crushing weight of existential dread?'

"Psst, Sheena," I whisper as I walk past the familiar stone gargoyle and its large talons. When she looks back at me, I partially shift my hand to add claws and recreate the iconic scene from E.T. Callum rolls his eyes at me, but Sheena's giggle is exactly what I was looking for. My girl is wound too tight.

"Good evening."

"*Shitfuck.*" I gasp as Mallory materializes out of the shadows like a fucking ghost.

She startles me so badly my claw jerks across the statue causing an ear-piercing scraping sound. We all wince. I mutter an apology, and Sheena's face turns tomato red from holding in her laugh.

"Is there a problem with the art, Gideon?" Mallory's tone is dry enough to send the whole state into a drought.

I immediately shake my head. "Oh no, ma'am. This little guy just reminded me of E.T. You know, the alien from that movie? 'E.T., phone home.'" I mimic the voice pretty fucking well, but Cal's mom doesn't even crack a smile.

"I don't think I've had the pleasure of viewing that film," she says coolly.

Mallory is wearing all white today, like she's heading to the dojo or a cult meeting. The look should make her come across as soft and welcoming, but she's really just giving off icicle vibes. To top it off, her blonde hair is wound into such a tight bun we may all leave here with a headache because of it.

She steeples her fingers together like a praying mantis and has the nerve to stare at me like I'm a bug she wants to squash. "That gargoyle has been passed down through Dimitri's family for the last seven hundred years. When demons first came to this realm, humans thought they could use stone figurines to ward their homes."

She smiles, but it's a creepy expression.

"They believed the gargoyles would come to life in the face of danger and prevent demons from infiltrating their house. They even carved their mouths open to better consume evil spirits."

Mallory points at the creepy thing's gaping mouth with a crimson-painted nail.

"Superstitious nonsense, of course. The demons got in no matter what." She turns and aims her smile directly at Sheena. "Hello dear, I'm Mallory."

Sheena introduces herself quietly, while everyone else ignores the freaky, demonic history lesson.

Mallory doesn't address Callum or Ciprian at all—as if two members of our group aren't her actual sons. Instead, she leads us straight to the formal dining room. My mom gives me an exasperated look over my gargoyle stunt before linking her arm with Sheena and catching up to Mallory. They pull my mate away before I can intervene, seating Sheena between them at the round mahogany table.

Somehow I end up stuck between the feuding brothers, who appear to have struck a temporary truce based entirely on booze.

Like he's trying to stress me out, Ciprian plops down next to his mom and chugs an entire glass of wine before starting on another. Without a word, he reaches across me and passes the bottle to Callum. I give the wine a longing look but choose to drink from my glass of water instead. Someone has to keep tonight on track.

Sheena seems torn between her own discomfort and glancing between the brothers with concern. The chatter is patchy and awkward. I try to break the tension with a joke, but no one laughs. My only saving grace comes from the plate of cheese cubes and salami on the table. I stuff my face to avoid speaking.

"Joshua and Dimitri should join us soon," mom says as she sets her phone down and picks up a cracker. "Mallory, these appetizers are wonderful. I just love a charcuterie board."

A little of Mallory's icy demeanor begins to thaw until she notices the small mountain of crumbs gathering around me. I brush them on the floor as soon as she looks away.

"Thank you, Sarah." Mallory rotates her desert fork to align with the plate. "I thought, since this was a family dinner of sorts, we could have something casual."

I choke down a laugh. Nothing screams casual like cloth napkins, crystal goblets, and staff darting around the room. When Sheena's water glass refills on its own, she lets out a concerned squawk.

"That's just the mazzikin, dear." Mallory's explanation does nothing for Sheena, who's now staring around the room with suspicion. "They're a type of lesser demon. Invisible but incredibly useful for running a household."

Mallory trills a laugh, like calling all her staff lesser to their invisible faces is not only acceptable, but also funny. Sheena nods politely, but her lips are pressed tightly together.

"How did you all meet?" Mallory asks, addressing Sheena directly.

"It was actually at a bar where I worked."

Our girl smiles, but I can sense Callum's mom charging up to deliver some cutting remark. "We met Sheena while working the case in Wyoming," I say, jumping in. "She was the only thing worth finding in that place."

"A *human* bar?" Mallory sounds scandalized.

"Well, yes." Sheena laughs. "Until recently, I wasn't aware there were any other kinds of bars."

We're saved from hearing Mallory's take on that by footsteps in the hallway. Seconds later, my father and Dimitri join us, and I'm surprised to see Idris trailing along behind them.

What the fuck?

Callum and I exchange loaded looks, but we say nothing.

"Sorry for the extra mouth to feed, Mal." My dad's voice booms across the table as he claps the fae on the back. Callum's mother grimaces. The only thing she hates more than surprises is that nickname, and it cracks me up every time my dad uses it.

"Idris was hoping to join us for dinner," Dimitri says.

Mallory gives her husband a cutting look, then motions in the air with her finger for the mazzikin to hurry up. The scrape of a heavy wooden chair punctuates the silence as another place setting appears.

"Of course, Idris. You have a standing invitation. I'm glad you finally used it," Mallory says.

The fae gives her a charming smile as he takes a seat in between Callum and Dimitri—directly across from Sheena.

"Gideon and Callum, I believe," Idris murmurs as though he doesn't know damn well what our names are. "I owe you both an apology for that awkward moment earlier. I must confess, when I woke up this morning, I never expected to encounter a full-blooded djinn. Much less one so beautiful and . . . undamaged."

Wait, what? We get about one full second of complete silence, then all hell breaks loose as everyone starts talking at once.

"A djinn, alive? Impossible."

"You met a djinn serving drinks in some reprehensible pub?"

"Oh, sweetheart. Are you alright?"

"Are you unbound?"

My chest throbs hard, but this panic isn't mine. Ignoring the parents, I focus on Sheena. Her face has lost all color, and her pupils have shrunk to pinpricks. She looks between all the unfamiliar faces, her head swiveling back and forth like she isn't sure where to start.

"Timeout," I say. It's a reasonable request, made at a reasonable volume, so of course no one listens. My hands clench into fists.

Callum shoots to his feet. "Shut up," he bellows, drowning out the combined voices with sheer volume alone.

Since I'm usually the one to lose my temper, I've rarely heard him raise his voice. I must not be the only one surprised because everyone actually listens for once. We all stare up at Callum. His eyes are black and hard as granite, and in that moment, he looks every bit like a creature from the demon realm.

Ciprian interrupts the stunned silence by popping a cheese cube into his mouth with a pleased hum and casually reaching across the table to clink his empty wine glass against the full one in Sheena's hand. "Congrats, friend. It seems like you're going to get some answers."

He grins drunkenly at her, unfazed by the tension in the room, but Sheena's grip on her glass is so tight her fingers have gone bone white from the pressure.

I'm kind of surprised the glass hasn't cracked.

The thought barely has time to bounce around in my head before the stem snaps off and tips over with a thud. Every eye at the table watches as the bowl lurches back and forth clumsily before finally reaching a resting place, tilted against the mahogany. A few drops of merlot trickle over the rim, dripping like blood onto the white tablecloth.

Sheena squares her shoulders and grips the remains of the cup in both hands. She takes a long look at it, then guzzles the contents in one go, setting it down with a thunk.

"What's a djinn?" She demands, looking around the table and focusing specifically on Idris.

Dimitri scoffs at her. "You mean to act like you don't know?"

Sheena meets his glare with one of her own, tilting her chin up. "I'm not acting," she hisses. "Obviously, I know I'm different, but it's not like I was raised in this world."

Her green eyes flicker to violet, and from the subtle, collective inhale, I don't think anyone at the table misses it.

"I discovered I wasn't just another unwanted kid when masked men broke into my foster home and dragged me out of bed. They used my abilities to make the family forget me."

Sheena glances at me then, and I hate that I'm not sitting next to her to support her.

"I escaped, and I've been running ever since. The only things I know about *your* world are the things I've learned since meeting Callum and Gideon," Sheena says, sucking in a breath. "So, unless you want to call me a liar again, I'll ask one more time: what is a djinn?"

Idris clears his throat.

"Djinn used to be an incredibly influential part of the supernatural community," he says, before Dimitri can put his foot in his mouth again. "They were always rare, mind you, and until I saw you, I had believed them to be extinct."

Callum falls back into his seat now that Sheena is finally getting answers. We all listen, horrified and spellbound as Idris explains how Sheena's kind were hunted ruthlessly for decades. According to the fae, many djinn lives were lost just to keep their power out of the hands of warring factions.

"Much of the generational wealth within the supernatural community is because a djinn made it so." Idris glances at the expensive furnishings around the room.

Dimitri and Mallory's interest is immediately piqued, but before I can speak up, Cal beats me to it. "This should go without saying, but I'll say it anyway." Callum's eyes lock onto his parents. "Sheena will not be the enclave's retirement plan or its piggy bank."

His words slice through the air like a knife. While Dimitri looks annoyed, Mallory is just appalled her son would bring up something as taboo as money in front of company.

"Of course not, kids," dad says. "But given what we know of the djinn's tragic past, I worry about Sheena's safety."

I know his concern is genuine at least, and I relax a little in my seat.

"There's something else," Sheena whispers, twisting her napkin between her fingers. "After my magic activates, I get sick. It drains me until I feel empty, and the last time it happened, it was worse than usual."

I watch the fae closely as she speaks, but his emotions pass over his face too quickly for me to identify.

"You have no talisman," Idris murmurs.

"What does that mean?" Callum demands, his black eyes digging holes in the side of the fae's face.

"A talisman is similar to a double-edged sword in the sense that it both protects the djinn and puts them at risk." Idris sips his wine, watching Sheena for her reaction. "It's a necessary evil."

"Like a lamp to be rubbed?" Ciprian snorts, but Idris ignores the interruption and continues his explanation.

"A talisman acts as a physical anchor for the djinn's power. A djinn bound to a talisman can choose which wishes to grant and avoid the intense sickness and draining that comes from granting a wish whilst unbound."

"What's the other side of the sword?" Sheena asks, her eyes narrowing with suspicion.

"Clever, little djinn," Idris says, smiling at her. "If someone else were to gain possession of your talisman, they would control your wishes and your free will right along with it."

He sounds cool and detached, but I'm not fooled. There's a gleam in Idris' eyes like he's running a bunch of calculations and really liking the results. I don't trust his intentions.

Sheena considers his words, then puts her napkin down. "What happens if I skip the whole talisman thing all together and never use my magic?"

Knowing this has been her plan all along, I'm not surprised, but Idris is visibly stunned.

"Besides the fact that someone could make an offhand comment in the grocery store and you could out the entire supernatural community?" Dimitri blusters.

"Yes, besides that." Sheena keeps her focus on the fae.

"You would die," Idris says simply.

Callum slams his fists down. The violent move jostles the table and forces Ciprian to steady his rocking wine glass.

"Is that a threat?" Callum bites the words out, but Idris only glances at him coldly.

"Hardly. It's simply the truth: an unbound djinn is living on borrowed time." He turns his shrewd eyes back on Sheena. "If some hunter or trafficker doesn't take you out first, you'll waste away before the year is out."

The fae's blue eyes glitter as he stares at my girl, and a growl bubbles up out of my chest. *Now is not the time for me to lose control.* I drag my twitching hands under the table.

"Face it, little djinn. Without a talisman—whether you use the magic or not—it will eventually consume you from the inside out."

SHEENA

"How do we get a talisman?" I ask, refusing to be cowed by the fae across from me.

Idris is the kind of beautiful you might find in a museum full of weapons—cold, timeless, and deadly. His cheekbones are sharp enough to cut, his blue eyes are piercing in their intensity, and even his black eyebrows slice across his face, bold and perfectly matched.

Who has matching eyebrows, anyway?

I add it to the growing list of reasons he makes me uneasy.

"That I don't know," he admits. "Much like a witch's grimoire, a talisman is typically a family heirloom. They're passed down through generations."

"Well, I'm sans family, so that's a problem." I grit the words out. His blasé attitude puts me on edge. "How do you even know all this stuff? Is it common knowledge?" I glance at the others, hoping anyone has a differing opinion to offer.

"Sweetie." Sarah jumps in. "I've never met a djinn myself. They were incredibly rare, even in my childhood."

"There was a djinn in my parents' community. The way I understood it, a rival clan killed him to remove his powers from the equation," Joshua says softly. He is gentle on my behalf, I realize, as he talks about the death of my kind.

"I knew a djinn." Mallory surprises us all as she speaks up, a brittle quality to her voice that wasn't there earlier. "Edith was powerful. You could feel it even when she was just a girl. Her family sent her to stay with us for protection. In exchange for keeping her safe, she agreed to join our community and help it thrive . . ."

Mallory's eyes lose focus as she stares down at her clasped hands. An uncomfortable silence falls over the table as we wait for her to continue.

"What happened to her, mother?" Callum prods. She clenches her hands so tightly it looks painful.

"She snuck out to meet with a boy in the village. I knew the risk, of course, but I covered for her." Mallory's eyes dip closed, then flicker back open. "Edith didn't make it home by dark, and I got scared. I went looking for her by myself because I didn't want to get in trouble. When I found her . . . It was already too late. I could smell the blood from a mile away." She fights back tears, choking up at the memory. "Someone had cut her throat and tossed her in a ditch outside town."

I stare at her in shock and horror. A quick glance around the table shows I'm not the only one. Mallory brushes her face off and excuses herself to see about the main course. A suffocating heaviness settles over the table, but I honestly prefer the dark energy. At least it's more authentic than the Casanells' earlier condescension.

"I've heard similar stories," Idris says. "The fear, greed, and violence of others forced the djinn into hiding decades ago. It was thought they were eventually hunted to extinction." He gives me a pointed look. "Although, clearly that was incorrect."

"We won't let anything happen to you," Gideon says, a serious look on his face.

I force a smile, my mind racing in a dozen different directions. *I wanted answers, but I never expected anything like this.*

The information we've learned tonight has sobered everyone but Ciprian, who is now well on his way to being sloppy drunk.

"It's fine for you to play guard dog or cat or whatever the animal of the week is," he quips, ignoring the dark looks thrown his way. "But if we can't find this mystical, not-a-lamp talisman thing, it sounds like Sheena is a goner."

Damn. That was blunt.

"Your bedside manner needs work, Ciprian." I respond before either Gideon or Callum can lash out at him.

"Oh, babe, you know nothing about my bedside manner." He winks at me as he reaches for the wine bottle again. Gideon tugs on the tablecloth, pulling it out of his reach. It's a practiced move that makes Joshua hide a smile, but it's Dimitri's expression that makes me want to laugh out loud. He's staring at his youngest son like he was just forced to swallow something rancid.

"Ciprian," Dimitri barks. "That's hardly appropriate conversation for mixed company at the dinner table."

"Oh loosen up, dad." Ciprian laughs. "Mom just talked about following a blood trail to her friend's body after helping her sneak out to get some. I think a little double entendre lightens the mood. After all, we're not at Sheena's funeral." He waggles his eyebrows at me. "Yet."

I let out an unladylike snort. "I'm going to make sure you're nowhere near my eulogy," I tease. "God knows what you would say."

"First, you won't get a say because you'll be dead. Second, the gods may not know what I would say, but I'm sure you've got an idea." Ciprian smirks.

Joshua and Dimitri exchange concerned looks.

"Relax," Ciprian says, rolling his eyes. "I already told Sarah— I'm not after the genie. She's the meat in Cal and Gideon's fuck sandwich. I have no interest in being the lettuce everyone picks off."

Dimitri chokes on his drink, although I don't know why he's shocked. *Has he met his son?* When Joshua pounds on his friend's back, an amused twinkle in his eye, Sarah and I have to stifle our laughter.

I want to see how the fae is reacting to this nonsense, but I don't want him to catch me looking at him. I can still feel his gaze drilling into my skull.

When Mallory comes back, her . . . staff are with her. Now that

I know they exist, I watch for the subtle flickering of the air as the not-so-subtle platters of steaming dishes float in behind her. My broken goblet disappears, only to be replaced with a sturdy, crystal glass typically used for sipping whiskey. It appears I'm no longer trusted with long stem glasses. Probably the right call if I'm being honest.

Joshua clears his throat pointedly.

"Let's table this conversation until after dinner." He glances around at the floating food, and we all get the message. No talking about my super secret origins while someone could overhear.

The problem now is no one knows what else to talk about.

"Idris, how are you adjusting to life at the enclave?" Joshua tosses the ball back into the fae's court.

"I'm settling in nicely," Idris says, picking up the conversation gracefully. "Both Sarah and Mallory have been kind enough to ensure a seamless transition."

He nods to the older women with a glittering smile. Both of them seem flustered by his attention, and I'm relieved I'm not the only one who finds him unnerving. Every time he looks at me, I want to run away.

I need to get Callum or Gideon alone so I can ask them about fae powers. They haven't mentioned mind reading, but I get the feeling this Idris guy sees way too much. There's a quiet stillness to the way he watches. It's like he's peeling back everyone's layers and expecting to find a rotten core.

"Has the scum we caught in the barn said anything useful?" Callum asks, shifting the conversation away from the fae. Idris actually seems relieved by the change of subject.

"Unfortunately, no." Joshua wipes his mouth with a fancy napkin. "He was a grunt like you suspected. He provided some locations, but there's been no movement at any of them so far."

"How do you know? You didn't call us," Gideon grumbles.

"Simmer down, son. We put some cameras up. It wasn't worth sending you two without confirmed sightings."

"I'm sure they're simply lying low after finding the barn burned down with their captives gone and henchmen dead," Dimitri says. He levels a stern look at Callum like it's somehow his fault. "They'll have to surface at some point. When they do, we'll be ready for them."

"Idris, have there been any rumors in the fae community about abductions or unexplained disappearances?" Callum's tone is almost neutral as he addresses the fae. But I can tell from the small twitch of Idris' lips, he's picking up on the frustration bleeding through.

"The short answer is no. The long answer is more complicated," he admits.

"It always is," Gideon mutters under his breath.

Idris pretends not to hear him.

"Unfortunately, fae are born and raised to be suspicious. After centuries of war and bloodshed, the folk are hesitant to trust any but those in their inner circle." Idris nods toward Callum and Gideon's parents. "I joined this enclave to prove there is strength when we stand together. I want my people to find a better way of life, but they can't do that unless I lead by example."

Callum gives him a look of begrudging respect, and I find myself pleasantly surprised as well. Maybe there's more to this guy than half-truths and calculated looks. Either that or we're gobbling up a load of bullshit.

Conversation trails off as we eat, and I tuck into the meal despite my churning stomach. The rhythmic clinking of forks and knives against the dishes relaxes me. The food is so delicious I don't even have to pretend. After I polish off a slab of strawberry cheesecake, Mallory calls for coffee. Once it's delivered, the parents wait a few minutes before reaching some unspoken agreement that it's safe to talk again.

"Given the information that's come to light, it would be safer for all three of you to move back home." Joshua's voice is firm. He crosses his arms over his chest, braced for pushback.

"Dad, we're grown," Gideon argues, furrowing his brow.

"A grown man doesn't let pride stop him from keeping someone they care about safe, son," Sarah counters. Her tone is softer than her husband's, but her words hit a lot harder for both men. Neither Callum nor Gideon will meet her eyes now.

"Thank you for offering me your hospitality," I say, genuinely touched that their offer includes me. I don't want to be pushed to make a decision right away, though. "We'll give you an answer after we've had time to discuss it."

Joshua and Sarah nod reluctantly.

"Mallory, did your friend have a talisman?" Dimitri reintroduces the topic gingerly, looking at his wife with a tenderness that surprises me. *Perhaps he's a better partner than father.* Despite his care, Callum's mother is clearly startled by the question.

"If she did, we never discussed it," Mallory says, eyes darting up to meet her husband's. "Given the importance, I suspect she kept it a secret. Even from me."

"If all the djinn are dead or in hiding, how are we going to get one of these things for Sheena?" Gideon snaps. He shifts around in his chair restlessly, the wood groaning under his weight.

"Can't we just pick something and make it her talisman?" Callum asks. He unclips and tosses his watch on the table. It lands with a muted thunk. "These things have to have an origin. You can't tell me they just popped into existence one day."

"You're probably right, but locating someone who knows more and is willing to share that knowledge with you is its own challenge," Idris says. His face twists slightly. "You could always ask the witches."

Apparently, he just stepped on a landmine because everyone freaks out and starts talking over each other.

It's so chaotic I'm tempted to cover my ears. I'm actually relieved when Idris holds his hands up in the universal supplicatory gesture people use when they've just offended almost everyone in their immediate vicinity.

"We can't trust witches," Joshua says. "They're more likely to drain Sheena's life force than help her."

"I didn't say it was a *good* idea," Idris admits.

"I'm scared to even ask this, but what's the deal with the witches?" I address Sarah, hoping she'll be the voice of reason. The last thing I want to do is stir them all up again, but this is my life and death we're talking about.

"Well dear, every supernatural can forge their own path," Sarah begins. "I mean that to say no species is inherently good or bad—"

Ciprian interrupts by spewing some sort of drunken chortle-huff noise. It's guttural and gross, and it makes me regret not cutting him off sooner.

"What Sarah is so delicately trying to avoid saying is witches are the fucking worst, but it's because they want to be." Ciprian finishes that eloquent statement with a hiccup that makes his mother's eye twitch.

"It's more complex than that," Idris says. He picks up the pitcher of creamer in one hand and the canister of sugar in the other and holds both containers at equal heights. "Evolution and altruism walk hand in hand in most modern cultures. The need for personal survival balances with the need to cherish, protect, and sacrifice for those you love."

I nod, following along with his explanation while avoiding eye contact.

"As Sarah and . . . Ciprian were saying . . . witches don't pursue that balance. They never have. Many covens are notorious for their capricious motives, pursuing chaos to the exclusion of almost everything else, including their own safety."

Idris drops both the sugar and creamer without warning, letting the crystallized cubes scatter across the tabletop. I brace myself for the liquid to splatter too, but an icy blue light catches the pitcher just before it makes contact, suspending it in the air. I watch it sway gently back and forth. One lone drop of cream drips down the side, its movement jerky and unpredictable, until it falls, sinking into the fabric of the tablecloth.

I stare at the magic, mesmerized, as Idris lowers the container to the table without touching it. He takes a casual sip of his coffee, and I blink, feeling heat rush to my cheeks.

"If they're just running around worshipping chaos all the time, wouldn't there be more witch mayhem on the evening news?" I ask, pointing to the scattered sugar cubes.

"Most people just assume they're eccentric or rationalize away anything overly weird," Callum says, shrugging.

"And the only rule their coven leaders force them to follow is the secrecy covenant," Dimitri adds. His dark eyes are tracking the way his oldest son looks at me, and I don't like the attention.

"Are there any trusted elders we could reach out to overseas?" Sarah diverts my attention from Dimitri's plotting with her question. "I doubt we want to involve any of the other North American enclaves. The temptation would be too close." She gives me an apologetic look, and I force a smile.

"That's not a bad idea." Joshua rubs his chin. "I'll think about it. Perhaps Magnus in Scotland."

"What about the academy?" Gideon asks, pressing his hand over his heart as he looks at me. The motion makes me realize I'm feeling the distance between us too.

"I don't trust any of the professors," Callum mutters.

"We wouldn't have to tell them what's going on, though." Gideon scrunches up his nose as he thinks about his alma mater. "Just come up with some excuse to case the library."

"That might actually work," Idris says. He seems impressed by Gideon's suggestion, but in a way that's almost completely patronizing. "It is the most comprehensive supernatural archive on this continent."

"I can't help with that. You know I'm banned from the campus for life," Ciprian says, grinning at me as if he's daring me to ask him why. I don't give him the satisfaction.

"Callum and I will go," Gideon says decisively. He stands then, his chair scraping against the floor with the sudden movement. "Now, we're going to bed. I can't listen to another word from any of you. You're all giving me a headache."

Gideon circles the table, clapping his father on the back and kissing his mother on the cheek.

"Mallory, the food was great." Gideon nods at our host, ignoring Ciprian, Dimitri, and Idris completely.

He slips his hand in mine and pulls me up from my seat. I barely have two seconds to thank the Casanells for the dinner, before my massive shifter half carries, half drags me from the room, Callum trailing after us.

The fae watches us leave with obvious interest. "Good night, little djinn." He purrs the nickname for the third time.

Gideon squeezes my hand a little tighter in response.

CHAPTER
SEVENTEEN

SHEENA

When we near the gargoyle statue, I remember Gideon's silly impersonation and some of my stress from dinner melts away. My lips tick up in amusement as I spot the claw mark he accidentally left behind while trying to make me laugh. I shed layers of tension with each step I take.

I must not be the only one because as soon as we cross into the winding corridor, Callum tugs me away from Gideon and into his arms. He kisses me with desperation, his tongue slipping in and dominating my mouth like he can't help himself. There's a new urgency in the way he holds me as though the things we've learned have shaken his control.

"It's okay," I whisper, trying to reassure him between kisses. He groans in my mouth, clinging to me tightly. Gideon crowds my back, dropping a warm kiss to my exposed neck.

"This is really fucking hot, but can we do it back in my room?" Gideon grumbles in my ear. "I still feel like that creepy statue is watching us."

I look over my shoulder. Even though the gargoyle is out of

sight now, I do feel something. I chuckle, a little unnerved, then put my imagination to better use.

With one hand still buried in Callum's dark hair, I stretch my other arm up, winding it around Gideon's neck, and arch back to whisper in his ear. "Better hurry and take me back to your room before it comes alive and you have to protect my virtue from a hungry demon."

My words impact him exactly how I hoped. Gideon's brown eyes melt into a rich gold, shining in the dark hallway. I push my lower body further into Callum, who is holding me so tightly I can feel exactly how excited he is. After years of haunting loneliness, seeing them burn for me thaws some of the ice around my heart.

"You don't get to leave us," Callum hisses, speaking for the first time since we left dinner. His words are raw and ragged.

"I'm not going anywhere," I reassure him, feeling a sting of regret over how my flight down the mountain damaged our fragile trust.

"That's not what I mean," Callum says, shaking his head. He presses his forehead against mine. "You don't get to die. No wasting away, no slit throats or cages. If your magic starts to drain you, I'll tie you to the bed and feed you my blood for the rest of time."

Callum presses another kiss to my mouth, swallowing my gasp.

"Unfortunately, that will make you unbearably horny, so Gideon will have to fuck you nonstop."

I groan and chase his mouth.

"As far as backup plans go, I'm a big fan," Gideon says, chuckling. "But let's try to actually get our hands on one of these talisman things before we commit to a lifetime of kinky hospice care."

Callum and I grimace.

"Kinky hospice care?" I snicker. "That's the least sexy way you could have described that."

"Yeah, I hope all your dirty talk isn't that bad." Callum frowns up at him.

Gideon bends down to rest his chin on top of my head and looks directly into Callum's dark, bottomless eyes. "If you help me get our girl out of this creepy hallway right now, you can grade my dirty talk firsthand."

I don't even have time to blink before Callum swings me up onto his back and takes off. He's moving so quickly I'm forced to hang on for dear life. I grab his shoulders to steady myself as Callum twists around a corner. His fingers grip the bottom of my thighs, tugging my legs forward. I take the hint and lock my legs around his waist.

When I look back to make sure Gideon is behind us, his eyes are glowing like beacons in the dark.

"Is he watching you?" Callum asks, panting slightly as he slows to a jog.

"He's watching us," I correct him. Instead of going in for the quick kill, Gideon is leisurely stalking his prey with the confidence of a seasoned hunter.

Callum chuckles. The sound is dark and raspy; it tickles the sensitive hollows of my skin.

Homey living room furniture passes in a blur, and I find myself in an unfamiliar room that smells like Gideon. I don't get much of a chance to take it in before Callum tosses me unceremoniously on top of a massive four-poster bed. He follows me down on the plush mattress, sliding his knee between my legs and grinding it against me with delicious friction. Moonlight from the big bay window bathes us in a moody grayscale.

When the door closes with a click and Gideon prowls toward the bed, I moan. He's never looked so feral.

Gideon's molten eyes slide over my body, stopping when he gets to where Callum is laying between my legs. For a minute, I worry he's mad. He's seen us fool around before, but not since all the mate stuff was out in the open. I know he said it was okay, but what if—

"Taste her," Gideon demands.

Callum grins and reaches for my shirt, but he waits to take it off until I nod my consent. Gideon stops at the foot of the bed, leaning against the post and hovering over us both where we lay sprawled together.

"I want to see her come apart on your tongue," Gideon says.

"I can make that happen," Callum assures him.

He slides my pants down, taking my underwear right along with them. My pulse races with excitement. If the fae is right, I might be dying, but at least I'm making the memories of a lifetime on my way out.

Callum parts my legs slowly, unmasked delight on his face as he looks over my naked body. I know he's feeding on my lust, but seeing his hunger and desire for me makes me feel like a goddess. I'm so turned on I can't even think about the fact that I'm spread out naked like a buffet in front of two men.

I don't want to miss a second of this.

I watch with rapt attention as Callum reaches for me. He rubs his thumb from my entrance to my clit, spreading my wetness all around before slipping one, then two fingers inside me, giving me time to adjust to the stretch. With no fumbling or guesswork, he curls them confidently, finding that spot I can never seem to reach on my own.

Callum pumps his fingers in and out at a languid, rhythmic pace, adding his tongue to the mix and bringing me to the breaking point in less than a minute. Before I can hurdle over the edge, he stops. I brace myself on my elbows. I'm preparing to voice my frustration when I see Callum offer his fingers, shiny with my arousal, to Gideon.

"I thought you might want a taste," he says, a devious glint in his eyes. Gideon doesn't hesitate, grabbing his best friend's wrist and bringing both of Callum's fingers into his mouth. He sucks them thoroughly, growling low in his throat as he licks them clean.

When Gideon releases his wrist, Callum turns his frenzied eyes on me.

I'm in for a ride.

He dives down again, sucking and licking enthusiastically, until I'm squirming in his grip, reaching for release. Then he changes up his moves. Again and again this happens. Every time I'm about to come, Callum eases me back from the edge. By the time I realize he's doing it on purpose, I'm desperate and frustrated, my hands fisted in his hair. When I buck my hips to get some relief, he stops completely, looking up at me from where he's laying between my legs.

"Remember, sweetheart, I can feel your lust." Callum kisses my thigh. "I can keep you hanging here all night if I want to." It's a threat if I've ever heard one. My hands clench viciously in his hair. He just chuckles. "If you want to come on my face, you're going to have to be good for us."

"Lay still, baby," Gideon purrs. "We'll give you what you want."

The moment I look up at Gideon's handsome face, Callum slides back into position. At the first swipe of his tongue, I flinch. I'm so sensitive. I don't know if I can handle any more teasing. Callum backs off, bringing me right back to the edge while avoiding any direct, over stimulating contact. When I'm floating once again, Gideon kisses my mouth softly. At the same time, Callum sucks my clit into his mouth. Hard.

I go off like a rocket. Writhing and screaming on the bed, I'm shocked to realize tears are streaming down my face.

I try to sit up. I feel boneless, but I'm eager to touch them.

"Not tonight." Gideon joins us on the bed and gathers me in his arms. He drops three kisses to the sensitive skin behind my ear.

"Are you okay?" Callum asks. He looks like a fallen angel hovering over me in the moonlight. He just conducted my body like an orchestra, but now he's clearly worried he took it too far.

"C'mere," I whisper, pulling him down to lie against my other side. "That was . . ." I kiss his cheek. "Life altering."

I feel him exhale and relax against my rapidly cooling body.

"That wasn't the only life altering event of the night," Gideon grunts. "Some of the stuff Idris said . . ."

"Ah, I get it now." I yawn, fighting sleep. My eyelids feel heavy. "That was my 'I'm sorry about the extinction and death diagnosis' orgasm." Both of their bodies shake with laughter, and I feel safe and warm sandwiched between them.

"That was really dark, Sheena," Callum hums. "I feel like we should probably unpack that."

"Tomorrow. After I return the favor," I say, my eyes drifting shut.

"Deal," he agrees.

I fall asleep to the warm rumble of their voices.

CALLUM

I REVEL IN THE WAY Sheena's body presses against mine, our legs tangling together beneath the sheets. I feel each of her deep, even breaths as she sleeps. Each puff is proof of life.

She's the last of her kind.

Hunted to extinction.

Living on borrowed time.

Despite all the body heat in this bed, a shiver runs through me. The legacy of the djinn is proof the supernatural world can be brutal. We may all look mostly human, but when you mix greed and magic with animal instincts and brutality—well, what happened to the djinn isn't the only horror story lurking in our history.

I won't let her story end in blood . . . How can I save her?

Her hair is spread across my pillow as she lays here, perfectly peaceful despite the magical kill code embedded in her DNA. Sheena has been forced to carve out a life in a world that wants her controlled or eliminated. My ribs constrict as my brain provides an endless supply of horrible what if scenarios.

How can I help her when I can't even make my family love me?

Watching my parents through her eyes tonight was painful. From my mother talking down to the staff to my father's scheming, Sheena took it all in, peeling back the numbness I've sheltered behind for a decade.

Shame clogs my throat, making it hard for me to lay still.

"Deep breaths," Gideon whispers. I turn my head and find him watching me with concern.

"I'm fine," I protest. We both know it's a lie.

"Talk to me," he urges. "It sounds like your heart is trying to escape your chest."

"I'm scared." I look at the woman between us. "What if I can't keep her safe? What if I'm not enough?"

"Enough to protect her or enough to make her happy?"

"I don't know. Is there a difference?"

"Yeah, Callum, there is. Sheena is not your parents. You don't need to be different for her to care about you." His words hit me hard. They aren't enough to heal the wound, but they stop the bleeding for now.

When I sigh, the sound is heavy.

"You know how they're ashamed of me?" I ask. Gideon dips his chin, but I can't look at him anymore, so I focus instead on the shadows the moonlight casts across the ceiling. "Tonight, I was ashamed of them for a change."

There's a beat of silence as he considers that.

"You don't want her to think you're like them," he says. It's not a question, but I nod anyway. Gideon groans. "Only an idiot would think you're anything like them, and our girl is smart." I look back at him then, needing to see the conviction behind what he's saying as well.

"Do you feel better now?" Gideon asks.

I nod without thinking. After a pause, I realize it's actually true. My breathing is steadier, and the pressure in my chest has eased up.

"Good, I'm glad," Gideon says. "But I'm pissed at you now."

"What the fuck for?" I whisper-yell, propping myself up on one elbow to see him more clearly.

"For saying 'I' so godsdamn much. *We* keep her safe. *We* keep her happy. *We* are a team." Gideon's eyes glitter in the darkness. "No matter what anyone's parents say, no matter how many libraries we have to tear apart for answers, and no matter how many fae fuckers lust after our girl."

"I knew he was checking her out," I hiss, lowering my voice when Sheena stirs between us.

"Yeah, he was." Gideon's tone is dark. "We can't kill him either. Even if we could pull it off, it would be too messy."

"Typical. I was over here about to have a panic attack while you were plotting the murder of an ally." I chuckle softly. "Although we could stage an accident. They are doing construction on his wing."

"We don't have time to organize that." Gideon groans, looking up at the ceiling. "We've got to find the silly talisman thing, and I'm a slow reader. Plus, fae anarchy would be a political disaster."

He's right about that. The folk are notoriously tricky. Idris himself says they don't trust anyone, and it's a miracle he keeps them as reined in as he does.

"Do you think he was telling the truth?" Gideon asks.

I consider how Idris crashed dinner and stared at Sheena. *What an asshole.*

"Some of the truth, yes," I admit. "The whole truth, hell no. He's either holding information back or he has some other motive."

"So we're on the same page—trust only each other?"

"Like always," I agree.

Gideon reaches over Sheena, and I grip his hand in mine. The movement triggers an instant replay in my mind of the moment he tasted Sheena on my fingers. *Godsdammit* . . . now is hardly the time to be thinking about that.

"For the record, I'm scared too," Gideon whispers, his voice a deep rumble.

I squeeze his hand a little tighter.

WHEN I WAKE UP, the sun is shining through the window, and I feel better. Gideon's hand is still loosely clasped in mine, resting in the dip above Sheena's hips.

"Are you two holding hands?"

I turn my head and see her green eyes sparkling with mischief.

"Is that a problem?" My question surprises me, but Sheena doesn't miss a beat.

"Not for me." She grins, batting her eyelashes at me. "I think it's super adorable."

"We aren't adorable," Gideon grumbles. "We are sexy, strong, powerful."

Sheena giggles but doesn't agree with him. To get her back, Gideon tightens his hold on my hand and scoots up against her, rubbing his stubble against the sensitive skin of her neck. She shrieks with laughter, wiggling away from him.

"Take it back," Gideon demands, blowing a raspberry against her neck.

"Never." Sheena barely gets the word out as she buries her face in my chest.

Their laughter echoes around the room, and my heart swells. *If I could wake up to this sound for the rest of my life, I'd do anything to make that happen.* I'm so consumed by the thought that I lose my grip on my powers. Not much leaks out, but it's enough to raise the temperature in the room and make both of them pant.

"Fuck, Callum," Gideon groans, eyes flashing to gold.

"Sorry, it just slipped out," I say, unable to focus. The sight of Sheena's pebbled nipple, exposed now because of Gideon's tickling, has me mesmerized.

"Don't be." Sheena's voice is husky.

She shifts deliberately, knocking the sheet to her waist. Like a man in a trance, I reach for the nipple closest to me while Gideon does the same on his side, gently rolling it between his fingers. Sheena's eyes drift closed and her lips part, her breath coming out ragged.

"Do you think we could make you come just like this?" I pinch the tip sharply, loving the way her back arches, bringing her even closer to my hand. "Look at me, Sheena."

"Callum," she moans, then meets my eyes.

"Yes, sweetheart."

"Do you remember when you said you wouldn't use your powers on me unless I asked for it?"

Immediately, I release her nipple and pull back, horrified. "Of course." My voice is stiff. "I'm so sorry. I promise, I didn't mean to."

"No, shit, that's not what I meant." She cradles my jaw in her hand. "I'm asking . . . Right now." A blush appears on her cheeks.

I pray to every god I can think of that she really means what I think she means. Still, I've got to be sure. "Asking for what, exactly?"

Her blush spreads, coloring her pale cheeks and neck a beautiful, kissable pink. She runs her thumb over my bottom lip, and I can sense how much she wants me.

It's addictive.

"Use your magic on me, please, Callum." The green of her eyes morphs to purple. "I want to feel what it's like."

I try not to freak out. I've never done this with anyone before, but I can't deny how much I want to. No matter what, I'm determined to make it good for her.

Returning my now shaking hand to her breast, I use my powers to gradually ratchet up her sensitivity. When I brush my finger over the tip, she shudders.

"If you want me to stop at any point, just tell me," I insist. She moans, nodding her head enthusiastically.

Her pleasure rushes into me, a loop of lust that takes us both apart bit by bit. Gritting my teeth, I feed her more and watch her writhe.

"Close your eyes," I rasp the words, and her eyelids flutter. "I bet you're dripping wet, clenching around nothing, desperate to be filled."

My powers take shape as shadows, a few degrees colder than the air around us. I make them dance across her body, watching her skin pebble in waves as my shadows discover new patches of unexplored skin. When I feel her hovering on the edge, I send the shadows to each nipple and push liquid heat into her hard.

"Come for me, now," I demand.

Her body obeys. Sheena bows under the force of the pleasure, wailing. Gideon swallows her cries with a deep kiss to keep her from waking the entire compound.

I don't give her a chance to come down. She's still riding the aftershocks of the orgasm when my shadows dip into the sensitive hollows behind her knees, brushing slow trails up her soft inner thighs. I stop them an inch away from her pussy and watch her face as she pants.

Gideon yanks the sheet off of all of us so he can see.

In chasing her pleasure, Sheena loses all inhibition. When I dip my shadows inside her, she draws both knees up, spreading herself open as wide as possible. *Gods above and below, she's fucking perfect.* Her trust, her passion . . . I could feed my incubus for years with memories of this moment alone.

Sheena's hips rock into my magic hungrily. Gideon groans as he watches her, licking his lips and clenching his jaw until something in him snaps. When he wraps his big hand around his thick cock, I feel his arousal sizzling against my skin. Overcome by the tsunami of lust I'm riding, I bring another shadow to life, letting it stroke up Gideon's thigh, pausing in an obvious question.

He looks over at me. His golden gaze is liquid with lust, but I don't see any worry or hesitation. He nods, letting his hand fall away from his length, and for once, I don't let myself overthink things. I direct the new shadow to wrap itself around his dick, pumping and vibrating it in time with the shadows inside of Sheena.

"Oh fuck, Callum," Gideon moans my name.

Sheena's molten purple eyes shoot open. As soon as she makes sense of what she's seeing, I feel her gush around my shadows. If any blood was still circulating in my body, it abandons that mission now and rushes to my hard cock instead.

"You like that, Sheena?" I double the pace inside her. "Seeing Gideon at my mercy . . . just like you?"

Sheena whimpers, Gideon hisses, and a rush of power floods my body. Before I know it, I'm trembling right alongside them. I'm used to absorbing lust in trickles here and there, so the deluge I'm feeling right now is overwhelming. I'm on fire with it, hovering on the edge of total ecstasy.

When Sheena slides her hand into my boxer briefs and curls it around me, I know I won't last. But I'm determined not to come before her, so I ratchet my power up another notch and let it grow into a steady crescendo before I slam them both with a sharp surge.

They aren't expecting it and both of them explode. Absorbing the pleasure of their orgasms sends me hurtling over the edge so hard I see spots. It's like nothing I've ever felt before.

For several minutes, the only sound in the room is our combined heavy breathing. Sheena lets her legs fall back flat against the mattress, wincing at the soggy aftermath she encounters on the sheets. Gideon chuckles and kisses her cheek.

"Dude. That was insane," he says, looking at me with a

dimpled grin. He inspects our hands one at a time, and then laughs out loud.

"What's so funny?" I ask, shocked by how hoarse I am.

"It's just—our hands are completely clean, but we're laying in the biggest wet spot of all time." I shake my head, and Sheena turns cherry red, burying her face in my chest.

"Did you like it?" I ask, feeling a surge of worry.

What if it wasn't as good for her as it seemed? She might never want to give up control like that again.

"It was incredible," Sheena says, smiling against my skin. "The only way it could have been better was if you were actually inside of me."

My confidence comes roaring back, and I puff out my chest.

"Oh, I will be, sweetheart," I tell her. "I intend to fuck you every way I can think of for the next century or so. When I run out of ideas, I'll start over and try them all again."

She shivers, a drop of sweat dripping from her temple down to my chest. I nudge her chin up and press a gentle kiss to her lips.

"Sheena, I will have all of you, and you'll have all of me, but the first time won't be while I'm using my powers or with an audience," I reassure her, and she smiles.

"Aw. That was sweet, man, but I don't like being called an audience," Gideon complains. "I may not have been headlining the show, but I was at least part of the band."

Climbing out of the soggy bed, we continue to laugh and joke as we strip the linens off. Sheena is deeply disturbed by the idea of anyone on the staff finding out what we've been up to. Neither Gideon nor I have the heart to tell her they definitely already know. Even if she wasn't incredibly loud, everyone in the place has supernatural hearing. I don't want her to be embarrassed, so I keep my mouth shut and toss the sheets into the hamper.

I follow her and Gideon into his big bathroom. Gideon heads to the walk-in shower, its frosted glass doing little to block our view of his tight ass. Sheena and I take up spots at the counter and begin our own morning routine.

After a few minutes, Sheena pauses while brushing her teeth and makes eye contact with me in the bathroom mirror. "We have to talk about it," she says.

"Talk about what?" Gideon asks.

I laugh at her exasperated look. "With all the shit going on, you could literally mean like seventeen different things." I drag my razor down my jaw, being careful not to knick the skin.

"I mean," Sheena starts, rolling her eyes at me. "Are we staying here or going home?"

I'm so delighted to hear her refer to the cabin as home I can't even get worked up about an extended stay at the compound.

"It's definitely safer here," I admit. "It's practically a fortress."

I finish up the right side of my face and start in on the left. Gideon steps out of the shower, wandering naked around the room in search of a towel.

"I would rather go home too, baby, but honestly, story time with Mallory freaked me out," Gideon says. He towels off his hair, then wraps the cloth around his waist. "I don't want you to end up with your throat cut in some ditch."

"Fuck, dude." I splash my face with water, hurriedly rinsing the shaving cream off so I can check on Sheena. I'm relieved to see she isn't upset by his bluntness.

"Yeah, I would like to avoid wasting away, slaughter, and captivity." Sheena's words are garbled by toothpaste as she ticks through the grisly options on her fingers. Once she's done, she spits into the sink.

The ease at which we're playing house with her should be weird, but it feels completely natural. *I like this.*

"Maybe we play it by ear and see how today goes," I say. Sheena glances at me then, worry in her eyes. I know why she's concerned. "Don't worry about me," I assure her. "I survived living with my parents for sixteen years just fine, and it would be nice to spend some time with Joshua and Sarah."

I don't mention my brother and neither does she, but I can tell she wants to bring him up. If Sheena had her way, we'd be hugging it out in no time. It's unlikely as hell, but who am I to crush her dreams?

"Okay, so what are we going to do today?" She scrapes her hair back into a high ponytail and secures it with a black band.

"I was thinking we could have a supernatural boot camp and teach you some self-defense, since you're new to all of this." I broach the topic carefully, unsure how she'll react.

"That sounds like a great idea." Sheena's face lights up in excitement. She drops into a boxing stance and holds up her fists. "I'm picturing a movie fight montage, except more awesome." She throws a jab, followed by a cross and a hook. I crowd her against the counter, sparring playfully with her.

Sheena and I are still going at it when Gideon's phone goes off. He saunters into the bedroom to get it, and I don't think anything of it until his ferocious growl rattles the door frame. Sheena and I rush in and find Gideon staring at the screen, trembling with rage.

"What's wrong?" I demand.

Instead of answering, Gideon angles the phone to show us both. Through our security app, we watch live as a masked figure ransacks our kitchen. The cheap skull mask is familiar. It looks just like the ones we found on the traffickers at the barn. To the side, I notice Sheena's worn duffle bag. I searched high and low for it in the woods the day after she ran, but couldn't find it anywhere. Now I know why, and I don't like it one bit.

Who the fuck is this, and how did he find our house?

Sheena shudders and covers her mouth with one hand. Gideon shoves the phone into my chest, rushing over to wrap her in his arms. It's only then that I notice she's completely frozen. *That's not good.* She can't shut down—not now, not ever. If she can't overcome this fear response, it could get her killed.

"Do you recognize this guy?" I ask.

I hold the phone where she can see it, ignoring Gideon's glare. The masked fucker looks directly at the camera. His eyes glow yellow. Sheena takes half a step back and blinks a couple of times, then nods slowly, her eyes fixed on the tiny screen.

"I can't be sure. I never saw his face, but I think he's the guy who took me," she says, her eyes wide and glassy. "Over the years, his guys have come close to catching me again. I don't understand how they keep finding me. Gideon, that's my bag. He must have been in the woods that night—"

"He can't get to you here, baby." Gideon tightens his arms around her, and she nods woodenly.

I harden my heart and focus on what needs to be done. The time for playing things by ear has passed.

IDRIS

I NEED TO DECIDE which side I'm on. Her existence alters the status quo. Sitting at my desk, I drum my fingers on the polished cedar as I consider my options. The little djinn seems moderately stable for now, but without a talisman, she could deteriorate at any moment.

Something heavy hits the floor above me. The whine of drilling starts up again, snagging the threads of my thoughts into a hopelessly mangled snarl.

Insufferable construction.

It can't be helped, I suppose. The alternative is to live indefinitely in this lifeless, stone mausoleum. But the volume of these improvements is grating in the extreme.

Studying the thick walls, I feel them closing in around me. *Would it be too much to ask for a window or two?* If the djinn harnesses her powers, she could bring light to this wing with a snap of her delicate fingers.

I close my eyes and imagine the large glass panels I would wish for.

The eastern windows would overlook a lush, garden paradise to watch the sun rise each morning. A riot of wildflowers grows nearby, guarded by honeybees and worshiped by exotic, dancing butterflies. Mother nature's divine magic nurtures her children's growth, blanketing my oasis in a thick carpet of grass. The sunshine is warm. The breeze is cool. The babbling brook sings a melodic song as I lay the djinn down on its banks and make love to her until the sun sets.

My eyes snap open and the vivid images fade to mist.

These thoughts are dangerous. My attraction—useless. I have displaced fae to lead and protect in this realm. They choose each day to follow me and pursue a future as a diaspora, instead of fighting over the bloody remnants of our homeland. I owe the folk my fealty, not some diminutive djinn.

If I can use her in my plans, that's fine, marvelous even. If not, well, the best course of action may be to eliminate her entirely. My conscience stirs from its long hibernation, disgusted by the idea. But I bury it. Much like I did the full extent of my knowledge of her kind last night.

Human lore—while fascinating—rarely portrays supernaturals accurately, and in many ways, djinn are just like any other enhanced species. Far from omnipotent, they have strengths and weaknesses just like the rest of us. According to legend, some djinn could birth civilizations, but many were limited to only granting wishes amounting to mere parlor tricks.

Until I know which category she falls into, it's too soon to play my hand. All I know for certain is that I cannot allow myself to become another of the besotted fools following in her wake.

A blood-curdling scream echoes through the thick walls of this fortress.

I jump to my feet, sprinting toward the courtyard where the wailing and shouting increases in volume the closer I get. *Are we under attack?*

When I skid to a stop by the space used for training and sparring, I'm confused by what I see. The djinn is clinging to the big shifter, weeping without restraint as she holds her hands over his throat. She's not choking him. Rather, it looks as if she's trying to staunch the flow of blood.

It's an action I've seen a thousand times during battle triage. But there doesn't seem to be anything wrong with Joshua's heir, besides his inability to comfort a distressed female. The buffoon grows increasingly frantic as he tries and fails to soothe her. As for the djinn, she seems to be trapped in a waking . . . nightmare.

"Ciprian, turn it off. Right fucking now." The shifter roars at the mouthy, blonde demon. "Her heart rate is way too high."

"Shit, I'm sorry." The nightmare is almost as devoid of color as the djinn. "Callum said to show her some stuff so she could practice mental walls. I just went with it. I didn't realize she'd take it so hard."

He stops the illusion, but the djinn continues to search for an imaginary wound.

"Blood. There was so much blood," she hiccups. "Gideon, your throat—it was torn out. I couldn't hold the blood in." She pats at the shifter's unblemished neck in confusion.

"I'm fine, baby," he tells her, his voice surprisingly gentle. "It was just an illusion. Ciprian was trying to see if you could force him out of your mind."

"You're okay?" She asks, the cloud of fear fading from her eyes.

"Yes, I'm healthy as a horse. I can turn into one and you can ride me around if you want more proof." He presses a kiss to her forehead, and she cracks a small smile, combing her fingers through his hair in a gesture so tender it makes even my heart ache.

"Weird kink, but okay, man."

I wince as the nightmare demon chooses that moment to open his mouth. The little djinn doesn't take it well either, her head snapping in his direction like a whip. She leaves the shifter sitting on the ground, stomping over to the blonde. He raises his hands to ward her off.

"Sheena, I'm really sorry. I took it too far," he admits, but she's not listening.

Her eyes are a luminescent purple as she glares at him, and

I'm not sure who is more stunned when she hauls back and slaps him in the face.

"You ripped out his throat," she screams. Her hands are shaking and several strands of her long dark hair begin to float. "You made me stand by and watch my mate bleed out with no warning. For what, Ciprian?"

Her mate? Surely she's talking about the silly human concept of soul mates and not referencing the matchmaking machinations of the gods.

"I thought you weren't telling people about the mate thing yet," the demon whispers. He glances around nervously at the audience that formed after hearing the yelling.

Rightly so. It's incredibly foolish to speak so openly about information that could be used against you.

The djinn's hair falls back down around her shoulders. Her bottom lip trembles as she realizes they are no longer alone. She looks back at the shifter.

"It's okay. I don't care if everyone knows," he reassures her. It's a gallant but foolish thing to do in the face of a bombshell of this magnitude. "Everyone, go away," he snaps at the bystanders. "There's nothing to see here."

His demanding tone is enough to scare people off. Instead of following suit, I cast a glamour that shows me walking away with the rest of the crowd, and then I turn myself as close to invisible as I can get. I bide my time, eager to see how this plays out.

"I'm really and truly sorry, Sheena. Callum said to check your mental barriers." The nightmare demon rushes to explain. His pale cheek burns red from her slap. "I should have talked with you first, but I was hung over. I just went with the first thing I thought of."

"Callum told you to do this to me?" Her face falls.

"I'm sure he didn't mean for Ciprian to show you . . . that." The shifter puts his hand on her shoulder. He's quick to back up his friend, but the djinn isn't having it.

"Don't protect him from this," she snaps and turns back to the demon. "What *exactly* did he say to you, Ciprian?"

The troublemaker looks uncharacteristically miserable—torn, no doubt, between throwing his brother to the wolves and covering for him.

"I'm really not sure I remember. I hadn't finished my coffee yet."

He avoids eye contact, and the djinn taps her foot impatiently.

"It was something like 'we're working on Sheena's self-defense skills. Make yourself useful and show her something to block.'" He takes a step toward her, arms outstretched. "Bestie, I apologize. It was a misunderstanding, a mistake."

"You know, I'm new to the whole adult friend thing," she says, considering him. "But whenever I imagined my future best friend, they were someone who'd watch my back, not attack my mind."

The blonde's face crumbles, but he doesn't argue. When the shifter reaches for the djinn again, she takes a step back.

"Look, I just need a minute. This kind of thing may be normal to you two, but I just watched you die." Her voice cracks. "I know this world is brutal and maybe I'm naive and useless, but surely there are better ways to teach me than whatever that was."

She takes one last look at the training ground then strides off, her spine rigid.

"I'm such a fuck up." The demon moans, his shoulders slumping as she leaves. "Everyone else already thought so. Now she does too."

"It's not just you she's upset with. And she's got a point," the shifter says, scraping a hand over his face. "If you'd shown me that, I would have been freaked out at first, but I would've known pretty quickly it wasn't real. Did she even know you could do that?"

The demon thinks for a moment, then shakes his head with a grimace. "I guess I never mentioned it. I just kind of assumed she knew."

"Ciprian, I heard your conversation this morning. Callum told you to scare her and see what happened. You could have blamed it on him when she asked."

"Yeah, sure, so you could tell him I'm a snitch the first chance you get? I already fucked up one relationship beyond repair today. I didn't want to make it two instead," he spits the words, then storms off.

I watch the shifter curse and kick a rock across the courtyard. It pings off something metal in the distance.

"I know you're there," he says, flaring his nostrils. "I can smell you, fae."

Damnation. I hadn't considered that.

I remove my glamour and shrug. "You can hardly blame me for my curiosity," I murmur. "And you must admit the training grounds are an odd place to hold an expectation of privacy."

My words earn a glare in response, but he hasn't tried to take my head off yet, which is mildly surprising given his reputation.

"I assume you've got some opinions," he says.

I raise my brow. While I have many thoughts about what I just witnessed, I'm shocked he's asking what they are. *This opening is too tempting to resist.*

"Are you asking for my advice?"

"Get fucked," he growls. "I don't know why I even bothered—"

"You're all actually correct," I say, before I can think better of it.

"We can't all be right. What kind of candy-ass, fairy bullshit is that?" He takes a menacing step toward me, but I refuse to be cowed by his brutish intimidation tactics.

"I'm not avoiding your question. I'm saying you're all correct. The djinn will need to toughen up if she has any hope of survival. As for the rest of you—you cannot simply treat her like you would each other. She's missing a lifetime of background information. You're going to have to communicate."

"My specialty," he groans, staring at the sky. I wonder which god he's bringing his case to, or if he even bothers with the old ways.

"I would think a fated mate bond would make it easier." I prod for details.

"Keep your mouth shut about that," he snarls.

I nod. The look on his face is genuinely terrifying. I've pushed my luck far enough for today. I have no need to share the information right now anyway. Part of me is even rooting for them.

"The road ahead will be fraught," I warn him. "If you want to keep her, you can never forget that."

"Thanks for the advice," he says, lowering his voice. "I'll give you some as well: Sheena is taken. Remember that."

His eyes flair golden, but he doesn't attack. I smile at the familiarity of male posturing. It's the same no matter what realm you're in. Instead of responding to his threat, I dip my chin and return to my wing.

Gideon can have the last word for now.

CHAPTER
EIGHTEEN

SHEENA

Blood gushing from Gideon's throat. His eyes glassy with pain. Knowing there was nothing I could do to save him. I blink, trying to clear the gruesome images from my head. It's no use. Every few seconds, I see Gideon bleeding out in front of me again.

Did Callum intend for Ciprian to do that? And if so, why?

Callum was quiet after the break-in this morning. He told us to get started on training without him while he talked over security options with the tech team. I didn't think much of it at the time, and I wanted a distraction from the masked man, but maybe I should have asked more questions.

Pushing my way through the door to the Therion home, I catch my hip on the console table in my hurry to be alone. Keys and coins go flying. The sharp pain rattles the tenuous grip I have on my tears. Another ragged sob breaks free as I stare at the mess.

"Sweetie, what's wrong?" Sarah comes around the corner, concern etched in each of the fine lines on her face. I've barely known her a day, but I rush into her arms like I have a right. She smells like cookies and comfort, exactly how I always imagine a mom should, and my emotional dam suffers a critical failure.

Absently, I hear the sound of my frantic breaths interrupted by hiccuping sobs as Sarah leads me into her cozy living room. She guides me down to the couch and drags a soft blanket onto my lap. I tuck it around my legs, remembering how Gideon did the same thing for me when I told him and Callum about my abduction. He must have learned it from his mom.

That makes me cry harder.

While I'm completely melting down, Sarah grips my hands between her own and waits patiently, giving me a chance to get myself under control without demanding answers. It takes a few minutes before I'm able to quiet my sobs, and then the entire story pours out of me. By the time I finish, Sarah is shaking her head in disbelief.

"Those stupid boys," she mutters. "I love them to death, but they can be completely clueless sometimes." She pats my hand and rises from the couch. "Hang on, honey. We need wine to work through all this."

Even though it's still early, Sarah comes back carrying a comically oversized bottle of chardonnay and two of the largest wine glasses I've ever seen. She pours us both a generous amount and curls up on the couch next to me. My ladylike sip quickly becomes a gulp once I realize how good the chilled wine feels after my crying jag.

"You're not just upset about the illusion," Sarah says, and I shake my head vigorously.

"It feels like they planned it together as some kind of prank on the girl that doesn't understand this world." I wipe another dumb tear off my cheek in frustration. "I'm trying so hard to keep up. When Callum suggested the supernatural boot camp this morning, I got excited. I wanted to prove I could belong. Instead, I completely broke down."

I take a deep, steadying breath to keep the tears at bay. I'm tired of crying.

"Sarah, it was so real. I swear I could feel his blood slipping through my fingers as I tried to hold his neck closed."

She shudders at my description, and I remember too late that I'm describing the fake death of her real child.

"Oh, I believe you, Sheena. Ciprian has always been a very strong nightmare demon. Even as a young boy—before he manifested—we saw flashes." She shakes her head as she reminisces. "One second I would be feeding peas to a toddler." She snaps her fingers. "Then a little dragon with needle-sharp teeth and scales made of bowtie pasta would be sitting in my lap."

Sarah chuckles at the memory. I can't help but smile as I picture it.

"He could never get it quite right, but even then, his illusions were believable. Of course, Gideon and Callum egged him on," she says as she refills my wine glass. "Ciprian wanted to impress them so badly."

"They were close as kids?"

"Inseparable." She frowns. "Things didn't change until their teens."

"When Callum manifested as an incubus?"

"Yes." Sarah sighs. "It was a tremendous blow for Callum. I think it came as a shock for Mallory and Dimitri as well. They didn't handle it well." She sips her wine in thought. "Ciprian was fourteen at the time. Overnight, all the pressure fell on him to carry on the nightmare legacy."

"He didn't want it," I suggest.

"He never wanted that kind of responsibility," Sarah says, shaking her head. "So he started acting out. Meanwhile, Callum buckled down to prove to them they were wrong about incubi. I think he wanted to show them that nothing had changed, that he was still a worthy son."

"But it didn't matter how good Callum was or how bad Ciprian acted because of their magic," I say, filling in the gaps. My chest burns over the way both brothers were treated.

Sarah hums in agreement and leans back, swirling the wine in her glass. "The boys fell out with each other because Callum felt like his brother threw away everything Callum had worked for but could no longer have." She takes a sip. "And Ciprian resents Callum for leaving him behind."

It makes complete sense, but I hate it.

"They both deserved better," I hiss, surprised to see Sarah nod in agreement.

"You're right, of course, but you have to understand, Sheena. Demons have a different way of raising their offspring," she explains. "I'm not saying it's right, but lineage, legacy, honor— those things are everything to them. I truly believe Dimitri and Mallory love both boys fiercely in their own way."

"I'm glad they had you," I tell her sincerely. "When I dreamed of having a mom, I pictured someone just like you."

I duck my head at my admission, but Sarah doesn't give me a chance to feel embarrassed. She envelops me in a warm hug as natural as breathing. When we finally pull back, both of us are laughing and weepy.

"There's plenty of me to go around," she says. "I'm just happy to have my babies back in the nest, no matter how badly they're behaving." She pats my back and offers me a watery smile. "Now, what's this rubbish about you not belonging in this world?"

I don't answer immediately, taking time to fully consider her question in a way I haven't allowed myself to do before.

"I just feel so behind, so off-balance all the time," I admit. "Today, it didn't even cross my mind that it could have been an illusion. If I don't even know the rules, how can I possibly keep up?" I drain my wine, and she fills my glass back up. "Like, I know I just found out I'm a djinn, but I'm not even sure I know how to spell that." I laugh a little manically, and Sarah takes my empty hand in hers.

"The truth is, I'm a liability for them both."

"That's bullshit." A deep voice interrupts me. Sarah and I turn to see Callum hovering at the edge of the room. "Sarah, can I have a moment alone with Sheena?"

If I weren't completely obsessed with her already, Gideon's mom turning to me for her cue on how to answer would have been what did it. She would toss him out if I asked her to. But I don't; I square my shoulders and give her a nod instead. This is a conversation I need to have. Sarah gives my hand a comforting squeeze before she stands and leaves the room.

Callum doesn't come any closer. He stays half hidden in the shadows, so I can't make out his expression. After everything that's happened, the distance between us stings. Still, I do nothing to erase it. While I'm feeling a lot of empathy for him after my talk with Sarah, none of the reasons I'm upset have magically gone away.

"I heard what happened," Callum says, finally breaking the silence.

"Is there anyone in this compound who hasn't?" I snort, frustrated by the rush of shame I feel.

"I fucked up, Sheena." He runs his fingers through his hair, tugging lightly at the ends.

"Yes, you did." I don't give an inch. I need him to understand how badly this hurt. "Can you tell me why?"

"Honestly, I don't even know."

"That's not good enough, Callum." My voice wobbles, and he shifts his weight but doesn't come any closer. I wait him out.

"I don't know," he groans. "I had maybe ten reasons, but all of them seem stupid now."

"Share some of them with me, then."

"To toughen you up—you know, prepare you for what we could be up against." He starts pacing, carving a short path back and forth in the small space of the entryway. Fury boils in my gut, but I keep my mouth shut as he explains his warped reasoning. "You fell asleep immediately last night. After you got off, you were out like a light."

I blush at the reminder. *What does that have to do with anything?*

Callum stops in a patch of light, staring at me like he can will me to understand.

"I could still taste you, sweet and perfect on my tongue, and feel you pressed against me. One minute I was watching you sleep, the next I was drowning in fear." He resumes his pacing, like a man possessed. "Sheena, I saw your death a hundred different ways. Each time, I couldn't stop it, wasn't enough to protect you. Then we woke up, but it was all like a dream. You were everything, and I couldn't get enough of you, of us. In the bathroom . . ."

He stares at me like it's all so clear.

"What about the bathroom, Callum?" I snap. "I brushed my teeth. You shaved. So what? You're not making any sense."

"We were talking, and you were happy, excited to train. You were shadowboxing in front of the mirror. It was cute, but then that fucking asshole broke into our home. He went through our shit and you froze. This whole situation—it's not a joke."

Oh, I know he did not just say that to me. My confusion fades, and the boiling rage inside me erupts, raining red-hot lava down on us both.

"Wait." I hold my hand up palm first. "You set this all in motion because you think I'm not taking this seriously? That I'm some kind of *idiot*?"

"No, no, of course not," he says, pausing in his pacing. "I don't know. I told myself it was a good starting lesson—something to put everything into perspective for you. Like supernatural shock exposure or something."

Callum waves his hands like that's going to make his motivations any less ridiculous.

"Oh, because getting yanked out of my bed on my birthday and being tossed in a cage too small to stand up in wasn't enough?" I reach for my wine, my hands trembling with anger. "My actual trauma didn't qualify as a good enough lesson, so you decided to manufacture some more to make sure everything sank in for me? Got it."

"Shit. *Fuck.* No. I don't mean—" He freezes, tugging viciously at his hair. "I just told Ciprian to rattle you a bit. It felt like a good idea at the time."

"Let me tell you something about fear, Callum." I lower my voice. "It's an addiction. If you give it room to grow, it will choke out every other emotion. I've lived a life where the only thing I felt for months at a time was fear. I became a flinching, terrified woman, ready to run at a moment's notice. My fear was always justified, but I let it become my only reason to go on."

A tear rolls down my cheek. I let it fall. I've got to get this out while I still can. I need to make him understand.

"That might have kept me alive for a long time, but something I've learned from Gideon—from you—is that a life of fear isn't worth living. *You* taught me that fighting back was worth it. *You* gave me something worth fighting for." I stand up from the couch, kicking the blanket off my lap. "Today, during that vision, Ciprian didn't just scare me, Callum, he took away one of my reasons to fight."

Callum takes a step closer to me then, shaking his head in agitation as he moves fully into the light.

"I want you to fight for yourself. You told Sarah you were our liability. But, fuck, Sheena—don't you see? We are yours. By hunting those traffickers, we put a target on your back."

"You're giving yourself way too much credit here. I was a target long before I met either of you." I jab my index finger into my own chest. "I'm some freak of nature with no control over my magic, no measurable fighting skills, and no knowledge of this world. I'm learning to live with the fact that I'm putting you both at risk just by existing."

"We don't care about that," he insists.

"That's easy for you to say." I roll my eyes. "You aren't the weak link."

"I'm serious, sweetheart. All those things you think are weaknesses are fixable with training."

He comes around the couch and reaches for me. I brace one

hand against his chest and hold him at arm's length. "Then teach me. But maybe clue me in on the goddamn lesson plan next time."

"Okay. I promise," Callum says.

He moves back into my space and takes my hand. I let him this time. It feels good to be close after that fight. Callum studies my hand for a moment, then his lips curl up at the corners.

"Why are you smiling at me like that?" I demand. Now that I understand his motivations, I'm less hurt, but I'm also not quite ready to let him off the hook.

"You really smacked my brother?" Callum grins fully, the expression sliding into devious territory.

Oh shit. I did slap Ciprian. I wince. In hindsight, maybe he didn't deserve everything I hurled at him.

"I did," I admit. "And if you'd been there, I probably would have slapped you too."

Callum chuckles, then lifts my chin and kisses me. It's a slow meeting of our lips, soft and sweet like an apology in physical form. When he pulls back, his face is pensive, the olive skin of his forehead furrowed in deep grooves.

"Seeing Gideon die . . . They say it made you fall apart."

"Like a woman in a soap opera," I whisper, shuddering as I remember the images. At the time, I felt like my heart was being torn from my chest. "I think people in the next town over heard me wailing."

Callum kisses me again, wrapping his arms around me until all I can feel is his body against mine.

"Would you cry like that for me?"

Tucked into his chest, I feel the vulnerability in his question and know I can't make light of it. Not this time. Even though he hurt me earlier, I summon up my courage to give him the truth.

"I'd fall down, and I don't know if I'd ever get back up again." My voice cracks, and his arms tighten around me. Callum may not have been kept in a physical cage like I was, but at his core, there's still a little boy who needs to hear he's enough.

"I'm sorry," he groans.

It's the first time since the start of this conversation he's said those words to me outright, but the apology feels genuine.

"I forgive you," I say. "Next time you're scared, though, tell me. We'll fight our fears together, yeah?"

He nods, burying his face in my neck. As we cling to each other, I don't think of my past or our future.

This moment is enough.

CALLUM

I'M A FUCKING IDIOT. Projecting my personal insecurities onto Sheena, I'm lucky she's even giving me a chance to make it right. Holding her tight, I sink into her warmth, letting her thaw some of the chill I've been feeling since hearing about what happened during training.

After I manifested as an incubus, I gave up on finding a long-term partner. As a kid with my world crashing down around me, being single didn't seem like a big deal. Now, a decade later, I barely stomach the one-night stands.

Most people in our community believe incubi need promiscuity to survive, but that assumption has become a self-fulfilling prophecy of sorts. We don't need variety, but being treated like an item on a sexual bucket list is enough to turn anyone into a relationship cynic.

I nuzzle Sheena's neck, pressing my lips against the soft, sensitive skin there. Moving her hair back to give myself more room, I leave small kisses and licks along her neck, loving the way her breathing picks up as I explore. When I graze my teeth over her earlobe, the energy shifts from cautious and sweet in the wake of our fight and make-up to something more sensual. When I pull back, the look on Sheena's face is so possessive I nearly drop to my knees.

"I want you," she says.

"I'm yours." I press a hungry kiss to her lips.

"Prove it."

Her taunt lands. I shoot her a dark grin, scooping her up and carrying her to Gideon's room where all our stuff ended up last night. Hopefully, my best friend won't mind me burying myself inside our girl on his bed because I can't wait a moment longer.

I kick the door closed, press Sheena against the wall, and step back to look at her. She leans back, heat simmering in her eyes. Power radiates off her in waves. She's so beautiful I can barely stand it.

I erase the space between us and nudge her legs apart, not stopping until the denim stretches tight along her hips and thighs. She lets me move her like a doll, but the challenge in her eyes is anything but submissive. Sheena isn't backing down; she's daring me to please her.

I trace a finger along the inner seam of her jeans and watch her eyelids flutter.

"It's the middle of the day," I whisper. "You'll have to be quiet or everyone will know what we're up to." I plant the idea that someone could catch us in her head. When her pupils dilate, I can tell some primal part of her likes the risk.

Using two fingers, I toy with the button of her jeans, but I don't open them. She cants her hips toward me, making her desires clear without saying a word. I pull my hand back.

"So demanding," I scold, watching her eyes spark with indignation. *How far I can push her?*

"Such a tease," she grumbles, a hint of a whine in her voice as she rests her head against the wall. "Maybe I should take matters into my own hands."

Her fingers drift towards the clasp of her jeans, but I stop them before they can reach their destination. Pinning both her wrists above her head with my left hand, I bring my right down to cup her pussy. She grinds down shamelessly.

My dick is hard as a rock, but I don't want to rush. I want her to remember the first time I fuck her for the rest of our lives.

I manifest a shadow to ease open the button on her jeans and draw her zipper down painfully slowly. It releases, tooth by tooth, until her pale blue panties peek out. I caress the skin below her belly button with my fingertips, watching her tremble at my touch.

"I'm going to wreck you," I promise her, my voice raspy.

Pressing a hard kiss to her mouth, I kick her legs back together and yank her jeans and panties down in two rough movements. Before she can recover her balance, I grab her by the hips and toss her face down on the bed. Displayed like this, she's almost entirely at my mercy, and I can feel the way her vulnerability feeds her lust. Cradling her hip in my hand, I make a few adjustments, pulling her back gently onto her knees with her cheek pressed into the mattress.

"You don't move until I tell you to."

I spread her pussy with my thumbs and admire how wet she is for me. I sink one finger inside her with no warning, loving the sound of her moan. Kneeling with her legs together, face down on the bed—it's a tight fit even for my fingers.

"I'm going to make you come until you forget how to do anything else. I won't tease. You won't have to beg. I'm going to give you as much pleasure as you can take." I pull my finger out and spread the wetness around her clit, rubbing her in firm, insistent circles with my thumb. "Then, tonight, when you're sitting at the dinner table surrounded by boring conversation, you'll only be able to think about how thoroughly I made up for my mistake."

She moans, pushing her hips back enthusiastically against my hand.

I keep stroking her, closing my eyes to better feel her reactions. She likes this pace, so I slip another finger inside of her, curling them until I find that special spot. I tap gently on the textured area. When she starts to buck away from the intensity of the sensation, I give her a break.

As soon as I feel her completely relax, I go back to that spot with a vengeance while dragging my thumb in lazy circles on her clit. When the first waves of her orgasm crest, energy rushes into me. Sheena turns her face into the covers to mask her scream. I stop putting pressure on her clit as soon as she becomes oversensitive, but I increase the force of my fingers thrusting inside her until she squirts all over my hand.

Giving her pleasure is the most addictive thing I've ever done.

I pepper her ass and back with kisses, unable to stop touching her. As her breathing returns to normal, Sheena turns her head to look at me, almost drunk with passion, and I can't resist sinking two fingers back inside her. She clenches around me like her body is trying to hold me there.

I fucking love it.

Starting all over again, I relentlessly push her higher, watching as longing, trust, and ecstasy flicker across her face. When she comes this time, she doesn't hide her face from me, and her mouth opens on a silent scream.

It's the most intimate thing I've ever been a part of.

When she reaches back for me, I take her trembling hand in mine. "I've got you, sweetheart," I say, interlacing our fingers.

I roll her gently onto her back, ditching my clothes and following her down. Her skin is silk beneath my fingers, her lips softer still as I steal kiss after kiss from her mouth. I don't tease or hesitate. Looking deep into her eyes, I line myself up and slip inside her.

The feeling is indescribable.

Even with how wet and relaxed she is after two orgasms, it's still a tight fit. I rock in and out with shallow strokes, burying more of my cock inside her bit by bit until I bottom out. I kiss her desperately, then rest my forehead against hers. This feeling . . . It's better than the first sip of water on a hot day. Better than anything I've ever dared wish for.

Sheena's eyes are glassy with unshed tears. For the first time in my life, I'm thankful for my magic, which tells me she's experiencing the same raw intensity I am. *I'm not alone; she's right here with me. This is so much more than physical.* I kiss her cheeks, her eyelids, her nose.

I brace myself on my elbows so I can give myself a deeper range of motion and kiss her at the same time. After the first few thrusts, Sheena wraps her legs around my hips, bracing her heels on my ass and using the leverage to create her own friction. The urge to pump myself into her at top speed is hard to ignore, but I'm determined to focus on her pleasure.

When she comes this time, I can feel her contracting on my cock. It's fucking exquisite, and I have to grit my teeth to hold my orgasm back.

Even though I'm inside her, staring into her eyes with her legs wrapped around me like a vise, I'm still not close enough. I want more. I sit up, pulling her with me so I never have to leave the warmth of her body. With her straddling my lap, I thrust up into her and watch the way her breasts bounce with the force.

Sheena murmurs my name, and I kiss her hungrily. When she scrapes her nails against my scalp, I pull one rosy nipple into my mouth. We trade caresses, touches, and nibbles until I feel another orgasm building inside her. This time, I know I won't be able to hold off, so I slip my hand down between our bodies and rub her clit.

"Just give me one more, sweetheart," I beg.

When she shatters in my arms, I let go, feeling my face warp as my climax roars through me. Every one of my nerve endings ignites then sputters out at the same time. It feels like an electric shock completely rewiring my entire nervous system.

I've never come so hard in my life. This one sexual experience gave me enough juice to last a month. Despite that fact, I can't wait for a repeat. I kiss her tenderly.

I'll never get enough of her.

We both tumble down on top of the sheets in a sweaty, exhausted pile of arms and legs. The purple in her eyes fades back to green, and my heart pumps unsteadily. I think I love her, but I hold myself back from saying it. I don't know whether it's timing or self-preservation, but the last thing I want is for her to feel obligated to say it back now and regret it later.

So I say everything but those three little words.

I tell Sheena how perfect she is and how amazing her body feels, punctuating each compliment with a kiss. She smiles, cuddling sleepily into my arms and resting her head on my chest. I'm surprised when she drifts off without a word. I pull the sheets over us and settle back into the pillows. Nothing could drag me out of this bed right now.

GIDEON

WHEN I GO to my bedroom to check on Sheena and Callum before dinner, I'm not sure what to expect. Maybe a defensive Callum or an emotional Sheena.

What I find is something else entirely.

The pair of them are sprawled naked on the bed, partially covered by a sheet. Callum's body is closest to the door, curled around her like a suit of armor. He's partially on top of her, his olive skin tone contrasting with her paler complexion. Sharing a pillow, strands of their dark hair are caught up together so it's hard to tell where hers ends and his begins.

Gods, they're pretty together.

I want to crawl into that bed and lose track of time, but if I do that, we'll miss dinner, and I don't want Sheena skipping meals. I remember the fae's warning and feel a sharp ache in my heart. *I can't lose her.*

Sheena must sense my worry because her eyes flicker open slowly, an expression of sleepy contentment on her face. One of her hands is buried in Callum's hair. She reaches out to me with the other, and I interlock my fingers with hers, dropping to the bed and cuddling her close. *A few more minutes can't hurt.*

"Are you feeling better, baby?" I ask, keeping my voice low.

"Mm-hmm. I had a good talk with your mom and then with Callum." She strokes a strand of his hair gently away from his face, her voice raspy from sleep. "Gideon, I'm so glad you're okay. That you're here with me."

I bend my neck, lowering my head to press a kiss against her lips.

"I'm right where I want to be, next to you," I whisper. "The nudity is just a bonus."

She giggles quietly but doesn't bother to cover herself. Since I'm propped against the headboard and looking down, I notice when Callum wakes up. His eyes blink open, but once he sees where his face is, he closes them again and pretends to be asleep.

Callum nuzzles her breast with his nose, and I stifle a laugh, not wanting to give away his game. Sheena looks down at him with a smile in her eyes and runs her fingers through his hair. When he eases the leg thrown around her hips between her thighs and grinds it against her deliberately, she laughs, pulling roughly on his hair to lift his head.

"I knew you weren't asleep."

Cal's eyes snap open and he grins at her, the joy on his face something I haven't seen much since we were kids. Peace sinks into me as they bicker playfully.

"Stop moving your leg." Sheena laughs. "I cannot possibly go again or I won't be walking to the dining room."

"Oh shit—about dinner," I say, pausing to check the time on my phone. They both turn to look at me.

"What about it?" Cal asks.

His voice is gravelly, and I'm shocked when my body responds to the husky sound. We're definitely going to be late, but I can't bring myself to care all that much. I love the way it feels to have both of them focusing their attention on me.

"It's about to start," I admit. "I was supposed to come get you both."

"Oh my god." Sheena gasps and jumps up in a panic. "So you just climbed right in and didn't say anything?"

I shrug and dodge a flying elbow, but Callum isn't so lucky. He takes a knee to the gut as she scrambles out of bed. Groaning dramatically, he closes his eyes and curls into a tight ball.

"Honestly, it smells better in here," I tease, inhaling deeply. Sheena lets out a scandalized gasp, and Callum chuckles and bumps his knuckles against mine. It's so fun and easy to rile her up. I could do it every day and never get tired of it.

"We can't miss dinner. What will your family think?"

She's getting really worked up now, tossing Cal's clothes at him as she searches for her own.

"People are late all the time, Sheena. That doesn't make them rude," he reasons.

"It does if they were late because they were . . . because they were . . ." Sheena's cheeks turn bright red as she struggles to find the words.

Callum perks up, a hungry look on his face.

"Because they were what, sweetheart?" He purrs at her like a cat chasing a mouse, and her blush spreads down her neck.

"You know what." She pulls on her panties, refusing to look at either of us.

"I do." Callum's groan is filthy. "But I so badly want to hear you say it."

He bites his bottom lip as Sheena shimmies into her jeans then stamps her foot. She glares at both of us while standing topless at the end of the bed.

"Fucking," she snaps. "I don't want your parents to think I'm the kind of person who blows off dinner and ignores their hospitality to get railed. Get up, please, before I'm too embarrassed to ever face them again." With that, she storms into the bathroom and slams the door. Callum watches her go, naked hunger stamped on his face.

"You better get dressed, dude, or you're going to be back in the doghouse again right after you got out." I adjust myself, then scoot out of the bed with a laugh.

"You're right," he agrees. "But making up for my mistakes is so much fun. It might be worth it."

After one last look at the bathroom door, he finally gets up and dresses himself.

"We're going through a lot of sheets," Callum says with a smirk.

I smile at the wrecked bed, clapping him on the back as he studies his handiwork. "Let's just buy more."

Sheena's cheeks are still flushed as we walk to dinner. Neither one of my parents comment on our lack of punctuality, but the knowing look and wink my mom gives Callum is enough to make even an incubus blush.

CHAPTER
NINETEEN

QUAID

They call it an alliance, a necessary evil. I call it verbal gymnastics. Last time I checked, our vows weren't designed to bend. Our rules are black and white—the Synod of Hunters taught me that. There shouldn't be any room for this grayscale hellscape they've dragged us into. But there's nothing I can do about it.

I have my orders, which is why I'm crawling around on pine needles like a goddamn snake, itching like a motherfucker, and desperate to escape the humidity and hypocrisy. It's just past five in the morning, and I can already feel the sweat dripping down my lower back from the muggy Missouri heat. I scratch at one of the bug bites on my neck and feel the scab give way. Blood dribbles out.

Wonderful. I might as well set off an air horn.

All around me, members of my team lay in similar positions, silently waiting, and likely itching too. We're a dozen across and three deep. That's thirty-six hunters strong, which is the biggest team I've ever been a part of.

Given how our numbers dwindle more each day, it's a colossal risk to commit so many to one mission, especially based on intel provided by the enemy. It makes me uneasy. I breathe a sigh of relief when dawn comes and the sun bathes the ground in fang-proof light.

We rise together, creeping out of the woods and across a field covered in coarse, chest-high grass. The brittle blades scrape my exposed skin. They've grown out of control, ungoverned by grazing animals and nature's checks and balances. It's another sign—if you know what to look for—that this territory has been claimed by something unnatural.

Surrounding the large, ranch-style house, we leave no exit or entrance unguarded. They have nowhere to run with the sun on our side. Once the light of dawn infiltrates every nook and cranny, it's time.

In sync, we charge from our hiding places, ripping off shutters, bashing in doors, and shattering the windows. After an hour of complete silence, broken only by the occasional trill of a bird or hum of a mosquito, the sudden noise is deafening.

Then terrified screams join the mix. The sound makes my skin crawl. I do my best to tune everything out, gritting my teeth and focusing on my orders: breach this house and kill everyone inside . . . permanently.

I climb through the nearest window, dodging shards of glass as I infiltrate what appears to be a simple living room. There are scattered books and a couple of worn looking couches.

An older female cowers in the corner away from the light. She looks like a normal human woman, her graying hair piled in a messy bun on top of her head. Her eyes widen with terror as they meet mine. Just as she's about to speak, the window next to her implodes. The sunlight reaches her instantly, and I'll never know what she might have said. She goes up in flames like an old newspaper doused in kerosene, her vestigial humanity wiped away by fiery justice.

I feel a grim sense of satisfaction.

Half a dozen piles of ash litter the room. My boots crunch on glass and ash as I make my way further inside, sending little puffs of desiccated vampire remains floating into the air. They clearly weren't expecting an attack.

I form up with the rest of the squad assigned to this side of the house, and we move out to ensure each room is cleared. We find several more piles of ash, then a male, barely more than a boy, cowering in a closet. He's covered in burns. Painful looking blisters run along the right side of his body.

"Where are the others?" I demand, watching his agony and fear fade only to be replaced by determination and defiance.

"Fuck you," he spits, using the last of his strength to lunge toward me.

Considering his injuries, he's faster than I expect, but I'm well trained. My body moves, muscle memory taking over. I drive my standard-issue stake into his heart without an ounce of hesitation, ramming it past his breastbone until I hear the grisly crack.

In death, his arms reach for me but his eyes are focused on something behind me. I look over my shoulder and see another door.

I kick the corpse away. As soon as my boot makes contact, the vampire crumbles to ash. I slam the closet door closed and head towards the room he died looking at.

Three teen girls are cramped inside a narrow bathroom, tears streaming down their faces and hatred burning in their eyes. Several hunters join me at the threshold and start arguing over who gets to make the kills. *Idiots. This isn't about clout—it's about justice.*

"We aren't animals," one girl says, placing her slight body in between us and the other two. "What gives you the right to hunt us down and slaughter us?"

I tilt my head and look her over. She's short—the other females stand at least a head taller, but her size doesn't stop her from trying to protect them. Despite the way her body trembles with fear and rage, she doesn't give an inch. Her hair is dark brown, her eyes a vibrant green.

The resemblance stops me in my tracks.

"Shut up, bitch," a recruit shouts at the vampire threateningly, but makes no move to attack. "You're a violation of nature."

I hear footsteps approaching behind me, but I can't stop staring at the girl—I'm gutted both by my memories and her ferocity.

"Quit fucking around and end this," a deep voice growls behind me.

I recognize it without looking.

Angus. A grizzled hunter, my mentor, and a meaner bastard than any I've ever met. He doesn't wait to see if we follow his orders. He tosses a can into the room, and it tips over. Gasoline glugs out of the nozzle, spreading along the cracks of the cheap linoleum floor in a noxious smelling delta.

The females have only a second to stare at the spilling fuel before Angus tosses a match on the ground. The vampires scream. He slams the door in their faces.

"Let's go. The entire house is about to go up." He grunts, narrowing his eyes at me. "Get moving. All of you."

My limbs feel wooden and hollow as I'm caught up in the exodus. The group jostles me until I can make my legs carry me, stumbling, out into the yard. Wails follow me outside, drowning out the sounds of crackling flames and my fellow hunters. I suck in the air greedily but immediately regret it. The pungent stench of accelerant and fire threatens to choke me as the agonized screams fall silent one by one. I hold my breath.

We took the horde of vampires completely off guard. More than a dozen of the dangerous creatures are dead and dusted. We suffered no casualties. On top of that, the intel I was so worried about turned out to be sound.

I should be thrilled, but I can't quiet the sick feeling in my gut.

This isn't our way; we don't do dirty work for the very beings we dedicate our lives to hunting. I look at the sooty faces around me. Most are grinning and chattering about our victory. No one looks the way I feel.

Why isn't anyone else asking questions?

My nausea spikes, and I stagger to an unoccupied corner of the yard, dodging a few burning clumps of grass. I lose the contents of my stomach on top of an angry anthill, grateful that I tied my braids back this morning. When there's nothing left to purge, I drag the back of my hand across my mouth. It's shaking. I will it to stop. I take a swig of water from my canteen as a bead of sweat drips off my chin and lands in the dust.

After I've managed a few deep breaths, I turn back toward the burning house. Angus stands at the corner, his arms crossed as he watches me. I say nothing and neither does he, but I feel his eyes on me for the entire march back to the rendezvous point.

SHEENA

BRUSH, SPIT, RINSE, AND REPEAT. Running my tongue over my freshly cleaned teeth, I pull my hair into a high, tight ponytail and square my shoulders. Supernatural boot camp is back in business. But there's a conversation I need to have first.

It's been radio silence from Ciprian since I called him out for being a bad friend. Now that I know it wasn't quite the premeditated ambush I first imagined, I'm eager to clear the air. Callum put him in a tough spot. Even with all the bad blood between them, Ciprian refused to throw his brother under the bus. That warms my heart.

I slide into my cutoff shorts and tank top and pull out my phone with a sigh. There's no point in stalling any longer.

Can we talk?

Why?

Because we had a fight

Blood... tears... yelling in front of an audience. Remember?

It's early, Sheena

Who's Sheena? This is bestie

Are you sure? I fucking scared you

Yeah you did

But you're a literal nightmare and I'm scared of everything

For the record, I am sorry

I know you are. I am too.

What the fuck for?

I was too harsh on you

ffs we need to work on your killer instinct

So, breakfast?

Ciprian suggests we meet at a nearby diner for breakfast. I'm a little—okay, a lot—nervous about going out in public, but he assures me the diner's owned and operated by the enclave and not very busy this time of year. Callum and Gideon won't like it if I leave the protection of the compound, but I'm not about to ask for anyone's permission to go out to eat.

Stepping out of the bathroom, I paste a cheery smile on my face. "I'm going to breakfast with Ciprian."

Gideon pauses in the middle of sliding into his gray sweatpants and smiles up at me. "If you'll wait two minutes, I'll walk down with you."

I admire his flexing muscles for a moment, then shrug. "It's actually a few miles away, I think. He says it's a diner."

Callum looks up from his phone, brow furrowed. Now that they know I don't mean Sarah's kitchen down the hall, I have their complete attention.

"Eggs N Bakin'?"

"Yeah, that sounds right." I slip into my shoes.

"I love their pancakes. I'll come too," Gideon says, dressing now at about twice the speed he started with.

"Well, Ciprian and I were going to talk," I explain, trying not to hurt his feelings.

"That's a good idea, baby. I want you two to make up." Gideon trails off, then he meets my eyes. "But I'm scared shitless for you to go out without me right now."

I feel his genuine worry echoing in my heart and consider backing out.

A muscle in Callum's jaw twitches. *Here it comes.*

"Sorry, I thought we were training today." He makes a show of snuggling back into his pillow, his voice dripping with playful sarcasm. "If I'd known you were going to throw yourself into the line of fire for a buttered biscuit, I would have slept in. Thank the gods you decided to bring a hung over idiot for backup."

"Your brother isn't an idiot." I cross my arms, feeling duty bound to defend my soon to be restored best friend. "And we don't know that he's hung over."

I hold Callum's gaze and refuse to blink, but winning a staring contest with an annoyed incubus is harder than it sounds, especially when he doesn't fight fair. Instead of arguing, Callum throws back the covers and crawls toward where I'm standing by the end of the bed. I see miles of naked skin, rippling muscles covered in intricate tattoos, and a filthy smirk I can practically feel against my skin.

I take a step closer, then remember my principles. *Snap out of it, Sheena.*

Channeling my inner strategist, I pivot and cover my eyes, cutting my losses and ending the staring contest. But it's a mistake, because now I don't know where Callum is—and fuck me, why is that so hot? Gideon's laugh booms somewhere to my right, and I feel a warm breath on my neck. I tense.

"Stop right there," I demand. "Callum, you can't try to win arguments by being naked and hot."

"I don't see why not." His voice melts in my ears. "I have to play to my strengths after all, sweetheart." He grazes his stubble against the sensitive skin of my neck.

"You could always take your clothes off and level the playing field, baby," Gideon suggests, and I groan in frustration.

"Can we be serious about this, please? I can't live scared all the time. Been there, done that—do not recommend."

"I don't want you to," Callum grumbles, running his fingers over my cheek. "I also don't want you to be the girl who runs into danger and dies first like in horror movies."

"Those women are usually blonde," Gideon says.

Our bedroom door clicks open.

"Whoa, did I walk in on some kinky role play?"

I drop my hand to see a grinning Ciprian standing in the entryway with two greasy paper bags clutched in his hands. He looks like a total fuckboy dressed in his dark jeans, a backwards cap, and a vintage band t-shirt. He scrunches up his nose at the sight of his brother kneeling naked in front of me on the bed.

"After I took some ibuprofen and knocked out my hangover," Ciprian says. Callum looks at me triumphantly, but I ignore him. "I realized it would be dumb to take baby Kazaam out in public while it's basically open season on djinn. So I grabbed takeout instead."

Ciprian hands a greasy bag to Gideon. Then he rattles one at me like I'm some sort of feral cat and smiles hesitantly. I snatch the bag from his hand, drop it on the coffee table, and then throw my arms around him. After a tiny pause, he sighs and squeezes me back, resting his cheek on the top of my head.

"I'm really sorry," he murmurs.

"It's already forgiven." I pull back from the hug and he groans.

"We need to add 'holding a grudge' to your lesson plan. I'm starting to worry about your fundamentals," Ciprian jokes, turning to look at the guys.

Gideon digs through his takeout bag with enthusiasm while Callum finally gets dressed.

"I grabbed you both your usual, but you're going to have to take it to-go." Ciprian points to the door as he sits down on the love seat, obsidian eyes sparkling with mischief. "This is bestie time."

"Yeah, yeah. We already heard we weren't invited." Gideon grabs me for a toe-curling kiss, then saunters out the door with his food.

Callum finishes dressing, covering his messy dark hair with a ball cap. I sink onto the love seat next to Ciprian, unwrap my breakfast sandwich, and watch both brothers subtly. With hats covering their hair and matching tense expressions, they look more alike than I've ever seen them.

Callum trudges over to us. "First, I told you he would be hung over," he says to me. It's not the greatest start, but Ciprian just shrugs and stuffs a home fry in his mouth. "Second, I'm sorry for putting you in that position, Ciprian. I was freaking out, and I made a mistake. I should never have asked you to do that."

By the time he's done, Callum's jaw is so tight I can practically hear it creaking. Ciprian sits there gaping at his brother, so I grind my elbow into his ribs until he snaps out of it.

"It's okay. Next time, I'll tell you when your plans are shit," Ciprian says, pushing my elbow away and standing to shake his brother's hand.

It's a good start for them, and I can't help bouncing a little in excitement.

"For fuck's sake, Sheena." Ciprian bumps me with his hip. "I can literally feel you overreacting. It's giving me indigestion."

I hide my smile around a huge bite of breakfast sandwich as Callum goes back to pretending his brother isn't there. He bends over and peppers tiny kisses all over my neck, making me giggle and squirm at the tickling sensation.

"Training at nine?" Callum asks.

I give him a nod and Ciprian sends him a sarcastic salute as he turns to leave.

When the door closes behind him, Ciprian turns to me, a long-suffering look on his face. "You two are gross. You should work on that."

CIPRIAN AND I WALK out to the training ground two minutes before nine. There are a few people milling around outside. They aren't paying us any attention now, but I know that could change, especially if I lose my shit again. People love a good supernatural meltdown.

"Why do we have to do this outside, anyway?" I gripe, swinging my foot at a pebble in my path. I miss and nearly fall on my ass. Ciprian's lip twitches, but he doesn't laugh. I pretend nothing happened. "It's not like we're fist fighting around your mom's precious gargoyle."

"No magic indoors. It's always been the rule." He shrugs. "Mother thinks it disturbs the energy in the house or something."

I level him with a disbelieving look. "But the energy is already . . ."

"Macabre? Insidious? Oppressive?"

I laugh as he rattles off synonyms. We enter the training ring together and find both Gideon and Callum waiting for us with matching nervous smiles.

"Hey, baby," Gideon says.

"When Ciprian pulls you into the vision, look for the edges."

Callum starts out all business, and it actually helps me feel grounded. "Once you can identify the edge—"

"It will ripple or shimmer slightly," Gideon interrupts.

Callum nods and continues. "Then you'll focus on peeling the illusion back. Like a sticker."

"Or pushing it away like a heavy piece of furniture," Gideon suggests.

I nod emphatically, bracing for whatever nightmare Ciprian has in store for me. "Ripples and shimmers, stickers and furniture, push or pull—got it."

I turn to Ciprian, expecting to see nerves on his face as well, but he looks absolutely diabolical. So much so that I take a wary step back. I spent enough time in foster care to recognize when someone is up to something.

His calculating wink is the last thing I see before the edges of my vision flicker.

I glance at Callum and Gideon to see if they notice anything, but they're not looking at me anymore. I'm about to tell them that nothing has changed when I notice a ripple around one of the puffy clouds above us.

Oh shit. We are in a vision. I start scanning the training ground for differences, determined not to fuck this up.

Gideon takes a step towards Callum and grabs his bicep in one of his massive hands. "Please, don't go. I've always been in love with you."

Gideon rubs his thumb across Callum's arm, then crowds him against the fence. When Callum yanks the taller man down into a hungry kiss, Ciprian's earlier wink begins to make sense to me. As I watch my boyfriends make out, the temperature climbs. I fan myself and grin.

"Oh my gods." Ciprian's disgruntled voice echoes inside my head. "This is my apology vision, Sheena, but you at least have to try to push me out before I'm scarred for life."

I choke on a laugh. There is literally no incentive for me to kick this illusion out. Instead of trying to peel or push like they suggested, I sit down cross-legged on the ground and watch the sexy tableau unfold.

When Callum yanks Gideon's shirt off and grinds against him roughly, a groan of appreciation escapes me. The sound must push him too far because Ciprian suddenly appears in front of me, blocking my view and glowering down at me.

"Ha-ha. You're hilarious. Now, are you going to train or get off in the courtyard?"

"Do I get a choice?" I ask, smirking up at him, then looking around his legs so I don't miss the show. Gideon unbuttons Callum's pants, and a drip of sweat trickles down his muscular neck. "This is fantastic, Ciprian. Cinematic even. Can you conjure me up some popcorn?"

He narrows his eyes at me like a wasp, then a full bowl of popcorn materializes over my head. Upside-down. Salty kernels rain down on me. It's so lifelike; I swear I can feel butter in my hair.

I pop a piece in my mouth and immediately spit it out. "The taste is off, Ciprian." I gag. "Your spell is broken."

"It's not a spell, and I'm not a fucking witch. I'm a demon," he roars down at me. "Now at least try to push me out, or this wet dream is going to turn into a nightmare really fast."

I take one last look at the steamy scene in front of me and sigh, standing up. "Fine. If you're going to be a dick about it."

Looking up, I find the fluffy cloud with the irregularity around the edges. I try shoving it mentally and manage to flatten it, but the vision doesn't end. I try again, furrowing my brow and pushing harder. It dissolves like a dandelion in the wind. Before I can celebrate, the cloud rematerializes with the same shimmering edges.

Maybe Gideon's idea of pushing isn't for me.

This time, I only focus on the edges. I imagine working my thumbnail under it like a sticker on a used book and tug gently. Part of the illusion comes loose, so I pull harder, unveiling strip after strip of reality juxtaposed alongside the illusion. Eventually, the real Callum and Gideon are standing next to their vision versions, staring at me with confusion and concern. Ciprian looks angry and slightly nauseous.

I muffle a giggle and focus on peeling back the last pieces of the illusion I missed. Some strips come loose easily and others hang on for dear life. By the time I finish, sweat is trickling down my back and a faint headache throbs at the base of my skull.

"Congratulations," Ciprian grumbles. "You're a voyeur and I'm a hundred years older."

"What the hell did you show her?" Gideon demands, taking a step toward me and flaring his nostrils. "Sheena, are you . . . horny?"

"Please, stop." Ciprian covers his mouth with his hand. "I'm going to lose my breakfast."

Callum stares between us with suspicion, his eyes narrowing on me. "What was the illusion, Sheena?"

"Well, it was you and Gideon." I smirk, looking them both up and down. Not knowing is killing them, and I really want to see how they react. "And you were feeling very affectionate towards each other."

Once my meaning sinks in, Gideon roars with laughter. Callum rolls his eyes at his brother, but I can see how flushed he is by the idea.

"Dude, no one attacking her is going to show her something sexy."

His criticism is the final nail in the coffin for Ciprian. He throws his hands up in the air, dislodging his hat in the process.

"I fucking know that. It was supposed to be a quick apology vision, a warm-up joke or whatever. Now I'm traumatized." He glares at us all. "You three are the worst. No helpful suggestions or thanks. It's always just 'Ciprian, your visions are too scary. Ciprian, your visions are too sexy.' Well, fuck you all very much. I should have just killed Gideon again and been done with it."

By the end of his rant, his platinum hair is standing on end, and the rest of us have given up fighting our laughter. Walking toward him, I pick up his baseball cap and dust it off, standing on my tiptoes to put it back on his head.

"Thank you, Ciprian. I definitely won't forget that vision," I say. His black eyes are still roiling with shadows like the night sky during a storm, but I see some of the tension leave his shoulders. "Could you show me something a little scarier so I can practice again?"

He nods at me gruffly. When his eyes lose focus, I square my shoulders and get ready to go again.

For the next three hours, I do my best to dismantle the mix of scenarios he conjures up with his illusions. I run through the woods with wolves biting at my heels. I dodge a witch trying to light me on fire. I even sword fight with a vampire pirate on the deck of a ship at sea.

The visions are so realistic; it's like being dropped in the middle of a movie. I feel the tree roots beneath my feet, the witch's flames licking at my skin, and taste the salty spray from the waves as I struggle to keep my footing.

Despite the distractions, I hunt down the weaknesses one by one, peeling back the visions a little faster each time. Once I manage to break through the imaginary sea and come back to the real courtyard, my shirt is sticking to my sweaty skin, and I can't ignore the throbbing in my head any longer.

Gideon must be able to tell I'm gassed because he's quick to step in.

"That's enough for now. You did an amazing job, baby." He wraps one big arm around my drooping shoulders, supporting me without making it obvious that I need it. The bond between us thrums happily with the contact.

I look over at Ciprian, and I'm somewhat relieved to see he looks just as exhausted as me. His pale skin is pink and splotchy, and with the way his brow is pinched together, I bet he's fighting a headache as well.

"Let's go get some lunch," Callum suggests, looking between

his brother and I. "I think you both might have pushed a little too hard."

Ciprian waves off the concern, but we all notice his hand trembling. "It's fine. I'll nap, then go see a horror movie or something." At my questioning look, he grins. "I feed on fear. I can do it through my visions if the reaction is strong enough, but that costs me energy as well. If I'm in a room full of scared kids, though, I'll be full to the brim in an hour or two."

"Sounds like a nightmare."

They all groan at my bad joke.

CHAPTER
TWENTY

IDRIS

The southern enclave just called in and reported a hunter attack in their territory. More than a dozen vampires killed by psychotic zealots during a cowardly ambush. Slaughtered in cold blood.

I close my eyes and grit my teeth. It's a terrible death for any supernatural.

The enclaves don't work together often, but we do share information on known hunter movements—the common enemy that continues to threaten our existence.

This time is different.

These victims weren't supernaturals in the wrong place at the wrong time. This was a coordinated extermination of a hidden halfway house. From what I've been told, it was for newly turned vampires worried about taming their thirst. They were there to learn how to avoid hurting anyone. Now, they're dead.

These kinds of facilities are becoming more common as we assimilate further into this world, but all it takes to ruin the progress and stoke up hatred is bloodthirsty and brainwashed humans. This cult may think they're protecting their kind, but all they're actually doing is breeding fear and promoting an endless cycle of violence.

Once a path is painted with blood, it can't be easily reversed.

I came to this realm as a refugee ten long years ago with nothing but the sword on my back. I limped through that portal, bloodied, beaten, and so tired of battle I could not fathom facing another fight. To my complete and utter shock, many of the folk followed me. Hungry for stability, they sacrificed near immortality in a realm ravaged by war for a chance at peace with me here.

I cannot fail them. Hatred is the harbinger of eternal battle lines, and war is hell. I won't let my people be sucked into another never-ending conflict.

Grabbing my notebook from the desk, I leave the constant banging of the construction behind. My desire to write things down in my own hand is a habit from another time. I know it dates me, but some things I refuse to leave behind.

While it is possible to walk from my wing of the compound to the shifter quarters and remain completely indoors for the duration, it is quicker to go directly through the central courtyard. It also gives me just a few blessed extra minutes away from the modern, artificial lights.

While I'm cutting across the open space, I see the djinn walking—no, stumbling—away from the training ground. She leans heavily on the tall shifter. My eyes narrow as I track their progress. Those fools don't have what it takes to keep her safe.

With their slow progress, delayed further by their incessantly childish levity, I catch up to the group quickly. All three males stare at me with suspicion.

"Hello, Idris." Sheena greets me with a tired smile on her face.

"Little djinn." I casually take her measure, noticing her normally vibrant green eyes are dull and glassy. "Working on your mental walls?" She nods, pride creeping into her expression. "I presume it went better than last time."

My comment is innocent enough, but I'm immediately the target of three glares and a sheepish look from Sheena.

"Much better this time," she says, standing a little straighter. "What brings you here?"

"There's been a hunter attack." I let my anger bleed into my tone. At everyone's concerned look, I clarify, "Not here. In the southern enclave's territory."

"Dimitri is out, but dad is here," Gideon offers. I already know that, but I congratulate myself on my self-control when I don't immediately tell him so.

"Lunch first. Work later," the nightmare demon complains, lurching into Gideon's unoccupied side. "Dude, you're huge. Give a guy a lift, would you?"

Gideon shoves the blonde away. "Knock it off, Ciprian."

"If you're too tired from all the humping, consider being on the bottom for a change." The nightmare sniffs dramatically.

"He lets me be on top," Sheena says, freezing when everyone stops to look at her. A blush spreads across her cheeks and neck like wildfire. "Don't look at me like that."

She tugs free from Gideon's arms and opens the door herself, strutting into the shifter wing with her head held high.

"Of course he does. He's not a fucking idiot," the incubus mutters, eyes heated as he watches her disappear down the hall.

For the first time since we met, I find myself in complete agreement with Callum.

SOMEHOW I GET CONNED into joining their luncheon, which is night and day different from the last meal we shared. The kitchen table is cluttered with bread, deli meats, and assorted condiments. There are elbows flying, discordant chatter, and an absence of any clearly delineated organizational structure.

Within seconds, I'm violently overwhelmed. Shame floods my

chest when I realize I'm not even sure how to construct a sandwich.

I'm trying to figure out a way to excuse myself without offending Sarah or Joshua when Sheena slides an occupied plate in front of me. She cuts the sandwich in half, smiling a bit when I stare. "Give that one a try," she encourages me.

I bite into her creation, pleasantly surprised to find it's not as bad as I expected. Sheena turns back to the chaos in front of her and starts assembling another sandwich. I watch, intrigued, as she grapples with the nightmare over the mustard and laughs at a joke Gideon makes. Even pale with exhaustion, she's radiant.

When she finishes making her own sandwich, I take the knife from her hand. She looks at me in confusion, but I simply incline my head, cutting through the bread and meat carefully just the way she did for me. When I pull back, I'm rewarded with a conspiratorial smile as she swipes a bag of chips from the melee. She tucks them between our arms and out of anyone else's reach.

"How are you so comfortable with . . ." I struggle for the right words, hesitant to offend her with an unfair characterization, and eventually settle for gesturing with a sweep of my hand to the mayhem.

"Foster kid." Sheena grimaces. "You learn how to get your elbows out pretty quickly in the system or sometimes you don't eat." She looks fondly at the people stuffing their faces around the table. "This is different, but the skills are transferrable."

She pops a chip into her mouth, but I can't keep my mouth closed. "It's not like this in my realm." I'm not sure what possessed me to say it. Sheena looks over at me with curiosity.

"I guess it's more formal." She prods gently while also providing me with an easy out if I choose to drop the conversation.

"Yes, that's true, I suppose. There are a lot of ceremonial customs that accompany most meals, even among family." I don't tell her about testing everything for poison or the constant assassination attempts. "Dining in the fae realm . . . Let's just say, this warmth is absent."

She nods at me, her smile falling. I curse myself for removing it.

"I haven't experienced much warmth in my life either." She looks around at the crowded table where multiple conversations are peppered with boisterous laughter. "Maybe this is a new beginning for us both." Her voice is soft, like she's afraid if she says it too loud, she'll spoil it somehow.

Perhaps she is right.

I grab a handful of the salty chips from the bag in between us and put them on my plate. We continue the meal until most of the assorted shifters who live in the compound have left the table and the noise reaches a more manageable decibel.

"Gideon tells me the hunters hit the southern enclave," Joshua says, his face grim as he turns to address me.

I wipe my mouth and take a sip of water, then pass on all the information from the earlier report, stopping only when someone asks me a question. Sheena listens in silence, her face crumpling as I give more details.

"They burned them all alive? Why?" She asks.

"The hunters are a very driven group," Joshua begins, tactful as always, although his jaw is clenched.

"It's a fucking cult," Gideon growls.

Joshua doesn't contradict him, and I pick up the explanation.

"Hunters have been around for hundreds of years, long before the enclaves formed. They're incredibly secretive, but from what we can tell, they raise each new generation to track down and kill supernaturals."

"This is a deviation from their usual pattern," Callum points out, and I'm impressed to see he picked up on that so quickly. "The leaders in the south keep their shit close to the belt. Very few people would have known about that house, right? So how the hell did the hunters find out about it?"

No one has an answer for him, a fact that's deeply unsettling.

"Could they have a mole?" Sheena asks, and we all weigh her words.

"It's a good idea, but I don't see it working," Sarah says, her lips pursed as she passes around a plate of cookies. "The hunters are zealots. I don't think they would partner with a supernatural willingly, even for a strategic advantage."

Nods follow her assessment, but Sheena's suggestion sinks into my brain and stays there. Hunters could become a real threat if they are indeed updating their tactics. Moreover, we have an even bigger problem on our hands if someone in our community is choosing to sell out our most vulnerable members.

As everyone finishes their meal and pushes back from the table, I catch Sheena's arm and press a kiss to the delicate skin of her wrist.

"Thank you for the sandwich, little djinn."

I leave the room without another word, enjoying her stunned expression and the waves of aggression coming off of her demon and shifter.

CALLUM

"But he kissed you," Gideon grumbles as he prowls around the bedroom after lunch.

"On the wrist," Sheena insists from the bed, waving her arm for emphasis. "He's kind of old fashioned. I bet it was just some weird fae custom."

Gideon scoffs. "Yeah, I'm sure it was just some weird fae custom . . . to get in your pants."

I'm inclined to agree with him, but I'm also not stupid enough to involve myself in a losing argument. From my spot on the love seat, I pretend to scroll on my phone and stay out of it.

Sheena groans and massages her temples. "You're being ridiculous."

"Or you're being oblivious." Gideon digs his heels in. "He definitely wants to fuck you. Why did you make him a sandwich in the first place? He's a grown ass man."

"Because I'm not an asshole." Sheena's voice is tight. "He was obviously overwhelmed, and I know what that feels like, so I made him a sandwich. It's not a big deal. You need to let it go."

Gideon should listen to her, but I'm starting to think he can't. The animal inside him sensed competition at lunch. With the bond still incomplete, the instinct to claim her is probably eating him alive.

"I don't want to let it go," he roars. "We found you first, and I'll be damned if I'm going to let him snatch you up."

I lift my eyes from my phone, trying to figure out a way to stop him before he takes this too far.

"Are you telling me you called dibs?" Sheena's voice is too quiet.

"You're my fated mate," Gideon says, crossing his arms belligerently. "The gods called dibs for me."

"Then why are you being so insecure?"

Gideon deflates, his shoulders sinking.

"Because I am insecure," he admits, all his anger gone.

Sheena's pinched face softens, and she reaches out to him. Gideon climbs into the bed, scooping her into his arms.

"You shouldn't be," she reassures him, her voice thick with exhaustion. "You're smart, kind, and sexy, and mate bond or not, you're mine. You shouldn't give a damn if some guy kisses my wrist."

Gideon peppers her arms with kisses, starting at her wrists and traveling up until he plants his lips on hers. She melts into the touch, pulling back only to suck in a deep breath.

"How long will you be at the library?" Sheena looks at me as she asks the question, and I give up pretending I'm not paying attention.

"We'll be back tonight," I respond. "I convinced the faculty to give us an alumni pass without admitting why we needed it."

Walking up to them both, I drop a kiss to her soft lips, ignoring how close my best friend is to the action.

"So I'll see you when I wake up?"

Sheena yawns. Close up, I can tell she's barely able to keep her eyes open. "Yeah, sweetheart. Get some rest. We'll be back before you know it," I say, speaking softly.

After her eyelids drift closed, I drag Gideon out of the compound, urgency building in my chest.

"Dude, you're way too eager to be holed up in that fucking library," he groans as we climb into the SUV.

I throw the car in reverse. "I'm not too eager. She's too tired."

"What do you mean?" Gideon snaps his seatbelt into place, worry in his voice.

"I mean, she worked hard this morning, but she shouldn't be that tired. She needs a talisman, and she needs it fast."

Silence settles over us, and we're lost in our own thoughts for the rest of the drive.

Neither of us is prepared to face the possibility that we could fail.

I RESIST A SHUDDER as we pass through the school wards. Being back on this campus feels risky. The feeling of witch magic on my skin has always made me itchy. It was unpleasant when we attended class here, and I still hate it.

"I don't really want to come here every day," I admit with a sigh, easing into a designated visitor parking spot. "I don't like leaving her at the compound."

"What if we didn't?" Gideon asks.

"Dude, have you not been listening? We need answers," I say, thrumming my fingers on the steering wheel.

Then I clock the calculated, devious look in his eyes and groan internally. Every time I see this expression, I end up having to clean up a mess later.

"What are you planning?" I ask, narrowing my eyes.

"Maybe we check the books out instead of coming back every day."

"You mean steal them?"

I glance around us just in case some wizened old hag from the faculty has materialized in the back seat. Since it's summer break, we're one of only a handful of cars in the parking lot, but this campus is never fully empty. Too many people have nowhere else to go.

"No, I mean borrow them." Gideon shrugs. "To be returned at a time more convenient to us."

I consider the idea, and it's actually not bad. We pulled tons of shit like this while we went to school here, but we're upstanding members of the community these days. I doubt they'll suspect us of a heist now.

"We'll have to stay a few hours. Do some bullshit research to make us less suspicious."

"I'm very interested in the healing property of herbs," Gideon drones. His voice is so dry and serious I choke on my laugh.

Now with a rough plan, we head to the library. I'm buzzing with nerves. I can feel Gideon's energy bouncing around too, although the look on his face is so bland it's impossible to tell.

The doors open automatically, then the floor shifts with a groan and deposits us in front of the reception desk. I feel a little nauseous from the sudden movement, but this school was constructed with more magic than actual building materials. Perfect for keeping tabs on unruly students.

"They told me you two were coming back." The librarian's tone is as dull as some of these dusty old tomes. "I prayed to the goddess it was a lie."

Damn, these witches have long memories.

I remember her vaguely. She's part of that boring coven that focuses on knowledge over everything else. Even though she's a low level witch, she'll still be able to notice and raise the alarm if I try to use my influence on her.

"I want to learn about plants," Gideon speaks before I can say a word, leaning over the desk and smiling down at the old woman. "Healing didn't interest me while I went to school here, but now I really want to know how to use herbs." He beams at her, and I watch in amazement as her shriveled heart grows three sizes.

"A worthy and expansive field of study, Mr. Therion. What remedies are you interested in?" She pulls a pencil from her hair, poised to take notes on his answer. I stare at the tight gray bun suspiciously. It's perched on top of her head like a third eye, and I wonder what else she has hiding in there.

Gideon freezes. My heart pounds faster and faster as the silence stretches. *Oh shit, we didn't talk through our plan this far.* I'm about to jump in and say gods know what when he finally speaks, saving me from a coronary.

"Sunburn, ant bites, and cholera," he says, rattling off the maladies with purpose. All I can do is try not to gape.

If the librarian thinks his interests are weird, she makes no mention of it, scribbling at length on a piece of paper she conjures from thin air. After an impatient gesture for us to follow, she leads us to a table around the corner, and then bustles off to collect the books.

As soon as she's out of earshot, I turn to Gideon and snort. "Cholera? Where the fuck did that come from? Isn't there a vaccine for that already?"

Gideon shrugs. He's so pleased with his improvisation that the dimples in his cheeks pop out of his smiling face.

"How the hell should I know? That's why I need these books." His voice cuts off as the librarian returns and drops a massive stack in front of us.

"These are on sunburn. I'll be back with the others soon."

She's quick for her age, and within minutes, we're completely buried in books. Once the librarian shuffles back to her desk, Gideon cracks one open with a grimace, then sneezes violently at the dust that blows up in his face.

At his long-suffering nod, I sneak away from the table and head to the creature section. It's alphabetized by species—thank the gods—so I skim past the entire shelf on demons, only to find myself immediately in another crowded section on elves.

Am I missing something? The djinn were hunted down, but surely they weren't erased from our history all together.

I retrace my steps, crouching to look closer at the spot where the books on demons end and the elf section begins. Tucked between two thick tomes, I spot a small, ancient-looking purple book with gold hinges and script on the spine. Looking closer, I make out the word 'djinn' and excitement builds in my chest. It's barely bigger than my hand and only about half an inch thick, but it's a start. I tug the book free and tuck it into my waistband.

I check the supernatural history and magical artifacts sections and even skim the fiction aisle. But this purple book appears to be the only one that mentions djinn in this entire monstrosity of a library. After hours of digging without any more luck, I head back to Gideon's table feeling deflated. His eyes are glazed over, but he's still diligently reading the medical books. I can't help but chuckle at him.

I put a hand on his shoulder and gesture to the exit. With a relieved sigh, he jumps up. We approach the desk to let the librarian know we're leaving, but she's busy talking to another visitor. Unfortunately, the woman is very familiar to me.

"Gideon and Callum in the library. Am I hallucinating?" She coos, her voice syrupy and sweet.

"Hey, Alina." I force a smile and offer her a stiff, awkward side hug.

Not good. Not good.

"How's life at the enclave?" There's a flash of something in Alina's eyes when she asks, but it's gone too quickly for me to get a good read.

"Everything is great. How have you been?" I ask.

"Fabulous, of course. I was in the neighborhood gathering some plants for the solstice celebration and thought I would drop by to tell Gretchen hello." She nods at the older witch, who's stacking books and pretending not to listen in. "Imagine my surprise when I run into two old friends. It must be a blessing from the mother."

Alina smiles. There's no bitterness on her face, but she always was a good actress.

"It's great to see you too," I say, trying to keep this short. I don't have any interest in getting into a conversation about her deity or anything else for that matter.

We make small talk for a few minutes while Gideon shuffles back and forth awkwardly. Glancing deliberately at my watch, I toss a disappointed look her way.

"Listen, Alina, I'd love to catch up more, but we've got to get going." I frown like I'm sad we have to go, but I can't tell if she buys it.

After another limp side hug, we take off. Gideon and I are halfway to the door when she speaks again.

"Remember, if you two need anything, I'm just a phone call away."

I shoot her a smile over my shoulder, but I don't respond. As soon as we're outside, I feel in my waistband, relieved to find the book exactly as I left it.

"That was fucking weird," Gideon whispers, and I shush him.

"Wait until we're in the car. This whole place has ears."

I don't relax fully until we're in the SUV, past the wards, and ten miles down the road.

"Fucking Alina. In the godsdamn library. Happy to see us." Gideon snorts. "I call bullshit."

"Yeah, it's strange," I admit, working the leather of the steering wheel between my hands. "Asking about the enclave was also weird."

"She's always fishing for something, but there's nothing we can do about that." Gideon brushes some dust from his leg. "Let me see the book you found."

I dig it out and pass it over.

"I haven't opened it yet. Is there a table of contents or something?" I ask, but a grunt is the only answer I get. "What?" I snap, glancing over at him before focusing back on the road. "Speak, man. I'm driving. I can't read your mind."

"I can't open it." Gideon sounds confused, so I take my eyes off the road again and see he's tugging on the cover with no success.

"Let me try then."

He hands the book back, but I have no luck either.

"Fucking magic," I mutter. "Let's just hope it opens for Sheena."

"It better, or I'm going to pry it open with a crowbar."

Gideon sighs and rubs his chest. His worry is making the air in the car feel hot and heavy. Cracking my window, I suck in a breath and ignore the anxiety eating at me.

SHEENA

I BLINK AWAKE to a hushed argument. The sun is fading, casting eerie, elongated shadows across the room, and it's making the usually cozy space look a little on the spooky side. In my half lucid state, the shadows look like evil spirits advancing toward me. I shiver, tucking the covers tighter around my neck and focusing harder on the conversation happening at the end of the bed.

"She needs more rest."

"But she's been napping for hours. I want to see if she can open it."

Gideon's husky baritone voice shushes Callum. "She can always try it tomorrow," he insists quietly.

"She could also try it now," I say, yawning and pushing myself into a sitting position. *It feels like I just fell asleep five minutes ago.*

Callum comes to my side of the bed, dropping a kiss to my

forehead and scooting in beside me. Gideon shuffles in on my other side. He hands me a small purple book, weathered with age.

"I didn't realize they would let you bring books home. That's great," I say. When neither of them responds, I look from side to side and sigh. "You stole it, didn't you?"

"Absolutely not. We borrowed it, which is how libraries are supposed to work," Callum assures me, his lips twitching as he fights a smirk. "Honestly, sweetheart, the gatekeeping of knowledge in the supernatural community is really fucking egregious. We're doing them a favor by forcing them into this millennium."

"I see." I shake my head, looking over at Gideon. "Do you feel the same way about the gatekeeping of knowledge?"

Gideon turns to me, a mischievous spark in his eyes. "I don't give a shit about that and I won't pretend I do." He kisses my cheek. "I just didn't want to leave you to go back there every day."

Just like that, my heart swells. Gideon never makes me doubt his affection. It's comforting like a warm blanket on a winter day or a deep breath in a field of wildflowers. I kiss him because it's all I can think about. Gideon meets my lips eagerly, and the kiss morphs from sweet to hot quicker than either of us intended.

"I can't believe I'm about to say this." Callum groans. "You both look very sexy, but can you make out later? I really want to know what's in that book." It's the whiniest I've ever heard him sound.

I break away from Gideon with a laugh. "If you wanted to know so badly, why didn't you read it in the car?"

"Because we couldn't."

"Why? Is it in some other language? Because if so, I hate to break it to you, but I'm not going to be able to understand it either."

"Maybe. I don't actually know. It's stuck," Callum says.

"What do you mean? How can a book be stuck?" I ask. *It's not exactly complicated technology.*

"It won't open for us," Gideon explains.

"I think it's magically sealed to only open for a djinn." Callum points at the book in my lap, his excitement buzzing when I pick it up again.

Sliding my thumb under the book's clasp, I try to flip it open. Nothing happens. I try again, bracing the spine on the bed and using both hands to pull. Still nothing.

"Shit." Callum sags beside me, and a pit settles low in my stomach.

"It's okay." I try for a reassuring smile. "Where are the other books? Surely they don't all have some super secret lock."

"That was it," Callum grumbles, throwing himself back on the bed. "It's literally the only book I could find mentioning djinn in the entire library."

The pit in my stomach starts rolling around. I didn't expect to encounter another dead end so soon. This book might be our only lead. If that's true . . . There is another option.

"What if you say the words I told you never to say to unlock it?" I suggest, bracing myself for their reactions.

"Absolutely fucking not."

"Hell no, you know what happened last time."

They both glare at me like I'm insane.

"It was just a suggestion." I sigh. "Do you have any better ideas?"

"Maybe put it up to your eyes when they're glowing purple," Gideon says. "I volunteer to get them going right now so we can test it out." He runs his hand up my inner thigh with a wink. I chuckle and tuck myself into his side.

"Do you really think this ancient thing has biometric scanning that will only work when I'm horny?" I flip the book around dramatically, eying it from every angle. "Oddly enough, I don't see any cameras."

"Smartass. You're still thinking like a human. All I'm saying is magic is wild and intuitive." Gideon strokes a piece of my hair between his fingers. "I think you have to convince the book it's safe to open for you."

Wonderful. My imposter syndrome is so bad even the book doesn't think I belong.

"I feel like you're telling me to befriend an inanimate object when I'm just now learning to do that with real people," I complain.

"You'll get it in no time with that attitude."

Gideon bumps his shoulder into mine, sending me rocking into Callum. My demon returns the gesture, and the guys keep it up until I'm jostling back and forth between them like the pendulum on a grandfather clock. Their teasing releases some of my tension, and soon I'm giggling so hard I can barely breathe.

"Look, don't stress about it now," Callum reassures me. "We'll figure out how to get it open. I promise."

CHAPTER
TWENTY-ONE

Callum is right about one thing: we're going to get this damn book open. He just won't like my plan to make it happen.

As I sneak through the courtyard, it's so dark I can barely see my shoes. The stone cobblestones are uneven beneath my feet, and I hear the decorative fountain gurgling and splashing to my right. I use the sound of rushing water to orient myself, irritated that I'm having to echo locate like a goddamn bat. Not everyone has perfect night vision. If they can afford a fountain, they should be able to invest in some outdoor lighting.

Two more reports of hunter attacks came in at dinner. So Gideon and Callum were pulled into a super secret meeting with their fathers, and Ciprian left town abruptly to deal with some sort of situation in Nevada. Their absence is why I find myself hustling across the courtyard alone, clutching the tiny purple and gold book to my chest like some kind of thief in the night.

They won't want me to talk to the fae, especially alone, but every time Gideon and Callum are around him, the entire conversation devolves into veiled threats and passive aggressive dick measuring. I know neither of them trust Idris, and given my background, I can appreciate their suspicion. But like it or not, he has been the only one able to tell me anything concrete about my heritage.

The entrance to the fae wing looms in front of me. I take a deep breath, square my shoulders, and step up to the threshold. A heinously bright LED floodlight switches on, and I stumble back as it sears my retinas.

"Shit," I hiss, my heart pounding.

I blink through the spots dancing in front of my eyes and grip the door's old-fashioned knocker firmly. It's cool under my fingers, a copper pentagram coated in a thick patina courtesy of time and the elements.

Before I can second-guess myself, I lift the knocker and bring it down against the wood several times. The sound is surprisingly underwhelming. If the fae is more than ten feet away, there's no way he will hear it. Just as I'm starting to think of a backup plan, the door swings open and reveals Idris. Dressed in sweatpants and a plain green t-shirt, I've never seen him look so casual.

"Oh good, you're home," I sputter.

"Little djinn." Idris tilts his head slightly to the side. If he's surprised to see me, he doesn't say so. "Please, come in."

He steps to the side to let me pass and closes the door behind me.

"Is everything alright?" Idris asks.

Is that concern flickering in his cool blue eyes?

"Yes, sorry. It's just—I have this book." I brandish the little tome as if that explains everything and immediately start rambling. "It won't open. I've tried pulling hard and opening my eyes really wide. I also told it I was a djinn and that it was safe to open. Nothing happened, so I was wondering if you had any ideas." I trail off, feeling like a complete idiot.

I'm relieved he doesn't comment on my word vomit. Instead, Idris leads me to a sitting room that's still in the middle of a major construction overhaul. A thin layer of sawdust blankets every surface. There's a protective sheet spread across the couch, but it doesn't help much.

Idris brushes some of the dust away. "I'm sorry everything is in such disarray. Please sit if you don't mind the mess," he says, gesturing to the couch.

I plop down with no hesitation, waving my hands around. "This is nothing." I smile. "The last ten places I lived were smaller than this room, plus a little dust never hurt anyone."

Idris cocks his head to the side, studying me like I'm some kind of oddity at the county fair.

"May I?" He holds his hand out for the book, and I hand it over.

When he attempts to open it, nothing happens. Even though I saw that coming, I'm disappointed. Determined not to run my mouth again like a fool, I sit quietly as he examines it from every angle. Idris runs his fingers along the golden clasp—his lips pursed in concentration—before assessing the back and spine.

With nothing else to occupy myself, I stare at his hands. They are pale and slender with long, tapered fingers—capable, demanding, and confident all at the same time.

What would they feel like on my skin?

Horrified, I banish that thought, realizing too late Idris has stopped perusing the book and is studying me just as closely.

"A curiosity," he says. I desperately want to ask if he means the book or me. "Have you tried your blood?" Idris' lips twitch. "Not all of your blood. Just a few drops, little djinn."

My blood? I scrunch my face up. *Right. I'm no longer part of the human world.*

"Blood magic used to be quite common, but it's fallen out of favor in recent years, especially here on Earth. I cannot imagine why." Idris smiles widely, and the effect is almost as blinding as the light by the door.

"Did you just make a joke?" I demand, wincing at how rude I sound.

"Apparently, not a very good one," he admits.

Idris rotates the book back to the front cover and holds it out to me, running his finger over a spot in the middle of the clasp where the color is darker.

"I would try putting a little of your blood here." His fingers brush against mine during the transfer, and I can't help my shudder. "The author of that book likely wanted to make sure it never fell into the wrong hands."

His arm falls back to his side and I nod, unsettled by the sudden static energy swirling around the room. When I stand, Idris rises with me, letting me lead the way back out. The skin on my neck tingles; I feel him watching me.

"Thank you for your help," I say when we reach the front door. "I'll let you know if the blood works."

I turn to face him and our eyes meet. Suddenly, I'm frozen by the intensity in his icy blue eyes as they search mine.

"You're drained," he says. It's a statement, not a question. He's giving my earlier bluntness a run for its money.

I can't stand the idea of Idris thinking I'm weak, so I square my shoulders and lift my chin. "No, no, I'm fine." I paste a fake smile on my face. "I had a long nap earlier, and I think I slept too long. It must have made me groggy."

"You don't have to lie to me," Idris whispers. His voice is so painfully gentle I flinch. "Without your talisman, it's only going to get worse."

I don't want to hear this.

"Wow, Idris." I force a laugh. "You're not winning any gold medals for optimism." His soft expression doesn't change at my obvious deflection.

"When humans talk of my kind, they often say we cannot tell a lie," Idris murmurs, his eyes cataloging my face. "That's rubbish, of course, but I've often wondered if there's at least a little truth to it."

He brings his hand up slowly, tracing the plane of my forehead with his thumb. The furrows I didn't even feel myself making relax under his touch. A cool sensation moves through my head like a gentle breeze, and the throbbing headache I've been trying to ignore since this morning disappears. My body sags in relief.

"I've seen many people I care for fall in battle or to betrayal." The mesmerizing lilt of Idris' voice sinks into my skin and takes root there. His thumb ghosts over my lips, just a whisper of a touch, before falling away from me completely. "As we speak, my home realm is ravaged by lies and greed, so I'm sorry if I cannot give you optimism, little djinn. But please don't mistake my truth as a desire to see you fail."

He steps back, and the only sound penetrating the night is the distant fall of the fountain's water. I have so many questions I want to ask, but I don't dare. Not now, maybe not ever. The only thing I'm brave enough to ask for in this moment is his silence.

"Please, don't tell them, Idris," I whisper. He frowns. "For the longest time, terror was all I had. Gideon and Callum changed that for me, and I don't want fear to be the only thing I leave behind for them to remember me by."

For a long moment, he says nothing. The silence stretches so long that I give up. I'm pivoting to make my way out the door when his voice stops me in my tracks.

"I can numb your pain, but I cannot heal what's causing it." He sounds frustrated, but I can't tell if it's with the situation in general or me. "Come to me when it becomes too much."

I nod, then yank the door open and hurry away. He didn't make me any promises, but for some reason, I trust Idris to keep his mouth closed. The fae may not be able to pull me from the magical current dragging me under, but he can give me the strength I need to keep my head above water.

It will have to be enough.

When I get back to Gideon's room, the guys are still gone. I take the opportunity to nick my finger with my razor. The blood wells up immediately, and I press it to the dark spot on the front of the book.

Nothing happens. I stare at it, frustrated.

I'm about to go to bed when the air around the book starts to blur. I squint as smoke curls up and out of the ancient pages.

Shit, is my blood flammable?

I drop the book on the table, and it flies open to the title page. Dark, golden ink glows across the weathered paper.

My heart pounds with adrenaline and triumph. Finally, something is going right.

GIDEON

Not a godsdamn thing is going right.

I massage my temples, sick of listening to my dad and Dimitri argue about the latest hunter attack.

The cultists ambushed a group of wolf shifters on a retreat. From what we can tell, it happened near the border between our enclave and the one to the south. Most of the casualties were practically kids, which is fucking sickening enough on its own, but the leader of the trip was also a good friend of dad's. The hunters left his broken body in the woods, so my father is out for blood.

I'll help him spill it when the time is right, but all this talking in circles isn't getting us anywhere. At the end of the day, we still don't have a clue how the hunters are getting this intel. With each new attack, it's getting harder to argue against Sheena's mole theory.

I glance at the clock on my phone's lock screen and smother my impatience. My chest is throbbing, and I want nothing more than to crawl into bed beside Sheena and pass the fuck out.

Ever the respectful son, Callum is giving our fathers his full attention. At least on the surface. Beneath the table, his leg is bouncing up and down beside mine. If he doesn't cut it out, everyone at the table is going to notice, and then we'll both be in for a lecture.

I clamp my hand down around his thigh, trapping the nervous movement beneath my palm. Callum flashes me a frustrated look. His patience is worn thin, which means I have to step up and handle this. As soon as there is a lull in the yelling, I clear my throat loudly. Dad and Dimitri both turn to look at me.

"This is serious," I start. "Obviously, we need to shut the hunters down and find out who is feeding them their intel. We cannot and will not show weakness," I parrot their words back to them, and they both nod aggressively. Good. I need them to chill out. "I think we should regroup tomorrow and see if Idris has anything to add to the attack plan."

My father squints his eyes in consideration.

"I thought you two didn't like him," Dimitri grumbles. "You've been complaining about the alliance ever since you came home."

As usual, Dimitri chooses to be a disagreeable fuck.

My dad booms a laugh, but it's missing his normal joy. "That's because they think he's after their girl," he says. "It's the jealousy of young men, plain and simple, Dimitri."

The accusation stings, but I won't hide how strongly I feel for her. "She's a woman worth getting a little jealous over," I admit. "I was skeptical at first. That's true. But I think Idris is a valuable ally."

"What do you think, Callum?" My dad asks. "You've been very quiet."

I barely stifle my groan. He's just trying to make sure Cal is included, but it's going to backfire. Every time my friend speaks in these meetings, his father jumps down his throat.

"I think Idris wants the folk to thrive here," Callum says carefully. "And I believe he knows being a part of the enclave is the best way to accomplish that."

"So you're saying he has ulterior motives and could turn on us?" Dimitri twists his son's words exactly as I predicted.

"No, that's not what I said at all." Callum's tone is measured but tight. "However, I do think leaving him out of meetings like this is the quickest way to erode his trust."

"Do you have something to say, boy?" Dimitri growls. "You think you can run this enclave better than me?"

"Now, now, everyone, calm down." My dad realizes his mistake too late and tries to diffuse the tension, even though Dimitri is the only one raising his voice.

"I am calm." Callum sounds exhausted. "As always, my words have no hidden meanings, and I have no interest in running this enclave." He sighs heavily and stands. I shuffle to my feet to join him. "I also have no more energy to devote to this meeting tonight. It's late, but I'll be happy to talk more about this tomorrow."

Dimitri leans back in his chair, crossing his arms. He doesn't apologize, but at least he shuts up.

Callum looks at my dad, his eyes softening when he sees how distressed he is. "Joshua, I'm truly sorry about your friend. I hope you know I will do everything in my power to help you protect this community."

"I know that, Callum." My dad nods. "We'll talk more in the morning."

Sadness carves deep brackets in the skin between dad's eyebrows and along the corners of his mouth. *He looks old*. It terrifies me.

After I tell them goodnight, I follow Callum out of the conference room. I'm only seconds behind him, but even with a solid six inches of height to my advantage, I have to jog to catch up. Following him down the deserted hallway, I keep quiet as he seethes. When he stops abruptly and kicks over a trash can, I wait.

"Why does he talk to me like that, Gideon? What have I ever done to lose his trust?"

His voice is anguished. It makes me want to turn around and beat the shit out of Dimitri. Instead, I shrug my shoulders, hating how helpless his dad's behavior always makes me feel. "Nothing, Cal. You haven't done anything to deserve this."

"I fucking hate being here." He throws his arms out, gesturing to the dark walls.

"I know you do, man," I whisper.

"It makes me feel . . . small." His hand shakes slightly, and there's so much vulnerability in the final word, it pisses me off even more.

"That's bullshit," I snarl. Callum shakes his head and turns away from me. I grab his arm, spinning him around so I can see his face. "It is bullshit. You can be mad. You can kick shit over as much as you want, but you don't get to feel small."

Callum's eyes are dull and lifeless as he looks up at me. "You can't control that any more than you can control my father, Gideon."

He's shutting down.

"Dimitri is jealous," I insist. Callum scoffs and I tighten my grip. "I'm serious. You're twice the demon he is. The community respects you, and he knows . . ." I hesitate, unsure if he's ready to talk about this.

"Knows what?"

"He knows he fucked up with you." I loosen my grip on his arm, but I don't drop my hand. "His own bias made him freak out when your powers manifested. He fucked up, and instead of admitting that and trying to make it up to you now, his ego tells him to tear you down."

"Godsdamn man, you're making a lot of eloquent assumptions about a demon who hasn't wasted a second thought on me in years." Callum chuckles, trying to play it off. "Are you sure that wish wore off?"

"No jokes, Cal. I need you to hear me this time."

"I hear you," he says, lifting his eyes to finally meet mine.

He doesn't seem like he's hanging off the edge of a cliff anymore, but I can't read the look on his face. I'm opening my mouth to drive my point home when Callum's lips crash into mine.

The kiss is rough and a little desperate. There's nothing soft about his mouth. By the time I unfreeze from the shock, he's pulling away, eyes wide with panic. I lick my lips, irritated that he didn't give me time to participate.

"I'm so sorry," Callum whispers, backing away from me. "I don't know why I—"

I don't give him a chance to freak out. I wrap one hand around the back of his neck and drop my head down to kiss him again. This time, when his mouth meets mine, the pace is less frenzied. It's like both of us are tiptoeing into the unknown.

At some point, I forget. I forget he's a man. I forget he's my best friend. And I forget to be careful. Instead, I just enjoy the kiss. I enjoy the way it feels to discover new things about a person I know better than myself—like the way his lips taste and how he fights me for control.

When Cal sinks his hand into my tangled curls and tugs, I growl, pushing him back against the wall and pinning him there with my body. We grapple for dominance, the air scorching between us, the kiss a physical escape from our argument and my long-ass list of pent up frustrations.

It's fucking addictive.

By the time I pull back to catch my breath, I'm not on the fence about kissing my best friend anymore.

"You don't have to apologize to me," I growl, responding a little late to his earlier panic.

"Was that weird for you?" Callum drops his head back against the wall. "I don't want you to feel obligated or pressured—"

"Stop acting like you're a predator or something. I didn't push you off, did I?" I point to our position, where he's clearly the one backed against the wall.

"No, but—"

"Relax, Callum." I interrupt him again. "We kissed. It was hot." I adjust myself in my pants. "I can't tell you I know what this means for us, but we'll figure it out."

Stepping away from his body, I give him space to process and pick up the trash can he kicked over earlier.

"Seriously, I'm fine. Are you good?" I ask.

"I think so," he mutters.

There's a familiar wrinkle between his eyes. I shake my head and smile.

"Do you want to talk about why you kissed me?" When he blushes, I waggle my eyebrows. "There's no reason to be shy and shit now, Cal. Thirty seconds ago, you were using my hair like a steering wheel."

Callum looks at the top of my head with a slight smirk. My curls probably look like a used mop at this point. Unfortunately, his smile doesn't last, and the wrinkle reappears as he sighs.

"I don't know. I was just upset, and you got it. You get me. You always have," Callum explains. "It's not like I've thought about kissing you a bunch of times before, but suddenly, I couldn't think about anything else."

His eyes drop to my lips again, and I don't hesitate. I lean in and kiss him. It's a hell of a lot softer than our first few kisses.

"What was that for?" Callum asks, so close I can feel the question on my lips.

"I was thinking about it, so I did." I grin and take off down the hallway for real this time. "Come on. I'm exhausted, and it's time for bed."

"What would your mom say if she knew you were ordering me to bed?" Callum trails after me, laughing lightly when I groan.

"Knowing her . . . 'I told you so.'"

CALLUM

WE SLIDE INTO BED on either side of Sheena. I wrap my arms around her, relishing in the feel of her soft body against mine and the way her scent relaxes me. She's perfect.

My demon agrees—nothing has changed there. Not that I expected it to. It's uncommon for incubi to be picky about the gender of their partners. A meal is a meal, after all. But I've never kissed a man before. Beyond that, I've never even thought about making a move on my best friend. Even when I was practically starving with the need to replenish my magic, it didn't cross my mind.

He's too important.

"Stop overthinking," Gideon grumbles at me, his voice low and irritated.

"I'm not," I snap.

"Yes, you obviously are. Your thoughts are so loud, I can't sleep."

He's not wrong, but I can't just turn them off. It doesn't work like that. "But what does it mean?" I ask.

"Gods, Cal. It means whatever we decide it means."

His confidence settles me. *It means whatever we decide it means.* I can live with that.

I FEEL EYES on me when I wake up the next morning. I crack mine open blearily. Emerald green greets me, burning with excitement.

"Are you awake?" Sheena whispers, the sound too loud for whatever time it is.

"I am now." I wipe the sleep from my face and smile back at her. "Do you feel better today?"

"Yeah, I'm fine."

Sheena blows past my question, reaching across Gideon to grab the purple book off the nightstand. In the process, she jostles him awake. Like a bear coming out of hibernation, he grumbles, latching on to her and dragging her down his chest.

"More sleep," he grunts, but already she's squirming free.

"No more sleep. I have to show you something," Sheena insists. Gideon cracks one eye open hopefully, but I don't think she has any plans to show him what he's imagining right now.

"Can I borrow a claw?" She asks, holding up his hand.

Gideon looks confused, but he transforms his nails into razor sharp claws. The look of confusion on his face morphs into horror when Sheena rakes her middle finger over one sharp tip.

"What the fuck, Sheena?" He yells, quickly transforming his claws back into normal human fingernails.

"Hush and just watch."

She waves us off impatiently, then presses her bleeding finger against the dirty old book. Before I can comment about how unsanitary that is, smoke rises from the pages and the book pops open. Gideon's jaw drops. He looks as shocked as I feel.

"Right?" She giggles. "I almost had a panic attack last night when it did that."

"How in the world did you figure that out?" I ask, impressed that she thought to use blood magic to get the book to trust her.

"Don't be mad." She dips her head. "I went to talk to Idris last night during your meeting. The blood was his idea."

Of course it was. That shady shit thinks of everything.

I take a deep breath. "I'm not mad," I assure her.

"Was he polite?" Gideon asks. "He didn't try anything, did he?"

Sheena groans, swatting at him with the book.

"Careful. That binding is like a thousand years old, and you're slinging it around like a used magazine," I tease.

"He was a complete gentleman." She hesitates. I tilt my head, considering her guarded expression. I don't think she's lying, but there's something she's leaving out. Before I can push for more, she fills the silence herself. "What happened to you both, anyway? I tried to wait up, but that was a really long meeting."

"Last night was wild, baby," Gideon says. "The meeting was boring and tense, but after it was over, Callum found out I'm a great kisser."

Gideon stretches his arms over his head with a yawn as I flinch. Sheena blinks slowly as she glances between the two of us and processes what he just said.

"Sweetheart, are you upset?" I ask, eying her carefully.

"Yeah, kind of," Sheena admits with a pout. My heart sinks

like a rock in my chest as I imagine a dozen ways to punish Gideon for his poor planning. "You two kissed in real life, and I wasn't there to see? Will you kiss again now? Please."

Sheena slides her index finger inside the book to hold her place and looks between us expectantly with wide eyes. Gideon bursts out laughing, falling back onto the pillows.

"I told you. You were overthinking it, Cal." Gideon laughs for so long I get a little offended. When I climb out of bed to get some distance, two sets of eyes follow me.

"I think you've hurt his feelings," Sheena says to Gideon. "You should kiss him to make it up to him."

My lips curl against my will at her one-track mind. Gideon follows me out of bed, stretching to his full height before stepping closer to me.

"You really think so, baby? You think I should kiss him?" He addresses her while breathing in my air.

Suddenly, I can't think about anything but the heat building in the room.

"Yes, please," Sheena whispers, biting her bottom lip.

Gideon grabs my neck with one hand, yanking my lips to his. I do my best to control the kiss. When Gideon digs his thumb into the hollow of my throat, I retaliate by sinking one of my hands into his hair roughly and rubbing my bare chest against his. I bite his bottom lip hard and he growls into my mouth.

It's only when I feel Sheena's lust spike and merge with ours that I groan and shove him away. "Are we going to read the djinn book or just stand around all day making out?" I try to play it cool, but my panting ruins the effect.

"I mean, if I really get a choice—it's option two, for sure," Sheena says, sinking back into the pillows with a huff. "You two are so hot. I'm not going to be able to focus on anything."

I shake my head and hide my smile as I walk to the bathroom.

By the time I come back, Sheena is sitting on the love seat and holding the book studiously. Gideon is staring at it over her shoulder.

"It snaps shut if he even thinks about touching it," Sheena explains without looking up.

"That's what she said." I snicker.

Gideon flips me the bird.

"If the book is going to be a prude, I guess you're on solo research duty for now," I say, wedging myself in beside her on the small piece of furniture. I point to the book. "Is there an index? Maybe you can read any sections that mention talisman magic first, so we can go get that handled for you."

I know I sound a little blasé. But it's that or release all of my worries on the two of them, and that wouldn't be fair. Feigning nonchalance is the best I can do right now.

"No index or table of contents." Sheena smiles to soften the blow. "Given that they probably assembled this book when dinosaurs roamed the Earth, it's not exactly organized tradition-ally. I'll let you know as soon as I see anything about a talisman. I promise."

I frown at the book, annoyed that it's still being difficult. "If it's so old," I say. "I'm surprised it's even readable."

"Yeah, that's odd."

"It's not readable."

Sheena and Gideon contradict each other at the same time. We share confused looks, then all together, we look back down at the book. Gideon is right. The only thing I can make out is the word 'djinn.' Everything else is completely indecipherable.

"Are you guys messing with me?" Sheena asks, tucking some hair behind her ear and pointing at the page in front of her. "It says, 'the djinn are a powerful and ancient race with a sacred mission to protect and preserve.'"

Gideon and I exchange a surprised look.

"It may say that, baby, but it looks like gibberish to us," Gideon says, squinting at the text.

"Maybe you being able to read it while we can't is just another part of the book's magic," I suggest. They both turn to look at me and I shrug. "I don't have any better ideas. Just keep reading."

Sheena nods and begins reading in earnest. After several minutes of silence, Gideon starts to fidget on the arm of the couch. He's so big she gets jostled every time he moves.

Eventually she's had enough. Sheena marks her place in the book and looks up. "I don't know how long it's going to take me to read this, and there's no reason for you to sit here all day waiting. Why don't you both go find something else to do?"

"Are you trying to get rid of us?" I ask, smirking at her obvious exasperation.

"Is it that obvious?"

"Yeah, but I get it, baby." Gideon grins, planting a sloppy kiss on her cheek. "We need to check in with our dads about the latest attack anyway." He gives me a loaded look, and I groan.

"Yeah, yeah, we'll go talk to the dads and let you read." I drop a soft kiss on her lips, smiling against her mouth. "But only if you promise to let us know as soon as you learn something about talismans."

She nods and waves us off, sinking back into the plush cushions to focus.

SHEENA

After years of hiding out in the middle of nowhere and bussing tables to get by, I'm sitting in an actual mansion, reading an ancient book written in a dead language. No more chipped laminate countertops for me. The tables around me now are all covered in linen tablecloths and crystal vases.

How did I end up here?

I inhale deeply, feeling a dull ache in my heart and head. Curled up on the couch reading in the middle of the day sounds relaxing, but there's nothing leisurely about it. It'd be easier to enjoy if everything wasn't a matter of life and death.

With the guys gone, I can finally concentrate on reading. I

know they want to help, but their anxiety made it impossible for me to focus. *Hopefully, this book has some answers.*

I make my way through the introduction and can't help but groan when I realize it's basically saying 'with great power comes great responsibility.' Spider-Man's dead uncle already taught me that. I thumb ahead, skimming until I get to a section on tiers.

This is interesting.

Apparently, djinn have different levels of power. The book says some can only affect physical objects. *Like wishing for a soda from the fridge.* Others can bend minds and warp wills, not just changing opinions but controlling actions as well. Even stronger djinn can modify reality itself, creating and manipulating the world around them and everyone's perception of it.

The book goes on to say it's not uncommon for djinn to have some combination of these skills, but the levels of power vary wildly. *Which apply to me?* I've changed some mental and physical outcomes against my will in the past, but it's difficult to gauge the scope. I rub the furrow between my brows when my headache becomes a persistent throbbing.

Whoever wrote this doesn't go into how to test your magic, but there is a small section about how all djinn must be assessed by an elder after they come of age. Evidently, the elders are the ones who give djinn their power rankings and placements.

On the next page there's an elaborate table. It takes me a second to figure out what it's showing, but eventually, I realize it's a guideline for djinn community placements. Once I find the djinn's power level column, I can see not only the suggested tithe but also standards for their protection detail. Stronger djinn require more money and more guards.

Here's a friendly neighborhood djinn. Now pay up and don't let anyone kill them. Given that I appear to be the last of my kind, I'm guessing this organizational structure stopped working at some point. I'm not surprised. It's cold and transactional and favors communities that are already thriving.

I flip to the next chapter and sit up a little straighter.

'Limitations' is scrawled at the top of the page in a gilded, looping script.

According to the text, my magic cannot take a life. *Thank god.* The idea of becoming someone else's killing machine . . . I shudder.

Changing the past is another impossibility. While it might be handy to wish for all the djinn to be alive again, it could also cause a lot of problems.

The book also notes that djinn can't grant any wish that imbues an object with magic or affects the belongings of another djinn, even a relative. That eliminates the possibility of wishing for a talisman.

The final limitation is the nail in my coffin: djinn magic cannot be used to affect another djinn or for their own direct personal gain. If Gideon tried to wish me better or Callum wished I knew the answers, nothing would happen. That brings me back to square one, and my heart sinks.

The next page has an ornate illustration that takes my breath away. The djinn in the drawing is beautiful and terrifying. Her hair is floating, her features angular and sharp—almost jagged in a way that haunts me.

Is this how I look?

Brushing my fingertips over the art, I feel her strength, her resolve, her pride in who she is. This djinn doesn't look like she spent her life hiding. She looks like the kind of person stories and songs are written about. *Was her life an epic adventure? Did she have a great love?*

The throbbing in my head ratchets up another notch as a cold, lonely feeling settles around my heart.

I'm the only one left.

When Idris and Mallory talked about the djinn, it all felt so abstract. I was just a bystander, someone observing a great tragedy from the sidelines. Now, staring at this image after adding my blood to the stained cover of this book, I feel grief not only for myself but also for my species as a whole.

There's no one else.

As the last of us, I can't help feeling as though I've inherited a greater responsibility. Like I'm carrying the burden of the past on my shoulders with no one to tell me which way to go.

I pull my eyes away from the nameless djinn, shocked to feel a tear slip down my cheek. I let it fall and scrub the heel of my hand over my eyes to clear the blur of exhaustion. The pressure opens up the tiny cut on my finger from Gideon's claw. Red blood blooms on the tip. I pop it into my mouth, wincing at the slight sting as I focus back on the book.

The next chapter details the ethics of wishing. It says the responsibility lies with the djinn to determine if the wisher is worthy or if their desires are within the bounds of what's right.

I scoff. *Who can make that kind of determination correctly each time?*

Reading further, I learn djinn are instructed to take any doubts or concerns to the elders for a final decision. No wonder my people made enemies. There's a lot of room for subjective moral interpretation here. I can imagine an infinite number of scenarios in which wishes were denied and the asker became furious.

I find a centerfold illustration of various ornate pieces of jewelry next. There are rings, necklaces, bracelets, and even a jewel-encrusted tiara. Turning the page, I see: 'Attuning to your Talisman.'

This is it; the answers I need.

My breathing picks up as my fingers tighten around the book. I skim the section quickly. It explains how to pick from among your family's cache of talismans to find the one that fits you and your magic best. There's nothing about creating a new magical anchor—only a minor note at the bottom of the page which tells you to seek help from an elder if none of your options feel right.

I throw my head back against the couch and groan. I knew we weren't going to be able to pick up a talisman at the mall, but this is bleak. With no family or elders, the odds of me locating and bonding with a magical, life-saving artifact are pretty slim.

Frowning at the book in my hands, I go back through the section more carefully, hoping I missed something. Then, I read through the entire book from front to back without skipping around this time. It's short, probably less than a hundred pages, so it doesn't take me long to finish it.

Unfortunately, the answer doesn't appear. While some things —like social structure and power dynamics—stand out to me on the re-read, there's nothing that gets me any closer to a talisman. There are also no helpful tips on ways to slow or stop my deterioration without an anchor.

No pity.

Falling back on my original rule holds my panic at bay. I've never given up before, and I'm not about to start now.

Ignoring the throbbing in my head, I flip back to the beginning and start again.

CHAPTER
TWENTY-TWO

SHEENA

I come to in hell. Painful light stabs my eye sockets, and I reach for my head with shaking hands. I don't remember falling asleep, but I must have dozed off. It feels like knives are burrowing into my skull, slicing my brain to ribbons. As I push myself up from where I'm laying on the love seat, I try to focus, but the room is spinning.

Idris. I need to find Idris.

I stumble out the door and make it to the hallway before I have to lean against the wall to rest. That's how Sarah finds me.

"Sweetie, what's wrong?" She rushes over and wraps her arm around my shoulders. "Are you hurt?"

I shake my head, but the sudden movement sends needles of pain into my scalp.

"Get Idris, please," I whisper, hating how weak I sound.

Thankfully, Sarah doesn't question me. She helps me over to the couch, props me up with a pillow, and starts speaking urgently into her phone.

"Don't tell the guys," I beg. Her worried gaze sharpens. "I don't want them to be scared."

Sarah doesn't make any promises, but she also doesn't make any more calls.

"You're fading," she says, rubbing my cold hands between hers.

She can clearly see I'm not okay, so there's no point pretending otherwise. "It's more painful than I expected," I admit.

"And there was nothing in the book?"

"Not unless there's a way to bring my family back to life and find their stash of talismans without djinn magic. Otherwise, it's a dead end."

I cringe at my unintentional wording. *A dead end.* That's what I'm going to be if we can't find some sort of breakthrough. Sarah squeezes my hand, and I let my eyes fall closed. I don't want to see pity when she looks at me.

Moments later, I hear footsteps coming our way. They stop in front of me. I force my eyes back open and see Idris. He appraises me with a tense look. Without a word, he presses his hands to my forehead, and the agony begins to fade. Slowly, the room comes back into focus, and I breathe a sigh of relief.

"You're not better," he says. "I only hid the pain."

"I know, Idris." I nod weakly and lift my hands, watching as they tremble in the air between us. "Thank you for making it bearable."

He stands and turns his back on me without a word.

"I opened the book," I tell him, desperate to change the subject. I don't want him to see me as a fragile, breakable damsel in need of a savior. Idris turns his head slightly toward me, his profile flawless in the low light of the living room. "It had some rules, tiers of power—that kind of thing. But it was clear a talisman has to come from a relative or the elders."

"Long dead, all of them," Idris says.

I already knew that, but his words bring a sort of finality with them. I sink a little further into despair. "I'm sure we'll think of something," I mutter, but I'm not sure I really believe it.

"Damn right we will," Gideon growls, stepping into my line of sight. Anger and hurt burn in his eyes. "I could feel your pain. It stopped." He rubs his chest and looks at Idris. "But the bond—it's weaker somehow."

Sarah gasps, her hand flying to her mouth.

I guess our last secret is out of the bag now.

When Gideon realizes what he revealed, he turns to his mom. "I didn't mean to blurt it out like that, but Sheena is my fated mate. I knew it the second we met." Gideon shifts his focus back to me, and I couldn't look away if I tried. "I followed her back then out of curiosity." His voice cracks. "I follow her now because I can't imagine life without her."

I hold my hand out, and he sinks down and wraps his arms around me. Safe in the cuddle, I indulge in the fantasy that everything will be alright after all. It can't last, though.

"Idris took the pain, but he can't make me better," I say. I wanted to spare him from seeing this for as long as possible, but Gideon deserves to hear the truth from me. "The book didn't have any answers, no treasure map, no loopholes." His arms tighten around me, and I choke down a sob. "Gideon, I'm fading. Fast."

"Then we will seal our mate bond now." He growls the words directly in my ear, but everyone hears him. Sarah makes a choking sound, and I know there's something I'm missing.

"I'm not saying no, but what will that do?" I pull back and meet his eyes.

"It will bind our souls together. It could cure you."

I'm excited until I realize no one else is cheering with relief. There's something else he isn't saying.

"It could cure me or?" I ask, bracing myself.

Gideon flexes his jaw.

" . . . Or it could kill him too." Callum steps out from the shadows with a look of pure unfiltered agony on his face. Gideon snarls at him. "If you bond now it could either save you or kill him, depending on whose fate rises to the top."

"It's worth the risk." Gideon stands to square off against his friend.

"It isn't," I insist, sighing as Gideon glares down at me. "I'm at peace with . . . running out of options if it's only me who goes. I won't be your death sentence."

His expression is hard, and I can tell his mind is made up. So I play my trump card.

"Would you leave Callum all alone?"

Gideon's face shutters, and he looks from me to Callum with a kind of helpless desperation. It's hard to see him brought this low, but there are people who need him. I can't be the reason his life is cut short. After a silent standoff, Gideon shoulders past Idris and leaves the room. I don't want him to be alone right now, so I shoot Sarah an anxious look, and she follows her son out.

"So that's it?" Callum's voice cracks through the air like a whip. "You're just going to give up?"

"She's not giving up," Idris snaps before I can argue.

"It's not like that," I say, keeping my voice gentle. "I'm just out of ideas."

"I can't . . . I can't . . ." Callum's voice breaks. "I promised to protect you, sweetheart. I swore that as long as you were with us, you wouldn't have to be scared anymore."

His devastation breaks the tight grip I had on my emotions, and a tear slides down the side of my nose.

"And you kept your promise. I'm not scared anymore, Callum, but there's no one for you to fight. You can't protect me from this," I say. If we can't find a talisman, I don't want him remembering me with a cloud of guilt.

"We'll keep looking for books, rumors, anything," he assures me, gritting his teeth with determination. "All these talismans didn't just fucking disappear. I'll find them."

I force a smile through my tears. I try to believe there's a way through this like he does. Despite how awful my body feels, I'm able to muster up a tiny sliver of hope. It's a fraction of the amount I felt last night when the book finally opened for me, but it's something.

When I reach for Callum, he falls to his knees, burying his face in my neck. He takes in deep lungfuls of air like he's trying to breathe me in and confirm I'm still here.

"I will question the folk," Idris adds. He stands as a silent witness above us, and for some reason, his presence doesn't bother me. "If any of my people know of a talisman, we will find it."

"If you save her," Callum says, lifting his head and giving Idris a long, searching look. "Gideon and I will pay anything." For once, his tone is completely respectful, but his words seem to offend the fae anyway.

"You will owe me nothing." Idris bites each word off angrily, but his face doesn't show any emotion.

He steps back into my space and slides his hands to my temples. I feel the cool rush of his magic, and a little burst of energy flairs to life in my tired body.

"I'll be back first thing in the morning," Idris assures me, and I smile gratefully. "If you give her your blood, demon, it will help her fatigue."

"I know that," Callum hisses, his polite cease-fire at an end after Idris' obvious dismissal. "Do you plan to stay for that part too?"

A blush spreads across my face as I realize Callum's meaning.

"I wasn't intending to linger any longer, but if you're concerned you won't be up to the task . . ." Idris drawls, rolling his eyes as Callum jumps to his feet with clenched fists. "In that case, have a wonderful evening, little djinn."

Idris takes my hand, kisses the back of it, and then flips it over to press another kiss to my wrist. It makes my pulse race, and I know he can feel it. Before I can think of something to say, Idris disappears.

CALLUM

As I carry Sheena through the hallway, my mind loops through a living nightmare. Her arms around my neck are proof that she's still here—still mine—but I'm running out of time to fix this.

Sheena is dying. What if I can't save her?

Idris wants to take her from me.

Walking into the bedroom, I kick the door shut with a grunt. I might not be enough to save her, but I don't know how I'm supposed to accept that.

"You can put me down, you know." There's a hint of teasing in Sheena's voice, and it unlocks the worst of my tension.

"What if I don't want to let you go?" I nibble on her earlobe, pleased to feel her shiver at my touch.

"You don't have to," she says, grinning. "But you do have to tell me why you got so annoyed with Idris."

"Because this is serious," I snap, remembering that smug fucker's face. "I'm going to share blood with you because you're sick, and that asshole thought now would be a good time to come on to you."

Sheena laughs, but the sound is a little off.

"Callum . . ." She meets my eyes. "Idris doesn't want me. There's no way."

Now it's my turn to laugh.

"Of course he doesn't, sweetheart," I say sarcastically. "Like we weren't both right there when he offered to come fuck you."

She smacks the back of my head, and I carefully slide her down my body to sit on the edge of the bed. Stepping in between her legs, I smile when she immediately knots them around my waist.

"There's no reason to worry about it," I assure her, smoothing out the furrow between her eyes. That's for me and Gideon to deal with—if he ever comes back from wherever he went to freak out. "Your only worry is staying strong until we find a talisman." I force a smile, not wanting her to see how scared I am that we might fail. "If Idris wants you and that motivates him to help, that's fine with me."

Especially if it keeps her alive.

"I still think he was just trying to rile you up," Sheena says, wrinkling her nose. "Now, about this blood thing. Are you just going to put it in a cup or something? Maybe add a straw? I'm assuming I have to drink it."

"Yeah, but it won't be as gross as you're imagining." I press a kiss to her forehead. "You'll probably enjoy it. A lot."

"Have you ever done this before?" Sheena asks me, two spots of color popping up on her cheeks.

I hope she never stops blushing because I plan to spend the next few decades riling her up.

"You'll be my first," I whisper, dropping a kiss to her full lips.

It was only meant to be a peck, but she's so soft, so perfect. All my intentions go flying out the window. We kiss lazily, like we have all the time in the world, and each taste is better than the last. Her nails trail over my scalp, and I explore her face with my fingertips, eager to map out every dip and curve.

My determination to find a talisman bubbles up and threatens to choke me. *Fuck the odds.* The gods, nature, whatever powers are still around—they can't take her from me. I won't allow it.

As my thoughts get more possessive, our kiss changes. I'm clinging to her now, my grip on her chin tight as I plunge my tongue inside her mouth. Sheena meets me stroke for stroke, and I can taste her desperation. *She feels it too—the fear that our time is running out.* Her hands fist my hair so tightly it hurts, but I'm not going anywhere.

The taste of salt seeps into our kiss. It's from a tear, but I'm not even sure who it belongs to. Our emotions are pulling me under, and I don't fight them. If we can't fix this, I want her to leave this life knowing how precious she was to me.

"I love you," I gasp the words. "I love you so fucking much, Sheena." My fear of saying it out loud is gone.

"I love you too, Callum," Sheena says. Her voice is raw and

anguished, and I know she's not holding anything back. "I don't want to go." She sobs, her fingers and legs shaking as she holds me close. "I'm not ready to lose you."

My heart breaks.

So I devour her, kissing this woman like I can erase her fear with my love—as if our passion has the power to change everything. For a while, maybe it does.

Her lust builds to a boiling point alongside mine. I can feel it threatening to set the whole room on fire. I'm dragged from the inferno when the door opens with a click behind us and Gideon shuffles in.

It's about time.

He comes up behind me, and I reluctantly pull back from our never-ending kiss. Sheena reaches her hand out and Gideon takes it, pressing a kiss to her knuckles and wrapping his long arms around both of us.

"Are you okay?" Sheena hums, her glowing purple eyes brimming with compassion.

Gideon puffs out a breath, dipping his chin down to rest on my shoulder. "No," he grunts.

And honestly, same here. I think that one word sums up how we all feel about this situation.

"We'll figure it out," I insist. "I won't lose either of you." It's the first time I've admitted feelings for him, but it's a relief to finally drop my guard. He's not allowed to hatch crazy plans that leave me all alone.

"Cal, I'm sorry," Gideon says. His arms tighten around us. "I didn't mean—"

"I know you didn't," I interrupt before he can beat himself up. "Believe me, I get it. Part of me even wants to let you try."

We all sag at the reminder of our reality.

"I have a request." Sheena lifts her chin, and we both direct our attention back to her. "No more worry, at least not for tonight. Can we just enjoy being together?"

The question and the way her voice trembles as she asks hit me right in the heart.

"Whatever you want, baby," Gideon says, voice raw.

He sounds like he's teetering on the edge of a cliff, so I step back and give him room. Gideon immediately takes the space. But instead of standing between Sheena's legs, he follows her down on the bed, kissing her and whispering words I don't try to overhear.

They need this moment, and I have a job to do.

I pull a pocketknife out of my jeans, flick the blade open, and drag it down my arm to make a shallow cut. It won't take much, so there's no need to make a mess. When I step back to the bed, Gideon is sitting behind Sheena. She's propped against his chest, eying the blood warily.

"Just a few swallows," I tell her, bringing my arm up to her face, but stopping a few inches from her mouth.

She leans down and hesitates, looking up at me and biting her bottom lip. I wink at her, and she tentatively drops her mouth to my arm. I know when she tastes my blood because I feel her stiffen in surprise. She laps around the cut experimentally. It feels so good, I moan. Sheena's head whips up in concern.

The cut closes up in seconds, but I'm falling apart from all the sensations. Sheena's pupils are huge, the dark almost completely eclipsing her vibrant irises. When they flash purple, I take a deep breath, letting her desire soak into my bones.

"Do you feel good, baby?" Gideon grins as he kisses down the side of her neck.

She shudders and writhes against him as I toss the pocketknife on the bedside table and crawl between her legs. My favorite place in the universe.

"How are we doing this?" I ask my friend, feeling all of my blood rush to my dick as he teases her. When he looks up at me, there's so much lust and affection in his eyes it nearly wrecks me.

"Well, for starters, everyone is overdressed," Gideon rasps.

Sheena takes his words to heart. She lunges at me, ripping my t-shirt over my head and tossing it to the floor. When her small fingers drop to my waist, Gideon takes advantage of the way she's leaning forward and palms her ass, smiling as she yanks at my pants with frustration. I choke on a laugh when she gives up on getting the jeans off entirely and shoves her hand down the front of my pants.

Her warm fingers wrap around my cock. I thrust into her hand, and she squeezes my length with the perfect pressure, rolling her thumb over the tip with each pass. When I look up, desperate to deepen our connection, her eyes are glowing purple.

"Help. Me. Now," Sheena demands, stroking me in time with each word while looking pointedly at my jeans.

Since I'm not a fucking idiot, I fucking help her.

We work my pants and underwear down my hips together. I moan as soon as her hot mouth finds me. In the dozens of times I've imagined her lips around me, she was always shy and took her time. In reality, Sheena dives in, swallowing me to the hilt and sucking enthusiastically. I'm thrilled to be wrong.

"Holy fucking shit," I groan.

I grip her hair, terrified by the very real possibility that I might explode after thirty seconds in her mouth. I look to Gideon for help, but his eyes are glued to where Sheena is licking me like I'm her favorite ice cream cone.

"Your mouth is so fucking perfect," I grunt, soaking up the pleasure and the view of her cheeks hollowed around me as she sucks.

When she gasps around my cock, I see Gideon has done away with her pants and has his thick fingers buried between her thighs. Watching Sheena ride his hand while she blows me has got to be one of the hottest things I've ever seen in my life.

Desperate, I slide my hands inside her shirt and bra, circling her nipples, then pinching sharply. She groans again; her vibrations the perfect torture. When she brings one hand up to play with my balls, I'm done for.

It's a race to the finish line, and I don't want to win.

So I do the only thing I can and call for backup. I lock eyes with Gideon. He winks at me, then does something with his hand that makes Sheena go rigid between us. She screams as she comes, the sound garbled by my cock, and I can't hold back any longer. I tap her head to warn her, but she sucks me deeper until I erupt in her throat. She swallows every drop, licking her lips and looking up at me from her knees with a smile.

"You're delicious, Cal," Sheena says. Her voice is raspy and low, so sensual and satisfied that I'm left speechless.

I'm supposed to be the sex demon here, but my girl just consumed my soul.

GIDEON

CALLUM'S FACE IS SLACK with awe, like he's about to build a shrine to Sheena's head game. While he floats at the foot of the bed in a post-o daze, I strip and pull her back against my chest.

"Are you proud of yourself, baby?" I whisper to her. "You sucked the English language right out of him."

She basks in the praise, and I give her a moment to feel smug. Wrapping my hands around her waist, I lift her up to hover right over my cock. She tenses, anticipating the drop, but I make her wait for it. Sinking just the tip inside, I hold her still as she squirms.

It's my turn now.

"I want you to remember," I growl. "Exactly how it feels when I stretch you open."

Her sweet whimper sinks into the neediest parts of me. Only when I feel her clawing at my thighs do I let her body sink down. Inch by inch, I fill her up until we're both gasping for breath. When I finally bottom out, I hold us both completely still and pull her hair to the side.

"You take me so well, baby." I nibble on her earlobe and feel her clench around me. "Do you know what you do to me? How I feel about you? Every second of every minute of every hour of every godsdamn day, I feel your heart beating inside my chest. It tells me I'll be yours forever. Even when our names are lost to time. Even when some meteor turns this planet into a ball of fire, I'll still love you."

I choke on the last words. It's the first time I've said them out loud, but I've known they were true now for a while. When Sheena twists her head to face me, tears are glistening in her lavender eyes.

"I love you too, Gideon."

Sheena presses her lips to mine, and I'm lost in our connection. Our bond pulses happily as our mouths meet. I'm obsessed with how we share oxygen between kisses. She pulls back and drops her head into the crook of my neck, and I can't imagine anything better.

"I love the way you protect your people so ferociously," Sheena says. I feel Callum's gaze burning against my skin and shudder. "I love how you make things simple when I'm over-thinking. I even love how you claim to be bad with words, then turn me into a puddle with your dirty talk."

She clenches around me again, and I groan.

"What about how I never have clean towels in the bathroom? Do you love that?" I ask.

Her giggle is music to my ears.

"Don't push it." Sheena teases me with a twist of her torso, so I thrust into her in quick, sharp strokes. "Fresh. Linens. Are. Important. Gideon." My name comes out of her lips in a strangled moan as I lift her up and shove her down, fucking her hard from the top and bottom.

Callum sinks to his knees in front of us and licks her clit with as much enthusiasm as she sucked his cock. He's so close to where we're joined that I can feel his tongue too. I go completely feral. Unable to hold back any longer, I fuck Sheena so hard she's bouncing up and down on my lap.

"Come for us, baby."

She moans. I bite down on her neck. It's not hard enough to break the skin and cement our bond, but it quiets the beast inside me. The feeling of her nails digging into my skin as she comes is the best fucking agony.

As her pussy tightens rhythmically around me, I slow down and give her a breather. But Callum isn't done yet. He licks Sheena through her orgasm until she's screaming. When I feel the pressure skyrocket, I lift her off my dick and watch as she soaks Cal's face. Sheena sags against me.

"Are you good, baby?" I ask.

She dips her chin in a half-assed nod. I get lost in the way her chest rises and falls with her frantic breathing, smiling at the glazed look in her eyes.

"Good. Because I'm not done."

Her eyes widen, but before she can react, I flip her on her back beside Callum and bury myself inside her once again. I'm so deep in this position, I can't tell where she stops and I begin. Her . . . me . . . *us*. It's everything I didn't know I was missing.

Picking up the pace, I lift her legs and prop her ankles on either side of my neck. I won't last much longer like this, but I want to bring her with me at least one more time.

"So tight," I mutter. "So perfect." I'm living for the sexy little sounds she makes every time I thrust into her.

Cal is kneeling beside us now, fingers toying with one of her nipples as he whispers filthy shit in her ear. The roaring in my head is so loud I can't make out what he's saying. From the way Sheena's blush is spreading down her chest and belly, it's got to be top tier.

"What are you saying to her?" I demand.

"I told her watching her wet little pussy swallow your huge cock was making me hungry." Callum's dark chuckle sends shivers down my spine, and Sheena squeezes me a little tighter.

"Dude," I groan. "She strangles my dick every time you talk."

The smug fucker just grins, bending his head back to her ear and resuming his nasty play-by-play loud enough for me to hear. He tells her he could watch her take dick all day, that nothing could be more gorgeous than her blush, and that he'll never get enough of her pussy or her laugh. The mix of filthy and sweet is taking us both apart.

When he describes how he can't wait until we're both buried inside her together, my rhythm falters. Sheena pulls Callum's hair and kisses him desperately. I slide my hand between our bodies and rub tight, firm circles on her clit like my life depends on it.

Sheena's mouth opens in a silent scream, her entire body strung tight from the force of her orgasm. With that fucking view, I can't hold off any longer. I finish inside her, dropping a final bruising kiss to her lips as I come.

When my arms start to tremble from the effort it takes to keep from crushing her, I pull away and flop onto my back. Callum curls around her other side, and for the next few minutes, we lay in silence, sprawled near the footboard in a messy heap of ragged breathing.

"Do you think the tub is big enough for three?" Sheena's voice is hoarse.

"I bet we can make it work," Callum says, pressing a smacking kiss to her shoulder. "We've certainly fit three in other situations that usually only call for two."

His dirty comment earns him a half-hearted smack that he easily dodges by rolling off the bed. As he heads into the bathroom to start the water, I can't resist pulling Sheena back into my arms.

"You know you mean more to me than I'll ever be able to say," I tell her.

"But you tell me all the time," Sheena insists, shaking her head. "When you treat me like I'm the only person in the room. In the way you hold me tight." She runs her fingers down my arm. "You make love to me with your entire soul, so how could I doubt you?"

I smile as I look down at her sleepy face.

Cal calls out to let us know the bath is ready. I press a kiss to Sheena's forehead and carry her to the tub. It's a tight fit, but we manage it. Laughing and splashing around, I let the warm water wash away the worst of my worry.

I don't believe the gods would bring us together only to tear us apart. We just have to have a little faith.

CHAPTER
TWENTY-THREE

IDRIS

My magic lashes out like an icy storm. Frozen bursts send the papers I've been sifting through flying across the room. I sip from my tumbler of whiskey, but only a trickle of liquor makes it through the sheet of ice that's formed in the glass.

The little djinn is going to die.

She is fading away like sunlight devoured by night, fragile as butterfly wings and just as fleeting. Soon she will be gone, and another ghost will haunt me.

Perhaps the gods have cursed me to stand silently by as an impotent witness to tragedy, saddling me with the weight of the cruelest of memories. I have knowledge, but it cannot help her. I have power, but it cannot save her. I can take her pain, but not the true poison siphoning away her life force.

Even now, as her magic consumes her from the inside out, Sheena clings to hope. *Insidious and slippery, I have no stomach for that particular emotion.*

I look down at the useless spread of papers with disgust, cursing myself for getting involved in the first place. There is neither word nor rumor of any magical objects or talismans kept hidden through time. Now, as her strength wanes, I am out of answers.

I wish she had never turned her green eyes in my direction.

A floorboard creaks, and I sense her incubus demon standing behind me. I turn to find him staring at my destroyed study, fear etched across his face.

"You really can't help her," Callum says, each syllable warped by pain. It puts a damper on the rage I feel at the invasion of my privacy at two o'clock in the morning.

"I cannot," I admit, forcing my fists to unclench.

"Do you know how long she has?"

His voice trembles, but there's an undercurrent of determination that surprises me. Perhaps I underestimated him. *If only that mattered.*

Meeting his stare, I shake my head. "No exact estimate, but from what I felt . . ." The demon's black eyes glitter dangerously in the dark. "She does not have long."

Instead of slumping in response, Callum stands a little taller. "I gave her my blood. She's resting now—"

"But it won't last." I finish the thought and he nods.

"I have to go," he says. I blink at his quick shift. "Will you manage her pain while I'm gone?"

Although the question is simple enough, the distaste he feels asking for my help is written across his face. I find it less satisfying than usual.

"I will give her all the relief at my disposal." I incline my head to assure him. It's a pointless exercise. We both know I would grant her that comfort with or without his request. "What could be so important to pull you away from her side now?"

I have my suspicions, but I want to hear him confirm them. While I don't expect him to answer, I find myself strangely frustrated when he simply meets my stare, and then turns to leave.

"Callum." I raise my voice. His name feels odd on my tongue. "What do you intend to do?"

He pauses but doesn't face me.

"Whatever it takes."

The demon leaves my wing without another word. May he find more success than the gods ever afforded me.

As soon as the sun rises, I creep through the shifter wing with my invisibility glamour firmly in place. I have neither the time nor the patience to answer questions about why I'm lurking around at dawn. I slip into their bedroom and find Gideon already awake. He holds her tight to his side as she shivers and moans in her sleep.

Just like in the courtyard, he smells me at once.

"I know you're here, fae," he whispers.

Fate is stealing his mate from his arms. It's cruel, but I'm still cautious. With the absence of an enemy to fight, he could turn his rage on me. Carefully, I remove the glamour and study him.

"Help her, please," Gideon begs.

His pleading startles me, but I don't hesitate to approach the bed and assess the situation. Gideon has the blankets piled high around them, even though the temperature in the room is already uncomfortably warm. Sheena's hair is damp with sweat, and when I place my fingers to her temples, her skin is icy to the touch. A shiver rolls down my spine.

It's worse than I thought.

I take Sheena's pain, watching as she relaxes into the pillows. Her head turns into Gideon's chest, seeking his comfort even in her sleep. He watches her like one might observe their salvation and damnation all rolled into one.

"Do you know where Callum is?" Gideon asks, glancing at me as he tucks the covers tightly around Sheena.

"I do not," I say. He looks down, defeat etched in every line of his body. Despite myself, I feel a pang of sympathy. "But I spoke to him earlier this morning. I believe he is working on some sort of plan."

Gideon perks up for a moment before narrowing his eyes.

"It wouldn't have killed him to say that," he mutters, and a muscle in his jaw twitches. "Sneaking out in the middle of the night and turning his phone off is fucked up."

Personally, I agree, but I keep my opinions to myself, sinking gingerly down into a seat near the bed. At his raised eyebrows, I steeple my fingers. "Callum asked me to ensure she remained pain free until his return."

Gideon accepts that without question, but he watches me with a calculating gleam in his eye.

"What?" I snap, fed up with his ill-concealed speculation.

"You said you don't know where he is." Gideon strokes his chin. "But you must have suspicions."

Certainly, but that doesn't mean he's entitled to them. Leaning back, I hold my ground against his probing eye contact.

"I would never venture to hazard a guess," I talk over his scoff. "However, from Callum's demeanor, I suspect his plan to be something he believes to be an unpopular choice."

Gideon sits on that for a moment, eyes narrowed in thought. If he has any suspicions about where his friend went, he doesn't share them with me.

CHAPTER
TWENTY-FOUR

CALLUM

Stomping on the gas, I listen to the abused engine whine and watch the sun rise. I've never hated these winding mountain roads more. When I round a narrow curve too quickly for the SUV to handle, I smell burning rubber. Gritting my teeth, I keep it between the lines and slow down a hair. I need to get back to the woman I love. A wreck won't help me get there any faster.

Holy gods. I actually did it.

Calling Alina last night was a desperation move, and when she demanded we meet in person to talk, I almost said no. Gideon and I haven't exactly been on speaking terms with her since her coven split with the enclave. Still, I had to try. We don't have any other leads left.

When Alina and the rest of the witches moved out of their wing at the compound, I was relieved. I think most of us were. The fighting—the constant, unhinged disagreements happening behind closed doors—it was toxic as hell. But Alina seemed over the drama when we ran into her at the library. She even hinted at our shared childhood like she wanted reconciliation.

I'm not a fool. I know she hopes for more from Gideon and me. While we've never reciprocated her feelings, I'm not above using them to save Sheena. Alina is a strong witch. I took a chance that she could help and it's paying off.

Alina has a talisman that could save Sheena.

Speeding up again, I grope around in the cup holder and turn my phone back on. I wince as I scroll over all the missed texts and calls from Gideon. It was a dick move to sneak out in the middle of the night, but when I felt Sheena's fever take hold, I had to do something. There wasn't time to argue.

I dial Gideon's number. He picks up on the second ring.

"Are you okay?" His tone is clipped.

He has every reason to be mad, but I barrel ahead.

"Yeah, I'm fine. I've got a lead. Tell Sheena to get ready to go."

"Cal—"

"I don't want to hear it right now, dude. You can yell at me later. Alina has a talisman."

"Callum—" He tries again, and I groan in frustration.

"Gideon, are you even listening to me? This could be the answer to everything. Get Sheena dressed. I'll be there soon."

"Fuck, Callum—she won't wake up."

His frantic words penetrate my brain, and my knuckles go white as bone against the steering wheel. "What? Get Idris over there."

"He's here. She's not hurting. She's just not . . . alert." Gideon sounds terrified. My heart rate spikes. "Why can't you bring the talisman here?"

I wince. It's the exact question I expected him to ask.

"Alina says I need to bring her."

"Well, fuck Alina's games," Gideon growls. "That's sketchy as hell."

"She doesn't want to come back to the compound. Which I get." Frustration rises within me. This debate is pointless. The alternative is waiting for Sheena's heart to stop, and that's not an option.

"Did you even ask why she has a talisman in the first place?" Gideon demands. "If the thirsty witch wants to help so godsdamn bad, why can't she just give it to you?"

I slam my fist into the horn. I knew he would do this; it's why I didn't bring him along.

"I'm aware," I snap. "But please—since you know everything —tell me the better choice."

"I don't know. How about anything that doesn't involve dragging my fated mate's limp body all over Colorado?" He roars into the phone, and I have to take a deep breath to calm myself. I know he's scared, but now isn't the time for either of us to melt down. Sheena needs us.

"We'll be right there. We'll keep her safe, Gideon, I promise."

For a beat, the only thing I hear on the other end of the line is his heavy breathing, then I make out another voice.

"What's he saying?" I ask, irritated Idris is at Sheena's side and helping her in a way I can't right now.

"That you're right. We're out of options." Gideon grits the words out, and I can just picture the stubborn look on his face. "Callum, if she tries to hurt her—"

"We won't let that happen. Get ready. I'm twelve minutes out." I hang up the phone, determination sinking into my bones. If Alina double-crosses us, there will be war.

———————————

I PULL INTO THE COURTYARD so fast the SUV struggles to keep all four wheels on the ground. Gideon carries Sheena toward me, her body hanging limp and lifeless in his arms. A shiver rolls down my spine. If I couldn't see her chest rising and falling, I would think she was already gone.

She promised not to leave us again. Sheena is a fighter.

I leave the key in the ignition and jump out to open the back door for Gideon. He lays Sheena across the seat gently and climbs in beside her. He doesn't look at me. Idris claims the passenger seat without a word, and I have to resist the urge to demand he fuck right off.

Joshua and Sarah step forward, and I raise my hands with my palms out. "I know what you're going to say. But we have to try."

Sarah looks between her son and I before nodding slowly, her face pinched with worry. Joshua sighs, folding his arms.

"Be careful, all of you. I don't want you boys to repeat our mistakes." Joshua's voice is uncharacteristically grave.

I spare him a quick nod before hopping back into the SUV and taking off. It's time to save the woman I love. If that means every supernatural creature on the fucking planet finds out what she is and comes looking for trouble, then I'll get my hands bloody. It's that simple.

"How is she?" I ask, glancing in the rearview mirror.

"She's still here." Gideon's voice is raspy and tired.

"There's no pain," Idris says.

Hearing his cool tone reminds me the fae just climbed into my SUV with no invitation. I snap my head around to look at him. "Why the fuck are you here?"

"I'm curious to know if you behave in this hostile way towards everyone you come into contact with," Idris says, his lips curving into a tight smirk. "Or is it a treat reserved for those trying to help you?"

I tighten my hands around the wheel to resist the urge to smack him. "I save it for people who want to poach my girl," I spit back.

"You raise an interesting point," Idris says. "But if someone can be poached, were they ever really yours to begin with?"

The bastard doesn't even bother denying he wants her. He's so smug, I want to pull over and kick his ass.

The only thing that stops me is a pitiful moan from the back seat. I twist my head to look at Sheena, but Idris reacts even quicker, his arm already outstretched and reaching for her. Gideon moves Sheena's head into the fae's palm, no questions asked. Their actions are familiar and practiced.

I focus back on the road as Idris sighs and slumps back against the passenger seat.

"Idris is here to keep Sheena pain free and back us up if things turn to shit. We're thankful for his help," Gideon grits the words out, and I nod reluctantly. "No fighting. No arguing. She's our only priority."

Dammit, he's right. I can't believe I needed the reminder.

"If Alina tries anything, one of us needs to get Sheena out of there," I say.

"It should be Idris," Gideon grunts. "Before you argue, he can glamour her. That's the best chance she has. You and I will be ready to fight."

I can't argue with his logic. Out of the corner of my eye, I assess Idris. He's as serious as I've ever seen him. *Good.* I meet Gideon's eyes in the rearview mirror and nod.

Together, we work out a loose plan for when we arrive. Gideon and Idris switch seats, and once that's done, we drive in tense silence. The only sounds interrupting the stillness are Sheena's labored breaths and the gentle hum of the engine.

When I pull up in front of the address Alina sent, I'm surprised. Far from the gaudy monstrosity I expected, it looks like any normal house you'd find on an average street in a middle-class suburb. There are white picket fences, carefully manicured lawns, and lots of Hondas and Nissans parked in driveways. There's absolutely nothing that stands out as supernatural.

I double-check the address of the two-story brick house just in case. It's the right one, so I take a deep breath and put the SUV in park. Gideon is so tense, I can feel heat radiating off of his body. With one final look at Idris and Sheena in the back seat, we get out.

As Gideon and I approach the porch steps, our hands brush. The brief contact makes me want to stop and wrap my arms around him, but I hold myself back. As if he can sense my conflict, Gideon throws his arm over my shoulder and looks at me.

"You did the right thing," he admits quietly. "Risk or not, we had to try."

His words unravel a horrible knot inside me and my shoulders sag with relief. I hated being at odds even for a minute. We've always been a team, and it feels right to be in sync again.

Hearts racing, Gideon and I climb the steps together.

GIDEON

My ADRENALINE ROCKETS into overdrive and every hair on my body stands on end when Cal knocks on the door. I don't like this shit. My animal fucking hates it. He thinks we're going into battle and wants to shift. It's getting harder by the second to convince him this situation calls for the man, not the lion.

The door opens with a high-pitched creak. My left arm trembles. I grip it hard to stop the shift. Alina stares up at us, a fake smile glued to her face.

I breathe deeply through my nose to check for any other scents. When nothing besides Alina's overwhelming perfume hits me, I release my arm but keep my guard up. If I learned anything growing up around a coven, it's that witches are unpredictable. The second you think you've got one figured out, they turn around and do the opposite of what you think.

"It's good to see you again, Gideon," Alina chirps. Her smile frays around the edges as she looks at me, but I can't bring myself to give a damn. "Where's your djinn?"

She talks about Sheena like she's a designer pet. I bite my tongue to hold back my instinctual need to put Alina in her place. If she's truly willing to help, I can't risk pissing her off before we get what we need.

"She's here," Callum says. He turns and looks over his shoulder—the signal we told Idris to watch for.

Where the SUV looked empty before, the fae suddenly

appears. He gets out, cradling Sheena in his arms with a blank look on his face.

"Ah, boys," Alina purrs and claps her hands with delight. "I see you're thanking me for my gesture of friendship with some new tricks."

Instead of being offended by the glamour, she seems pleased to learn we hid things from her.

Fucking witches.

Silently, Idris climbs the stairs, carefully supporting Sheena's head on his shoulder. Alina ignores him completely, turning her full attention to my mate.

"You weren't kidding. She doesn't seem well at all." She clicks her tongue, but the sympathy is as fake as her smile. "Perhaps I can do something about that."

Alina reaches for Sheena. Callum and I step together to block her path. She laughs, the sound grating and way too fucking loud given the circumstances.

"She really is your djinn after all then. How curious that you would protect her from an old friend." Alina pouts, but I'm not falling for her antics. Neither is Cal.

"I followed your instructions. She's here. You've seen her," Callum snaps. "Now where's the talisman?"

He sounds dangerous, but Alina just rolls her eyes and pulls a ring from her pocket. I don't have a clue if it's actually what Sheena needs to harness her power, but it looks old. When Callum reaches out to take it, Alina snatches her hand back.

"Not so fast, darling. I didn't ask to see her. I asked to meet her." Alina tuts, tapping the ring against her chin. "We can hardly meet if she's not even awake to say 'hi.'"

I swallow my growl, already sick to death of Alina's games. We could try to overpower her and take it, but only the gods know the hell the witches would rain down on us if they thought we were stealing from the coven. Playing along is still the best choice.

Even knowing that, it takes me two tries to get my body to

obey my brain and step aside. As the witch advances, I block her with my hand and speak for the first time. "If you hurt her, Alina, I won't rest until you're dead."

I lock eyes with her, and she finally loses her fake smile.

"Always so rude," Alina huffs at me. "Threat received, Gideon." Pivoting and walking into the house, she tosses her hair over her shoulder. "At least bring her inside so we're not causing a spectacle for every bored human in the neighborhood."

One by one, we follow her in. The door swings shut by itself.

When Alina reaches for Sheena again, I allow it, ignoring every muscle in my body that demands I stop her. The witch places one hand against Sheena's temple and the other against her heart. I've seen Alina use magic before, but when her fingers begin to glow a hazy green color, I stiffen. Watching anyone cast so close to where the mate bond lives feels wrong.

Color returns to Sheena's chalky cheeks and her breathing becomes less ragged. Her beautiful green eyes flutter open, and Alina steps back, chest heaving and shoulders slumped. Whatever she did took effort.

Sheena blinks as she looks around and takes in the unfamiliar house, the stranger, and the tense looks on all of our faces. When she realizes Idris is holding her, she seems even more flustered.

"So you're the last djinn," Alina says in a dry tone.

"I'm Sheena," she says, tapping on Idris' neck until he puts her down. As soon as her feet hit the ground, he shifts to hover behind her like a silent watchdog.

"I'm Alina, the witch that just wrapped you in a magical bandage and bought you some time." She pats her pocket. "But I think I have something you've been looking for."

Alina pulls the ring out. When I first saw it on the porch, it looked like the witch found it buried underground using some weirdo's metal detector. Now, it's glowing.

"Is that a talisman?" Sheena's eyes light up as she pieces everything together.

"It would certainly seem so," Alina says with a smirk. "My

coven has had this ring for hundreds of years. The old ones say it once belonged to a powerful djinn."

Sheena's eyes flash purple when she looks at the talisman. It takes some effort for her to tear her focus away from it and meet Alina's eyes instead.

"And you're just willing to give it to me?" Sheena studies the witch with suspicion, and my chest swells with pride. "Why would you do that?"

"Consider it a gesture of friendship," Alina says with a tinkling laugh. "Your boys and I go way back. It's the least I could do."

She implies a familiarity that neither of us had with her. When Sheena doesn't give her the reaction she's looking for, an angry glint appears in Alina's eyes. Warning bells go off in my head.

We all hold our breath when the witch offers the ring to Sheena. The closer her fingers come, the more the thing glows. It's so bright I have to shield my eyes.

Before Sheena makes contact, her feet leave the ground and her hair begins to float. It's exactly like the time I activated her powers in the kitchen—a moment so pivotal to our relationship that I don't think I could forget it if I tried. I know without looking that her features have sharpened to match her dazzling purple eyes.

Sheena's fingers close around the ring.

A blinding light shoots out in all directions. Dark spots cloud my vision.

I hear a muted apology, then a crackling sound. I reach for Sheena, but it's already too late. They're gone.

My heart rips in two.

EPILOGUE

QUAID

Sheena is alive.

Nothing could have prepared me for this. I stand frozen by the window as she disappears with the witch. I'm so stunned by the sight of my failure that I don't even feel the disgusting chill that usually runs through me when I encounter magic.

After fighting my misgivings, I broke rank today and followed the informant. We've slaughtered dozens of targets since the witch showed up. But it doesn't feel right. Hunters aren't weapons for abominations like her to use to further their own plans.

We've been blindly playing into her agenda.

When she came to this house, I suspected the witch planned to attack some humans who lived in the area. Then I saw her greet two males on the porch and thought it was some dirty hookup.

Never in my wildest dreams did I expect to see Sheena. Once I recognized her, it took all my discipline not to reveal myself. My former friend . . . within my reach after all this time. She looked grown up and as dangerous as I always feared she'd become. Glowing purple eyes. Face monstrously warped.

I'm not sure if she's working with the witch, but she's certainly not my friend anymore. She's living proof of my weakness. I feel a pang of guilt. It's my fault she even made it to adulthood.

I have no choice but to destroy her.

From my hiding place, I watch the three males react to Sheena's disappearance. The huge freak is destroying furniture and tearing at his chest like a madman. He came unglued as soon as the light cleared. Meanwhile, the one with tattoos clings to the doorframe, his black eyes wild as he scans the room. The third male holds himself apart, his posture like something from a different time. When he snaps his head in my direction, cold blue eyes lock with mine, and I see the pointed tips of his ears peaking out from his hair.

Fuck. He's fae. I've been made.

It's tempting to take them all on, but I retreat. One is having an emotional breakdown, but the other two make me pause. All three can wait for now. They'll meet their end soon enough.

It's time to right my one wrong and regain my perfect record.

My mission is clear: hunt Sheena down.

AUTHOR'S NOTE

Don't panic. Everything is going to be fine.

**Lost Legacy Book 2, The Last Dream,
is available now.**

If you enjoyed The Last Wish, please consider leaving a rating or review. These make such a difference for indie authors, and I love hearing from you!

Download Deleted Scenes, Sarah's Chocolate Chip Cookie Recipe, and receive updates on my next series by signing up for my newsletter or scanning the QR code below with your phone's camera.

ACKNOWLEDGMENTS

Hot damn. This page feels a long time coming because this book would still only exist in my head if not for the amazing support system around me.

First, for Gabe, the love of my life. Dating you was the best decision any 20-year-old has ever made. Thank you for spending the last decade proving that real life men can not only live up to book boyfriends but also surpass them. You don't read romance novels or urban fantasy, but you've read this one about ten times now and never hesitated to talk me off the metaphorical ledge. There's a little bit of you in every hunky hero that I write.

Next, for my momma. This is the only page of the book you're allowed to read, but it wouldn't have happened without you. When I told you at 10 years old I wanted to be an author, you never once doubted me. Your confidence and support during the times I didn't believe in myself are what got me to this point, and I wouldn't be who I am without you.

For my 2nd Lieutenant. This book wouldn't exist without you. You've put almost as many hours into these pages as I have and dealt with every high and low of the process as well. The wind beneath my sails, the chortle to my huff, and the best damn editor out there. Your blood, sweat, tears, and friendship are more appreciated than I can ever put into words.

For Alyssa, my big sister, best friend, lifelong cheerleader, and the busiest woman I know. Your schedule is insane and terrifying, but you still always make time for me. Thank you for inspiring me every day. I know you wanted this book to be more angsty, but you'll have to wait for the sequels for that.

For Madeleine, for looking up at me from behind a book one Saturday, thumping the cover, and saying, "you should do this." I started writing again the next day, and now here we are. You're an expert at spotting homophones and knowing exactly what to say when I'm discouraged. I love you so much.

For Lisa, for being as confused by commas as I am and believing my stories are wonderful no matter how I punctuate them. You're such a wonderful hype woman and friend, and I look forward to consuming your beta reader feedback more than my morning Diet Coke.

For Krista, for being the least flaky person in all of Los Angeles. Your writing inspires me, but I'm most grateful for our coffee meetups where we talk about life, fix plot holes, eavesdrop on awkward first dates, and weave some fun, amazing dreams together. Thank you for always listening.

For Caleb, for all the joint writing sessions and understanding my creative mania the most. You've clocked a lot of hours listening to me ramble incoherently in the car on the way to and from fencing class. You promised you'd read my book when I put it in your hands. That time has finally come.

Finally, for all the friends who kept checking in for updates and cheering me on. You didn't have to do that, but every time you did, it gave me the energy to carry on. Thomas, Meg, Chris, Kelsey, Kourtney, Dillan, Valz, and Danni (in no particular order; this isn't MySpace top eight)—your friendship means the world to me. I'm so lucky to have you all.

ABOUT THE AUTHOR

ALANA KAY is a romance author with a soft spot for imperfect heroes, tough heroines, and steamy love stories. She made her debut into paranormal romance in 2024 with her novel The Last Wish (Lost Legacy Book One) and completed the trilogy in February 2025. Alana Kay fell for romance novels in the early aughts after sneaking bodice rippers from her mom's dog-eared collection of paperbacks. A big believer in happy endings, she likes her love scenes on page, her adventures nonstop, and her magic off the rails. When she's not typing feverishly, she's either snuggling with her dog, cats, or husband in sunny Los Angeles or impulsively signing up for a sporting event she's not nearly athletic enough to commit to.

Author of the Lost Legacy series, including The Last Wish, The Last Dream, and The Last Djinn. Her upcoming Radiant Legacy series releases its first book, Darkest Valley, in 2025.

For updates, follow @AlanaKayAuthor on social media or head over to AlanaKayAuthor.com.

ALSO BY ALANA KAY

LEGACY UNIVERSE

LOST LEGACY

The Last Wish

The Last Dream

The Last Djinn

RADIANT LEGACY

Darkest Valley
(Coming 2025)

Shadow of Death
(Coming 2025)

Fear No Evil
(Coming 2026)

9 798991 291811